THE
FAMISHED
LAND

A Novel of the
Irish Potato Famine

By the same author

IMMORTAL QUEEN
THE FLOWERS OF THE FOREST
THE GHOSTS IN MY LIFE
A STRANGE AND SEEING TIME

THE
FAMISHED
LAND

A Novel of the
Irish Potato Famine

ELIZABETH BYRD

J. B. Lippincott Company
PHILADELPHIA AND NEW YORK

U.S. Library of Congress Cataloging in Publication Data

Byrd, Elizabeth.
    The famished land.

    I. Title.
PZ4.B995Fam   [PS3552.Y67]   813'.5'4   72–3878
ISBN–0–397–00949–6

For Margaret and Robert Gore-Browne
and
Leonard Byrne

Prologue

13 June 1845

It was a Friday evening much like any other. The hills purpled with twilight and swans on the river tucked their wings toward sleep. Woodcock sought the alders, foxes slipped into leafy lairs and moles tunnelled upwards. Jackdaws which had quarrelled all day in chimney pots flew off as turf fires were lighted. Between mud huts and rock fences potato plants flowered white and through the deepening grey of the dusk the candles of Bally-fearna welcomed men home from the fields.

In her cottage Moira McFlaherty plaited her long red hair and bound it with a ribbon for love of Liam Lenihan. Across the road Granny Cullen took a penny from the thatch and polished it on her shawl. Down the gently rising wind John the Basket waded from the river and laid his reeds on the bank to dry.

In the abbey cloister young Father Leary strolled under the wild cherry trees and pondered Eileen Finnigan's strange confession. Nearby in the priest's house Eileen cleaned trout for his supper. On the road Paddy the Pawn closed shop and stopped next door for a dram at Murphy's Hotel. Across the bogs Jesus Finnigan delivered a jug of illicit poteen to the Widow Dumbie. Up the hill at the Crossroads of the Shoes Mary the Midwife put on her stockings and laced her boots to make a fine appearance in town. In the woods Bridget Reilly and Liam Lenihan straightened their clothes and took separate paths to their homes. Three miles east, two nuns journeyed into Ballyfearna by donkey cart.

At seven o'clock all of them met at the wake of James Dumbie, the blacksmith. They streamed through his yard bearing gifts for the widow — potatoes, oatmeal, cabbages, salt fish and blood puddings. Most of the villagers had arrived earlier, bursting the seams of the kitchen and spilling out into the bedroom. Dogs and children romped in the fowl yard and baby guests were bedded in the pig sty.

Near the hearth, circled by candles, the corpse lay in state on a table. It wore a black frieze tailcoat, a white shirt and a black stock that came high to the whiskers. A top hat rented for the occasion from Paddy the Pawn lay upside down on a stool beside it, an innovation noticed by everyone as elegantly subtle. Granny Cullen placed her penny in the hat and it gradually filled as sixty-eight mourners filed by. They knelt and prayed, then rose and moved on. Father Leary blessed the house and the two nuns told their beads. The widow passed jars of poteen to the guests who stood or sat on the straw.

The first formalities had all been observed, from the keening of the women who had laid out the body to the roasting of the pig. The coffin, nearly finished, reposed in the hen-run where Michael O'Shea's hammer could be heard above the laughter of the children.

It was not customary to speak of the departed at such a time since, in a manner, he was guest of honour. But the widow could not help it.

'Himself is somehow on me mind,' she said apologetically. 'I never thought the cough would take him so fast, and he so strong. But praise be, he lived the longest of the lot.'

Her guests were respectfully silent, remembering that she had buried four.

'A grand man,' she said.

'He was that,' said Dennis Murphy, 'and may God lift the darkness on your soul.'

For over an hour folk drank and smoked and spoke of

8

Dumbie's noble character. Those who could not recall his kind-
nesses invented them for Ballyfearna was on best behaviour at
wakes. Besides, they felt that they owed the widow for wonderful wakes in the past.

'What were his last words?' asked Sister Charity.

The widow reflected. 'He said, "Mind the ass." '

'A lovely sentiment,' said Mrs John the Basket. 'Sick as he was,
thinking of the poor humble creature.'

'You can see the goodness fair on his face,' said Bridget Reilly.
'Oh, the sweet look of him! You'd think he was only asleep.'

'And how,' inquired the widow sharply, 'should you be knowing how he looks asleep?'

'I only meant —'

'When have *you* seen him asleep?'

'In church,' said Jesus Finnigan swiftly. 'We've all seen the dear
man exhausted from his labours dozing through Mass like a
child.'

'Oh, yes,' said Bridget. 'In church it was.'

The widow was not pacified. 'That may be, but I resent your
remark, Bridget Reilly, and I may add I do not consider that
bonnet of yours proper to this occasion.' She took a gulp of
poteen from her jar and glared across the corpse at Bridget. 'Why
didn't you wear decent black?'

Bridget touched the glory of primroses and red ribbons that
hid her glossy black hair. 'It's me only bonnet, Mrs Dumbie, as
God's me witness.'

'Is your head too proud for a shawl like the rest of us?'

A tear rolled down Bridget's nose.

'Now wait,' said Liam Lenihan. 'Let us be fair, Mrs Dumbie. It
is Bridget's Sunday best and she wore it not in vanity but to
honour the corpse and for her great respect of your sorrow. Is
that not right, Bridget?'

Bridget sniffled. 'That's so.'

'Well!' said the widow. 'It's men defend that creature every
time. What do *you* say, Father?'

Father Leary's mouth thinned. 'I say it's a bloody flaming shame
that your minds are on a bonnet at a time when a soul is rising to
purgatory and requires your prayers.'

'Aye,' said Sister Angelica, 'we should set our minds to holy matters . . . I've often wondered, Bridget, where you came by that bonnet?'

Bridget stroked the red satin bow at her chin. 'It was given me by Mrs Pond when I was housemaid there.'

'*I'd* not take charity from an English woman,' said Moira McFlaherty, 'not if it was the last bonnet in Mayo. I'd sooner go bare.'

'Ah,' said Jesus Finnigan, 'and sure I'd love to see you so.'

Liam thrust out a great fist and cracked him in the jaw. Jesus staggered and fell on to Mrs John the Basket. Liam rushed to help her and met her husband in mid-rescue. The two collided, dumping the widow from her stool. As the three fell, Jesus leaped on to Liam and Moira smashed her shoe on to Jesus' head. Eileen Finnigan ran to defend her brother, pulled Moira by the hair and swung at her wildly, hitting Mary the Midwife who threw poteen in her face. The screams of the women excited the dogs, who yelped in and out of the rooms and set up a howl of children from yard and pig sty. Father Leary hurried the nuns to the safety of the yard and returned to assist the other women whose panicked flight through the door swept him outside again. There by the blackberry bushes the crowd talked of summoning the bailiff from Ballydonny but no one cared to journey ten miles lest the shame of the scandal reach the ears of the land agent and they be evicted or their rents raised.

'God be praised,' said Granny Cullen. 'I think they've quieted now.'

'The quiet of death,' sobbed Bridget. 'It's Jesus has killed Liam.'

'It's Liam has killed Jesus!' screamed Eileen.

Paddy the Pawn peered cautiously through the door. 'No one has killed no one. The two are lying peaceful as lambs, stunned side by side and no blood to speak of.' He gave way to Father Leary. 'See for yourself, Father.'

The priest opened the door an inch wider. 'Jesus, Mary and Joseph! The terrible shambles of it!' He turned and whispered to Paddy. 'Quick, go in and set up the corpse before the widow sees it and get the coins back in the hat. Splash the two of them with water and mind they don't go at it again.'

10

As Paddy went in Father Leary hushed the weeping widow and turned to the crowd. "It's the drink that did it, it's the curse of this parish as I've warned you a hundred times. I'd hate to think what the bishop will say when I tell him.'

'Well, now,' said Sister Charity, 'it will be a most dreadful blow to him — and he sick abed of eating the green gooseberries.'

'Oh, my,' said Sister Angelica. 'It could be the death of him.'

'Him delicate at best,' said Sister Charity.

'They say,' said Sister Angelica, 'that his old father do be dying in Tobercurry.'

'I had not thought of it that way,' the priest said slowly. 'It does seem a cruel thing to tell him at this time. . . . Now we'd best all get home and thank God it was no worse.'

'Aye, Father,' said Michael O'Shea, 'but it seems a pity to end so early before the pig was passed.'

'Slaughter your own pig,' said Father Leary, 'if it's only food on your mind.'

He shepherded the nuns to their donkey cart and drove away. The guests offered the widow formal condolences, plucked their babies from the pig sty and their lanterns from the grass and took their separate paths home. The widow went inside. Only Bridget, Moira and Eileen lingered in the yard.

'I'll wait to see me brother home,' Eileen said.

Bridget said, 'I'm going in to me poor Liam.'

Moira blocked her way. '*Your* poor Liam? And since when are you owning Liam Lenihan?'

'Now mind me,' said Bridget, hands on hips. 'I've took enough talk this night on account of me bonnet but only for respect of the grieving widow. One word — just one more — will set me off proper!'

'So? Then here's the word: Dilsy!'

Bridget gasped. Then she removed her bonnet and laid it carefully on the grass. 'Say that once more and I'll crack you one!'

'I'll not drop to fighting with your like,' Moira said haughtily. 'I'd not dirty me hands on you.'

'The pair of you is cowards,' jeered Eileen.

'You keep out of this,' Moira said. 'It was your brother Jesus insulted me that caused the fuss to begin with.' She turned back

11

to Bridget. 'If he was *your* Liam then why did he hit Jesus for insulting me?' she asked triumphantly.

'He'd hit Jesus for anything,' Bridget said. 'He's hit Jesus since they was confirmed together. So don't be taking the compliment to yourself.'

'Why,' asked Eileen, 'don't the pair of you go in to Liam and ask him to choose between you?'

'He's in no condition,' Bridget said warily, 'not tonight he isn't.'

'True for you,' agreed Moira.

'The pair of you is cowards,' Eileen repeated gleefully.

A sudden commotion stirred in the house and Liam and Jesus emerged at the point of the widow's broom, followed hastily by Paddy.

'. . . . and never dirty me doorstep again and don't you be coming to the funeral tomorrow and ruining the peace of the church. Nor you, either, Paddy Nolan, slopping water all over me tidy house. A fine thing, Himself askew from collar to boots worse than he was in life!' She saw Bridget and her voice shrilled higher. 'Get off me land and take that damned hat out of me sight forever!'

Moira moved timidly forward. 'Now I've done you no harm Mrs Dumbie and I want you to know me and me family is sore for your trouble.'

'Then why aren't they here? I'd be glad of your mother's comfort.'

'It's the child in her.'

The harsh voice gentled. 'Give her the kiss of me heart, Moira. And a good night to you.'

She closed the door. Bridget picked up her bonnet from the grass and ran to Liam. 'Poor soul, is it badly hurt you are?'

'No,' said Liam.

Her hand caressed his cheek, her black eyes were soft with sympathy.

'Well, now,' said Liam, 'if the truth be told, I'm terrible.'

Moira came up swiftly. 'But alanna, there's not a scratch on you.'

'It's me insides,' he said, 'me belly.'

12

'Where I hit him,' Jesus said, spitting out a tooth.

'Where I hit meself on the stool,' Liam said.

'You're a black liar! Me fist caught your stomach fair.'

'It's God's truth I never felt your touch, like petals it was. But I got your eye and your mouth.'

'Sprained they are,' Jesus said contemptuously, 'from me own exertions. When the floor slipped me.'

'You hurt Liam bad,' Eileen said. 'I heard him squeal.'

'Squeal, is it? Me? *Squeal?*' Liam appealed to Paddy. 'Did you hear me squeal, Paddy Nolan?'

'I was drunk,' Paddy said prudently. 'And now, a good night to you all.'

He walked off down the road. Eileen took her brother's arm. 'It's a marvel you were tonight, Jesus, and I proud of you. Let's go home and have a nourishing jar before I put you to bed.'

'You heard Father Leary say that drink is a curse on us,' Moira said, 'and you, the good man's housekeeper, do be encouraging your brother to take another jar when he caused the whole fuss.'

'I did not,' Jesus said indignantly. 'I paid you the courtesy of a fine compliment and Liam in his drink took it wickedly.'

'I? Drunk?' Liam laughed. 'It's you were drunk from the first sniff o' the keg. And you are still.'

'I am not. I fought meself sober. Come,' he said to Eileen, 'it's to home we'll go and drink and do as we please. Or I'll have a pot at Murphy's.'

They moved with dignity down the dark road.

'Him!' said Liam. 'It's not so much a liar I mind as a braggart. He never touched a hair of me head.'

'Of course not,' said the girls.

Moths flapped about the candlelit door. Wind rustled the elder trees and far off they heard the rattle of the Castlebar coach crossing the bridge.

'You'll see me home, Liam?' Moira asked.

'You'll see me home?' Bridget asked.

He stood momentarily baffled. There was Bridget's lush body, her black curls; Moira's tall slenderness and long, copper-coloured hair. Bridget's slanty black eyes and Moira's the colour of shamrocks. The most beautiful girls in Ballyfearna, the most beautiful

13

he had ever seen. He had glimpsed the Countess O'Toole at the Roscommon horse fair, famed for her loveliness in four counties. Not even she had hair and eyes and lips like these. . . .

'Well, now,' he said, 'you know it's me insides were smashed on that stool and me in terrible pain. But none the less I'll go with you as far as the Crossroads of the Shoes and watch there on the hill to see that no harm comes to you. You've lanterns?'

They nodded.

'Then you'll not stumble and there's nothing about to harm you.'

Moira said, 'Wild hogs.'

'Wolves.' Bridget shivered.

'You know they're not about in this season.'

'Owls,' said Moira. 'Their very sound puts me heart crosswise.'

'Hares,' Bridget said hopelessly.

Liam groaned and placed his hand on his stomach. 'I can only just reach the crossroads and me so weak I can scarcely stand.'

Hastily they raised their lanterns from the grass and, one on either side, supported him out to the road and along the leafy lane. A few stars spattered above the hills but there was no moon.

The girls were deeply solicitous of his condition. Moira insisted that his father summon Dr Thrush from Ballydonny but Liam protested and they praised his courage. Bridget suggested that he would require nursing such as his old mother could not provide and begged to visit him tomorrow but again he refused. They were the blessed darlings, he said, but they did not perceive that a man needed to stand on his own two feet — if he possibly could. Better to die with some pride. . . .

The girls wept as they patted his cheek at the crossroads, where they left one another in disdainful silence. Liam stood looking after them as their lanterns bobbed across the hill and over the bog. Then he took out his pipe and lit it and sighed. It was a sad thing to leave either one alone to cross her doorstep unkissed. It was a terrible hard thing to make a decision about life, and him only twenty. Women, in fact, were terrible.

He could not see their lanterns now but in Ballyfearna the candles were alight at Murphy's Hotel. There he could find men to talk to, men of great wisdom and good sense. The peace of

14

the dark, wood-panelled bar, the comfort of slow-curling smoke from a dozen pipes, the spark of drink. But mostly, the kindly understanding of men.

Almost any man would do, he thought, as he hurried down the hill. Mike O'Shea or Peter the Thatcher or Paddy Nolan. John the Basket or Kevin Ryan — philosophers all. Larry Donahue or Danel Powderley. Or even Jesus Finnigan.

Part One

Seven sad leagues past the last lonely fountain,
A mile from tomorrow, the dead garden lay

—Michael Innes

Chapter 1

Moira McFlaherty awakened to the mists of early morning. Her brothers Colum and Sean, three and four years old, curled beside her on the rags. Across the room her mother and father lay asleep on their bed. Everything was quiet save for the stir of chickens in the kitchen flying down from the beams where they roosted at night.

She arose and dressed stealthily, anxious not to disturb her brothers. They were not bad boys but forever underfoot and needful of care and she treasured an hour of solitude at dawn. God knew she would not have such hours when her mother birthed in August. An infant in the cottage would destroy what little privacy she had.

Privacy to ponder and dream. First, of course, the dream of Liam Lenihan, herself in his arms and his kiss on her mouth and his pledge of love. Then their marriage in the abbey and the frolic afterwards with Larry the Fiddler playing out his heart. The cottage Liam would take her to — surely the one near the Pool of thc Waterdogs where wild roses tangled from roof to door stone. A place remote from the village yet near enough

19

should one be lonely for company. Not that she would need one soul but Liam. . . .

Of course, she thought, I'd want to see my family but I'd soon have one of my own. Three boys and three girls. . . .

In her old blue bodice and red petticoat girdled by string she tiptoed into the kitchen, hushed the two dogs who greeted her and shooed the hens into the back yard. Then she released the pig from his prison of piled logs. He was sluggish and stubborn and she prodded him with a stick until finally, grunting, he followed the hens outside. There he rolled in the damp grass, freeing himself from lice. She threw him potatoes and parings and filled his trough with potato water from last night's pot. She shook out a bit of grain for the hens, drank a cup of buttermilk and hurried out the front door. The dogs followed, then turned back to chase a hare.

The mists which had shawled the hills were lifting and across the road smoke was rising from Granny Cullen's hut. Moira skipped through the dew-heavy grass, pleased by the coolness on her bare feet. Silvery spider webs glistened on the bushes. A blackbird called.

'Moira McFlaherty!' Granny Cullen hobbled from her potato patch and peered out between slitted fingers. 'You've done it again! Now it's bad luck I'll be having 'til sundown.'

It was bad luck to see a red-headed woman at the top of the day and Moira apologized. 'But I have to pass here for there's no other path I can take to where I'm going.'

Granny snorted. 'And where should you be going? It's home you should be at your cook fire and your poor mother in her seventh month —'

But Moira was off down the road and up the hill. At the Crossroads of the Shoes she looked out over dew-stippled meadows. White-blossoming potato gardens lay before Ballyfearna like a flowery quilt patched with the pink of roses and knotgrass, goosefoot and yarrow blossom. Poppies reddened the grainfields and along the river wild iris bloomed gold to the banks of Lough Sorm.

Where should she go to daydream? To the Pool of the Waterdogs, of course. She crossed the little wooden bridge over the river and entered thick woods.

Here were dark, fern-hidden caves where she had played as a child and an underground river which joined the great Loughs of Sorm and Daree. Ahead lay Poll na Sigheog, the Fairies' well, and she paused, startled by the sight of Jesus Finnigan drinking from a bucket of water. No one had ever known Jesus to be astir at dawn, much less drinking water.

'Good day to you,' she said.

He lowered the bucket and she saw his wet, beard-stubbled face never handsome at best with its protuberant nose and the scars of ancient battles, but now purpled about the mouth where Liam had hit him.

'Glory be,' he said, and crossed himself at sight of her red hair. 'What are you doing here?'

'Just a-walking.'

He set down the bucket and groaned. 'It's walked I have clear from me home and me weak as a stuck salmon. Last night's drink did it and now it's raising a thirst like a giant's.'

'Was there no water at your house?'

'Only a jar. I could drain the river, I could. It's that Dennis Murphy did it at the hotel, giving me drink for each song I sang and they kept me at it till after twelve. Ah, well, it's a comfort to know that Dennis and Liam have heads as sorry as mine.'

'Liam! Was Liam at Murphy's?'

'Sure.'

'And what was he doing there?'

'Jigging with the girls.'

O, Liam, the liar, the betrayer! 'What girls?'

'Actresses they were, a whole coach of them. They were on the way to Castlebar but the coach had got down in a bog and they had to walk back a mile to town. They could dance and sing both, and all beautiful as angels and friendly, too.'

'Friendly?' she asked. 'To Liam?'

'And why not, then? He's a grand fellow. It was he pulled me out of the ditch and carried me home and put me on to me pallet. Eileen says he stayed a full two hours to sure himself I was all right.'

21

'And what was Liam and Eileen doing them full two hours?'
Moira asked fearfully.

'Should I know, who was asleep the minute me head hit the straw?'

Oh, triply betrayed! She had never thought of Eileen as a rival — God knew Bridget Reilly was sufficient — but now she must mistrust Eileen too. And atop the two of them, all the actresses from the Castlebar coach.

Jesus sensed her mood. 'I think Eileen and Liam was just having a friendly jar,' he said tactfully. 'Or maybe a few.'

'And where may Liam be now?'

'Likely at home or maybe at the hotel for these actresses asked him to come back today and see them safe to the coach as they're so afraid of the bogs . . . poor girleens, I never saw women so dirtied. This Katie, she said all of her petticoats was black to the knees.'

'*All* of her petticoats? And how many did she be wearing?'

'Seven,' said Jesus.

'And I suppose you and Liam saw them, all seven?'

Jesus seemed hurt. 'Now, how could you think such a sin of us?'

She eased a little. 'You didn't leave the bar? You didn't go to the rooms upstairs?'

'How could we, with Dennis' wife there at the staircase with a terrible axe? No, she made the girls sleep in the common room, piled like dolls on the floor they was, without hay to their heads or cover to their bodies. Likely she'll charge them tuppence apiece and I doubt they even get breakfast.'

Moira could appreciate Biddy Murphy's behaviour but her conscience labelled it unfair. Guests who had mired on the road should at least receive the hospitality of the house. Saddened as she was by Liam's perfidy, jealous and uneasy, yet a corner of her mind judged Biddy Murphy as niggardly.

'I'd ask you the honour of walking with you,' Jesus said, 'but me head is too big to carry.'

Anxious to be alone, she went on through the woods, past oak and holly groves until she came to the Pool of the Waterdogs. There otters played, frisking through the water and chasing one another on to the banks. Just beyond, in a cluster of sycamores and beeches, stood the small rock hut she visioned as someday hers. The Big Wind of 1839 had levelled huge oaks so that it stood in a little clearing, thickly curtained by lichen and wild roses. Once long ago it had been a secret schoolhouse where a priest taught the parish children, but a band of English soldiers had ridden into the clearing and booted into the house — and the Father was dragged off to prison. Thereafter the house was deemed unlucky, and no one had lived there.

Moira thought, with its two rooms emptied of twigs and leaves and its fireplace cleaned it would make a snug home. But now the dream seemed remote. It was obvious that Liam had no love for her. He had lied and gone to Murphy's to consort with strange women. Likely only Biddy's axe had saved him from mortal sin. But had he been saved from Eileen?

She stood in the gathering sunlight and the beauty of the old flowered hut and the peace of the woods seemed a mockery. Likely she would never live here, but age and dry like a leaf in her parents' home.

At thought of her parents she started home by way of the stone bridge that crossed the river on the western edge of town. A river of leaping salmon, of brown trout. Passing the great ruined abbey on its carpet of cherry blossoms she saw smoke curling from the priest's house. In the back yard Eileen Finnigan was throwing slops to the priest's three pigs. Seeing Moira, she came to the fence.

'And why are you abroad so early?'

It was more like a gibe than a question, Moira thought, and a sneer on the face of her.

'I might ask the same of you,' Moira said coldly, 'considering you was up all night drinking.'

'And why on earth would you be thinking that?'

'Jesus told me. I met him in the woods.'

'Oh, my,' said Eileen, 'no girl should meet me brother in the woods if she values her virtue.'

'I didn't meet him!'

'You said you did.'

'By chance.'

23

'That's likely.'

Now I have never warmed to her, Moira thought, nor she to me, but never before have we higgled. It must be that she's taken with Liam, and if so then something *did* happen last night. In wonderment she studied Eileen as though she were a stranger.

What do I see that should shiver me so? A tall, full-breasted woman of twenty with broad shoulders and narrow waist. Dusty oat-coloured hair snarled uncombed to her apron strings. A thin red mouth, cruel as a gash. Blue eyes bright with malice. No, more than malice. Hate.

'I met your brother by chance,' Moira repeated, steadying her glance. 'God knows I'd not be taking up with a Finnigan.'

For the Finnigans were lowest of the low and all the folk for miles around knew their history. Twenty-one years ago James Finnigan, begging afoot through the bogs, had come to Bally-fearna and asked food of the young Widow MacNamara. She had taken him in, fed and clothed him and borne him a daughter — Eileen. Old Father O'Connor had threatened them with ex-communication unless they married and the ceremony was per-formed on a windy Easter. But it was not long after that when James left town with his wife's scant egg money, the abbey poor box and the Cross of Gold that had adorned the High Altar since 1206.

Mrs Finnigan went wailing to the priest to say that she was not only abandoned but again pregnant — and with the coughing sickness. He comforted her and asked nuns from the convent to tend her needs, for the village women were hostile. Three months later when young Mary the Midwife delivered Mrs Finnigan of a son she sent for Father O'Connor.

Mrs Finnigan said, 'I'd be obliged if you'd christen the boy now before my eyes, for death is upon me.'

The priest glanced at Mary the Midwife, who nodded.

'And what name would you be wanting for him?' Father O'Connor asked gently.

'Jesus.'

But such a name would be blasphemous, especially for the son of a church robber. He named the boy Terence, but Mary was so moved by the wish of a dying woman that she felt that the name Jesus should be used — at least in private. And so did all the other women who heard the tale. Thus Terence Finnigan was called Jesus from then on — and the priest not hearing.

Eileen was cared for in the convent until she was fifteen, of age to keep house for the new priest, Father Leary. Jesus lived at the workhouse near Ballydonny, tending the gardens until, at seventeen, he was dismissed by the Work Master as impossibly lazy. He joined Eileen in her woodland cottage and idled about for a year or more. The whim for drink, bred from ale stolen at the workhouse, brewed mischief in him. Treated to whiskey at Murphy's hotel, he could be depended on to furnish splendid fights, even taking on the champion from Ballinrobe and winning, so that betting men of Ballyfearna profited in shillings. Dennis Murphy saw further profit in Jesus' natural inclination toward an easy life. One night at the bar he said, 'Jesus, do you know the high cost of whiskey?'

Jesus, who had never bought any himself, said he did not.

'Folk hereabout cannot afford it, but I'm forced to keep a few bottles for the strangers who come through by coach. It's ruining me. Sometimes it sits on the shelf for half a year.'

'Oh, my,' Jesus said. 'That's terrible.'

'Now, it should not be so costly,' Dennis said. 'Made of praties, it is, and easy to brew. You peel the praties and crush them and add sugar or malt to ferment them. . . . It's a bloody shame I've no time to do this simple thing from a cave in the woods. Would you like a whiskey now, Jesus?'

Jesus would.

'I could make better,' Dennis said, 'if I had the time. If I were a young lad like yourself without a trade or a family, I'd brew it and sell it to someone like meself with a hotel, or to those folk who need it for theirselves, being sad or happy or requiring it as medicine. But,' Dennis sighed, 'I'm too old for public service.'

He poured Jesus another. 'Of course it's against the law. It's the English would keep us in perpetual thirst. I'm thinking it's patriots we need who'd not be afraid of the authorities. . . .'

So Jesus rose to the need of the people. Moira knew where his still was hidden; she had stumbled on it in St Cecilia's Cave, but she never revealed that secret to anyone. No one in town was so low as to inform. In fairness to Jesus she thought, even if it profited him to inform against himself, he wouldn't.

'Ha!' Eileen said, 'so you'd not be taking up with a Finnigan. And are you imagining me brother would take up with a Mc-Flaherty?'

Why does she hate me so? What had so suddenly caused this change from indifference to loathing? It could only be that Eileen had learned love of Liam last night, and a girl does not learn without knowledge or encouragement. Bridget Reilly, at least, had fancies to build on, for Liam had twice escorted her to frolics when Moira was ill. But he had never so much as glanced at Eileen. Could it be that he had changed from a fine religious boy into a rogue who not only pursued actresses but descended to the favours of a slattern? Aye, Eileen kept Father Leary's house in order but not her own cottage nor her own self. Her hair was a dirty spill, bits of food spotted her waist and her ankles were bog-black.

Moira looked into the blue eyes that were so bright with hate and hoped that her shiver was not obvious. As calmly as she could she said 'I've nothing to say to you,' and was about to move on when Father Leary came down the road from the abbey. Eileen, delinquent with his breakfast, turned and rushed into the house. Moira waited by the fence as he called a greeting.

With the eye of a devout parishioner she noticed the worn breviary he held and the dark shabby robes that swept the still-wet grass. With the eye of a woman she thought, Despite his small stature he is a handsome man. Twenty-eight? Thirty-two? No one knew. But his brown hair curled against a romantically pallid brow. His features were delicate, perfect, yet there was no weakness, no trace of femininity in his face. And his voice was rich and deep as the velvet that veined his hat.

'Good day, Moira.' He smiled at her. 'Perhaps I should be naming you Miss McFlaherty now you are so tall.'

But until two years ago she had been his pupil. 'It's Moira I am to you, Father.'

'And how old are you now?'

'Sixteen.'

26

'Ah, time rushes.' He studied her face. 'What's amiss? You seem troubled.'

Now how did he know that? Did her eyes or her voice betray her or was it not his own holy perception?

'It's Liam,' she said (and Eileen, too, but hateful as she is I'd not tell him). 'I am wondering if he loves me.'

'Oh,' he said. 'Liam.'

'He has not pledged himself. I think he has changed for the worse.'

'And how, Moira?'

Indeed, she would not tattle about Bridget or Eileen or the actresses. 'It's only me sense of something.'

'Lads do change,' he said mildly, 'and to grow from boy to man is sometimes a stormy matter. At least he's a good, hard worker.'

That was true. The Lenihans' two acres thrived despite the fact that Liam had no help from a lazy father and a sickly mother. And right or wrong, he knew his own mind and was even planning to plant turnips and cabbages on the slope behind the potato field — unusual in Ballyfearna where the major crop was lumpers.

'If he doesn't take care,' she said, 'Mr Pond will raise his rent for improving the land. He's even built a shed.'

'I saw it last week.' Father Leary lowered his voice. 'It's sorry I am to say that Mr Pond is coming to me house for tea next Wednesday. Invited himself, he did. But he'll not be passing by way of Liam's shed.'

'True,' she said, 'but he might see other things. It's the way of him to notice everything, even a bit of fence like John the Basket's, or the new roof of Mike O'Shea. Do you mind when he raised the rent of Molly Ryan when she inherited her cousin's pig? And she taking in her cousin's three children?'

'Is it that I'd forget?' he asked grimly. 'I've no doubt he's here to snoop around. Tea, is it? Me company he wants? And he godless?'

Eileen poked her head out of the kitchen door and called, 'Your meal is hot, an' it please you, Father.'

'Will you be joining us, Moira?'

She thanked him but went on her way past the House of the Protestant Poet (no cook fire here till past noon!) on to the road. There at the Market Cross was the hub of the village — the Public Well, the cobbler's and the shed of Michael O'Shea, stone-cutter and coffin-maker. There was the Cattle, Egg and Poultry Market and the blacksmith's shop with its horseshoe-shaped door hung with a funeral wreath of whitethorn tied with black string. Opposite were the shops of John the Basket and Paddy the Pawn and next door Murphy's Hotel and the coaching stop with its tethering posts and horse trough.

Despite its smoking chimney the hotel looked deserted and Moira hoped that the actresses had left. But likely they were still asleep, 'piled like dolls' in the common room. She imagined them jealously, each with seven petticoats over high-heeled red-laced boots over white cotton stockings. Last year Biddy Murphy had shown her pictures from *The Ladies' Illustrated Paper* left at the hotel, so she knew what the fashions were in Dublin. Dresses with shocking low necks, but ah, so pretty with their scalloped frilled skirts, the mantles with long silky fringe. Parades of buttons, regiments of velvet frogs, waterfalls of ruffles. Yet surely those actresses would not be looking so elegant should Liam be seeing them now, curls awry, eyes bleary, pettish over misplaced gloves and reticules. And it was said that if a woman painted, the skin was poisoned and bleedy-like . . .

Biddy came out to shake her broom and called a good morning.

Subtly Moira asked, 'Are you the only one about?'

'Aye, Himself has gone back abed, he has the head on him.'

Moira assumed ignorance of last night's orgy. 'A head from the wake, and it ending so early?'

Biddy's freckled face pinked with anger. 'From that and later things I'll not be talking of. But I'll say this to you, Moira Mc-Flaherty, it's lucky you are to be having no husband — and one who passes the jug as though it were water! Who hosts strangers as though he were Lord Mountjoy himself! And what do we have in the till at the end of it? Nothing!'

She brushed a red hairbow off her doorstep with such violence that it whisked half-way across the road. 'I'm not talking, but it's thinking I am — and deep. I took him for better or for worse and for worse it is and I hope Father Leary gives him penances from now to Christmas, that I do.'

Moira said, 'It must have been terrible. But then it's other people do be helping Dennis into trouble?'

'True for you. But now, thank God, they're all gone. Not till an hour ago did I get the lot of them out of this house and on to the road — and Himself offering a door-drink!'

Moira soothed her, reminded her of Dennis' many goodnesses. Biddy grudged them, then finally nodded. At heart, he *was* good but the tool of troublemakers whom she would not deign to mention. Like Jesus Finnigan, Paddy Nolan. Michael O'Shea. Liam Lenihan.

'Liam?'

'Ah, alanna, I know your long love but you'd best forget him. He's wild as a blue hare. It was him overset the cabinet with all me yellow china in chase of that dilsy —' She stopped abruptly. 'I'll not say more.'

But Moira had to know. 'Did he catch her?'

'Sure, of course he did. But a hat pin she had and stuck him proper right in the chin. But it's not an informer I am as you know. It's only me wise heart telling you to forget him.'

How could one forget a boy one had loved these three years? Together through the playtime of youth they had explored the mysteries of loughs and woods, caves and pools. He had fashioned her a rod and line and taught her to fish; he had shown her how to trap and skin rabbits. He had even saved her life when, at ten, she had fallen into the river and his big hands had wrestled life back into her body before he carried her home to her parents. You could not forget such things, part of your breath and bone, a glory in your heart and an ache in your belly.

What had changed him now? The four years' difference in age had never mattered between them. Perhaps, as Father Leary had said, to grow from boy to man was a stormy matter. Well then, she would wait out the storm.

'Biddy,' she said, 'I thank you for your counsel, but it's Liam I love.' And she went on down the street and turned toward the path.

The sun, like a huge bakestone, was drying the grass and making a glare to the eye. She followed the wind of the river seeing the dark bulk of the grain mill in the distance. Tiny potato fields scattered about — the Widow Dumbie's, Mary the Midwife's, Granny Cullen's and the two acres of her parents. Southeast was the road to Ballydonny, ten miles of rough green grass to the convent, the workhouse and the estate of Lord Mountjoy who owned most of the county. No one in Ballyfearna had ever seen him, for he lived in England, but Mr Pond, his estate agent, came every six months to collect rents. And God help a family if it had not sufficient potato crop or a pig fit for market, or if the land was worked over-well. Eviction or rent-raise. Folk tried to keep a middle course.

One must keep a middle course of the heart too, she thought, neither to love nor hate too much lest one blunder to one's own hurt. Eileen, now, hated too much — it was plain in her eyes. Father Leary loved too much, fretting over everyone in the parish. And she, Moira, though God knew not holy, loved too much too. Liam, her family, the dogs, the pigs, the silly chickens, all that crept the woods or climbed the slopes or stirred the trees. That dozy bee that lazied in the clover, this baby blackbird which was making timid flights from the hedgerow. There were times when she wanted to cuddle the plump, soft cushions of the hills — aye, even the world beyond them which she had never seen.

As she approached her hut the dogs ran to meet her. She passed the manure pile where the pig was wallowing and entered the kitchen. It was, like most, the common-room of the hut. There were stools and a table, pegs for clothes, and cupboards to hold pots and cutlery, and above, a loft for the turf. A long bench, high out of reach of the dogs, held flour, sugar, salt, eggs, oats and the bit of tea saved for special occasions when the priest or the nuns called. Each evening the milk jar was filled and when her mother Cathleen was in the mood to churn, there was butter or she and Moira made curds. Sometimes during the summer the family ate fresh fish but in all seasons and at all meals they ate potatoes from the big barrel that stood at the back door.

Potatoes roasted in the ashes or boiled in the pot or fried in pig grease or cold in their own skins with a touch of salt.

Sun-blinded, her eyes grew accustomed to the windowless dark of the hut. Now she could see her parents and brothers seated at the deal table. Cathleen brought potatoes from the boiling pot and served them on one large plate.

'Where have you been?' her father asked.

'Only a-walking.'

He frowned. 'Where?'

'In the woods and by the abbey. I met the priest.'

Sean McFlaherty's eyes softened a little — eyes green as Moira's but small and scantily lashed. He was a small man with a face rutted as a field and a flow of rough, sandy hair. He wore faded grey breeches and his grey shirt sleeves were rolled high to sun-browned elbows.

'Father Leary said Mr Pond is coming to town on Wednesday.'

'For what?' Sean asked sharply. 'The rents are not due!'

'It's for tea at the priest's house.'

Cathleen's shoulders slumped in relief. 'Tea, is it?'

'Tea,' said Colum parroting. 'Tea, tea, tea,' and little Sean took up the chant. They pounded the table with their milk mugs until their father slapped his fist between them and demanded quiet.

Cathleen brought a wooden bowl of salt water. The family peeled the potatoes, dropped the parings to the dogs, then dipped the potatoes into the salt water and ate. Moira poured more buttermilk.

'You should have stayed home to help me," Cathleen said. 'The sickness was on me again this morning.'

So late as the seventh month? Moira regarded her mother worriedly. Normally slender as herself, she was, even allowing for her condition, frighteningly fat, though she ate sparingly. Grey eyes stared out from a swollen face and her very legs were puffed. The luxuriant red hair, once so like her own, was tarnished and lightless. At thirty-six she moved as slowly as Granny Cullen.

'I'm sorry,' Moira said.

31

Sean's voice was harsh. 'You should be. What's devilled you these past months?'

She could not explain her restlessness nor her need to dream in secret places. Once so close to her parents she realized that she had built a bridge away from them even though she loved them. And it was true that she evaded her chores whenever she could.

'Last night,' Sean said, 'I forbade you to stay at the wake more than a few minutes. You were to pay our respects and come home. You did not — and I waiting up for you two hours.'

'But I told you. The fuss —'

'If you'd obeyed me there'd been none, for you say it was caused by yourself.'

I should not have told them, she thought. You grant the truth, you confide it through years of love, and then it is held against you.

'You've become heedless and lazy, with no burden on your mind. You did not milk the cow last night, but left it to your mother. You did not graze it this morning. You did not even stir the fire before you ran off.'

She could not deny her behaviour nor defend it. She thought of a word used in one of Father Leary's sermons: *Irresponsible.* He had explained its meaning with particular reference to the government of Ireland by England. Not deliberately cruel, perhaps, but remote, uncaring.

But she did care about her family — the thin, rosy-cheeked boys with their thatches of red-blonde curls, her sweet-voiced mother pathetic in her fat, and Sean himself who worked so hard to protect them from need.

Cathleen said, 'Ah, Sean, have you no thought of our own youth? Of the time you left the harvesting to take me to Ballydonny? Of the days we shirked our work to roam the hills?'

Their eyes locked in memory, softly and secretly.

'But she must do better, alanna. She must spare you the work.'

Little Sean said, 'I want to go out,' and, grateful for the reprieve, Moira led him outside to the bushes behind the hut. The sun was hotter, the grass had dried, it would be a fair day for the funeral. She put her father's scolding from her mind and pondered what to wear in the church. The 'new' red petticoat (two

32

years old) and the white bodice. She and her mother shared one good black shawl but naturally Cathleen must wear it. Still, it did not greatly matter how she looked, since the widow had forbidden Liam to the church.

She pulled up little Sean's breeches and brought him back into the house. Cathleen was vomiting into the hearth, Sean hovering beside her and Colum tense with fright. Moira ran to her mother, patted the jerking shoulders. Child sickness was always hard but she did not remember Cathleen so ill with Colum or Sean.

She thought of the midwife. 'Shall I go for Mary?'

Cathleen shook her head and told Sean to take the boys to the field. They left, and she gradually eased and went into the bedroom to lie down on her pallet. Moira bent and kissed her.

'What is it you'll be needing?' she asked.

'Nothing.' She tried to smile. 'A new stomach. You'll tend the chores?'

'Of course.'

This time she would prove her — what was the word? Responsibility. She needed water to wash the dish and mugs and took a bucket across to the well they shared with Granny Cullen. As she lowered it a shadow fell across the rough cheek of the well and she turned, startled, to see Liam standing behind her.

'Dear God!' she said, 'where did you come from?'

He motioned to Granny's hut. 'I was after mending the hole in Granny's thatch.'

'And you so sick,' she said sarcastically, 'with your insides smashed.'

'They healed in me sleep thanks to me prayers.'

Angrily she said, 'I'm hearing you need prayers after what happened last night at Murphy's.'

'Ah, yes,' he said calmly, 'it taxed all me strength it did to get down that hill to help poor Jesus in his drink.'

'And who else was there, saving poor Jesus?'

He hesitated. 'Oh, a few folk came off the coach. Strangers, they was.'

'Women?' she asked, assuming innocence.

'Well, in a way of speaking I'd guess you'd call them that — ugly as they was.'

33

'Don't you lie to me!' she said. 'I saw Jesus this morning and he said they was actresses with seven petticoats and beautiful as angels. Dancing, you was —'

'Och!' Liam struck his chest. 'It's what I feared, he's got the drink on his brain and if he keeps on he'll be seeing the snakes in his jar. O, poor Jesus, friend of me youth, to come to such a shame! Angels! And them so pocked you could scarce see their faces? Actresses? All bald, with wigs over? Dancing? And them poor creatures on crutches?' He shook his head sorrowfully.

Well, she thought, perhaps Jesus *had* exaggerated. . . .

He pulled on the rope and brought up the bucket. 'I'll take it home for you, then you'll come to me field.'

How often she had helped him dig or fern the potato pits, or just sat nearby, entranced by his talk. Now she was uncertain what to do. Her mind said, 'He's a black liar and Biddy is right. I should forget him.'

But liar or not, I love every hair of his head.

Crisp, black-curling hair, soft to the touch, soft to her lips when she kissed it. Large black eyes, soft too, and heavy-lidded. But no softness elsewhere. His body was hard and tall, with an animal grace and strength that seemed effortless. She found joy merely in watching him sow or dig for he seemed in rhythm with the earth he tended.

She trotted behind him to her hut where he set down the bucket inside the door. From the doorway they could see across the hedges, her father working in the potato field and the boys pulling weeds.

Liam took her arm. 'Come, alanna, I must get to work.'

And so must I, she thought. The fire to replenish, the water to boil, the pig straw to change and the lime to spread on the floor against its stench. . . . But it was not yet nine o'clock. There was plenty of time before noon, and her mother likely asleep. . . .

She followed him up the hill to the Corner of the Shoes across the bridge past the grain mill into the woods. At Miller's Cave they paused to look at the bank of heavy ferns which hid a canyon so mysteriously dark that no one ever ventured there after dusk.

'Do you really think it haunted?' Moira asked.

34

'Not by day.'

'But at night?'

'You recall me grandmother said the wee miller folk grind their grain there.'

And indeed there was a soft, odd sound from the depths. But it could be the underground river.

'Did she ever see them, Liam?'

'Often. Tiny as grassblades they was in green aprons powdered with oats. Once they left a little wheelbarrow outside here but when she took it in her hand it changed to dandelion fluff.'

No stranger would suspect the cave's existence, for ferns, dockweed, and laurel concealed its mouth. Under the heavy foliage, natural rock steps, wetly mossy, led a hundred feet down to two large chambers. Even by day one needed a lantern to grope one's way, so dark it was. Moira had not explored there since she was twelve and she had no wish to do so now. Haunted or not there were surely bats and the thought of them tangling in her hair made her shudder.

'If there are ghosts, they're holy ones,' she said.

Here, years ago, priests had hidden from the English authorities and there was a smoke-blackened hearth in one of the chambers where they had cooked what they dared to hunt. Twenty years ago human bones had been found, removed and buried in the abbey yard.

'Let's go down,' Liam said.

'Oh, no!'

'I dare you.'

'We are not children.'

'You are afraid!'

'I am not.'

He shrugged. 'I'd thought braver of you. Other girls do.'

'What other girls?'

'Oh — others,' he said vaguely, indicating the village with a sweep of his hand.

'Bridget Reilly?'

'Maybe.'

'With you?'

'Now it's a poke-nose you are.'

So! If Bridget was brave enough to descend into that hellish black, then she could too. If only she had a shawl to keep her hair from the bats. . . .

Liam went ahead, holding out his hand to help her down the treacherous moss-slippery steps. Her toes clamped to the crevices, her free hand clutched the rock wall. Down they went and down until finally there was only a phantom of daylight and no sound but the soft, secret rush of water.

They came to solid ground. There was only the dank creeping moisture and the grave-dark.

She shivered. 'Let's go back.'

Her voice echoed, mocking along the hollow corridors. *Go back.*

'Now why would you want to be going when we've only been here one minute?'

'Because I'm afraid.'

Not of bats, for she had seen none. But of something far worse, something unknown but imminent. Her fear was primeval, instinctive as fear of fire or flood.

'Afraid of what, darling?'

Of death. For this was a tomb wreathed with lichen and wildflowers. This was a dark, closing coffin.

His arms went around her and she felt his mouth on hers. Dear God, she thought, clinging, another such kiss to confess to Father Leary. Yet through her guilt she felt something different in this kiss, less a passion to caress than a will to survive.

She pulled away as his hand touched her breast and he laughed and kissed her again and helped her up toward the steps, up through the wan slant of daylight, up to the hot, safe sun.

The sun was high and she said, 'I should be home to me chores,' but when he kissed her again she made no move to leave. She could smell the wild of the woods and the sweet sweat of his body through the thin blue shirt. And when he bade her come with him, she followed him to his field.

At noon she was barely home in time to cook the dinner. Sean slapped her for the first time in years, but the drug of her love for Liam made her impervious to the pain. Lazy, he called her,

36

and wilful, but his words were lost in the memory of Liam's.

For Liam had said, 'My beloved.' No promise, no pledge of marriage. But for the time, it did not matter.

At three in the afternoon, dressed in their best, the McFlahertys attended the funeral at the abbey. The entire village was there save those barred by the widow. Outside in the hot sunlight of the graveyard the coffin was lowered into the pit and the widow threw in the last flower. Moira tried hard to weep but was unable. She had no affection for the blacksmith and her heart was too happy of Liam for tears.

Eileen Finnigan followed her as the crowd straggled out to the road. She said, 'Who do you think I met in the woods but an hour ago?'

Liam, Moira thought. But no, he'd still be at work in his field.

'Liam and Bridget,' Eileen said. 'So surprised she was she had still to button her bodice.'

The deep core of happiness splintered. She had no words to match the venom of Eileen's smile.

Eileen said, 'But of course you're not caring at all, at all?'

'No,' Moira lied, cold in the scorch of the sun. Cold and hopeless and fearful, aye, even sick to her belly. For something told her the truth was in Eileen. 'No, I'm not caring.'

Eileen laughed and sauntered off toward the priest's house. Moira's family joined her for the walk home. Her brothers loitered on the rickety wooden bridge to throw stones into the river.

'It's queer weather,' Sean said, sniffing the windless air. 'Queer.'

'A storm?' Cathleen asked. 'Is it a storm coming?'

He did not reply. A salmon leaped in a bright, sun-silvered arc.

'I'm thinking,' Cathleen said, 'that someone should comfort Annie Dumbie with supper. Go after her, Moira, and ask if she'll kindly join us.'

Grateful to be alone, Moira crossed the bridge and followed the western bank of the river but there was no sight of the widow on the path. Presently she saw a cart approaching. Horses' hooves raised the dust and she stood aside on the grass. My God, she thought, what a rattle and clank! Then she saw the glitter of pots and pans and knives and mugs and bangles and she knew that this was a tinker a-travel. He checked the horse and as the dust settled she saw a young man, his dark skin shiny with sweat. A red kerchief covered his hair and his brass ear rings caught the fire of the sun.

'May the day joy you,' he said.

She said, 'May you travel in peace.'

His face was thin, his nose aquiline, his eyes a merry brown flecked with gold. 'Is it far to Ballyfearna?'

She pointed back in the direction of the road. 'Less than a mile.'

He flung off his kerchief and mopped his face. His hair was black as sea-coal and hung straight to the collar of his open shirt. A fine lad, she thought, though strange-like as gypsies were wont to be.

'Now, Madam,' he said, 'You'll be wanting some pans for your hearth.' He patted a plump-bellied pot and thumped it. 'Sound and sweet as a sovereign, but only a shilling.'

'But I've no need —'

'Ah, but you've never tasted praties so good as from a pot like this! Or this for your fish.' He showed her an iron skillet. 'It pampers trout as no other on earth, straight from Dublin it is. And do you know who bought three? No other than the Lord Mayor's wife, as God's me witness.'

'But I've no money and I've no home of me own.'

'No home of your own?' He seemed incredulous. 'A beautiful young lady like yourself is not married?'

'No,' she said.

'My God, you could marry anyone you've a fancy to so you'd best prepare for it with buying your household goods now. Or,' he added tactfully, 'if you must wait on the paltry matter of money why you can find me anytime for it's here I shall be for the summer.'

'Here?' she asked, astonished. 'In Ballyfearna?'

'Aye, I've heard it's a fine town with a coach stop. I'll find meself a decent hedgerow and sleep in me cart. . . . But allow me to introduce meself.' He made a little bow from the cart seat. 'Tyrone Schwartz.'

'Schwartz,' she said. 'It's a name I never heard.'

'It comes from me father, God rest his soul, who was born in Germany of a Jewish family. A banker he was, and he came to Dublin and married me mother out of her tribe and they took to the road lest she be murdered.'

'Murdered! Why?'

'She was a princess of her tribe and he only a banker as I said.'

'Oh, my! And was she murdered?'

'No, they escaped to the road. But she fell down a grain pit in Skibbereen, bless her memory, and he died of the shock so it was only me alone in the world. . . . You'll not be having one of these exquisite pots? Or a knife for peeling the praties?'

'Me mother has pots. And a peeling knife — do I not have ten fingers?'

'Ah, well.' He sighed and shrugged. 'Where can I find me a dram for me thirst?'

She pointed in the direction of Murphy's Hotel and he said he would stay the night there before finding himself a hedgerow for a summer home.

'We've had a dry summer,' she said, 'but how will you live when it rains?'

He showed her clever canvas flaps that lifted up from the sides of the cart and buttoned on an arch of wire. 'It's dry as dust I'll be. Now may I ask your name?'

She told him, thinking that if it were not for Liam he would lift her heart. No fly-by-night pedlar but one who planned to settle in a proper hedgerow, and of royal birth.

'And are you pledged to anyone?' he asked.

'No,' she said, 'but though he's not spoken, me heart is pledged.'

He was too much of a gentleman to pry, though he looked puzzled. Then, tipping a non-existent hat, he drove on and she watched him until dust-swirls hid the cart from her sight.

She brought Annie Dumbie back for supper. Surely Liam would come by as he did nearly every evening. But at high starlight she gave up hope, took the ribbon from her hair and blew out the lantern in the kitchen. She tiptoed into the bedroom, undressed and lay sleepless beside her brothers.

In the morning Liam sought her out in the potato garden. She knew better than to face him with accusations, for no man craved a jealous woman. Yet she could not help it, and spilled out Eileen's story.

He was indignant. A trouble-making liar was Eileen and Moira was mad to believe her. Bridget Reilly? Why, he'd not seen her since the wake. And how could he look at another woman when Moira's image was always before him?

'You've faith in God,' he said. 'You've faith in your father and mother. Why have you none in me?'

She looked into the black eyes, the strong face tensed with the need to make her believe. And she believed.

Throughout July County Mayo burned in heat. Toward the end of the month new potatoes were coming in and good crops were predicted from Sligo to Kerry. In August the heat was brutal, oppressive. Folk found it difficult to breathe and lagged about their work. Children played quietly, heartlessly.

In late August came a strange stillness. From coast to coast the sails of ships drooped windless. Ponds and rivers were silent and sullen. There seemed no life to the land. Nothing scuttered or sang or tunneled up through the baked earth. The woods were lifeless as scraps of tapestry that hung in old churches, fixed as tarnished green silk.

Rains began, drumming thatched roofs, flooding brooks. Then the sun rose, steaming the reeds of the roofs, hardening ditches and potato pits. Mildewed clothing was stretched on lines between trees. And the trees were silent for there was no wind and the crows flew away from the land and sought the sea.

The rains resumed like warm swill.

Chapter 2

Rain and high winds kept Ballyfearna indoors spinning, weaving, tale-telling at hearths. One night at Murphy's a plot was hatched to invade England. Instigated by Danel Powderley, the Protestant poet, it inflamed the men at the bar, who agreed to collect arms and ammunition and store them in Kelly's Cave until fair weather, when they would row a boat from Galway Bay and land by night on English soil. No one seemed clear as to what port would be invaded or what the invasion party would do when it landed, but these were minor points for future discussion.

That night at the bar great speeches were made, so resonant that they aroused the hens from the beams. Dennis Murphy provided free drink to the conspirators so that eighteen men pledged themselves to the mission. They would meet in the cave at dawn. But at dawn it was still raining, and God knew it would be foolish to carry a cache of arms to a wet cave. So the liberators went back to sleep.

Word of the plot, however, reached the ears of Biddy Murphy who told Mrs John the Basket who told Annie Dumbie who told Father Leary. He was aghast; and in chapel on Sunday he sternly warned against the enterprsie.

'Ireland,' he said, 'has had enough troubles with England without this parish making them worse. Now I'm absolving you all, for patriotism is a dear, lovely thing and freedom from tyranny is close to me heart. But *it won't work*. And if I hear of any one of you setting out for the coast it's excommunicated you'll all be.'

The male congregation, deprived of heroism, found solace in the fact that at least they had tried, and that their women considered them spiritual martyrs. Then the episode was forgotten in a new excitement. Granny Cullen's widowed daughter arrived from Boston America.

Sally Mullen was fifty, thin as a twig but wonderfully stylish in a buttoned black dress and feathered bonnet. On her second night home, despite driving rain, she held court in Granny's hut but graciously, as befit a former resident who knew better than to put on airs. The younger folk who did not remember her were deeply impressed. Everyone asked questions about America, though the answers were not always believed. Surely no man could earn a shilling a day driving a horse car! Nor a woman servant be paid tenpence a week with room and board! Imagine the marvels of inside privies! Sally had seen them, she said, and the rich people for whom she worked had a bathing vat of mahogany wood lined with marble. Even the poor ate bacon once a week and golden potatoes that were sweet as sugar.

'Do you swear this is true?' asked Father Leary.

'May God strike me dead if it ain't.'

'It sounds like heaven,' Mrs John the Basket said, 'so I'm wondering why you did leave there.'

'To die in me own land,' Sally said, 'when me time comes.'

They understood. For all the wonders of America, they too would want to be buried here on the earth of home.

As they talked, wind shook soot down Granny's roof-hole and the rain was a rage at the walls. In the turflight Moira saw her mother's face pinched suddenly in pain, her underlip caught between her teeth. It was surely not yet her time. Perhaps the baby kicked in her belly . . .

But Cathleen leaned toward Mary the Midwife and whispered and Mary rose quickly and crossed the room to Sean who hurried

42

to light a lantern. Moira roused her brothers who slept on the hearthstone and spoke softly to Liam.

'I think the pain is on me mother. I must go.'

'Then I'll go with you.'

Gratefully she said, 'May the Lord bless you. But it may be hours.'

'No matter.' He snatched up his coat and cap.

Granny said, 'Is it leaving you are, and it only early and the food not passed?'

'It's me time,' Cathleen said.

'Then I'll be sitting up with you.' Granny reached for her shawl and turned to her daughter. 'If I'm not home by morning, mind you feed the chickens and stir up the fire.'

Biddy Murphy stroked Colum's curls. 'I'll be keeping the little boys for the night, Mrs McFlaherty.'

Cathleen thanked her. Women clustered and petted, offering help, and Father Leary promised to come round after morning prayers. Moira thought, It's love I have for them all, for there's never a thought for themselves if a friend is in trouble or need. For all the grandeurs of America I'd not give tuppence this night . . .

The little group crossed the road to the McFlaherty hut while Paddy the Pawn scurried off to Mary's cabin to bring back her fardel of medicines. The women made Cathleen comfortable on her bed, undressing her and combing the lice from her hair. When Paddy returned, Mary gave her a brew of herbs to drink. Presently the swollen red eyelids drooped in sleep and Mary said, 'Let's go in to the fire.'

Liam had brought more turf from the loft and the fire was smoking against the chill of the night and the chill of their fear. Fear was in Granny's eyes, for she had lost three daughters and two sons in childbirth. Fear was in Liam, whose own mother had lost two — and she still sickly. Moira saw her own fear reflected in her father's face. Neither would forget that when Colum was born three years ago Cathleen had lost her mind in pain and nearly died.

Moira had neglected to sew more than two little shifts for the baby, so now in guilt she brought an oat sack to the fire and cut

43

it to the proper size. As she stitched it Liam watched her from his place on the hearth straw, one hand caressing Granny's hound pup. It was cosy with the animals all around — the two Mc-Flaherty dogs, Mary's old collie, the pig in its logs and the chickens roosting in the rafters. The wind screamed down from the hills but here it was snug, with the pot a-chuckle on its hook.

Mary, as befit her profession, had a fund of stories garnered through thirty years of lying-ins. There was the woman in Ballinrobe who had borne a fair child — Mary herself had breathed life into it and slapped its pink bottom. Yet not an hour later the fairies had stolen it and left a dark crumpled imp in its place.

'Sure,' Granny said wisely, 'because you'd left no gift for the fairies.'

'I was young then,' Mary said defensively. 'I didn't know.'

'What gift is it you'll be leaving tonight?' Sean asked.

'She's bedded with salt and flax and the boat ticket me daughter used from America,' Granny said.

Moira blessed them silently. They were taking no chances. For even if the fairies did not steal the child they could taunt the mother with pain.

She saw her father rise and go restlessly to the door, turn and pace back. Love lay on him like a shawl and worry like a shroud. She tried to divert him.

'Tell us the story of Finn McCool.'

'Do,' said Liam. 'I've not heard it since I was a lad.'

'Well . . .' Sean lit his pipe. 'Finn McCool was thirty feet tall, the biggest giant in Ireland. But in Scotland there was an even bigger giant who was fifty feet tall and he came to the village of Finn to challenge him to fight. When he rapped on Finn's door — a sound like thunder it was — Finn was mortally afraid and he said to his wife, "What shall I do? He'll kill me sure."

'Finn's wife hid the baby and told Finn to jump into its cot. She covered him with oat sacks and stuck a sucking jar in his mouth. Then she opened the door to the Scotch giant who said, "Is Finn McCool here?"

' "No," she said. "Only me and me baby."

'The Scot looked at the length of Finn in the cot and he said,

44

"By Jesus Christ if that's the babe how big is the father?" And out he ran as fast as he could. Finn, seeing him a coward, got out of the cot and chased him and tore off a turf sod and hurled it and killed him. That night was a great storm and rain pooled that sod-hole. You can still see it, only now they call it Lough Neagh. And the sod fell into the sea between Ireland and England to form the Isle of Man.'

'It's an education to hear you,' Mary said.

'Aye,' Granny said, 'they was great men in the old days, strong as oxen they was.'

Mary tiptoed into the bedroom and returned. 'She's sleeping peaceful . . . What's outside?'

There was a rapping on the door and Sean rose to greet Tyrone Schwartz and Danel Powderley, the Protestant poet.

'We was asked by Dennis to bring you a jug,' Danel said, handing it to Sean, 'and to ask if there's anything you need.'

Sean unplugged the jug and brought mugs. 'It's kind you are to come on such a night but it's only your company we need.'

As Moira brought their wet coats to the fire Tyrone said, 'If you'll be wanting the doctor I have me horse at Murphy's.'

'Doctor?' Mary asked angrily. 'Am I not here meself?'

'So I told him,' Danel said mildly. 'But he's new to this place. He meant no harm.' He lifted his mug. 'Slainte.'

The men drank.

Danel glanced at Moira. 'Someday I shall write you a poem, Moira of the Scarlet Hair, for beautiful you are.'

'Ah, now,' she said, embarrassed but pleased that Liam should be hearing the compliment.

'Tell us a poem,' Sean said.

'No,' Danel said, 'I do not tell my own.'

'Why not, then?' Mary asked.

'It is too poor they are, barefoot and uncombed.'

'Then why do you make them?' Granny asked.

'It's a fault I cannot help. It's like drink. I say to meself, "I'll not make another poem," but sure as the sunrise I am making another.'

'Ah,' Liam said, 'but he tells fine stories. Tell them the one you told us at Murphy's — the one about the pudden.'

The mug of poteen met Danel's lips through the curly grey-brown of his beard. 'Once upon a time the fairies bewitched a pudden because the woman who made it was courting with a Protestant like meself. They thought she deserved all the mischief they could invent, so after she'd tied up that pudden and put it on to boil they cast a spell on it. They made it fall from its hook and burst its lid and caper out of its pot and wobble all over the house so that her sweetheart Jack was near to a fit and jumped up on the table in fright. Maggie said her prayers for she knew a fairy was in that pudden and she told Jack to treat it respectful and maybe it would stop its pranking.

'So Jack says to the pudden, "Your honour, I'd consider it highly a favour if you'd stop cavorting about and hop back in your pot." But the pudden went leaping out the door and along the lanes and the minute the neighbours saw it they suspected the truth — that this was a betrothal pudden (for it had currants and all) and it protesting the marriage of a Catholic and a Black-mouth and they feared it would bring them all bad luck. So they rushed after it with pitchforks and shovels and sticks and scythes and finally they trapped it on the grass between the two opposing churches.

'The minister came out and the priest came out and the pudden lay quiet at their feet. Out popped a fairy wearing green knee-breeches and a silver-buttoned coat and a red cap and it said, "I've been chased near to death and toward death a fairy sees the error of his ways. I ask your forgiveness for trying to prevent the marriage of Maggie and Jack for these two is in love and love needs no faith but its own self."

'And with that the fairy went back in the pudden and split it in a hundred pieces and hopped into every mouth in town and was eaten up. And since then in that village there's been no animosity between Protestants and Catholics, not even when they're fighting.'

Granny crossed herself. 'That's a fine, moral story. But would you be marrying a Catholic, Danel Powderley?'

'I would,' Danel said, 'but now it's too old I am — fifty years of age.'

Mary sent him a long look and a flutter of eyelashes. 'It's only in the autumn of your youth you are.'

Cathleen called from the bedroom and the women rose swiftly and went in. Cathleen was sitting up, her forehead wet with sweat, and red veins mottled her cheeks. In her calico shift she looked as if she would burst, so distended was her stomach. Moira held her hand which she gripped hard. Mary ran for the hearth kettle. Granny lined a little box with clean oat sacks.

'Is Larry here?' Cathleen asked.

'No,' Moira said.

'No one to fiddle? Then the company will hear me.'

'No matter,' Mary said. 'It's all friends here.'

'But Sean — he must not hear.'

'Nonsense,' Mary said. 'Your own husband.'

'He'll sicken. He always does.' She appealed to Moira. 'Get him out of doors or send him to Murphy's — quick!'

Moira hurried back to the kitchen and whispered to her father.

'No,' he said, 'I'll not go.'

'But you always have.'

'Not now, alanna.'

'Why not? She wants you to.'

'Tell her I've gone, then. She'll not know.'

She reassured Cathleen that he had gone, then resumed her sewing, fingers clumsy as paws. The poteen lowered in the jug and Danel and Tyrone and Liam went off for another. Moira and Sean were alone in the turf-glowed dark.

They rarely talked of more than practical matters — planting, harvesting, or the rent. Sometimes they savoured the gossip of bog-trotters who brought the villagers infrequent mail. But now Sean was flooded of talk as though a dam had broken.

He spoke of his first meeting with Cathleen when she came from Ballinrobe to be maid at Murphy's Hotel. 'She was only fourteen but full as an opening flower and beautiful, with her hair to her knees. I had stopped into the bar for a jar and it was she who served me, but foolishly, not knowing one jug from another. I told her where the poteen was and I raised me jar and said, "To me future wife," and drank to her grace. And do you know, she took it truly. She said, "That's meself, is it not?" and I said, "Aye, it's me pledge."

'So we were betrothed at a glance and married a month later. It's the way love comes on you, swift as pain or death and once it's on you there's no leaving it even if you wish.'

She knew only too well.

'But you never wished to leave her, Da?'

'I have, each time she births. I long to run away lest I hear her screams but I can't. For her pain is mine to share.'

'It's to Granny's you went last time.'

'It was not, though I told you so. I was sitting outside, sick in the grass.'

'Do you know,' he said, 'it's me mind I'm losing in times like this. If God should ask me me name tonight I'd say, "Cathleen McFlaherty." '

Screams began, soaring up to the rafters, dying down in gasps only to begin again. Moira moved to her father's side and held his hand but his hand on hers was hurtfully tight and she withdrew it.

'Go,' she pleaded, 'go out.'

The rain and the wind would be better than this . . .

'She may need me . . .'

'No,' she said, 'only women can tend her. Go, darling.'

He hurried out the door, heedless of a coat, and tears spilled down her face and she put her hands to her ears to still the sounds of agony. She took the dogs in her arms for comfort. They had rolled in the pig-dung but she did not care for they were warm and loving and trembling as herself.

Screams and cessation . . . Sean came back, Liam, Danel and Tyrone returned with a jug. Moira put the little shift aside, unfinished.

Just before dawn Granny, grey-faced as her hair, came in and said over the sound of squalling, 'A little girl,' and sat down on the floor and went to sleep with her head in Moira's lap. Sean ventured into the bedroom and came back smiling and settled to sleep with a little sigh of content.

All that day neighbors brought food and drink — hare stew and oatbread, fish and potato puddings. Shyly, Bridget Reilly came to the door with a pot of hen soup and what could Moira do but ask her in? Thank God Liam was safely back to his field for Bridget not only wore her flowered bonnet but a new red frieze petticoat and a yellow bangle on her wrist. Somewhere, Moira thought, I have seen that bangle and when Tyrone Schwartz reappeared at dusk she remembered. There had been a row of them on his cart, strung on a knife, clinking against the cutlery.

Not that she cared if Bridget and Tyrone had met but Bridget was a threat to any woman. The thick black hair, the slanty black eyes . . . My God, even Dennis Murphy and John the Basket looked at her as no husbands should, and their wives only a whisper away.

The house was honoured by Sister Charity and Sister Angelica who brought pears from the convent. Father Leary blessed Cathleen and the baby and took a glass of sloe wine. Returning from the bedroom Mary said, 'She's no name for the child as yet.'

The guests in the kitchen pondered the matter. Cona was a beautiful name, Moira thought, and that of Sean's mother. But Tyrone Schwartz suggested a name as befit a Queen.

Father Leary frowned. 'Victoria?'

'Ah, no,' Tyrone said. 'I had in mind Deirdre.'

Bridget said, 'If I had a girleen I'd not name her for any person but for something beautiful I admired.'

Bonnet, Moira thought scornfully. Bonnet McFlaherty. 'Sunset,' Bridget said dreamily.

As Moira moved about the room serving food she heard snatches of talk. Biddy warned Dennis to mind his drinking. Sally Mullen, with a cold eye on Bridget, informed the women that flowered bonnets had not been worn in Boston America since before the Revolution. Father Leary and Danel discussed the similarity between prayers and poems. Paddy the Pawn agreed to exchange breeches for two jugs of Jesus' poteen. Mary confided to Sean that she never expected remuneration for her services as midwife but people were always so generous it was embarrassing . . .

At dusk the company dispersed. Moira showed the baby to her

brothers and told them to handle it gently. Small, stubby fingers stroked the bald head and silky toes. Round-eyed, they watched it try to feed at its mother's puffed breast.

Moira washed the dishes and straightened the room. Sean went out to milk the cow which they shared with Granny Cullen. The rain resumed, drumming against the roof.

Sean returned, tossing his wet jacket on the hearth stool. 'I met with Brian O'Donnell in the lane. He said he had seen The Gorta.'

'God save us!' Moira clasped her rosary. 'Where? When?'

'In the woods near the waterfall. But Brian is old and his head is crazy so we'll not worry.'

But crazy or not Brian was gifted with second sight. 'What did The Gorta look like?'

'He was seven feet tall but thin as a reed and his face was a skull. He wore a black ragged cloak over his bones and he asked Brian for alms.'

'Did Brian give to him?'

'No, he had not a penny on him so he ran as fast as he could. It was after panting he was when I met him. Feared he was for sure, but he could have been chased by dogs or children.'

'Aye,' she said, taking comfort. The cruel little ones often chased the old man and she had often slapped them for pestering him.

But as she finished her chores she thought of the many evils abroad in the woods, the bogs, the mountains. Old evils born thousands of years ago in cairns, evils which had never died. There were bad fairies who stole beautiful women for brides on St John's Eve and bonfires were lit against them. Again on November Eve the bonfires burned from hill to hill to frighten them away from the villages. Old evils lived in pools and rivers. Merrows reached out scaly hands to pull in fishermen, mermaids sang so sweetly to men that they left their wives and sweethearts to drown in darkness. There was the banshee, a female fairy who wailed before the death of someone of importance. She rode in a huge black coach drawn by headless horses and if she knocked at your door and you opened, a bucket of blood was hurled in your face.

50

Pray God The Gorta was only in Brian's mind.

Sean tapped his pipe against the fire-stones. 'Don't tell your mother about this. She must rest from her labour and her heart be at peace.'

Moira agreed.

'She's not as strong as she was when she bore Colum, it may be near a week before she's up. Mary tells me to have another child might kill her.'

'Dear God!'

'So you must not shirk your duties but spare her all you can.'

Oh, she would do better! She would nurse her mother like a baby and tempt her with good breads and potato pies. But in the morning when Liam came to the door she thought, What harm to leave for an hour or so? I'll make the bread later.

They walked through the misty woods to his wet field. There they packed dry turf over the potatoes and placed cut weeds on the pits to soak up the moisture. Then the air turned heavy with thunder, rain lashed the field and they rushed to the shelter of his shed. It was shadowy, steamy with cow and pig dung. Chicken feathers tickled her bare feet.

She said as he kissed her, 'I must go home . . .'

But it was a long, dark rain and how should she go home through treacherous bogs? Close in his arms she closed her eyes and raised her mouth for his kiss.

Sean's anger was slow to brew but that night he struck Moira hard on the face, so hard that she reeled against the wall. The boys ran shrieking into Cathleen who rose from bed to pacify her husband and comfort her daughter.

Moira wept in her arms, full of love and guilt. Fury at her father died quickly for her trust in him was fathomless and she knew he was right. She put Cathleen back to bed and quieted the boys. Alone with Sean she asked if he thought her a dilsy.

'No,' he said, as though surprised by the question. 'It's your goodness I doubt, not your virtue. Liam's a wild lad but he's not one to harm you. Still, I'll not have him coming here for a morning and charming you off from your work. I'll tell him me-self that you'll see him but two nights a week.'

She had to be content with that. Deprived of his company the days of September passed slowly. Cathleen was up now but she moved with a strange sort of lethargy as though still heavy with child. Father Leary christened the baby Grace and Moira loved it for the wee thing rarely cried and often smiled. Since Cathleen's milk was scant it was also fed from the cow and it made no complaint.

Harvest time was delayed by rains and thunderstorms until finally one morning Sean said, 'Wet or not, we'll spade up the praties.'

Moira shawled her head, took her spade and joined him in the fog-filled garden. They stood sniffing like dogs for there was a strange smell.

'What is it?' she asked, sickened by the stench.

Sean said nothing but ran past the fence and she followed him blindly for he was obscured in swirling fog. She stubbed her toe on a rock but hurried on, heedless of the pain. The stench was nearly unbearable and she pressed her shawl to her nose.

The fog lifted in a sudden breeze. All around them were the green stems of potato plants but the leaves were spotted brown. Sean bent to touch the foliage and a stem fell into his hand. He took his spade and dug into a trench and uncovered three tiny blackened potatoes.

'Da,' she asked, 'what has happened?'

But he did not reply. They went to other trenches. Some potatoes were fat and sound, others half-rotted, still others a soft mass of decay. Then the fog crept over again and she could see nothing beyond her own extended hand.

'Da! What is it?'

He said, 'Get your mother and tell her to bring a barrel and the boys to help fill it. Then go to Granny's and look at her field and if it's rotting tell her to spade them up fast as she can and store the sound ones in a pit.'

'But what *is* it? What's happened?'

'The blight,' he said.

The white evil-smelling fog crept into Antrim, Armagh, Wicklow, Tyrone. Sound potatoes rotted to slime within a few days and the animals that ate them sickened. From the Scientific Commission in Dublin pamphlets came to landlords and priests advising them to instruct the people how to salt or soak or bake the diseased potatoes for cattle and pig food. But most of the people did not understand the instructions and those who did found them useless.

The people of Ballyfearna were not panicked because of Father Leary's calm reassurance. This was not the terrible blight the old folk talked of but only a partial one. They must thank God for the remains of last spring's plentiful crop, but they must tighten their belts and hoard. On no account must they eat the precious seed potatoes but save them for the next planting. They must supplement their meals with fish.

From the abbey pulpit he asked the people if they had any questions.

'Aye,' said Granny Cullen. 'How am I to eat fish and they sickening me?'

'You ate it in 1830, did you not? And it kept you alive.'

'Fish is not fit food,' said Brian O'Donnell. 'Me wife died of it.'

'Meal, then,' Father Leary said patiently. 'Berries, nuts. And there's plenty of game hereabouts.'

'Hares are tough,' said Biddy Murphy. 'They upset the stomach something terrible.'

'True for you,' agreed Mrs John the Basket. 'It's cramps they bring.'

'Heed me now,' the priest said, still patiently but with an edge to his voice. 'It's the pratie you're used to but my God, it's not the only food on earth. Why did the good Lord give us rabbits and moorhens and birds? Cabbages and turnips? *Eat them.* Keep your praties for one meal a day only and mind what I said about the seed praties, for if you eat them up you'll have nothing for the spring.'

'How will we pay our rents?' Annie Dumbie asked.

'With the pig, if need be, but I'll be after asking Mr Pond to give an extension. Trust in God and you'll not want.'

And so October came with little change from the years before except that men fished and children gathered nuts and traps were laid for moorhens. The young men shot woodcock and partridge but few folk ate them — the flesh was boiled for the animals.

The weather turned dry and the foliage reddened and gold-ened. There was little change on the land. Blackbirds ate the sloes at first frost, stray cattle were blinded by thistles as they roamed the high slopes of the hills. And as always when the wet cold tightened the people huddled to their fires. There was nothing to do but feed the stock. In the dark of winter there was nothing to do but bed and breed, visit and gossip and long for the spring.

It was shortly after Christmas when Annie Dumbie shed her wet shawl on the hearth of the McFlahertys' where it steamed like a sprawled black pudding.

'And what brings you here this terrible night?' Cathleen asked, honouring her with the next-best stool for Granny Cullen had the soundest one.

The widow's plump face dimpled. 'Oh, just a-visiting I am. It's lonely when Himself's not with me.'

'Aye,' Sean said. 'You was married in happiness.'

Cathleen and Granny and Moira exchanged amused glances, for all the women knew that the widow was spoken for.

'It's Peter Kane is courting me,' Annie said, fluffing her damp hair. 'The weaver from Ballydonny, bereft like meself but not so often. It's two wives he's buried, and a year lived in sadness.'

Sean pulled at his pipe. 'And shall you marry, then?'

'At the time of the cowslips.'

She must be near fifty, Moira thought, a dumpling of a woman with three chins and the grey on her hair yet she's snared her fifth husband while I . . .

'It's me old trouble I came about,' Annie said. She appealed to Granny. 'What shall I be doing about it now?'

'What trouble?' Sean asked.

'Her dress,' Granny said, gently but impatiently for even a man should recall Annie's recurrent problem. 'She has had the same marriage dress these thirty years. First it was white —'

'Then I stained it with haw-juice.'

'And then we put on the blue embroidery.'

54

'Was it the red sash then?' Cathleen asked.

'It was the black ruffle,' Granny said. 'I'd enough left over from me husband's casket cover. And we let out the seams, she plumpening as she did.'

Sean interrupted. 'Is it not fearful you are to marry again, knowing the short life of them?'

'No,' Annie said, 'for bad luck must pass. I'm afraid of nothing.'

'I wish that was true of me,' Granny said. 'Them birds. I see them, I hear them and me heart chokes me throat. If one of them should light on me I'd die of the fright and I dread every spring that comes. That's why I keep me cats. But sometimes they catch the birds and bring them to me, the terrible bloodied feathers.'

The toothless mouth worked to explain, the pale eyes dilated. 'It's so hard to go to me patch of a fair day for I hear them, I see them there in the trees and if one should come down on me —' She shuddered. 'It's not me age, for Eileen Finnigan has the fear too and she only twenty. But it's dogs she fears.'

Moira leaned forward. 'Dogs?'

'She never said, but I know.'

'But the priest has dogs.'

'She keeps them fenced outside when he's away and she'll not let them in until he comes home. She told me it's fear of the fleas but I know better for she's not afraid of them on herself.'

Moira thought of Father Leary's two gentle hounds. If Eileen fenced them it was for some lazy purpose of her own, perhaps to keep their droppings from the house so she need not clean the floors.

'Have you no fears?' Granny asked Cathleen.

She hesitated. Then she said, 'The blight. You mind how it was fifteen years ago.'

Granny said, 'It's hard times we had but it's always been hard. It's the Lord's will to punish us.'

'It's the railroads,' Sean said, 'the steam and the smoke spread out over the land and rot the praties.'

'There wasn't no railroads in thirty,' Annie said. 'Himself says it's the fallings of the sea-fowl that poison the earth.'

'We're far from the coast,' Sean said. 'Twenty-five miles.'

Moira said, 'Liam says it's these hot old things deep in the earth — vol — volcanoes.'

'All I know, it comes with the rains and the thunder,' Cathleen said. 'And it falls in a mist from the heavens . . . Moira, fetch the pudden and cut a bit for each.'

Moira was proud of her pudding, made with oatmeal, sloes, eggs and sugar, then boiled in the iron pot. A pity Liam was not here to share it but Sean had been adamant. They could court but twice a week.

Annie tasted the pudding. 'It's a fine wife you'll make, Moira.'

Granny chuckled. 'Fine wife! She's not quite long enough for a man to seed her!'

'She would,' Cathleen said, loyal before company. 'It's young she is.'

'You were only fourteen when you married,' Granny said. 'Or was it fifteen?'

'Fifteen,' Cathleen said.

'A quiet one you were and tending your house like it was the priest's own. I mind you had the clothes line out two days after you was wedded.'

'It's different now,' Annie said. 'Times change. Moira will have the easier work.'

It was easy now, Moira thought, for in the dark of winter folk had little to do but feed themselves and the animals. They ate when they were hungry, slept when tired. Save for those few men who laboured at looms or in the shops no one wound a clock until spring. One could tell the hour well enough by the roosting of hens at dusk and the grind of the grain mill of a morning. Once a week one could know the hour of eight by the sound of the Castlebar Coach as it pulled into Murphy's yard to the yells of the waiting children. But mostly winter was a time of sleeping, lightened only by the visit of friends.

'Is it Liam Lenihan you'll be marrying?' Annie asked.

'It is me hope.'

'Maybe it's brides we'll be together.' Annie licked pudding from her fingers and wiped them on her petticoat. 'But what am I to do to fancy me dress? It's not a bit of calico I have nor a ribbon bow nor nothing.'

'Could you not ask Paddy to give you a bit?' Sean asked.

'Och, he'll give me no more for I'm deep to him already for cost of me husband's wake and all.'

They talked of Paddy — pawnbroker, shopkeeper and usurer. He was kind by night, generous of drinks to the men at Murphy's and sometimes lavish as a host in his own hut. But by day in his shop he was hard and mean. If you had a fine coat to pawn, not even three years old, he'd lend you half its value. Was it just a loan you wanted he'd fee you tuppence to the shilling. Or suppose you wanted to trade a pig-bristle broom for a bag of meal. He'd cheat on the weight if your eyelid flickered. Clearly, Paddy was no solution to Annie's problem.

'I can't wear me marriage dress the same,' Annie said. 'It wouldn't look right in the eyes of the church.'

The women considered. Finally Granny said, 'Now I'm not sure she'll agree but me daughter Sally has a bit of white tarlatan she brought from America. I could just ask her.'

'Glory be to God! Is it enough to collar me?'

'Enough and more. It is how the rich people cover their windows in America.'

'And why should they cover such fine things as windows?' Cathleen asked. 'Is it ashamed they are to have them?'

'It is to keep folk from looking inside,' Moira said. 'Like the shutters of wood at Murphy's.'

'I don't like them shutters,' Granny said. 'It's against nature. You can't look out and see what people is doing on the road. But tarlatan curtains is nice, I'd be thinking. You could peep through them.'

Annie turned to Granny in sudden inspiration. 'Sally should marry again and Himself has a brother. You tell her if she can see her way to give me the tarlatan for the dress I could see me way to having her meet Patrick Kane.'

Granny looked dubious.

'He's got an acre, a goat and a sheep.'

'Ah, well.' Granny shrugged.

'A fine brown beard, curly it is.'

'Oh?' Granny dismissed the beard with a wave of her hand. 'And what else?'

Annie thought hard. 'A shed a-building.'

'Chickens?'

'Aye. And my God, I near forgot — a gold tooth.'

'Hm,' said Granny, unimpressed. 'Teeth cut food but they don't feed nobody.'

'He's got a big barrel of praties.'

'You're sure?'

'I seen them with me own eyes. And seedling too.'

'A pig?'

'He shares one with Himself. With me Peter.'

'Well now,' Granny said, 'Sally's in the prime of life, like a rose she is. I'm thinking she could find a better man. But I might just ask her.'

'Good,' said Annie.

'Now wait,' Granny said, 'how old is this Patrick Kane?'

'Oh — who's to be knowing, him with the brown of his beard?'

'Is it snuff he takes to tip the burden of it?'

'Snuff? Not he.'

'It's costly, snuff is,' Granny said.

'Maybe he takes just a little then for he owns enough to buy it should he choose. He having no wife to lavish on,' Annie added.

'Well now,' Granny said, 'I might just ask Sally, though I doubt if she'll be wanting to meet him. Shall we be going over to me house to see if she might agree? It being in a way a favour to yourself?'

The McFlahertys thanked them for coming and watched them walk down the path through the rain. Cathleen cut another slice of pudding and heaved her bulk back on to the stool.

'It's so hungry I am,' she said, 'that I think I'll be birthing.'

They stared at her.

'Maybe it's only me hunger, but me breasts are sore too and I've not had me bleeding.'

Sean pulled Cathleen to her feet and took her into the other room. Moira could hear them talking softly through the drum of the rain and the swell of the wind in the trees. She sat on the straw by the fire but though it was embering she did not stir it. Her heart beat jaggedly and she put her hand to its pulsing.

58

Sean came in and sat down. 'I pray it's not true but I feel it is so.'

'Why did you do it?' she asked.

He was silent, tapping his dead pipe in his hand. His silence grew long and she studied his face and saw for the first time the lines of age on eyes and brow but she felt no pity for his silence and his sadness.

'Mary told you — you knew. Yet you did it.'

Still he said nothing. She felt that he was looking beyond her.

'You knew it could kill her!'

He smashed down his pipe and it broke on the hearthstone.

'Is it an animal you are?' she asked.

He spoke on a sob. 'Hush, you don't know what you're talking of. When you love someone —'

'Love! Is it love you'd kill her with?'

His curse shocked and sickened her and she ran to the end of the room but it was not far enough and she opened the door and fled outside heedless of the rain. Smoke still puffed from Granny's cottage and she hurried there, not thinking what she would say, only wanting warmth and a refuge from Sean.

Sally opened the door. 'Come in, Moira. Annie's just left and me mother's abed and it's lonesome I am — what's wrong?'

It did not matter that she scarcely knew Sally or that years lay between them. She told her what had happened.

'. . . and he cursed me for saying the truth!'

Sally shook her head. 'It's not for you to judge him. Your mother could have put him off.'

'She can't refuse him anything.'

'It's her love and his and you should not poke-nose.'

'But it's her life she could lose!'

'It's her life to spend as she pleases. And Mary may be wrong. In Boston it's doctors women go to. Midwives only help. So when her time comes, send for Dr Thrush.'

Moira could imagine Mary's jealous fury and the long friendship shattered. But a small price to pay for her mother's life.

'Doctors in Boston do miracles,' Sally said. 'I seen with me own eyes. Mrs Brown, the rich lady I worked for, was young and frail and too small for her first child. It's in terrible pain she was until

59

the doctor came and gave her laudanum and she slept through the pain and the child was born before she knew it.'

'Laudam?'

'Laudanum. It's a few drops you drink.'

Moira repeated the word so as to remember. Dr Thrush had never been called to Ballyfearna for childbirth, only accidents, but he was renowned throughout the county. Comforted, she said, 'You've cheered me.'

Sally smiled. 'You cheer me, too. It's strange I feel here, though I was born and raised here. And it's lonely too. Me husband is gone, me mother is old. And I am not — old.'

She did not look her age, Moira thought. Her small-boned body was neat. She had Granny's sharp chin and pale eyes but her skin was fresh and rosy, dotted by freckles. In the candlelight in her stylish brown wrapper with her brown hair down her back she could have passed for thirty. Yet, Moira thought, she is twelve years older than my mother.

'Annie tells me that she is after marrying again,' Sally said. 'It's me intention to give her me tarlatan curtain —'

'Ah,' Moira said. 'It's good you are.'

'— after I have met this man at her house. I'm not giving of the goods until I have seen him.'

'It's wise you are. And if you don't like him?'

'Then I'll only lend her the curtain and no harm done if it's not cut.' Sally lowered her voice. 'I've a worry — me mother.'

'But she wants you to marry —'

'It's not that troubles me. But you mind what the priest said of saving our seed praties to plant?'

Moira nodded.

'We've had many meals of praties since. Too many, I'm thinking.'

'But you *have* planted.'

'I made the trenches and spread the ash and manure and then you recall me tooth pain came on and I went to Dr Thrush in Ballydonny. I was gone from dawn to dusk.'

Moira remembered seeing her drive off in the hired cart of Tyrone Schwartz.

'Did you see me mother plant that day?'

60

'She was there in the patch for a while, but I took no notice really. You think she did not plant, only pretended to?'

'I don't know,' Sally said. 'I don't know . . . but I think a sickness is on her mind.'

Granny was eighty-one but Moira had noticed no addlement. 'Why?'

'She thinks birds are waiting for her, ready to spring down from the trees. She says they come into the house and steal the grain from the jug. She screams of them in the night. And I fear she did not plant because she is afraid of the birds. And because there were no praties to put in the earth, them being eaten.'

It was Moira's turn to comfort. 'Ah, well, it's a fine crop we'll have and plenty to share so don't worry. And maybe you are wrong.'

'Maybe I am wrong,' Sally said.

Cold rains ushered in March. The folk of Ballyfearna were eating their last stored potatoes; by April the potatoes were gone even from the shop of Paddy the Pawn. But the days were warm and dry and plants bloomed in miles of little gardens. No one could recall lusher blossoms nor finer weather.

One day a bog-trotter came to deliver a letter to Father Leary and stopped afterwards at Murphy's Hotel. Bog-trotters were an exciting event and word of his arrival scurried through town. Sean paid one of his rare visits to Murphy's bar.

Moira and Cathleen waited up for the news he was certain to bring. Births, marriages, deaths. Scandals ardently hoped for. But when Sean returned he had little to repeat. A bad storm in Longford. A fisherman drowned at Black Sod.

'What else did he say, Da?' Moira asked.

Sean shrugged. 'Nothing. He was off early.'

'Was Liam there?' Moira asked.

'Aye, he was.'

Cathleen said, 'And who else?'

'Oh, the same as ever. Jesus and Paddy and John.' He seemed preoccupied. 'Father Leary.'

'Father Leary at the bar!' Cathleen exclaimed. This was news indeed. 'Why?'

'For the love of God! Is it the priest can't take a glass of porter?'

'Who was his letter from, then?'

Sean's voice climbed. 'How the hell should I be knowing? Is it talk you live for?' He strode outside banging the door behind him.

Moira and Cathleen exchanged puzzled glances. Sean loved gossip as much as they.

The next evening, when Liam came to take her walking in the moonlight Moira told him about her father's strange reaction to their questions. 'He's always told us what the bog-trotter said.'

'Ah, well. There's times a man can't be plagued.'

She paused on the wooden bridge. 'What did the bog-trotter tell you?'

'Oh,' he said casually, 'there was a storm, a drowning. A woman had twins in Ahascrogh.'

'And —?'

'A storm.'

'You said that. How long was the trotter at Murphy's?'

'Three hours, I think.'

Men were so *unhearing*. In three hours a listening woman would have had enough gossip to last all the months of spring.

'And Father Leary was there at the bar?'

Sean's impatience was in Liam's voice. 'Aye, he was. He was wearing his robes and hat, and shoes on his feet. He drank an inch of porter from Biddy's best glass. I mind he sneezed twice. What else must you know?'

Quickly she caught his hand in hers. 'It's no harm I meant but you won't *tell* me anything.'

He turned to look at her. 'I will. It's beautiful you are with the light of the moon on your hair.'

She saw Jesus Finnigan next day near St Cecilia's Cave. Clearly he had tested his own poteen for his voice was slurred as he greeted her. 'Moira, me dear love, and how is it with you? So lovely you are you shame the flowers.'

She cut through the flowers of his speech. 'Was you at Murphy's the night before last and heard the bog-trotter?'

'Oh.' He stiffened. 'I think I was, sure.'

'What did he say?'

He scratched his snarled blond head and cursed the lice.

'I said what did he say?'

'Who?'

'The bog-trotter!'

Jesus's voice turned clear and sharp. 'I don't remember. How should I, and me in the drink?'

As the days passed there seemed a true renaissance of the earth and Father Leary bade the parish thank God for their flowering fields. In June he formed a pilgrimage to St John's Cave and most of the village went.

Moira remained home to tend baby Grace and the baby slept. In the quiet hut she slipped, as always, into daydream. If Liam had not marriage in mind why did he call so regularly under her father's eye or bring her that shamrock? Once more she visioned the house near the Pool of the Waterdogs and furnished it lovingly. A wedding dress would be the principal problem . . .

She heard horses' hooves and the barking of her dogs and ran outside to see Mr Pond descending from his gig.

'Where is everyone?' he asked testily.

'Oh, Your Honour!' She dropped a humble curtsy. 'It's off to pray they are at the Cave of St John and offer praise to God.'

'For what?'

'For the good blooming, sir. To give thanks for it.'

'Is your father 'ere?'

'No, sir.'

He swore softly. 'It seems I must send my calling card ahead to find folk 'ome.'

She did not know what he meant. 'Sir?'

'When will 'e be 'ome?'

'Before the milking, sir.'

'A wasted day for us all. 'Ow can you lag in your duties?'

'Duties? And what should we be doing, sir?'

For the fields stretched full and fair, the willow fences were neat, the cow grazed the green slope and the pig was fat.

'You should be paying your rent,' he said. 'It's not a rent I've taken these ten months.'

She feared him but she had also a deep disgust bred of old stories. Landlords could be somehow romanticised, those who lived in castles or great houses. But their agents were mean, like this one with his prim tight-buttoned face and scraggy moustache the colour of dirty straw. He wore a bowler hat and high stock and his breeches were tight on his skinny legs. He was English, and Father Leary said he came from the parish of Cockney and these Cockneys were hired by the landlords because they were shrewd and drove a ruthless bargain.

'Rent!' she said. 'Father Leary said you'd granted us all another month, sir.'

'The month is up.' He pulled a little vellum book from his pocket. 'You owe one pound five.'

'Five shillings, sir? It's always been a pound the half-year.'

'The five is for your defaulting. Your failure,' he explained impatiently.

'But the blight —'

'Is not 'is Lordship's concern. Is 'e to wait on your 'arvest? And was it not your own lazy ways brewed the ill?'

'We've not lazied,' she said. 'If you'll tell His Lordship, please your honour, that as soon as we dig the praties he'll have the rent —'

' 'E's in England and 'e's 'earing these stories and 'e wants 'is rent or 'e'll sell the land. You think the gentry is rich? Rich with praties and pigflesh?' His voice held a whine. 'What of myself?'

She knew he had a tall, snug house with a chimney, five acres sown in oats and praties, pigs and cows and sheep and a wife with a maid servant.

'If I'm not collecting the rents then me and my family starve.'

'Oh, sir, it's none of us will starve.' She indicated the flowery expanse of dozens of little holdings. 'We'll pay as soon as we dig.'

His voice rose querulously. 'And why are you so sure? Is it you're the chosen people? Did some fairy ring the town with a

64

magic spell? Are you so smug you can't look a mile beyond your own 'ill? Do you know what's 'appened in Ballinglass? Three 'undred people have been evicted.'

Evicted. The most terrible of words . . .

'Yes,' he said, 'their 'ouses tumbled and themselves set to begging on the roads.'

'But,' she said through her shock, 'Ballinglass must be miles away. I never heard of it.'

'Ballinglass is in the next county.'

'Dear God! They could not pay their rents?'

'They could. But Mrs Gerrard, knowing their laziness and knowing the pratie crop might fail again, 'as turned the land to grazing. And so may 'is Lordship do that 'ere if you don't pye your rents.'

She stood chilled in the sunlight.

'You don't know what's 'appening around you,' he said with satisfaction. And as she shook her head numbly, he told her.

In village after village the sound potatoes were gone and folk were sickening of diseased ones. Many were too weak to catch the fish of the streams or — strong enough to fish — vomited the food because of the sickness on them. People were selling all they owned, even to their clothes, for a few pounds of oatmeal. Old folk and babies were dying of fever.

He looked into her astonished face and his own face softened. 'No one 'as told you? No one 'as been through these five weeks?'

'No, sir, we've had no news. A bog-trotter only, and he said nothing, else me father would have known or the priest would have —'

She paused, her memory nagged by that night at Murphy's and all the men evasive of news . . .

He raised his hands. 'God! And you're giving thanks, making a 'oliday at some cave for some s-s-saint —' He was stuttering with exasperation. 'I think this town is a lunatic asylum without b-b-bars!'

She wondered how to pacify him. What would her parents have her do? Inspired, she said, 'Why don't you be coming inside to have a nice cup of tea?'

But his temper flared higher. That, he said, was just what he might have expected! Improvidence. Reckless expenditure. 'Tea! And 'ave you got oranges and champine wine and seed cykes too? And maybe a suckling pig to roast? But you can't pye the rent.'

'But your Honour, the tea is only for special folk like yourself. We've had it this two years.'

Still sputtering he got into the gig. 'Tell your father I'll be back Tuesday and if 'e can't pye then it's the eviction piper will be in my pocket. And that's the same for all of you, all of you.'

She had not wholly realized her fear until, watching him drive off, she turned to go into the house and her knees buckled so that for a moment she held to the wall.

She tumbled out her news when her parents returned and the little boys were asleep on the hearth straw.

'Can we pay him, Da?' she asked Sean.

He nodded. 'With the pig.'

To give up the pig was like giving part of the house.

'It's in luck we are,' Sean said. 'Some have no pig at all.'

She said accusingly, 'You knew. The bog-trotter must have told you what's happening. Why didn't you tell us?'

Cathleen said, 'Peace, alanna. Himself told me in secret but we wanted to spare you. Besides, the good father told the men at Murphy's to repeat nothing — he did not want the women and the old folk to fret. He said it would cause —' she appealed to Sean — 'what was the word he used?'

'I forget,' Sean said. 'But what he meant, old folk would start a-talking of '30 and pass the terrible stories about and the town would freeze into fear. And he said fear could be the hurt of us, chilling our hearts just when the springtime is on us and we needing all our faith to pray for the good harvest.'

Moira understood but she was puzzled. 'Why is it lands about us are so bad with the blight and we struck lightly?'

'It's that I asked Father Leary,' Sean said. 'He told me the country is like a chessboard. You've seen that board?'

'Aye.' There was a chessboard for coach guests in the parlour of Murphy's Hotel. 'Black and white squares it is.'

'He says Ireland is like that, some counties white in plenty or black in blight. I'm thinking we here are like white only just touched by the black.'

'But Da, how can that be?'

'Who's to know? I say it's the smoke of the railroads —'

'It's the will of God,' Cathleen said. 'The fog comes at His will. But alanna, you've only to look at the fields to know we are safe. And oh, so beautiful was the service at the Cave!' She described it, with the lit candles of the pilgrims and the blue cathedral hush of the sky. 'And Father Leary blessed us all, and every living thing and a peace came on me heart.'

Comforted, Moira thought: So we give Mr Pond the pig for rent but when the praties are in why we buy another — maybe two . . .

They roused the little boys and ate and Cathleen brought the baby in for feeding. Cathleen was gay; perhaps the ribbon in her hair or the comfort of the pilgrimage and her faith renewed.

'Bridget Reilly was there with Tyrone Schwartz,' she said. 'It's courting I think they are. And Eileen Finnigan — but alone. Now there's a strange one. She'd not even bend her head in prayer and she wore her hair uncovered though it was like in church . . .'

Something rumpled Moira's mind. A word unsaid — a word her parents had not remembered.

'Da,' she said as Sean came in after milking, 'what was the word the good father said would bring us worry?'

He shook his head. 'A word?'

'A word that would fear us.'

'Oh,' he said. 'Panic.'

The McFlaherty pig was paid as rent and Sally's savings from Boston kept Granny from eviction. Perhaps, Moira thought, there was indeed a spell cast on Ballyfearna for though the harvest was not yet in no one lacked the pound or the pig to pay Mr Pond. A happy time it was, with neighbours happy. The mare Liam shared with Paddy the Pawn foaled; Annie Dumbie introduced Sally to Patrick Kane and the tarlatan curtain was given, not lent. Sally's mistrust of her mother vanished, for the potato garden flourished high and white as any in town.

Old Larry the Fiddler died, but in his sleep, softly as music. Danel Powderley sent a poem to a Dublin paper and received four shillings. Bridget Reilly and Tyrone Schwartz walked hand in hand. The bishop gave the convent nuns a plough mule. Jesus Finnigan won a fight against the Ballinrobe champion and Dennis treated the bar. Liam was lovesome of Moira as never before and made for her a ring of clover — surely an unspoken pledge? And she felt with a lift of her heart that her mother was happy with the child growing in her and that all would be well.

Only Father Leary seemed thoughtful and grave, and of the young women only Eileen Finnigan walked alone. It was she who stoned John the Basket's dog which, she said, fanged her as she crossed the reeds of the river bank. But John forgave her for he had sold six baskets to coach travellers.

So it was a time of happiness, these days of the bright flowers and quick-scattered rain and golden sun. These days of the spring of 1846 in Ballyfearna.

The early morning air was sultry and thunderous. Moira awakened slowly, numbed from a dream. What had frightened her so? Her brothers lay beside her and she took Colum into her arms for comfort.

What had been the dream? A road, she remembered, a cold unending road grey without trees. Piles of black dead crows and Granny there screaming.

She sank back to sleep.

'Cathleen! Moira!'

The shouting was real, Sean's voice blurred from the distance of the room between them. Moira and her mother sprang up and ran to the kitchen where he stood at the open front door with a spade in his hand. And through the room came the white evil fog, the smell of death — lush, overripe, overblown. The smell of a corpse of a garden.

They followed him out to last night's white blooming, now scorched and blackened. Cathleen bent and a stem brittled in her hand. Moira lifted her night shift to cover her nose. The boys came out and stood in silence.

Moira moved close to her father. 'Da?' Like a child she struggled against certainty, hoped without hope. 'It's no worse than the last?'

It seemed to her that her voice was unreal. It was all unreal, she thought — her family half-glimpsed through the drifting fog, the tall phantom spade and the green phantom grass. And all around her the smell of her nightmare, grey without trees though she knew the trees were there.

'The hunger is on us,' Sean said.

Chapter 3

All that remained of the gardens were a few sound seed potatoes more precious than money, the one insurance against eviction. These potatoes were planted hopefully and prayerfully and Father Leary blessed each patch. He rode to the outlying farmers who had poor crops of wheat, barley and oats and prayed for abundance. On the few acres seeded with turnips and cabbage he asked the mercy of God.

Drouth came and the game left Ballyfearna and sought the mountains for food. Birds fell dead on the wing. The streams and rivers relinquished scant fish and the few people who had fishing gear sold it for bags of meal.

Sun baked the hills to hard golden loaves and the grain mill was forced to close for lack of water. The farmers had no work for the people. Hares and moorfowl, once scorned as inedible, became delicacies. There were no eggs, for folk had eaten their chickens.

Slowly, slowly, tables and chairs and beds were seen at Paddy the Pawn's, bought cheaply by the gentry who in turn were carting their heirloom furniture to sell in the cities. In many a manor house a family sat down to eat turnips on dishes ringed with gold and drink the last of their claret from eighteenth-century goblets no dealer wanted.

Often there was the tease of thunder, a stab of lightning, but no rain fell.

On a hot grey Sunday, as lightning hissed through the broken windows of the abbey, Father Leary brought good news to the congregation.

'The English, my God, have seen fit to help us. I have had a letter . . .'

Everyone knew, of course, that the bog-trotter had visited again but he had hastened away not even stopping at Murphy's for a dram.

'. . . which says that the Relief Commission through the Board of Works will build a canal here to join Loughs Sorm and Daree and this will put our men to work.'

There was a sigh through the church as though people holding their breath too long had finally exhaled.

'The pay is sixpence a day from six of the morning to six at night saving the Holy Days.'

'Praise be!' said Molly Ryan, not meaning to speak but unable to help herself.

'Amen,' said John the Basket. 'But what is a canal?'

'It's a passageway for ships,' Father Leary said, 'and it will take a long time to build.'

'But we ain't got no ships,' Paddy said.

'It's the ships will come to us,' Father Leary said, 'from Galway Bay and maybe other ports.'

'May I ask Father Leary what them ships is to be doing here, then?'

'Carrying cargo. Bringing supplies and taking them away.'

'And what will them ships be taking away?' Granny Cullen asked suspiciously.

'Praties,' the priest said firmly. 'Cattle, hogs — in time we'll have plenty to send on the ships and money to buy what they bring. It's in trouble we are, you're thinking, but as sure as the Lord taketh away, He giveth back. Even now He is promising men work.'

Mary the Midwife asked, 'Can the women work too?'

71

Father Leary glanced at the letter, 'It says "able-bodied persons from sixteen to sixty." Aye, I'd say strong women can work, those that can handle a pick axe or help cart stone.'

I could do that, Moira thought excitedly. Da and me together could earn twelve pence a day!

Michael O'Shea spoke. 'I'd say this thing that brings ships is better than what they put us to doing in '30. We was building roads to nowhere and when them roads was finished nobody wanted to go where they went so nobody used them roads and the grass took over and the bushes and it was like there'd never been no roads at all.'

'You can still walk one of them roads,' Jesus said, 'part way to the workhouse. But when does the ship thing begin, Father?'

'The English engineers come next week. I'd guess they'll be measuring and figuring and all, so I'd say work could begin in a month maybe.'

'Oh, God,' said Tyrone Schwartz, 'and what do we do until then? It's not a spoon I can sell these days, much less a pot.'

'Do what you have been doing,' Father Leary said. 'Go up to the mountains and hunt and set traps for the birds there. Fish the streams when it rains, for rain it must.' He looked down on the upturned faces. 'I've heard of pratie sickness among you and I'm warning you once more — do not eat the white parts of the sick black praties — it's dysentery they cause.'

Innocent eyes looked up, puzzled.

'What's that?' Bridget asked.

Father Leary strove to explain. They would get sick and weak from a running of the bowels.

'What's them?' Annie Dumbie asked.

The congregation waited. Father Leary hesitated. 'Just take me word for it and don't eat the diseased praties no matter how fine and white they're looking inside.'

Granny said, 'It's your word I'm taking, Father, but in all me life I never heard of no pratie hurting nobody.'

Father Leary sighed. 'They do, but I can't explain in front of ladies.'

'Oh!' said Jesus, 'and sure I know what comes from eating

72

only four. It's — ' He looked at Father Leary, saw the barely perceptible nod, and explained in a word.

'Oh, *that*,' Mary said softly, 'it comes from green berries too but milk is the cure.'

'What cow is left?' Cathleen asked bleakly.

Again the lightning sizzled, hissing like a gander. 'Think on your blessings,' the priest said, 'think of the blessed rain to come, and the mill opening and the canal. Think of everlasting things like love. Why, only last year some of you young ladies was asking me if it was proper to pray for a good husband.'

'And is it?' Bridget asked.

'Aye, it is. Some of you young ladies over thirty have asked that too and I say it is proper but you should have started to pray sooner.'

The congregation laughed — unheard of in church. Moira laughed too but she thought how strange the sound of laughter close to weeping. For all the priest's cheer there were the terrible facts. Before the mill reopened, before the canal started, families might be begging on the roads.

'God has spared us the misery of our neighbours.'

'Aye,' said Brian O'Donnell, 'but I saw The Gorta with me own eyes — '

'The eyes of eighty,' Father Leary said swiftly, 'and you tricked by a shadow or a bit of fog to believe it true.' He bent his head. 'Let us pray.'

As the velvet voice prayed for the village and the surrounding farms Moira thought, Father Leary himself believes in The Gorta else he'd not have silenced Brian but paid respect to his age. He'd have smiled as though at some All Hallows tale. No one could deny The Gorta as shadow or mist; he had walked among them from the very birth of Ireland, bony in his rags, wandering from garden to garden through the grey centuries. Aye, he came in mist but he left a scorch and a stench and rot that was proof in your hand. Even the English knew him. They called him The Famine.

Paddy's cart stood outside and Sean was loading it with what

73

they could spare for a stone of oats. First the stools had gone, then the bench, now the milk can.

'Well?' Paddy asked from the dust motes in the doorway. 'It's still another shilling I'm wanting.' He looked further into the room. 'I'd give you a shilling for that table.'

'Then how in the name of God are we to eat?'

He shrugged. 'You've a bed, then.'

Cathleen hesitated, for a bed was indeed a luxury but Moira turned angrily to Paddy. 'Is it my mother will birth on the floor?'

'Hush,' said Cathleen. 'Paddy Nolan, will you pay three shillings for that bed?'

Sean came in to hear her question. 'Sell the bed? By God, I'd sooner sell me soul to some other Devil. What's it you're up to, Paddy?'

'It's only a shilling I'm needing,' Paddy whined, 'and kindness I'm doing for your insult. For the milk can I'll pay a farthing.'

'Then,' Sean said, ominously gentle, 'I'm thinking you've come in charity and that we can't accept. Take your oats and thank you and a good day to you.'

'Who else will sell you oats for a song?' Paddy demanded. 'And where will you be buying them then? From the gombeen man in Ballydonny?' Paddy asked, as Sean was silent. 'He weights the bag with rocks and charges you four and six to boot.' He went over to the table and tapped it. 'Now, if you'd be throwing in this table I'll give you the oats and a stool.'

'A stool!' said Moira, who was still unused to rocks and barrels. 'One of our stools back?'

'Yours are sold,' Paddy said, 'but I've another one.'

'What's wrong with it?' Sean asked.

'The finest cherry wood it is, shiny as a apple.'

'What's wrong with it?' Sean repeated.

'It's maybe a little low, I'm thinking, but grand for the little boys.'

'So it hasn't any legs,' said Sean.

'You might say that, but it could have. Three pegs of wood, why a child could do it . . . Is it agreed?'

'Agreed.' Sean sighed. There was never a way to out-trick

Paddy by day and when he turned soft at night nobody wanted to. So the table joined the milk can on the cart, and the fourteen pounds of oats were placed on the cupboard out of reach of the dogs.

At sunset Liam came with news that the English engineers had arrived and would sign up men within a week. The work was too hard for women, they said, and Moira was disappointed but Cathleen refused to worry. The pratie crop to be dug next week was sure to be good and the rent was not due till December.

'You'll stay to supper, Liam,' Cathleen said, 'and we'll celebrate.'

Her excitement caught the little boys whom she sent to search for berries — she would use the last cups of flour to make a pudding. Moira mixed the oats with water for bread and Sean lit the wax candles used only at Christmas and Easter. Liam went home and returned with a glorious cabbage. 'Save it,' he told Cathleen, but she was in party mood and cooked half, placing the rest on a barrel to admire like a flower.

After supper rain began and the boys danced outside to welcome it. Moira took the empty plates from the floor thinking that the loss of the table was not tragic, only awkward. There was much to be thankful for — the rain, the promise of work. Her mother, though heavy with child, was not so bloated as she had been with Grace; and Grace, without milk of any kind, was healthy and happy, gurgling now through her sucking jar as she watched the dying cookfire. Liam sat beside Sean on the hearth rock. Their silence was as companionable as that of father and son-in-law as they shared Liam's pipe and his last tobacco.

When the children were asleep and the house was soft with rain and cricket-song Jesus came to visit, bringing a jug of poteen.

'And why not?' he asked, as Sean remonstrated at such bounty. 'I'm not selling it, for who can buy? Would you be having me drink it all meself and going mad in the head?'

So they drank to maintain Jesus' sanity and they talked of the English engineers. Jesus and Liam agreed they were not bad fellows at all, though expecting more comforts than they got at Murphy's where they lodged.

'It's pig meat they were asking for,' Jesus said, 'and not but two pigs left in town and they the good father's. It's strange to think it's him could be evicted like the rest of us.'

'Oh, no,' Cathleen said. 'He do be getting a bit from the church.'

'Eileen says there's not a shilling saved in his thatch — you mind how he gives to the squatters.'

They knew how often during the past years Father Leary visited the derelicts who lived in caves — old folk abandoned by their families. Often they saw him driving home a corpse to bury on abbey ground.

'It's not all of them deserve his help,' Liam said. 'Some is not so old they can't earn a penny but only lazy.'

Like his father, Moira thought. Liam never mentioned his father's shiftlessness but the neighbours knew only too well. Among themselves they called him Lazy Lanihan.

He must have been in Liam's mind too, for he said, 'There's not much to do until the praties are ready, so me and me father is going to work at the mill or on the canal, whichever starts first.'

Sean nodded. 'So will I. But even at sixpence a day it will be hard to pay the rent unless the crop is good.'

'It's only too much rain would fret me,' Liam said.

There came a tapping at the door and the dogs roused, barking. Sean opened to three strangers, women clad in rags. Moira caught her breath in horror and pity for their faces were scarcely fleshed and their eyes receded like slits in their skulls. Two were about her own age, one old.

'God keep all here,' said the old woman, 'and for the love of God give us a bit of bread for we've not eaten these four days except for a —'

She swayed and would have fallen but Sean caught her and brought her to sit on a barrel by the hearth. The two girls stood at the door in fear or timidity. Cathleen made them welcome and they sat down side by side on the straw.

'Quick, Moira,' Sean said, 'bring the bread and the rest of the pudding.' As Moira obeyed, Cathleen took their poor damp shawls, then hastily replaced them around their shoulders for

76

they wore nothing above their tattered petticoats. They ate ravenously. Then the old woman blessed the family and sank down on the floor to sleep. Cathleen covered her with a quilt from the bedroom. The girls sat, eyes listless, but open.

'Where is it you come from?' Cathleen asked.

'Gort.'

Moira shuddered.

'That's not far from Galway Bay,' Liam said. 'Could you not get fish?'

The smaller girl said, 'Who's to know how to catch it? And who's to give us a boat and tackle and all?'

Jesus asked, 'Were you evicted?'

'Aye.' Tears came. 'Our house pulled down about us and nowhere to go. It's on the road we've been these eight days.'

Cathleen interrupted as Sean's mouth shaped a question. 'We'll not be asking more of your troubles. Rest here and quiet yourselves.'

But even as she spoke the sisters had curled together in sleep.

Later, after her parents had retired and Liam and Jesus had left Moira stirred the fire and added more turf to warm the women until morning. She tried not to look at their sleeping faces, for one could almost count the bones. At the little painted picture of the Virgin which hung on the wall she offered a prayer for them before she tiptoed into the bedroom to join her brothers on the pallet.

Before dawn the women were gone and with them the half cabbage and the bag of oats.

It was a queer kind of frolic, Moira thought, without food to eat or poteen to drink; but Sally Mullen had got herself engaged to Patrick Kane and that was enough to set the village a-dancing, with Larry's son Terence playing the fiddle so fine and loud you might have thought his father's spirit stroked the strings.

It was a nine-mile journey back from Patrick's cottage to Ballyfearna; the old folk left in Paddy and Tyrone's carts, the young ones courted home on foot, loitering in the glow of the August moon, kissing in darkened hedgerows. It was almost three in the morning when Moira and Liam reached the Corner of the Shoes and began to descend the hill, hand in hand.

He stopped, suddenly rigid.

'What is it?' she asked. The pressure of his hand hurt her and she cried out.

She strained her eyes to see what had alarmed him but there was only the flash of the fireflies through a thickening white mist.

'Moira,' he said, 'tell me I'm wrong for the love of God.'

She stared at him blankly.

'Don't you smell it?'

'What?' she asked. 'I don't know what y——'

Then the mist moved toward her, rank with the decay and corruption of coffined potatoes.

They ran down the hill. Granny's garden, green at dusk, had blackened into Moira's. Half a mile further they came to the horror of Liam's. There they separated to rouse their families and sleeping neighbours. They must save the healthy potatoes for seed.

But they knew by dawn there was nothing to save.

Hundreds of refugees swarmed into Ballyfearna from Ahascragh, Ballinasloe, Kinvarra and from as far as Athlone. The pinch-faced swollen-bellied children were too weak to cry, dragged by their begging mothers from hut to hut. The men settled like ragged vultures on the site of the canal, pleading for work, but many were rejected as too weak to swing a pick axe. Alfred Nevin, captain of engineers, reduced the daily wage from sixpence to fourpence so as to put as many as possible to work. The boring and blasting began through four miles of limestone rock.

Heavy rains came and the work was halted. The grain mill could employ only thirty, Liam and Sean among them. Day after day Moira and Cathleen were forced to turn away dozens of starving strangers for they had only barely enough to feed themselves. The cupboard had gone to Paddy for another bag of oats.

One afternoon a father with two shivering little boys came to ask food and Cathleen met them at the door.

'It's sore to me heart I am,' she said, 'but we have nothing for you.'

Moira went to lend her the courage for rejection. 'It's true me mother speaks,' she said.

The man's lips moved wordlessly and his eyes pleaded. His little sons, naked save for grimy grain sacks, stared lethargically at Sean and Colum who stared back.

'I wish,' Cathleen said on a sob. Her arms stretched toward the boys, then fell to her sides. 'We've no pig, no cow, no chickens, we've sold all but our bed, and it the last to go. So you see . . .?'

The man bowed his head. Slowly he turned away, shuffling off through the mist with his sons.

'Who was they?' Colum asked.

'Beggars,' said his brother. 'They was hungry.'

Cathleen sat down. 'It tears me heart, it does. I think we'll not stir next time we hear someone at the door. Neighbours will come in by themselves.'

Moira nodded. 'Aye.'

Cathleen stared into her lap. 'Those children,' she said. 'If it's not hunger kills them the wet mist will — and slowly.'

Slowly, slowly. Sean had seen children dead in the ditches with grass in their mouths.

'Moira, they're not our neighbours. We owe them nothing.'

'No,' Moira said.

'And yet, they came to us, so now they're not strangers. We know them. He spoke and asked, the father did, and so we know him.'

She reached for Sean and held him close but he squirmed away to play with Colum in the corner. They had a game of Whisk the Feather that led them a chase into the bedroom and set the dogs to barking after them.

'The boys is thinner,' Cathleen said.

'No, mother. It's always thin they've been.'

'Not as thin as those poor children but —'

79

'Hush.'

'Shall we be forgetting that man and his children, you and I?'

'Not forgetting, no. But trying not to remember.'

Cathleen rose, her body heavy with child. 'Moira — there's yet time. They could not be far, slow as they were to walk. Get your shawl, and quickly. Oh, God, quickly!'

But Moira had already snatched her shawl from the peg and was running.

It was sad to let these folk go or the others who came later; to give them food and rest and then to have to tell them to leave.

But there was never a protest at leaving; there seemed no protest in them. They rose obediently from the straw with a sigh and a shiver and a blessing and their eyes looked out with the puzzlement and pain of children who had somehow erred but could not fathom their error. And quietly they went back to the long wet road between the whin and gorse of early autumn.

Paddy the Pawn said, 'We can't dare let them in, Sean.' He sat by the McFlaherty fire and spoke in his kindly night-voice. 'It's food and clothes I've given them, but only from me door. I'd not let them in nor must you for they carry the Black Fever.'

Cathleen said, 'But —'

'There's no buts about this fever,' Paddy said, 'them that gets it dies.'

'We spread lime,' Sean began.

'Lime! You might as well spread clover. It's something on the beggars or in them and it sickens all they touch, even folk well-fed. You must not take them in. You can't. It's not fair to your own children and a danger to us all.

'Do you think I don't know?' Paddy asked as they were silent. 'Folk come to me shop from all over, gentry needing to buy what we need to sell. They know more than we do, they's educated people and they say the fever is everywhere. They say Dr Thrush has been at the workhouse all this week tending the dying and him so busy he couldn't even go to Lady Fitzwilliam's and her in her deathbed. Aye, from the fever she died and two of her servants with her.'

'But was it from the beggars she got the fever?' Moira asked.

'Aye, she fed them herself, not throwing scraps from the door but bringing them in.'

'God rest her,' Cathleen said. 'I know how she felt. To throw them food as if they was pigs or dogs could not comfort the heart. It's comfort they need as well as food, I'm thinking.'

'And will it be a comfort to you if your family sickens and dies?' Paddy asked. He rose, tall, stoop-shouldered. 'I'm warning you, that's all.'

'And it's kind you are,' Cathleen said, 'but there's no fever in Ballyfearna.'

'Is there not, then? Do you know how it starts? Queer-like, sometimes, for it makes you think things that isn't. Michael O'Shea, he came to me shop yesterday and asked me did I have a hammer so he could make a coffin for his wife.'

'My God!' Moira said. 'And she dead these three years.'

'And he had a hammer,' Paddy said, 'in his hand.'

'Then the fever is on him?' Sean asked.

'I'd think so, yes. What else could turn him queer in the head, and he in good health two days ago?'

'Poor soul,' Cathleen said, 'alone in that house . . . I'll go to him tomorrow.'

Paddy swore and Cathleen stared at him in astonishment. 'Go to him then if it's the fever you crave. Go put his face to yours, kiss his mouth —'

'You'll not speak to me wife like that,' Sean said, rising.

'— take in the beggars, the roadlings, aye, take them all, rub their spit on your children, it's all one to me for I'll not be here to see it.'

He left, slamming the door behind him.

Late the next day the pains came on Cathleen and Moira put her to bed with a warm stone to ease her. As she returned to the kitchen Sean was drawing on his boots.

'Let's pray Mary is to home,' he said.

Moira had dreaded this moment. 'It's not Mary we're calling on, Da, but Dr Thrush. No!' she said, as he started to speak, 'there's no time to waste in arguing. You mind this birth could kill her. Go to Tyrone's and get his horse and ride to the workhouse where he's treating the fever.'

'If he'd not go to Lady Fitzwilliam's he'd not be coming here.'

'He will, Da. I *know* he will. It's a feeling in me strong as prayer, it's like God has told me so I *know*.'

He looked at her for a long moment. Then he nodded and ran to the door.

'Wait, Da! Mind you tell him to bring laudanum.' She made him repeat the word twice, then hurried back to the bedroom where Cathleen was talking with the boys.

'Come,' Moira said to Sean. 'You and Colum must go to Granny's and stay the night.'

'But I want to see the baby come,' Sean said.

'So do I,' Colum said. 'I want to give it a present.'

'He got a toad for it,' Sean said, 'up in the loft.'

'Shoo with you both or it's a whipping you'll get.' She thrust a quilt into Sean's hands, dragged them into the kitchen, gave them oat bread for their supper and warned them not to ask Granny or Sally for any food. When they were gone she went back to Cathleen and told her that Sean had gone for the doctor.

'The doctor! Oh, alanna, whoever heard of the doctor coming for this!' She laughed. 'It's joking you are of course.' She caught her breath for a moment as pain knifed her, then lay back. 'Wake me when Mary comes,' she said drowsily.

Moira went back to the kitchen and mindful of what Mary always did she heated a pot of water and lined an old box with clean rags. Grace awoke from her nest of quilts and she fed her a supper of thin oatmush. She longed for other tasks to keep her mind from torment. If Cathleen's pains came suddenly and strongly she was helpless to ease them. Mary at least had brews of herbs; she had nothing.

She did not doubt the doctor would come but would he come in time? There was the worry about payment for God knew what he would ask. There were only five shillings saved toward the rent and it due in November . . .

Grace slept. Moira sat close to the fire chilled by her own apprehension, listening for some sound from the bedroom. The dogs came to her in sympathy and she thought: they always know my sadness. Her wet, tongue-lapped hand stroked them. Poor darlings, they were gaunt and their brown coats wrinkled loosely. Their brown eyes looked out from deep fleshless sockets. No praties and peelings to nourish them now, only a bit of meal and what sparse game they could catch. How old were they, she wondered. Ah, yes, the litter had come soon after her seventh birthday. Granny had hurried over to say that Molly was having babies and Moira had returned with her to count them as they appeared. 'One, two, three . . .' Granny had kept One and now Two and Three were ten years of age.

'Old ladies you are,' Moira told them. Yet they were still puppy-hearted, forever a-caper with the children and rarely too weary to chase sticks. Though of late they moved more slowly . . .

She was picking burrs from Two's coat when Granny came in. The dogs ran to greet her as Moira rose.

'How is she?' Granny asked, slipping her shawl from her head to her shoulders.

'Asleep.' Moira took Granny's lantern and extinguished it. 'You'd not be needing a light so early?'

'It's a bad fog this night.' Granny tiptoed into the bedroom then came out, whirling on Moira. 'Where's Mary?'

Moira explained.

'Jesus God! Is it out of your mind you are? How do you know the doctor's still at the workhouse?'

'Paddy said he was there all this week.'

'By day, girl, by day! Is it not to his own house he'll go as dark falls and it more than ten miles from here? Even if he comes —'

'He will!'

'It's only your hope talking. Go for Mary or I'll go meself!'

Granny's authority collapsed her own. Like a child she went obediently for her shawl, lit a lantern and left the house.

The dusk was so heavy with fog that she could not see the candles in Granny's hut though she knew Sally was there. She swung her lantern toward the well to assure her direction and followed the path that led to the Corner of the Shoes, seeing only the narrow ridge of light ahead. There seemed nothing outside or beyond that ridge, only the grass and the stones of the path. She could not see the hill she climbed and when she reached its summit she stared in dismay for the lights of Ballyfearna were totally obscured.

She struck out blindly toward the right and down to what must surely be the river though she could not see it. Then her light revealed the wooden bridge and she crossed it hurriedly and turned left. Soon she would see the lights of Paddy's hut. But when she swung her lantern there were only oak trunks and browning hedges she should have left far behind.

Yet Paddy's hut must be here, perhaps only a few yards through the fog. She must find out if she were on the right path.

'Paddy!' she called. 'Paddy!'

Far off a dog barked.

Dear God, she thought, I cannot be lost in a place trod these many years by my own feet. She walked on, calling for Paddy, listening, but hearing nothing but the snap of a twig or a rolled stone under her heels. Then the path grew narrower, hedged in by ferns and moss and she smelled the deep woods.

'Paddy!' she screamed. She flashed her lantern to one side and saw a heavy curtain of laurel and dockweed. She was at Miller's Cave.

She turned and fled the way she had come, her errand forgotten in terror of seeing the wee men, of hearing their pursuing footsteps. Then suddenly a breeze swept the fog and she saw a lantern bobbing toward her and heard someone singing.

'When I was a young man in Dublin town . . .'

'Jesus, is it yourself?' she called, for that was the song he sang in his drink.

He came closer and blinked as she held up her lantern. 'Moira!'

'Oh, God, it's lost in the woods I've been and looking for Mary to take to me mother for birthing she is, and like to die . . .'

He smelled of Murphy's beer and smoke but for a marvel he seemed sober and led her to his cottage to rest while he

84

brought Mary to her. 'I'll guide you both to your house then.'

Hearing their voices, Eileen opened the door.

'Give Moira a jar,' Jesus said, 'it's lost in the woods she was looking for Mary to take to her mother's birthing.'

He left them and Moira followed Eileen into the house. It still smelled of pig, though it had been paid in rent these five months. Chicken dung and feathers carpeted the floor. Dirty dishes piled on the hearthstone were explored by a gaunt cat.

Eileen spoke grudgingly. 'Sit down if you want.'

Moira sat on one of the smooth-topped rocks. Eileen brought her poteen and she sipped it slowly, hating its taste as always but grateful for its easing.

'What happened to your feet?'

Moira looked down indifferently.

'I never seen your feet so black. Where is Your Ladyship's slippers?'

She was too weary to mind the gibe. Eileen stood leaning against the loft ladder, her long fair hair loosened from the plait that fell to the front of her bodice. The bodice was white and soiled above a red petticoat banded by fraying black braid.

Her voice lisped of poteen. 'How is it with you and Liam — and Bridget?'

Moira shook her head. 'I've no thought of anyone tonight but me mother. Da went for the doctor but —'

'The *doctor?*' Eileen snickered. 'Do you think Himself would come for a baby-pull?'

'But he must! Mary said another birth could kill her.'

'What's one death to him now? The priest was there to the workhouse only Friday and he says the paupers is dying off like flies, ten in one day and the crowds waiting outside, them that's been sick on the roads.'

'Then —' She would not cry in front of Eileen, 'it's God will help Mary to save me mother.'

'Does Mary be knowing you sent for the doctor?'

'No, I'd not want to hurt her feelings.'

Eileen smiled. 'If she finds out, it's devil a McFlaherty she'll be helping again.'

She would not beg Eileen's discretion nor could she trust it. Again she wondered, why should she hate me so, who never harmed her in any way?

'Remember if you should marry Liam you'll be needing Mary.'

So Liam is the nub of it. It's deep in love with him she must be though never encouraged surely . . .

'Well? Will you be marrying Liam?'

'I don't know,' Moira said.

'More likely *he* doesn't know. But sure he must marry someone for sons. It's a hard life you'd be having, seeing as women is his meat and drink. He'd not pass up a petticoat on the way to his own funeral.'

This was too much. 'I'm thinking he's passed up a real one with black braid. It's only jealous you are.'

'Jealous of you?' Eileen asked contemptuously. 'If I whistled Liam would be at me door this minute but I've better things to do than lower meself to a chaser.'

'And what do you do then that's better? Seeing as you can't get the man you want?'

Eileen's pupils dilated so that the blue eyes were suffused with black. Her hands clawed a rung of the ladder so tightly that Moira could see the white, bloodless knuckles. Her upper lip bared her teeth. 'Get out of me house before I kill you.'

Moira picked up her lantern and went to the door, forcing herself not to run. Safe outside she did run, grateful that the fog had lifted. Only on the path to Mary's house did she stop and sit down on a stile.

Eileen was mad, she thought, perhaps from the strange fever or from the drink. She had known drink to do that, though not in folk so young. Michael's wife, Kate, had died of the drink, screaming that a ferret was eating of her belly. Rory O'Donnell had shot himself in terror of the snakes no one else could see. And there was the man in Ballydonny who had killed his brother in the madness of drink and been hanged in the jailyard. Aye, only drink could account for Eileen's hatred of her; it had started last year long before the fever had even been heard of.

At last she saw lanterns shining on the path. Mary had her

fardel of medicine and a bit of food for herself, for folk no longer offered nor accepted hospitality.

They talked little on the journey, hastening to keep up with Jesus' long strides. Finally they descended the hill and saw the lights of home. But there was no horse outside. Obviously the doctor had not come.

Sean was alone in the room with the sleeping Grace. His eyes lit as he saw Mary. 'May the Mother of Mercy reward you. Screaming she was not a minute ago.'

Mary shed her shawl and went into the bedroom. Jesus said, 'Come, Sean, we'll go to Murphy's.'

'Even if I would it's no money I have to be spending on drink.'

'Now, Dennis is sure to be treating an expecting father and it's company we're both needing.'

'No.' He was so nervous that Moira could see the apple of his throat as he swallowed. Suddenly she realized how thin he was, the breeches loose on the string about his waist.

'Then I'll be going,' Jesus said, 'with a prayer for the dear lady.'

Moira thanked him for his kindness and he left. Sean said, 'The doctor was in the fever shed but I never got near him, no one is allowed in but the sick.' He shook his head as though to clear it. 'Terrible it was, maybe two hundred folk out in the yard begging for Himself to help them or for food . . . I was afraid of catching the fever meself so I took the way back to Paddy's.'

'Paddy's? Was it not Tyrone's horse you took?'

'I met Paddy on the way to Tyrone's and it was his own horse he lent me to spare me time. He even gave me this.'

She had not noticed that Sean was smoking a new pipe until he extended a paper of tobacco.

'He's a good man truly,' Sean said, 'after dark.'

Granny came in.

'Is she worse than before?' Moira asked.

'Not worse, but better, I think. It's quieter she is and the pains shorter.'

'Thank God. But if we only had the laudanum she'd not feel the pains at all.'

Granny said, 'That's only one of me daughter's tales, I'm

thinking. There's nothing soothes a woman in birth, not even in America, for it's against nature.' She manoeuvred on to one of the barrels but it was too tall for her short legs and she moved to a rock so that her foot met the floor in dignity. 'There's times I wish Sally would stop her talking of America.'

'Why?' Sean asked.

'It's food she talks of. Praties cooked every way, even in soup. Beef and lamb and pig, and my God, chickens to eat, not in hunger as we did but just for Sunday dinner. They's more eggs in America than people can eat. She says it isn't just seed cakes they eat every day but great tall cakes with —' she stretched her hand from thumb to third finger '— this much frosting of butter and sugar and maybe strawberries. And after all them big dinners the men has nuts and wine and the women leave the table.'

'Why should the women do that?' Moira asked.

'Women knows when they've had enough,' Granny said, 'but it's the men eats like pigs.'

'I'm thinking we forgot Sally worked for rich folk,' Sean said. 'Maybe the poor don't eat much better than we did.'

'They do! You heard her talk of the golden praties and the bacon —'

Granny paused. A thin dew of saliva oozed from her lips. Moira could feel the flow of her own saliva. To have just one pratie now, only one! Thin as it was the oatmeal didn't hold from one hour to another.

Sean echoed her thought. 'I'd give all the golden praties of America for a barrel of ours. Meal —' He shrugged. 'It's like Tyrone says. Meal is like a fancy woman stays with a man an hour and then goes and leaves him.'

'True for him,' Granny said, 'but meal might do if we could have it thick, maybe with buttermilk . . .'

Three, the dog, moved from Sean to Moira and back again, then went to the front door and whined. Moira let her out. The fog had closed in again and she could not see Granny's cottage.

'Once I was in Newport,' Sean said. 'It's there I went by donkey car to bring back the scythes for Callahan and he give me a shilling for me fun. I went to this place and had a dish of fish, only it wasn't fish, rightly speaking, it had butter on it and maybe cream and eggs, brown on top and soft like inside.'

Sean paused as Moira let in Three and closed the door.

'It's fifteen years ago,' he said, 'and I've never lost thought of that fish.'

'Once,' Granny said, 'I had some cherries in me own tree — it was before the Big Wind come and blown it down; and I took them cherries and made a pudden with milk and flour and all.'

Two put her face into Moira's hand and she stroked her, feeling the hard ridge of the ribs. Three lifted a paw on to her skirt. She shifted her glance from their begging eyes to the pot of water that simmered high above the flame.

'There was apple trees at the Corner then,' Sean said. 'Me mother used to —'

'OOOOOHHHhhhhhhhh!'

It was Cathleen's voice pitched to a peak of pain, sliding to a harsh gargle. They rushed into the bedroom and Sean cried out.

But Moira had no voice, only eyes to see the blood-bathed thighs, the blood-soaking blanket and Mary's dripping red hands splashed to the elbow and the ends of her braid wet with blood. Her mother screamed again and the dogs howled and ran from the room.

'Moira.' Mary did not turn. 'Fetch the priest.'

Moira blundered out of the room, out of the house, before she faced the fog and turned back to snatch a lantern. The oil was low but she had only time to catch a spill from the fire and light the wick, her hands impeded by the dogs' need to lick her fingers. She had started again for the door when Granny stumbled in from the bedroom with her petticoat over her face and the burble of the keen on her mouth.

So she is dead.

Moira went out slowly. No need to hurry for the priest. She fumbled through the fog as though sleep-walking and everything around her seemed strange — the brassy golden trees, the tarnished hedges, caught in her light, were fixed and motionless in a death of their own. She had not thought to ask Granny if the child lived; only Cathleen had mattered.

Strangely she could not remember her mother's face, only

89

her voice and her words. A memory haunted her, an episode she had not thought of for years. She was eight years old, walking home with Cathleen from a neighbour's house. A dark thing was scuttling along the grass ahead of them.

'What kind of bug is that?' Moira asked.

'It's not a bug, alanna.' And then with a world of sadness in her voice, 'It's a baby bird.'

'It's too small for a bird.'

'But it is. It has fallen from its nest.'

'Will its mother put it back?'

'No.'

'May I have it? May I keep it?'

'Not long. It's dying, alanna.'

Moira bent and stretched out her hand and picked it up. Its feeble fluttering tickled her palm as she carried it toward the house. Then it was still and stiff in her fingers.

'Don't mourn,' Cathleen said. 'It's safe from Granny's cats and from hunger and all the trials of sky and earth. The dead are happy — never weep for them.'

'Do they weep for us?'

'If we are sad they do. It's their tears are the rain.'

Now the fog was turning to mist, wet on her face. And Cathleen was weeping, for the rain began and lasted throughout the night. She sees us in the depth of our grief, Moira thought, she hears the silent tears of Sean alone in his bed. She cannot comfort the little boys in their first knowledge of death nor hold the daughter she had borne of her blood.

Father Leary christened the baby Cathleen.

Folk came to the wake bringing no food nor expecting any. There was only a bit of Jesus' poteen to cheer the mourners. Cathleen lay in the crude coffin Sean and Liam had made for her for Michael O'Shea was deep in the fever. No one dared go near him but Father Leary who saw to his needs each day. He said that Michael's face was dark and swollen, his body covered by a rash and his mind a-wander. It was whispered he would soon join Cathleen under the abbey willows.

The next day Cathleen's coffin was lowered into mud. When

the earth was heaped upon it home-made wreaths were laid —
heather and harebells from the convent garden. Father Leary
ended his prayer in heavy rain.

Sean and the boys walked toward the gate and the crowd
followed. Only Moira lingered by the grave and Liam turned
back to join her.

'Come, darling,' he said. 'You are wet through.'

'I don't want to go home,' she said, though it was not fair
that Granny should be minding Grace and Cathleen and missing
the funeral to boot.

'Then we'll walk over to Murphy's. Likely Biddy will give you
some tea if it's any she has.'

They walked through the wet falling leaves over the bridge on
to the road. A little knot of people had gathered in the open shed
of the Market where hogs and poultry used to be sold and were
staring at the house next door.

'What's amiss?' Liam asked.

Bridget Reilly said, 'It's John the Basket has the Black Fever.'

'Mother of God!' Moira crossed herself.

'We was trying to get Kitty to come out and go to visit her
children but she slammed down the window and told us to mind
our own business,' Biddy said.

'It's a wife's place is with her husband,' Moira said.

'Not at such a time,' said Mary the Midwife. 'How can she
help him if she gets the fever?'

'Some folk recover,' Annie Dumbie said. 'The priest said so.'
She put her arm around Moira. 'I'm sore for your trouble, child.
Sadness comes all at a time, death and fever and the hunger. And me
and Sally has put aside our weddings.'

Moira was stirred out of her own grief. 'Oh, no! Why should
you, then?'

'Because after the rents Patrick and Peter has not a pig between them. Where shall we know to lay our heads next spring?'

If Liam and I were betrothed, Moira thought, I'd not care if
my bed was of turf and me cover laurel leaves. It's no roof I'd
need but the shelter of a holly hedge. But then, older women
were set in their ways. Plump Annie (not so plump now, with the
skin loosening on her bones) likely married through long habit,

and Sally, though less privileged of husbands, was accustomed to the comforts of America. They were guided by prudence, not passion, and she felt sorry for them.

'. . . . and I'd not live with Himself in Ballydonny,' Annie was saying, 'with all them sick paupers about.'

They glanced uneasily at John the Basket's house.

'At least,' Biddy said, 'we can thank God when the rain stops so the men can work on the ship thing.'

'Canal,' said Tyrone Schwartz. 'It will be coming along grand, and the work lasting years . . .'

Moira was half-listening for Liam had sauntered up the street with Bridget. She saw him bend to shawl the rain-wet black hair, a gesture so tenderly and casually possessive that she felt the stir of illness in her stomach. And now my God, he was kneeling to draw a burr from Bridget's foot. The way they stood was worse than flirting; they might have been man and wife. Tyrone turned to watch them, doubtless jealous as she. To spare them both the loneliness of the moment she drew him aside and thanked him for the spray of ferns he had placed on her mother's grave.

'It's all I could find in the woods.'

As though by agreement they stood with their backs toward the couple up the street.

'How is it with you, Tyrone?' she asked.

He said, 'I'm thinking to go to Dublin while me horse is not too weak to get me there. Me wares is useless so long as Paddy sells second-hand. I'd thought the gentry — but no.' He sighed. 'I'd be sorry to go, for it's a village I love.'

'And Bridget?' she asked.

He puckered his mouth. 'I've nothing to offer.'

'Would she not go to Dublin with you?'

'No. She thinks things will be better here.' He smiled wryly. 'Poor girleen, it's like a babe she is, not a penny in her thatch, and her rent soon due. Not a living soul to help her but meself, and it's little enough I've done — yet she hasn't a worry of the future. If she was eighty instead of eighteen I'd say she was soft in the head.'

'But does she love you, Tyrone?'

92

'In a bit of a way, maybe.' Bluntly he added, 'I think it's Liam she hopes for.'

She had known that for months but to hear it spoken made it harder to bear. And now Bridget and Liam were strolling back to join the group.

'Well, Moira? Shall I be taking you home now?' he asked.

'If you want.' As they walked up the road she was fearful of speaking lest her anger be uncontrolled. It was bad enough that he had been so husbandly with Bridget — and in public. But worse, not an hour after Cathleen's burial.

She thought, I don't matter to him in his heart's core. I am only someone to kiss on a whim, to tease and frolic with. Disappointed in his own family, he enjoys mine as a second home. And all this less a need than a long habit.

'Time will ease you,' Liam said, taking her silence for grief.

'In some things,' she said coldly.

'She'd not have wanted you to sorrow so . . ."

'Damn you!' she said, 'Don't speak of me mother!'

She started to walk ahead of him but he caught her arm and pulled her back. With her free hand she turned and slapped him hard on the mouth.

His look of incredulity changed to anger, then to concern. 'Is it sick you are?'

Mad, he meant. Fevered.

'I am not! Must I be sick to want you out of me sight?'

She flounced on ahead of him. The rain grew suddenly heavy and as she ducked into the little entrance way of Paddy's shop she saw Liam cross the street to Murphy's Hotel.

Paddy's shop was closed, his window fly-specked and grey. Rain rippled down it but the glass was impervious to years of dust. There in a tangled turmoil were pans and pig-bristle brooms, quilts and clothes, a wall altar, a cradle, spades and shoes. Far to the left she saw a bunch of silk flowers — no, it was a bonnet made of primroses and red satin ribbon half-concealed by an iron pot.

She looked at the bonnet for a long time, her nose pressed against the wet window. Then she crossed the street to Murphy's and waited in the common room while Dennis summoned Liam from the bar.

The turkey-cloth curtains were pulled aside so she could see the bar, long and dark and glossy. A few men smoked; others held empty pipes. There was not a mug or a glass in sight, though a row of bottles stood on a shelf near the mirror.

Liam came through the door and she ran to meet him. 'I'm sorry,' she said. 'Truly I am.'

'For what?' he asked, and smiled and rubbed his mouth. 'I've still me front teeth.'

'I'm sorry for —'

But she could not name her sorrows. One slept under the abbey willows, two blackened in fever, six sat at a bar cheerless without drinks. And though she feared and mistrusted Bridget Reilly, the primrose bonnet pulled her heart with red satin strings.

John the Basket and Michael O'Shea died the same day. There were no wakes, but services in the abbey late in the afternoon. It was there that Moira realized the change that had befallen her neighbours.

It was not merely the shabby, grimy clothes of the men who had worked on the canal, nor their thinness, gradual as the shift from dusk to dark. It was their behaviour; they seemed restless as stalled animals scenting storm. Dennis Murphy, oblivious to sacrilege, absently tore a page from a missal and littered it on the floor. Patrick Kane, sitting beside Sally, moved from side to side as though for a better glimpse of the priest, though no one impeded his view. Sean fiddled with his scrap of a cap and jumped when a fly buzzed his ear. The women fingered their buttons or shawls, fussed with their hair, pulled at their fretful children. Their uneasiness infected Moira. She heard not a word of the Mass.

The sky was ambering as they moved outside to watch the coffins lowered. The churchyard had once been part of the inner abbey, now roofless. The cloister walks survived under trellises of browning vines, and brilliant green moss grew up through the stones. The great Gothic windows, torn with age, filled now with a gold mist from the distant loughs.

94

'Look to the hills,' Father Leary was saying, 'whence cometh thy salvation . . .'

He meant the hills of heaven, Moira thought, not these darkening hills beyond the mist. She and the boys and the dogs had hunted there yesterday. Two and Three had caught a sickened rabbit but there was no food for humans, no salvation from the hills of this autumn.

The final prayer was offered, the graves filled. Father Leary took the path to his house. It was then that the altercation began — unheard of on holy ground.

Eileen turned on Mrs John the Basket. 'You should not have come here.'

The widow stared, startled.

'You should not have come,' Eileen repeated.

'Not come to me own husband's funeral?' Kitty the Basket asked.

'It was your stubborn will to stay with him — you might have spared us your fever.'

'You lie I have the fever!' Kitty said furiously.

'I say you may have. To mix among us you could make us all blacken and die.'

'May that lie strangle your throat, Eileen Finnigan!'

The crowd, which had been moving off, paused to listen. Sides were taken. Mary the Midwife was appealed to.

'Aye,' she said to Kitty, 'I'm not sure of these things but I think you should have stayed alone to yourself a week or two.'

'You could have stayed to *your* home.' Kitty shouted. 'It's Himself's funeral, not yours — more's the pity. Who asked you to come here who'd grudge me your help? It was me laid him out by meself and put him in the coffin with me own hands, aye, and it near broke me back it did!'

Liam took her part. 'It's Mary O'Hara and Eileen Finnegan should have stayed home.'

'Me sister goes where she pleases,' Jesus said, pushing out his chin. 'Is it you going to stop her, Liam?'

Knowing how swiftly a fight could begin, Sean stepped between them. 'Let's not higgle,' he said mildly. 'It's a question of shall Kitty consort with us. I say she shall, for if the fever's on

95

her it's on us, and if not, there's no harm done.'

'So!' Mary said, 'I'd like to see you touch her, Sean Mc-Flaherty and her hands not dry from his rot!'

Oh, God, Moira thought — Mary may be right.

'Aye,' Eileen said. 'It's easy enough to say, pretending you're brave.'

'Pretending, is it?' Sean asked, still mildly. 'Well, I'll be on me way.'

As he came to the widow he paused, 'It's sad for your trouble I am, Kitty.' He drew aside her shawl, held her tear-wet face in his hands and kissed her lips.

A murmur went through the crowd but no one spoke. Moira and her brothers followed him from the churchyard and took the path home.

'Why did Da kiss her,' Colum asked, 'if she got fever?'

'No matter,' Moira said. 'Run ahead and see if you and Sean can find berries on the path.'

'There's no berries,' Sean said, a cynic at four. But they ran ahead, kicking at stones and rousing a whirl of fallen leaves.

'Da,' Moira said, 'it's a hero you are.'

He smiled wanly, the merest movement of his pale, thin lips. She realised suddenly that there was grey in the flow of sandy hair and though his face had always been deeply rutted she could almost see its skeleton.

'No hero, alanna,' he said. 'It was Cathleen I was thinking of, for she always liked Kitty. Poor Kitty — and her own children afraid to come from Castlebar to share her grief.'

'Da.' She hesitated. 'Will folk be afraid of us now?'

He shrugged. 'Some. But in a while they'll forget their fears.'

Unless . . . but she killed the thought that Kitty had the fever. Despite her dark-circled eyes, pouchy from sleeplessness, she was a healthy-looking woman, no thinner than any and with fresh ruddy skin.

Smoke rose from their cottage where Granny was tending the girl-babies. Sean paused at the well.

'Go in and tell Granny what happened, Moira. She must have the choice to fear us or not.'

Reluctantly Moira went into the house, making a fuss of the

dogs before she gathered courage to speak. It would be hard to lose Granny.

Granny listened intently as Moira blurted the story. Then she said, 'What did me daughter Sally say?'

'Nothing.'

'She did not defend the poor widow?'

'No.'

'Well, then,' Granny said, 'it's a slap of me hand she'll get this night if she *is* fifty years.' She went to the door and called to Sean, 'Come in! I've news!'

She told them dramatically, squeezing the last juice from the drama. 'Danel Powderley was here. And what he had to say was so grand I gave him a cup o' your tea.'

'Well? What did he say?'

But Granny would not be rushed. It took half an hour for them to learn that the English were giving away turnips from a shed near the workhouse, free to all who wanted them from sunrise to dusk.

Before dawn, before their day's work began, Sean and Liam set off on the five-mile walk carrying buckets for the turnips. At sunrise Moira heated a big pot of water in preparation for the feast. She was dizzy with hunger but a glance into the oat barrel steadied her. The scant meal must be saved for Grace and the infant. It was merciful, she thought, that Sean and Colum had not awakened. It seemed to her that they slept longer each morning as though reluctant to face the day; and during the day their play was quiet and they dozed often, almost like old folk.

She eyed the oats again — less than three cups left. The turnips would be providential, she would cut them small for rapid cooking and the peelings would nourish the dogs. Now they watched her every movement, whining, nosing her hands. She opened the door and let them out to their hopeless hunting.

She thought of her own hopeless hunting — the endless, futile search for a sound potato in the pits, for berries in the woods. She had sold her fishing gear to Paddy for tuppence, home made as it was, and useless. There was nothing in the river, the brooks, the ponds. Liam thought the changes from flood to drought and the sudden storms had killed the fish or sent them away, but no one knew for sure. Inland folk were not fishermen and pretended no knowledge of the mystery. She remembered how indifferent folk had been to fish in years of plenty. One offered it apologetically before pratie harvests. Now she thought of fried brown trout and drank a cup of water to ease her longing.

Cathleen awakened and cried, arousing Grace. Moira gave them sips of the watery meal mush, praying that the boys would sleep on. But they stumbled in naked from their pallets as Grace consumed the last spoonful.

'I'm hungry,' Sean said.

'So am I,' Moira said. 'Get back to your bed.'

Colum looked into the empty pot and began to cry.

'Get you both back to bed,' Moira said, 'and stay there till I call you. It's food you'll have later.'

'I want it now,' Sean wailed.

'Now isn't that the terrible thing?' Moira said, feeling a rise of fury that astonished her. 'And are you the only one? Get back to bed!'

Her voice, splintered toward a scream, set the little girls to crying.

'Jesus God!' Moira shouted over the howling, 'Stop it or I swear I'll whip you all four.' She pushed Sean toward the bedroom. 'Get out of here!'

He fled, followed by Colum. Ignoring the bawling girls she put her hands to her ears and ran outside. *Let* them wail — their stomachs were full. As for the boys, they'd soon be fed and happy again. What did they know of worry, the eternal struggle to pay the rent, the threat of future eviction? She ran beyond the sound of their voices to the end of her garden which adjoined Granny's.

The trees were tawny in broadening sunlight and the hills were round and rosy as apples. Moira sat down with her back to an oak, spent of her fury, ashamed, repentant. She could not understand her behaviour or why, at least, she had not tried to comfort the boys and explain about the turnips.

She strained her eyes for a glimpse of Sean and Liam. Surely they should be home soon. Or perhaps they had been delayed and forced to go direct to the canal to begin the day's work. If they did not return in half an hour she would go there and bring back sufficient turnips for the day's needs.

Two and Three came up to lick her hands. They were all ribs, poor creatures, all ribs and eyes. Granny's cat sidled up, mewing, but the dogs, once inimical, ignored her. She prowled the potato plants, caught a moth and ate it.

Granny came out of her hut. 'Are they here yet?'

'They are not. Moira rose and went to her. 'Maybe they had to go to their work.'

'Sally left only an hour ago. It was all I could do to rouse her. Lazy, she is.'

'Not lazy,' Moira said. 'I think it's the hunger on her.'

Granny said nothing, watching the cat in the potato plants. Two came up close to it, retreated and lay down with Three.

'It's queer, the creatures,' Granny said. 'There's no heat in them, they ain't themselves. That cat ain't let me pet her these eight years. But last night it was she on me shoulder all the night long, sweet as a kitten. And Brownie' — she referred to the young dog who drowsed on the doorstone — 'he was lively as hoppers in May. Now he just lies. He don't chase nothing.'

She looked up at the sky. 'Anyways, there's no birds to plague me, I can come outside with me heart steady. I'm telling you, Moira, if a bird should fall on me and I'd feel its feathers I'd lose me reason —'

'Look!' Moira said, 'it's them!'

Sean and Liam were coming down the hill, baskets swinging.

'You'll take some of our turnips till Sally gets back,' Moira said. 'Is your water hot?'

'Aye.'

Moira ran to the men and the dogs suddenly stirred to barking and leaping between them.

'Da, you've got them?'

Granny came sprinting behind her. They looked into the buckets and saw only a few packets of paper.

Liam said, 'The bastards. The goddamned arsecockled English bastards.'

'It's seeds,' Sean said. 'The turnips is just seeds.'

99

Chapter *4*

To the folk of Ballyfearna Mr Pond was the Grim Reaper, inescapable, unavoidable; but unlike death, coming twice a year. For a small man he cast a gigantic shadow. For years he had been considered each time a tenant planted; or when a woman pondered the purchase of a hair bow, a frill or a needless button. A storm brought him instantly to mind lest a roof cave in or a willow fence collapse. And in glorious weather, with the sun blessing the plants, there was the fear that he would raise the rent on a bumper crop, for nothing could be hidden from him. He was omniscient. How else could he have known that John Duffy (might he rest in peace) had concealed seed praties under his floor boards and gone to that very spot? And John pushed off the land he had tended so long to die in a ditch near Ballinrobe.

Even the children felt his shadow. They used him as the fright-man in their games, or as a boogie with which to bully younger brothers and sisters. But only the children spoke of him freely. The older folk, understanding death, preferred not to speak of it.

But now, as November approached, they talked of Mr Pond as people do who face extinction together. Nearly everyone had been forced to choose between rent for him and food for themselves, between oatmeal and shelter. For most there was no choice. The thought of eviction was sad enough in spring, but now they risked it in winter. And winter with its hail and freezing rains, its threat of snow, was bleak enough inside a hut by a fire of boiling praties. And so as the leaves fell and the days shortened, dread of Mr Pond became terror. But unlike death his appearance was certain. November tenth.

In the face of death men carted turf from the bogs and spread it out to dry on the heatherbeds of the moors, as though by some miracle they would have need for it. They could not believe in their hearts that there might be no hearths this winter, no food to cook. Their effort was wasted for the long, dark rains began and they were forced to use their last stored fuel. On All-Hallows Eve no bonfires could be raised on the sodden hills to frighten evil spirits but Biddy Murphy lit a candle in the hotel window to symbolise exorcism through fire. A few days later she stopped by Moira's hut and invited her to a frolic celebrating the twentieth anniversary of her marriage.

'Dennis and me do be thinking it may be the last time we're all together.'

It was not a happy way to contemplate a party but Moira was happy, for Liam asked to accompany her even before she had a chance to worry that he might ask Bridget. There was no choice of what to wear. She had sold all of Cathleen's clothes but the black shawl, which they had shared for years. She only had her red petticoat and blue bodice, and they ragged. The family's shoes had brought only a shilling but surprisingly Paddy had paid well for the bed. Thank God there was nearly a pound saved for the rent. Shifting between the grain mill during the rains and the canal in dry weather, Sean was able to earn his fourpence a day, and Liam too. Ballyfearna was not overburdened by industrious workers, so good ones were appreciated.

She looked into the scrap of mirror which she had not the heart to sell for a penny and mourned the loss of her hairbrush yet she saw thankfully that her hair had not lost its sparkle. Her

101

face was thinner so that her eyes seemed larger in contrast. Her lips were still red, her skin soft and moist. She thought, I'm not ageing too badly . . .

She covered the children who slept on the bedroom floor and went into the kitchen.

'Da,' she said, as Sean came down from the loft with a bit of turf, 'If there's any food at all I'll bring you some.'

'There'll be a bit,' he said, 'if only for the Murphy's guilt in having more than most. Not that I grudge them.'

'And they've no children to feed.' She took a rag from the peg and placed it in her waistband to clean her feet before she entered the hotel. Then, hearing Liam's whistle, she put on her shawl and joined him outside.

'An evil night,' he said, guiding her through the rain. It was cold rain and she shivered despite her shawl. To her dismay she found that she had nothing to say for her thoughts were all on food. Would there maybe be oatcakes? A pudding? Or, ultimate in generosity, some of last year's praties saved for this very occasion? Hotel guests fared well at Murphy's and since there had been none in months save the English engineers there should be a cellarful of food. Crates of eggs wrapped in meal-dust. Hams. Bacon . . .

'How is it with you and the rent?' Liam asked as they sloshed down the hill.

'We lack only a shilling. And you?'

'Just enough. But I'm guessing there are only three others that's safe. Dennis, Paddy and Father Leary who still has the pig.'

If only there would be roasted pig tonight, but that was the wildest reach of dream. The hotel hadn't served pig for a year or more.

Once blazing with lights, the hotel was lit only in the parlour by oil lamps set in the walls. Still, Moira thought, it had always been a grand room, papered with pink roses. There was a black horsehair sofa, three chairs shawled by antimacassars, a sideboard, a chess table and a brown piano. Dennis had brought stools and benches in from the bar so that nearly all the guests were seated; and praise be, a great fire crackled in the hearth.

There was no food on the sideboard but Dennis passed a tray

102

of glasses and Moira took one and tasted the sweet nectar of sloe-wine.

'You're just in time,' Biddy said, motioning Moira to a stool. 'We was beginning St Martin's Wishes.'

All wishes stated on St Martin's Eve came true unless they were wicked. None might be trivial, for St Martin listened only to the deepest need of the heart.

'I started,' Biddy said, 'by saying me wish is for another child.'

There was something defiant in the set of her stocky body and the thrust of the square, freckled jaw. My God, Moira thought, she must be forty-five and she's had her share of children, grown now and away north. But the longing still in her . . .

'And your wish, Dennis?' asked Annie Dumbie. 'Is it for a child too?'

'I'd not bother me wife's wish,' Dennis said. He stood by the fire, tall, gaunt, a roll of loose fat flapping his chin. 'What I wish is the old days back, and coaches a-pulling up and merry people in and out and enough in me till to give them a door-drink, and all of you too. I'd wish for them Dublin pedlars back so as to know all the news of the world. And —' He pointed up to the dead chandelier '— wax candles to burn there. To have folk say from here to Ballyness Bay "Murphy's is the grandest hotel in Ireland, linen sheets it has." '

'It is the grandest hotel in Ireland,' old Kevin Ryan said loyally, 'sheets or not. And me wish is the same as yours for the old days back, with me shed full of cows and pigs and the women bringing their eggs to trade for a ham or a joint.' He pushed back his spiky grey hair to scratch at a louse. 'But more than that —' he lifted his chin with some of Biddy's defiance and faced his wife Molly, '— I'd wish for a acre of me own.'

'You'd never raise a nettle,' Molly said with the promptness of long argument. 'It's a town man you are with no green to your hand and I'll have none of it.'

'It's *me* wish,' Kevin said, jealous of it. 'It's in luck you are I'm not wishing me a younger woman.'

'At your age,' Molly said good-humouredly, 'you couldn't seed her neither.'

The people laughed, but abashedly, for Father Leary had come

103

in and was shedding his wet cloak. Eileen sprang up to take it and smooth it and hang it near the fire.

'We're wishing to St Martin, Father,' Biddy said. 'What would be yours?'

He accepted wine, sat down by Annie and closed his eyes for a moment's reflection. Moira admired the sensitive, chiselled profile and thought 'What a waste to a woman,' then chided herself.

'The wish must be for you, Father,' Biddy said, 'not for anybody else.'

He opened his eyes and smiled. 'Well, then, it's books I'd want — lots of books to answer me questions. Books to line the whole wall of me cottage in a case with glass to keep them from the mice.'

'I'd wish that for meself,' Danel Powderley said, 'only I could borrow them from you, Father. So I'd wish for a printer in Dublin to gather up all me poems and bind them in a leather book tooled in gold and give me five hundred pounds for them; and I'd thatch me roof and get back me desk and stool and tell Mr Pond to go to —' He paused, embarrassed.

'It's all right, Danel,' the priest said, 'I'm thinking he'll go there in time. But I wonder would St Martin be approving a wish for so much money?'

'Poems don't bring none anyway,' Danel said morosely. 'Look at Goldsmith.'

Biddy turned toward the door, but seeing no one, appealed to Jesus for his wish.

Jesus hesitated, glanced down at his big bog-black feet.

'Come,' Dennis said, refilling his glass, 'we're all friends together.'

The big mouth opened, closed. The blue eyes looked out shyly. 'I guess it's not for saying.'

'Is it *that* wicked?' Kitty the Basket asked.

Jesus said nothing.

'Go on,' encouraged Annie. 'If you don't say, your wish won't come true.'

'It won't anyway,' Jesus mumbled.

'Come,' Paddy said, 'there's lots for young fellows to wish. A acre of his own, a horse and cart, a wife maybe.'

104

'They'd be nice,' Jesus said, 'but what I want is to do something big, like Liam when he saved Moira from the river, like O'Neill when he pulled Tim out of the fire, like Sean when he kissed Kitty. Only there's never no chance.'

'You're brave enough,' Dennis said kindly. 'You've won a lot of fights.'

'And lost some too. But that's not what's in me mind.' He leaned forward, tense with the need to make them understand. 'Every time I'm in church I look at that altar me father robbed and I think, "Someday I'll do something so grand nobody will remember him — only me." It's *respect* I want.'

How strange, Moira thought, to know a person so long yet not know him at all. Not to realise that the shame of his father's memory and his years as a pauper in the workhouse had burned so deeply as to hurt even now. She glanced at Eileen wondering if she shared the hurt but she sat impassively, eyes hard. Now she swirled back her long oaten hair and spoke contemptuously: 'It's wine-talk,' she said. 'All he can do is drink big.'

'And you,' Moira asked coldly. 'What do you wish?'

Like Jesus, she hesitated. For the first time in her life Moira saw her blush. But the softness vanished swiftly and she said, 'Me wish is the only honest one here, barring Father Leary's. Why do you beat about it with your talk of acres and animals? Is food a dirty word, then? It's food I want.' She threw the word like a dagger. '*Praties.*'

No one spoke. It was as though, linked in the common wish, they were somehow guilty of it for they did not look at one another. The room was so still that they could hear the fall of soot from the chimney in the bar. Then Bridget gave a little nervous gasp of laughter and the wine trembled in her glass and splashed on to her skirt.

'And your wish, Bridget?' Biddy asked quickly.

'Well, some day —' she bent her head and rubbed at her skirt — 'a husband and babies.'

Annie asked gently, 'And you'd wish your bonnet back?'

Bridget sent her a timid, grateful smile. 'It was all I ever had was pretty.'

'It was,' Liam said, 'and who knows but some day you'll be

105

having it back? Sure, Paddy will be raising the price so high the Countess O'Toole herself could not be buying it.'

She laughed. 'And your wish, Liam?'

Like Father Leary he sat in thought for a moment and Moira could feel the heavy thump of her heart as she waited for him to speak.

'I would like me garden safe,' he said finally. 'Safe not for six months, and me in fear of the landlord, but safe always.' He turned to the priest. 'It's not for wealth I'm wishing but just good crops and new things to try like me cabbages and maybe corn and goats.'

So I am no part of his need, Moira thought. It's as well I know and accept it. There is no other man I could marry, even if I would. No babies to cherish, no one of me blood to bury me.

She saw Eileen looking at her and smiled serenely.

Liam's mother whined, 'A proper son would wish for me health so I'll have to wish it meself. Ever since I lost me baby I been tied to me pallet missing all the frolics and funerals and no one coming to visit so I come here in the rain, and me stomach hurting so bad I —'

'I wish,' said her husband grimly, 'that you'd hush about your pains.' He stood and stretched by the fire, tall and arrogantly handsome as Liam, Moira thought, but sluggish, slow-moving. 'I wish to move to some other place, England, maybe, or America, and have a proper house and horses to ride and a hired girl to cook me food.'

No one admired Lazy Lenihan but he had had at least the virtue of predictability. Now they stared in disbelief. To leave his land? Not only that, to leave his country? Aye, a few of the young folk had married and left Ballyfearna but only to venture a county or two away, and always with the dream of returning.

Sally Mullen said, 'I followed me husband to America, but only in me duty. When I came back, when me boat reached Galway Bay and I got on land I fell on me knees and kissed the very furze on the bank and thanked God I was home.' She looked at her betrothed. 'It's nothing I've to wish for now but to marry Patrick in better times.'

Granny said, 'Aye, daughter, I wish it too. But there's some-

106

thing else.' She licked the lip of her empty glass and Dennis refilled it. 'I got me a funeral dress nobody but Sally ever seen. It was to surprise everybody when they passed by me coffin at the wake. Stitched it meself back in '28, me entering me sixties. You never saw finer — black frieze, it is, with six buttons and a neck frill. But now I got to sell it. Sally and me don't have the rent and only meal for another day. So me wish is — I wish I could find some way to keep that dress. It don't seem right a living woman should wear it.'

Paddy said, 'Come to me shop Monday and I'll give you a stone of meal.'

'But me dress is worth three stone,' Granny said. 'It was never worn.'

'I'll give you the meal free.'

'My God!' Granny said. 'My God!'

'When you die,' Paddy said, 'I'd naturally bring a wake-gift, wouldn't I?' She nodded. 'So when you die I won't, and it's even we'll be.'

Granny rose and embraced him and people laughed and applauded. Father Leary laughed too but he said, 'It's not Paddy did it alone; I'm thinking St Martin pushed him. And it's a good omen for all our wishes that one should come true tonight.'

Moira thought, no one has asked me mine — and better so. But she sent up a little prayer to St Martin.

'Two wishes have come true,' Dennis said, smiling at Eileen. 'Food!'

Biddy's hired girl brought in a tray of hard-boiled eggs, ham, oatbread and pudding. In normal times, Moira thought, it would have been enough, for everyone would have had their supper. Now it was a tease and a torment. And though guests usually helped themselves, Biddy served each one as if she knew the temptation to take more than one's share.

Moira ate her sliver of ham, her oatbread and egg so quickly that she scarcely tasted it. And the thin slice of pudding was halfway to her mouth before she remembered her promise to bring something to Sean.

Loathing herself, Moira said, 'It looks and smells so grand — but I don't mind giving it up for Da.'

107

'Right,' Biddy said, 'wrap it in your shawl.'

Terence the Fiddler played, songs were sung and a final toast drunk to long years of marriage for Biddy and Dennis. At midnight the guests departed in the rain.

'You're quiet as mice,' Liam said, as they came to Moira's hut.

'Aye?' She paused at the door.

'What's wrong?' he asked.

Hunger. Two hungers. And to her horror the need for food was stronger than the other. At this moment it did not greatly matter that Liam's wish was for land, not marriage. What mattered was the slice of pudding held under her shawl. Perhaps Mary was right in saying that paupers given a bite were hungrier than if they had had nothing.

'Nothing's wrong,' she said.

He drew her close and kissed her but she could not respond; his lips roused no warmth, no feeling. Impatient to be rid of him, desperate to be alone, she said, 'I promised Da I'd be home early,' and pulled away.

In the kitchen Sean had Cathleen on his knee, feeding her mush.

'And how was the frolic?' he asked, as Moira let out the dogs.

'Grand,' she said. 'Wait — I'll just hang up me shawl.'

They never used the bedroom pegs for outdoor clothing but she went into the bedroom now, not caring if it seemed strange to him, anxious only to hide. She stepped over the sleeping children and went to the far dark corner and opened the poke. The smell of spice and currants knifed her stomach and saliva spilled down her chin.

She heard Sean's voice as he coaxed the infant. 'Come, alanna, you must eat.'

She felt a sudden rage at the baby who could eat all it wished, the baby who had killed her mother, who was now depriving her father, her brothers and herself. A cup of mush a day meant seven a week, and more later on.

'Cathleen . . .' Sean was chiding the child.

Moira's flood of love for him was as swift and savage as her hatred for the baby. She tossed off the cloak and ran into the kitchen with the pudding in her hand.

'Look what I brought you!'

He peered at her hand. His mouth made a little O. 'Pudden?' he asked. His voice was soft, almost timorous.

'Aye, and good. Take it and eat it and put down Cathleen. God knows *she's* eaten, with porridge to her ears.'

'I'll not be eating.' Sean said. 'I never liked Biddy's puddens.'

'I never heard you say so.'

'Sure you must have. Them spices ain't good for old stomachs.'

'Please, Da. You've had nothing but nettles all day.' She extended her hand. 'Smell it.'

'No!' He shrank back. 'Eat it yourself and don't be pestering me. See, you've made the baby cry.'

She would not eat it. Strangely, her hunger had vanished save for a little ache. She felt light-headed, but her wits were about her. She placed the pudding on a stool within Sean's reach.

'I'm going to bed,' she said, yawning. 'Mind, before you let the dogs in, to move that pudden or they'll grab it sure. Now mind. But it's so forgetful you are . . .'

She kissed him and left him.

The next day, Sunday, was unusually warm and sunny and Mass was well attended. And Father Leary told the congregation of three marvels: the bishop had petitioned Lord Mountjoy for a month's grace on the rents, scarcely hoping he would grant this for a second time — but he had.

'. . . so Mr Pond will not come here until December tenth.'

Jesus, who was drunk, cheered and was admonished by the priest but no parishioner blamed him.

'Our cups runneth over,' Father Leary continued with a twinkle. He told them that a shipment of curry powder was on the way from England to relieve the hunger of the people of Mayo on the advice of the Duke of Norfolk who stated that this powder, mixed with water, had nourished thousands of starving Indians. And the third marvel — boatloads of corn meal from America were on the way and would be free to all.

It was a happy day for Moira for Liam seemed more loving than he had in many weeks. On the way home he kissed her at the bridge, again on the hill, even at the well in full sight of Granny. In the afternoon they set out alone to search for nettles.

Nettles were cruel, stinging the hands, but if you boiled them a long time you could eat them. They were tasteless as grass and could not satisfy hunger but they dulled it. So did ferns — veined and stringy but edible when cooked with cress and wild garlic. Leaves simmered five to six hours made a nourishing broth combined with the tiny plants that grew by ponds. One must gather all these now before the frost set in.

With their buckets filled Moira and Liam sat down on a heatherbed and watched twilight steal across the hills, robbing the sunset. Moira said, 'It's like me whole body bore a weight and now it's off. I ain't even hungry. But tomorrow we can buy oats!'

'Aye, but mind, a month is not long. You must save the rent money.'

'Have I not? But now I know how to make the meal last longer. You mix it with the greens and the greens don't taste so bad.'

'Me parents can't eat the greens,' Liam said. 'It makes them run till they're weak.'

'Aye, me brothers was terrible sick the first time but they got used to it. They's thin but strong as oxen.' The thought of all she had to be thankful for emboldened her. 'Liam, was it the whole of your wish you told last night?'

'No,' he said, 'I'd want cows and a mare again and a bigger shed but the priest's eye was on me and I feared to seem greedy.'

Greatly daring, she asked, 'Won't you ever be wanting children?'

'Oh, I don't know. Children pester a man.'

'But sons to linger your name?'

'I don't know one man in his true mind ever really wanted sons except them lords and dukes so as to raise more of themselves. It's only women want children.'

'I do,' Moira said softly.

So softly, perhaps, that Liam didn't hear? He rose and stretched and hummed a tuneless little song. Mother Mary, but he was thin, yet handsomer than ever with the shoulders seeming wider in contrast to the narrow waist. She could never decide what part of him she loved the most; the great shoulders or the big eyes that were so shiny you could almost see yourself in them; or the heavy black waves of his hair. Or the full mouth that drowned you in a kiss. No, it was all of him together and the way he walked as if he owned all the acres of the world.

Maybe, she thought, it was enough just to love him, to see him every day. To know that no matter what happened he would always be there, like the hills and the stars.

On Thursday Father Leary had more good news. The English were distributing rice, a pound to a family, from the shed near the workhouse.

At first people were mistrustful for no one had ever heard of rice, not even the priest. But Alfred Nevin, captain of engineers, calmed their fears. He had never seen any but he knew for a fact that it fed whole countries like China and India. He advised everyone to get some.

Sean went out early and returned with a pound before going to work. Moira pounced on it.

'Do you cook it, Da?' she asked.

'Nobody said to.'

She ran it through her fingers, then tasted a grain. 'It's hard as little pebbles. It got no flavour.'

'Well, all I know is the woman at the shed, the one giving it out, said it was fine for children.'

Moira tried to chew a morsel, gave it up and swallowed it. Surely it would not hurt to cook it, at least soak it a while to soften it. She shook it all into a pot of water to let stand until suppertime.

The afternoon was balmy. The boys played outside in their quiet new way, not chasing or running but building with stones and sticks. Granny sat under a tree with Cathleen, teasing her nose with a weed and making her gurgle. Grace dozed with the dogs on the doorstone.

In the bedroom Moira shook the lice from the pallets and swept the floor while Sally kept her company.

'Patrick found four frogs last night,' Sally said. 'He made me

111

swear not to tell, but like Granny says, you're like the family. Only if I tell you where they are do you promise to keep it secret?"

Moira promised.

Sally lowered her voice. 'They're at the Pool of the Water-dogs.'

Me own pool, Moira thought, outside me own little house. Yet since spring it had seemed deserted of all life, the fish and otters gone and the birds silent.

'Maybe it's a omen,' Moira said. 'The creatures coming back.'

'Maybe. Anyway, you go there tonight and get you some frogs. But don't you tell Liam.'

'But Liam is me heart, like Patrick is yours.'

Sally frowned. 'Patrick's spoken for me. Liam ain't done you that honour.'

'But he'd not inform about the frogs.'

'I'm not so sure, Moira.'

'What do you mean?'

'Bridget Reilly's got nothing. He'd tell her, wouldn't he?'

They heard a crash in the kitchen, a scream, and ran in to see Grace lying on the floor beside an overturned barrel. A quick glance showed Moira that she wasn't hurt, only frightened, and she pulled her to her feet with a playful slap for her mischief. Then she noticed that Grace's mouth and chin were wet. Tiny white pellets dribbled down her dress. Moira looked up and saw the rice pot on its shelf.

'Why, you imp of hell! Thieving, was you?' Her slap on the little rump was not playful. 'I'll teach you to steal,' and she picked her up, laid her over the barrel, raised the ragged skirt and spanked hard.

'My God, Moira,' Sally said, above the howling, 'she's only a babe.'

'Old enough to steal,' Moira said grimly. 'Sly and secret too.' She placed Grace none too gently on the hearth rags. 'She knows better, even the dogs know, though they'd steal if they could. There'll be no theft in this house.' She added more calmly, 'Can't you see how it would be if the children were let to steal from their own kin in times like these?'

112

'She was hungry,' Sally said, bending to soothe the sobbing child. 'She don't understand.'

'She *must* understand. It's me that's got to *make* her understand. Suppose your mother gets queer in her age — would you let her steal food?'

'She'd never —'

'She would, like the children. Da whipped Sean for finding a apple and not sharing with Colum. It was a old ratty apple but Da was right. Families has got to —'

She stopped short. Grace was retching. Rice and water poured from her mouth, her face flamed and the tiny cords of her neck seemed taut to bursting. Moira held down her head while Sally brought a pan to put under her chin.

'It's shamed, she is,' Moira said, 'and all me fault for the scolding.' She stroked the fair curls, murmured endearments. 'It's a good girleen you are and you'll never do it again, I know. . . .'

'She ain't got much on her stomach,' Sally said, 'it's all she can bring up.'

Moira set the child upright, cradling her and crooning.

'Her face looks queer,' Sally said.

'True for you,' Moira agreed, alarmed. Queer indeed. Not the colour of it but the twist of it as though she were in pain. 'Quick, Sally, go for Mary.'

'She'll not come here for anger at your Da.'

'Oh, God. But she knows we're not fevered.'

'I'll beg her.' Sally ran to the door, calling for her mother.

Granny hurried in, carrying Cathleen, and the boys and the dogs followed. As they approached her, Moira said, 'Listen to me, and do what I say and don't come nearer.'

Granny halted, the boys behind her.

'Grace is sick, she got to be quiet.' Moira spoke slowly and distinctly. 'Sean, you and Colum get them dogs out and stay out with them till I call you in.'

She was so strangely sure of herself that she was not surprised by the boys' instant obedience.

'Granny, put Cathleen in the bedroom.'

'But she's only just awoke. She's hungry. She'll cry —'

'Let her.'

And Granny obeyed.

'Now,' Moira said, as Granny reappeared, 'come and take Grace.'

They exchanged places. Grace whimpered and clutched her stomach.

'Holy Mary,' Granny said, 'her face is like it's bent.'

'Aye, it's the poison of the rice she ate.' Moira took down the pot, carried it out the back door and dumped it. The bastards, she thought, echoing Liam, the damned English bastards. It's not enough to taunt us with turnip seed, they've got to poison us as well.

'Her little body is shaking,' Granny said. 'Have you got a drop of poteen?'

'You know we've not.'

'I've a jar hid,' Granny said. 'Look in me first pratie pit where the dockweed is.'

Moira brought it and Granny forced a spoon of it through Grace's lips. 'I was saving it in case of the fever,' Granny said. 'It's poteen kept us healthy in the '30's. Why, I know more about what's good for fever than Mary ever knew. If Kitty had asked me to help lay out John I'd not have said no. All you have to do to keep yourself clean is to wash your hands in your own body-water.'

Grace whimpered, but softly. And Moira's heart lightened, for the cramped face eased, the eyes closed. She will have Mama's lashes, Moira thought, like little silk curtains.

'I wonder,' Granny said, 'how ever on earth she got to that shelf?'

'By the barrel. But I never knew she could climb on that barrel. It's strong she's getting.'

'At that age you got to be watching them every minute.'

Mary the Midwife came in, followed by Sally who carried her fardel of medicines.

'God bless you for coming,' Moira said, 'but I think she's all right now.'

Mary bent to examine her.

'She's just asleep this minute,' Granny said.

'Aye,' Mary said, 'in heaven.'

114

Long before suppertime word of the lethal rice spread through Ballyfearna and folk threw theirs away, thankful to be spared. Their mourning for Grace was a measure of their gratitude toward her. No child's funeral had ever been so splendid. Sister Charity and Sister Angelica stripped the convent gardens of winter jasmine. Paddy provided a real pine box with silver handles. All the men in town vied to be pall bearers.

It was rumoured that Father Leary would recommend the child for sainthood; she had not only spared Ballyfearna but Ballydonny and Ballinrobe as well. And so it was a shock and a surprise when Father Leary celebrated an ordinary Solemn High Mass. He did not dwell on the means of her death nor hint at possible sainthood. He did not take his text from 'Suffer Little Children' nor 'A Little Child Shall Lead Them.' Most folk felt that he was saving his shaft for the graveside but when the convent flowers were piled on the mound next to Cathleen's, he gave only the usual blessing.

The ceremony over, he spoke consolingly to the McFlahertys, then mingled among the others in the churchyard. Jesus, moved toward tears, said, 'It's in my mind Grace McFlaherty done something bigger than anybody ever did here.' And he asked Father Leary the imperative question. 'Do you think we might have a saint, Father?'

'If you mean the child, no. She ate that rice as a hungry wee one would, without thought for us. A saint must have intention and discipline. There are young angels, aye, but no saints her age.' He patted Moira's shoulder. 'Don't fret, she'll be an angel sure.'

'Maybe a martyr?' Jesus asked hopefully.

'You could say that. But the rice wasn't poisoned, it was only boiling it needed — Dr Thrush ate some himself. The crime is, the English didn't instruct us. It's their old sin — negligence, indifference. They've used Ireland as a garden these long years and now the garden is ruined. But they might need us later, so they send us little presents to keep our anger down.'

'That powder in bottles they do be sending to nourish us,' Biddy said, 'would you be trusting it now?'

'Aye,' said the priest, 'if the government sends proper instructions.'

115

'And what of the corn-meal from America?' Dennis asked. 'Shall we be trusting that?'

'Sure, and why not?'

'That was a stupid question,' Sally said to Dennis. 'It's not the Americans would trick us and hurt us, and it's meself should know. I never ate their meal — Indian meal, they calls it — but I'd trust it like mother's milk.'

'Now would ye?' asked old Brian. 'You was away, you never had the meal of corn they sent us in '31. Sour it was and we all got sick and the children, some of 'em died. Your mother will remember. Ask her when you get home, don't she remember that terrible sour meal.'

But Sally didn't ask, for Brian was crazy in the head. And besides, nobody wanted to hear anything fearsome or sad. There had been four deaths in seven weeks.

At home Moira smoothed Grace's little oat sack dress and put it away for Cathleen, whom she fed. Then she boiled the last of the oats with nettles for Sean, herself and the boys. But when suppertime came, she could not eat, and took her grief to bed.

Several times during the night she heard her father moving about and the closing of the kitchen door; but she sank back to sleep. In the morning Sean refused breakfast, for the nettles had made him ill with cramps and dysentery. Despite her insistence that he stay home he went to work as usual. Moira accompanied him into town where she bought oats at Paddy's, thankful to have them for the healing of Sean's stomach.

But they did not heal. He was forced to remain at home, cursing himself, alternately dragging outside to the bushes and spewing up the food in the hearth. Mary the Midwife doctored him with herbs to no avail. In two weeks he was no better and Moira suspected that fear kept his sickness alive, for soon they must make the choice between rent and food.

'If I'm not to work soon,' he said, 'Nevin will give me place to somebody else.'

'Ah, no, you and Liam is the best workers he got.'

'The Kane brothers is strong, so is Kevin. And Jesus has turned queer, he isn't lazy any more. Some of them roadlings, now they're feeding, can do a good day's labour. Moira, I must get there tomorrow.'

He got there but was too weak to swing an axe and was sent home at noon. In desperation, Moira went to Mary's house to beg advice.

'Is there nothing more you can do?' she asked.

'Not I. It's blood he needs, meat. If you've got a shilling to spare, go out to Houlihan's Ballinrobe way and they'll sell you a bit of cow.'

She had the shilling, but only to complete the rent so she dared not spend it. 'What in God's name will I do?'

'What I did,' Mary said, not looking at her. 'It's hard but I done it. Afterwards I sickened and thought I couldn't, but I ate it.'

'Ate what?'

'Me cat.'

'Oh, no!'

'More folk has done that than's telling. It's what the creatures are for, Moira. Where do you think Granny's cats and dog has gone?'

'Off somewhere searching for food.'

'They were food for her and Sally. I'd not be after informing, alanna, only to show you what you've to do.'

Moira swallowed, willing back the salty rise of nausea. 'How could I kill me dogs?'

'It's that or losing your Da.'

'He'd die else?'

'Not die of the dysentery maybe, but if it goes on he'll lose his job and then you'll all hunger toward death. You got to give him blood and bones so's he can work again.'

Moira took a deep breath. 'How am I to do it?'

'I strangled me cat.'

'But Two and Three are big dogs. I couldn't — I — me hands is too small.'

'Well, then. You've seen a pig stuck —'

'Never! I always hid with me head under the covers so as not to hear the screaming or I ran off to the woods with me mother, she was the same as me, she could never look.'

117

'Well, you've got to do it. All I can say is, don't let anyone know. Take the dogs to the deep woods and a hatchet for cutting them up after you've used a knife to their throats. When you've done that come here to me house and cook them. Then you can carry the pot home and tell your people I've given you hare stew.'

'Nobody's caught a hare in months.'

'No matter, you've got to say so.'

Lying . . . murder. 'I can't,' Moira said. 'Them dogs —' Tears spilled down her cheeks. They're old, too —'

'They are meat,' Mary said.

Meat. Life. So she told herself as she took Two and Three through the woods to the Pool of the Waterdogs. But she would spare them if only she could find frogs, which were rich and nourishing as chicken. Or if she saw an otter she could surely force herself to hatchet it, provided she could get close enough. They were strange frisky creatures moody as moonlight, rarely still in human sight. They scampered off at sound of your footfall only to peer at you from behind the very rock you sat on. If you were quiet they might mischief in reach of your hand but before you could lean to touch them they were perking the pool or shaking their whiskers on the opposite bank.

The pool was full, sluggish with dead leaves and lily pads and a brown slime of flies. If the insects were there uneaten then the frogs must be gone. She knew they were dusk creatures yet she sat for a long time, watching and listening. But there was no sound save the fall of leaves and the scuffle of the dogs exploring the bushes.

Behind her was the small abandoned hut curtained with ivy. Someone had once planted flowers. There were the bare stems of climbing roses, old man's beard and red-berried holly.

Moira tossed her shawl on a bush. As the sun lost its warmth she lost hope and took ropes from her bucket and made collars for the dogs. Despite their age they had a puppy innocence and they thought it a game, tugging and teasing and pretending to bite her hands. With more rope she tied them to strong young

118

saplings. At first they barked and strained but finally they lay down in acceptance of their ropes. When they were quiet she took from the bucket a pan and a sharp knife.

Please God for the croak of a frog or the splash of an otter.

But nothing stirred. There was no sound but the long sigh of wind in the trees and the whisper of falling leaves.

She thought of Liam who could do this quickly and cleanly but she had not asked him, had not told him. Because he might never feel the same about her as she might never feel the same about herself.

God, don't let me hurt them too much.

She removed her bodice, petticoat and undershift. Naked, carrying the knife in the pan, she went to Two, sat down beside her and clasped her close, burying her face in the rough burry coat. Then she straightened and turned the dog so that its rump was firmly against her knee. She took the knife from the pan, held the blade to Two's throat and pressed.

Two whined, squirmed around and licked her cheek. Moira pressed the blade harder but the neck fur was heavy, heavy and tough. The dog yelped and struggled, turned her head and looked into Moira's face. Moira pushed the head around so that she could not see the eyes. Again she slashed at the throat and Two screamed and tried to lunge away. Moira grasped the head and lifted it high, holding the loose skin taut but the collar of rope was in the way. Finally she felt the knife penetrate, and slid the pan under the throat to catch the flooding blood, moving aside so that her vomit watered the leaves.

Three was howling, straining at the rope. Moira rose and went to her with the pan and the knife and this time it was quicker because she knew what to do. After that she moved slowly, as one mired in nightmare. She poured the blood-brimming pan into the bucket. With the knife she stripped off the dogs' coats as Liam had taught her to skin rabbits long ago; and she kept the entrails for nourishment. Then she chopped the meat into pieces with the hatchet. At the pool she washed the knife and the pan and placed them in the bucket with the meat, covering the top with laurel. She buried the dogs' coats under the leaves.

119

She knew that Mary was waiting with the water-pot boiling but waves of illness kept her retching in the pool. Finally she washed the blood from her body, dressed and slumped on to the bank, digging her nails into the moss, pressing her face into the little pond plants. She was cold, cold to freezing though the sun lingered warmly. She felt that no quilt could warm her, no bed-brick, no poteen. She was too cold to move her legs.

She lay there for a long time, b.yond thought, beyond tears. Leaves crisped down on her hair and she smelled the sweetness of viburnum and dying clematis. Then she forced herself to stand. She draped the shawl over her arm to conceal the hatchet and picked up the bucket. As she left the pool she saw a frog on the pad of a lily and a hare scampered from her path.

Moira waited until the children were abed before she served Sean the meat, for he needed it more than they. She had expected astonishment when she told him that Mary had found hares in the fields but he accepted the story apathetically, nor did he seem surprised that she ignored the food. It was as though he ate in a stupor, unaware of her presence.

The sight and smell of the stew was nearly unbearable. Finally it was over and she washed his dish and stored the pot on the shelf to reheat for him tomorrow. There was enough for six or seven more meals, for his appetite was small; and Mary had warned not to force his feeding lest he sicken.

Strangely, as though the food had the swift warmth of poteen, he began to talk and his face awakened to its old awareness.

'Since I've been home,' he said, 'I've been seeing how it is with the boys. Sean's a thief.'

'Oh, now, Da — sure he took the apple. But it's only the hunger on him. And he'll not do it again after the whipping you gave him.'

'He did do it again — not a apple, it was Cathleen's porridge he ate today and pretending to feed her, with his back to me.'

'Maybe only a spoonful —'

'No, alanna, she got nothing. I made her more. And I took Sean outside and whipped him again — hard.'

From old habit he reached for his pipe, realised there was no tobacco, stroked the stem and put it down. 'He didn't cry. He only looked at me like I was dung. And then, my God, he smiled.'

'He was after forgiving you then.'

'No. For that smile was like —' he gestured helplessly '— like cold. Like broken ice. And it froze me heart. I was almost —' he lowered his voice '— scared of him.'

She realised his addlement and tried to cheer him out of it. 'Nothing's so fearsome as a five-year-old. I mind the time he put the mouse in Granny's shawl —'

'But this was no prank.'

'He was hungry. So was Grace.'

They both looked at the little box placed at the hearth for Grace and the barrel stool for Cathleen, for where should lonely spirits return but to their own homes?

'It's more than hunger,' Sean said. 'It's cruel the boy is.'

I know, Moira thought. I've known a long time but washed the knowledge from me mind like bog-dirt from me body. I would not see it and I do not want to see it now.

'Ah, well,' she said, yawning, 'we'll teach him better. Now it's late —'

Sean said, 'He hurts things. Animals.'

She wanted to close her ears. 'Da, please, it's tired I am —'

'You must know.'

She knew, or did she? She remembered the mutilated frogs . . . Granny's cats, fearful of him, and Two and Three patient with the mischief that was not entirely mischief.

'You mind the dogs have been gone all day. I think he's done something — frightened them away.'

'They're off hunting,' she said.

'They've never been gone so long before.'

'Da —' she tried to keep her voice level, 'it's not we can blame Sean for all the creatures going off. They're seeking food. It's only natural.'

'Maybe.' He spoke almost in a whisper. 'But Sean — he's not natural.'

121

'That isn't so!' But her mind had whispered it lately and so softly she had scarcely heard. 'He's just a boy and boys have the whims on them.'

'Colum hasn't.'

No, Colum was gentle and shy and sweet.

'He doesn't hurt Colum, that we know. He's not cruel to Colum,' she said.

'No. Your mother saw to that.'

Perceiving Sean's jealousy of his brother at the age of three Cathleen had told him that the baby was his birthday gift, for Colum had been born only two days after Sean's birthday. Moira could remember her words: 'He is yours, Sean, to care for and protect and a gift to cherish your life through . . .'

And the jealousy had vanished like magic and the gift, like a toy, accepted with love. Sean did protect Colum to the best of his young abilities. Their wranglings were never fierce and Colum grew in the sun of his brother's devotion. Last year when an older boy had bullied Colum, Sean had attacked him viciously, trying to rake his eyes, screaming, 'You can't! He's mine, he's mine!'

'We'll not fret,' Moira said. 'It's cruel many children are but not for long. Was Liam not cruel? Did he not used to tear the wings off moths?'

Sean sighed. 'You're like your mother, God rest her.'

'Like mother!' It was too great a compliment, and undeserved. 'Why?'

'She never saw evil, she stopped her ears and bound her eyes.' He rose heavily, as though he bore ten times his slender weight. For a moment he stopped by Cathleen's barrel, touched above it as though she sat there, patted at the air. 'Good night.'

'Good night, Da.'

After he left she lingered, weary yet reluctant to go to bed. Then she looked up at the stew on its shelf. Sick at heart she took it down, climbed the ladder to the loft and hid the pot under a pile of oat sacks.

Two days later Sean returned to work and Moira marveled that meat could cure so quickly. Hoping for more she went each day to the Pool of the Waterdogs but though she often waited until dusk she found no frogs. The weather had turned bitterly cold and she wore a quilt over her shawl and fastened oat sacks on her bare legs.

Early on the day Mr Pond was due she went over to Granny's to leave her rent money. 'It's a coward I am,' she said, 'but I'd hate to see him, so nervous he makes me. I'm going to hunt the hills before the weather worsens.'

Granny put the money in a pot. 'It's no rent me and Sally has. We'll be evicted.'

'Ah, now, it's two months' notice he'll be giving, you know that.'

'He gave no notice to the Tumultys and the Boynes.'

'But he gave Bridget Reilly *six* months last time.'

'I know why, and so do you.'

Moira said, 'We can't be sure of that.'

'Why else, then? And why did his wife dismiss Bridget as maid? Because she didn't want a dilsy in her house.' Granny shrugged. 'I'm beyond caring about that but it do seem like good folk have no chance.'

Sally came in from the bedroom, eyes puffed with sleep. Gone was the stylish brown wrapper from America. She wore a tattered quilt over her nakedness.

'Dress,' Granny said sharply. 'Suppose Mr Pond comes and sees you so?'

'It's only sunrise.' She turned to Moira. 'Is anything wrong?'

'No, I'm off to hunt and I've left me rent with you.' She wished now that she hadn't; it seemed a taunt to friends who had none. But she was anxious to escape to the woods. 'And I wanted you'd keep an eye on the children.'

'Sure,' Sally said, 'I'll bring Cathleen here.'

'They've had their mush,' Moira said.

'Oh, God!' Granny said, 'are the two of you uncaring what's to happen? Himself maybe giving us the eviction paper, ordering us out to the roads?' Tears poured down the raddled face and her voice rose. 'Is it mad you are not to know what this day may bring?'

'Hush,' Sally said, 'of course we're knowing but it's no good to be keening on it. Moira's right to go hunting and it's I will be cleaning this place.'

'For what?' Granny asked. 'It don't stink.'

'For something to do. And to show Mr Pond we're not lazy.'

Granny spoke on a sob. 'I seen a pretty weed down near the fence. Maybe I'll get it and put it in a cup.'

'And maybe we'll give him a drop of the poteen,' Sally said.

'No!' Moira explained about his fury when she had offered him tea. 'He'd chide you for being ir-irresponsible. He'd say if you can't pay your rent you shouldn't have nothing nice. So don't you offer him nothing.' She kissed Granny's wet cheek, caressed the thin gray hair. 'If I can find food I'll bring you some.' She went to the door. 'May God stand atween you and all harm.'

'May He bless your hunting,' Sally said.

The sun reddened the distant hills but died in a slate grey sky. Moira shivered and her hands were cold. She carried the hatchet and a net Liam had fashioned for frogs. There *must* be creatures somewhere in those hills. A badger, perhaps, or a hare or rabbits. Surely they had not fled the high ground, only the blighted gardens.

She climbed slowly, clumsily, hampered by the oat sacks on her feet. The fields below were silvered by hoar-frost, the trees stretched bony arms above wind-bare bushes. Now she was above the town, two miles beyond the familiar, on one of the roads to nowhere built so long ago.

Often she paused in the chill silence hoping for sight of a rabbit or a squirrel but nothing moved. Walking on, she came to a log bridge over a brook but though she lingered there she saw no water creature. To keep warm she began to walk faster, up and up into the shaggy green of a pine forest where the needled ground was soft and level beneath her feet.

Here she was in a dark cathedral hush where the great heads of the pines bent together to hide the sky. She stopped to sit on a rock. And in the quietness she heard a scratching which seemed to come from a cairn ahead.

Silently and swiftly she rose, grasping the hatchet in her right

124

hand, and crept toward the mound of stones. A skeleton fox streaked across the path and was gone in a swirl of dead leaves.

She stared curiously at the stones, piled neatly as though by a human hand. With the hatchet she poked and dislodged a few. She poked again and again until the stones fell away and she saw the flesh-hung carcass of a child.

She ran in terror, not homeward, but upward, on and on through the green fragrant woods until she came to a little clearing. There was a sod cabin with smoke puffing through the roof and she went to the door and rapped, unthinking of who might live there, anxious only for the sound of a voice and the shelter of walls.

The woman who opened the door screamed at sight of the hatchet and the scream burst through Moira's hysteria and steadied her to explain her presence. 'Come from Ballyfearna . . . hunting these woods . . . I saw, I saw — something terrible.'

'Come,' said the woman, calm now. 'Come to the fire. What was it?'

'No, it was —' She choked on the words. 'It was —'

'Sit down.'

Moira sat on the bare earth floor beside the little fire of sticks and the woman sat opposite her, gaunt-faced, pale-lipped, wearing a ragged quilt like her own. Her brown hair spilled down her back, one emaciated arm stretched out to press Moira's hand. 'Peace on you, catch your puff before you try to speak.'

Moira nodded, shivering.

'It's a bit of broth you'll be needing.'

The woman rose, poured something from a pot into a wooden mug and handed it to Moira. It was the familiar brew of ferns and nettles and Moira sipped it gratefully.

'Now, tell me.'

Moira told her.

'It's me child,' she said, with the glisten of tears on her eyes. 'I thought to dig a little grave but I'd no spade, no strength in me hands. I just piled stones, thinking to keep him from the creatures, but . . .'

She said he had died of the hunger, he could not keep down the broth. 'He was the last to go.'

125

'The *last!*'

'Aye, me husband and me two little girls before him.'

'Are they, too, buried in the woods?' Moira asked.

'It was the back end o' the year and the leaves heavy. I burned them. For the fever was on them, you see.'

Moira said nothing for she had no words to comfort.

'Is it true they're a-building down below?' the woman asked.

'Aye, it's a thing for ships to go through, a great wide path in the woods.'

'So I heard. If I could work —' She stared at her long, bony hands. 'If only I could work! It's mad I'll be if I can't leave here.'

'Women aren't let to work on it. And then, it's a long way.'

'That's why I didn't come. Once I tried, I got down beyond the woods, then I had to come back. It took me an hour to crawl back.'

'How do you live?' Moira asked.

'The plants. There are no animals up here now, I'm surprised you saw that fox.'

'But I'm going to look,' Moira said. She felt suddenly and oddly strengthened — the broth, the warmth of fire and this woman's helplessness combined to lend her courage. 'I'll be back.'

'God and Mary with you.'

They were with her, Moira thought, for she had not gone forty yards before she found a dead stoat. It was partially eaten but it was fresh and she took it back to the woman who thanked her and begged her to stay for the stew.

'No,' Moira said, 'I'll be hunting for meself now. But before the cold comes I'll be back again. Maybe some Sunday I'll bring me sweetheart to set traps.'

'Then hurry. It's snow I smell.'

'Ah, no!' Moira could remember only one day of snow, and that winters ago, a day of lark and caper for the village children. 'It hasn't snowed for years.'

'It's strange years,' the woman said, and blessed Moira, and stood at the door to watch her out of sight.

By late afternoon Moira had found a dead owl, a dying hare, and a rich clump of pond plants. Moving down the hill she saw the far, toy village of Ballyfearna cuddled like a cup in the valley. There was the abbey white as a sprawled tulip on bright grass; the winding ribbon of the road and red sunset across the bridge.

But there was no sun. It was fire that reddened the fields of home.

She hurried down the hill past the huts of the O'Dowds and the O'Garras and the Regans. As she rounded the slope she heard shouting and saw a crowd outside Granny's house. Outside what had been Granny's house, now a tumble of stone, of flaming wood and thatch and the bone-ends of doors and shutters, cupboards and barrels and beams. Soldiers were mounting their horses, coats red in the firefury, cursing the eye-smarting smoke and the screaming women and the rearing fire-panicked horses. Then they were gone, riding off toward the village where, through the night, new fires were lit and new crowds gathered to watch in despair the funeral pyres of homes.

By dusk the next day only six houses stood in Ballyfearna — Moira's, Liam's, Paddy's, Father Leary's, Bridget's and the hotel. Biddy and Dennis turned the hotel into a temporary refuge for the homeless but they could not feed ninety people and gradually, family by family, they took to the roads. Jesus, Eileen, Tyrone and Mary the Midwife remained, welcome to stay because they could feed themselves. Kitty the Basket, Annie Dumbie and other single women walked to the workhouse, joining fifteen hundred other paupers in the makeshift sheds of the yard where they sometimes received a cup of soup a day.

Granny and Sally moved in with the McFlahertys, sleeping on the floor in the kitchen. Moira stretched the oats to its limits, feeding seven people on Sean's fourpence a day. There was no hope of saving for the spring rent. And when January came with alternate rain and dry cold there was no hope of turf for fires.

'I should have cut the wood last summer,' Sean said one night as they sat in the faint light of hoarded turf. 'But my God, I never thought . . .'

Moira bit back the words, 'You never do.' He had once accused her of being irresponsible but so was he, in a different

127

way. For all his goodness he had leaned too heavily on Cathleen's strength and resourcefulness; now that she was gone he had constantly to be reminded of any chore besides the one essential — his work on the canal. It was only the hunger on him — he had always been so, living in the moment with no prudence for the future. But then, she thought, excusing him, nearly every family in Ballyfearna had lacked wood. No one had considered the possibility of storms, that the ever-present turf would be unavailable.

'None of us thought we'd be evicted, neither,' Sally said, 'even with the warnings and all. It's like nobody really believes they'll die until old age is on them.'

'I did,' Granny said triumphantly. 'I made that dress for me funeral.'

Moira felt the rise of her temper. 'You should sell it. It's three stone of oats we'd have for it.'

'I won't.' Granny's little eyes flickered angrily, her sharp chin jutted. 'I won't.'

'You got to,' Sally said. 'It isn't right to be taking from neighbours and giving nothing.'

'That dress is all I've on this earth and I'm not selling it. Besides, who's to buy it? Paddy says even the gentry have nothing, them that hasn't moved away.'

'You should sell it for what he'll give you,' Moira said. 'Isn't that right, Da?'

'Aye,' Sean said, but softly, uncertainly.

'Even if it's only one stone of oats,' Moira said. 'You should be sharing with us.'

Little Sean who had been dozing on the floor next to Colum lifted his face from the straw. 'Has Granny got oats? Where?'

'I have none,' Granny said sharply.

Little Sean's voice turned sly. 'You have them hid.'

'She does not,' Moira said, 'she only has a dress to sell. Now you hush.'

Sean gave her a long, contemptuous stare. How odd, she thought, that a child could look so wise, so all-knowing. He and Colum could be twins save for the difference of expression. Both had thick red-gold curls, high cheek bones, deep-set blue eyes heavily lashed. Both had thin lips. But Sean's mouth was petulant as Colum's was upcurved and happy. Colum's eyes were soft and full of mood, Sean's were hard and sheenless as blue glass. And the thin little bodies were carried so differently, Colum's slow in movement, Sean's quick as a cat. Now Sean stared at Moira with those strange, lightless eyes and she fidgeted uneasily.

He said, 'I seen Granny bury something in the garden.'

'Aye,' Granny said furiously, 'I buried back me poteen, and what's it to you?'

Sean's eyes were hooded under the heavy lashes. '*Maybe* it's poteen.'

'Give over teasing Granny now,' his father said, but with that weak note in his voice that Moira had noticed of late, as though he spoke without conviction. 'We'll only be needing Granny's dress if the storms shut down the canal.'

Moira had seen the men working through this queer winter, chipping through ice to the hard ground, breaking rock, standing barefoot in thin oat sacks, warmed only by cotton quilts and their own effort. Since Christmas three had died of pneumonia, others sickened in sheds, caves, ditches. Her father dragged home on frost-cracked feet, with cruelly bruised hands. Liam, strong as he was, sometimes went straight to bed after supper instead of coming to see her. Or did he lie? Did he go to Bridget?

Jesus tapped at the door and came in. He was wearing one of Father Leary's old cassocks, pulled out at the seams and lengthened with bits of patchwork. He carried a jug of poteen.

'May God bless all saving the cat,' he said.

'We've no cats now,' Granny said, 'more's the pity.'

Sean rose to welcome him and to protest the generosity of the poteen.

'I've *told* you,' Jesus said, 'it's not a drop I can sell, and them kegs freezing in the cave. Only two people has bought any this month, them engineers, and they'd not pay me price, the bastards, but give me only tenpence. The bastards. Tenpence they give, and smiles on the face of them and a question, too — did I want to keep me work on the canal?'

He sat down on a rock next to Moira's as Sean poured and

129

distributed jars. 'I'm not drinking except for me head, that's God's truth. It was celebrating I was.'

'Celebrating what?' Sally asked.

'Why,' Jesus said, 'no one's tole you? The English has sent clothes, they's at the Workhouse and we can all get them at the abbey tomorrow. Free!'

'Clothes?' Little Sean asked. 'For me?'

'Sure and why not?'

'Praise God.' Granny crossed herself.

'It's Tyrone will fetch them in his cart. The good father himself told me, when I was after meeting him in the lane. They'll be fine clothes from them rich people in London who maybe change their clothes two, three times a week, in and out going to see the Queen and she liking to see them all dressed different. Warm they'll be, with fur and all . . .'

They were silent, awed.

'. . . and the Indian meal, it came too, two ships is at Galway Bay so we should have it maybe this week.' He took a long gulp of his drink. 'And it's free too!'

Colum awakened, poked his head out of the quilt-nest and smiled. 'Is it yourself, Jesus?'

'Aye,' Jesus said, 'I think so. This drink's done me a world o' good.' He emptied his jar. 'It's like another man I feel, in truth I'm meself again.'

Moira lifted her jar. 'May you live to eat the goose that scratches your grave.'

He smiled, showing big broken teeth, then frowned. 'Let's not be talking of graves. The good father is after having me bury three roadlings tomorrow, and them without coffins or shrouds.'

'Who were they?' Sally asked.

'Folk of the roads, no one we know.'

'Oh, God,' Sally said. 'Do you be hearing anything of me Patrick?'

'No, but I'd guess he's still in his house. They wasn't many evictions in Ballydonny.'

'Why?' Sean asked.

'Most folk had left to beg or to squat at the workhouse. He

isn't going to tumble good houses if people has left them.' Jesus turned to Granny. 'You should have left your house and hid in the woods till Mr Pond had gone.'

'Are you mad?' Moira asked. 'He'd know. He'd come back to make sure.'

Sally said, 'I'm wanting to walk to Ballydonny to see Himself but each morning I go just up the hill and it's so tired I am I turn back. But I used to walk ten miles like it was one.'

'It's easy you'll be with warm clothes,' Moira said, 'and Patrick too. Likely he'll come here to see you.'

'If he does we'll marry and me and me mother will go to live with him so's not to burden you.'

'Good,' said little Sean. 'We haven't enough food.'

Moira rose swiftly, slapped him and dragged him into the bedroom. He bit her finger and she cried out in pain.

'What's come over you?' she asked as he sat sullenly on the floor. 'How can you be so bad?'

He gave her the contemptuous stare. His eyes were dry.

It's the hunger on him, she thought, it's twisted him somehow, made him cruel. And how's a child to govern it?

She knelt beside him. 'Is it the hunger makes you this way?'

'What way?' he asked, eyes evasive.

'Like a little cruel animal, taunting people.'

'What's taunting?'

'Hurting. Like what you said about Granny and Sally.'

'I said true. They're taking our food.'

She restrained her anger. 'Granny's helped care for you since you was born and it's many a pratie they given you before the blight, and milk and pudden too. They're part of the family and we must share what we have. Would you have them on the roads?'

He said nothing. She faced the bright blankness of his eyes and shook her head. 'How would you like to be told to go out in the dark cold and no place to lay your head?'

He shrugged.

Colum came in shyly, anxious to help if his brother were in trouble and Sean's eyes came softly to life. It's only Colum he

131

loves, Moira thought, the rest of us could be dirt. But he had loved Cathleen. There was love in him if only she knew how to draw it.

She kissed both boys. 'Sleep now, and tomorrow we'll have clothes. It's no quilts we'll be wearing any more but suits and shawls, and maybe even shoes.'

Colum's arms crept about her neck. Sean lay down, drawing· up the straw to hide his face.

She returned to the common room and finished her jar but the poteen did not warm her. There was a cold knot of fear which it could not thaw, a fear she could not fathom. Starvation? Eviction? But she had lived with those fears for months . . .

Jesus was talking of Boston America. 'Is it true,' he asked Sally, 'that men like me has maybe two suits apiece?'

'Aye, and more. And the women, my God, their red flannel petticoats is made of satin.'

'Have you ever thought,' Jesus asked Sean, 'of trying to get to America?'

'And leave me land?' Sean asked incredulously.

'It's not ours,' Jesus said.

'It is till we're evicted.'

'It's Paddy is going.'

'It's only his talk,' Sean said. 'It's a year now he's been going on his tongue.'

'Well, they do say Danel Powderley took the road to Galway Bay to try to work over on a ship.'

Without a goodbye, Moira thought. But then, neither had Annie nor Kitty, Kevin nor Molly, nor any of the others said farewell. Perhaps they had neither time nor strength, but fled their homes like burned-out animals. Perhaps they had no heart for it lest they weaken and stay. If I had to go, she thought, I'd hurry off and not look back.

Sean said, 'We'll never leave here. Things has got to get better.' He sucked on his empty pipe which Paddy would not buy for surfeit of them. 'They have to.'

'I'd say things would get better if we only had the seed praties,' Jesus said. 'Anyway, we have the turnip seed.'

'Where did you plant?' Moira asked.

'Now, that's a queer thing,' Jesus said, 'We'd have planted in our garden, Eileen and me, it being our land then. But the priest, he was afraid of blighted ground so he told us to plant somewhere else, and we did — behind the hotel. Dennis has no garden there. So it's turnips we can give him for the shelter he gave us.'

'I planted beyond our pits,' Moira said, 'only the same as I do for praties.'

'How else?' Sally asked. 'Seed is seed, good ground is good. We'll all get plenty of turnips once it's spring.'

Granny nodded. 'Once it's spring.' The bony brown-veined hand reached out as though toward April, the old eyes gleamed. 'It's even me will live till then, God willing.'

'Sure,' Jesus said, 'it's jig at your wedding I will.'

The old woman chortled, took a sip of poteen, choked and had to be slapped on the back to regain her breath. Tears born of laughter ran down her cheeks. 'Me,' she said, 'me wedding! And who'll I be marrying, Jesus?'

'Lord Mountjoy. He's sure to be coming here someday.'

She was off again, helpless in laughter.

'He'll see you in your garden and tip the hat of him and say "Missus Cullen, may I have the honour of your hand . . .'

'Oh!' said Granny, 'you'll be the death of me —'

'. . . and you'll live in his big house and eat off plates of gold, pig and goose and chickens fried in butter . . .'

Moira felt her stomach cramp, the terrible hollowness that had somehow to be ignored. We should never talk of food, she thought, we torture ourselves. And at night when we should be at peace in our sleep we dream of it.

Granny had stopped laughing. She was looking up at the shelf where the oat sack was. Then she glanced at Moira with begging eyes.

No, Moira told her silently, not until tomorrow noon. One bowl a day is all we can have, and the green broth at night.

Granny said, 'Onc't at a wedding in Ballinrobe I had me a duck all to meself . . .'

133

The next morning Moira and Sally set out for the abbey where a little crowd had gathered in the churchyard, all that was left of the village. The roadlings who worked on the canal, once resented, were now tolerated, for without them work would stop. They lived in abandoned huts or in caves. A few had wives and children but most were lonely men who had lost their families months ago, on the cold brown roads of autumn.

The crowd in their quilts moved about between the tombstones, stamping their feet for warmth, blowing on their hands, waiting for Father Leary to come and distribute the clothes. Gossip traveled. Eileen had seen Tyrone Schwartz bring a loaded cart to the abbey last night, piled to the top it was, more clothes than they could ever use. Nevertheless the great oak door was locked against stealing strangers, and this only right and proper.

Presently the priest came up the path from his house and Moira noticed with horror that he too wore oat sacks on his feet. In the week since she had seen him his face had thinned to bones. Even his smile was different, as though painful or pinched by cold. He took a key from his belt, unlocked the massive door and bade them enter and be seated in the pews.

Near the altar Moira could see a great pile of clothes, red and green and blue and pink like the stained glass above in the high window. A shaft of sunlight settled on something golden and she tried to guess what it might be.

'Let us pray.'

Heads bowed.

'Let us pray for understanding of others, for this is to forgive . . . We must try to realise that what was sent to help us was sent, not in malice, but in ignorance. The good people of London who gave these clothes did not know our need, nobody told them, I think. It's like we wouldn't be knowing what *they* needed. So I ask you in God's name to accept in charity what was sent in charity and to use these things as best you can.' He tried to smile. 'Save them for the good times ahead, for the frolics and the weddings and the lovely christenings and thank God for them . . . Amen.'

Moira felt the slump of her heart; yet the clothes looked so bright, so beautiful . . .

'The women's clothes are in the middle pile, the men's on the right, the children's on the left,' Father Leary said. 'You'll come up the aisle in order as you're sitting, the ladies first. Mrs O'Hara?'

Mary the Midwife approached the altar, riffled through the middle pile. Moira saw her take something red, something black, and what looked to be shoes and a shawl.

'Miss McFlaherty?'

Moira went up the aisle trying not to seem too eager. As she reached the pile of women's clothes she drew in her breath at the glitter there. Gold-tasselled shawls of silk. Gold and pink and green satin ballgowns, white kid gloves, dancing slippers, reticules, plumed bonnets and a froth of lacy undergarments.

But nothing warm. Heedless of size or shape or colour she rummaged for flannel, frieze, anything of weight. She touched only muslin, satin, chiffon, calico. There were mitts of silk and kid and net, slippers and hose for ladies who walked on lawns. Thin aprons for their maids, and dimity petticoats. Ah, here was something heavier — a little velvet capelet banded with mink tails.

She looked up into the sad eyes of the priest. 'Take something pretty,' he said, 'for your marriage box.'

She chose the capelet, a pale blue silk dress, a white shift and petticoat trimmed with blue satin ribbon, a blue bonnet with white plumes.

'Shoes,' he said.

The sturdiest in her size were pink velvet tipped with feathers.

He motioned her on to the children's pile where she found two linen dresses for Cathleen, dark silk suits for Sean and Colum, ruffled shirts, patent leather slippers. Praise be, there was one warm coat. But for her father she could find nothing but thin riding breeches, a brown velvet jacket and frilled shirts.

'What is this?' she asked Father Leary, holding up something long and silken.

'A robe, I think'

'Then it should be for yourself, Father.'

'It's not that kind of robe,' he said. 'It's a gentleman's dressing robe.'

135

'It's silk, but it's heavy.'

'Take it.'

She had never seen anything like it, flowered in petals of red and gold, collared in dark fur. She took it over her arm with the other garments and seated herself at the end of the church to wait for Sally.

They walked out together quietly, silent until they reached the bridge. Then Sally said, 'I never seen such clothes, not even in America. But dear God, such *cold* clothes. It must be terrible hot in London.'

'They don't live like us.'

Sally peered at the blue silk over Moira's arm. 'That's pretty. I got me a red velvet, it has pearls on the sash . . . a muslin bodice. But nothing has no sleeves, only little puffs.'

'I know.' Moira pulled up Sean's brocaded robe, which was trailing the ground. 'What have you for Granny?'

'A good black dress, buttons of gold it has, and sleeves too. Likely now she'll sell the woe-weed. And a bonnet, black straw with pink roses on.'

Moira shifted the weight of her garments. 'I am thinking the English men aren't very big. I didn't see anything would fit Liam or Jesus.'

'I saw Mrs Lenihan get a tall hat,' Sally said, 'like the one Paddy rented Annie for the wake. Silk it was. It'll be grand on Liam.'

'That's no use to a man, when it wouldn't even cover his ears.'

'But so grand!'

'For a wedding or a wake.'

Leaving the bridge, they followed the ice-grey river.

'Sally —'

'Aye?'

'Wait till you see me dress spread out. It has diamonds on top and little violet bunches on the skirt and something back behind like angel wings. Do you think —' her breath steamed and her face ached from the cold — 'we'll be wearing these dresses at our weddings?'

'And why not?' Sally asked.

'It's white I should be wearing.'

'There's no law says so.'

'And Liam has his tall hat. It's like a omen, isn't it?'

'Sure.'

'They say God moves mysterious-like. Maybe He made them English ladies send us our marriage dresses.'

'Sure,' Sally said.

But she had a vacant look in her eyes, a look Moira knew and could feel in herself. She and Sally were not thinking to the months ahead, to the abbey bells, the Nuptial Mass, the crowd and the kisses, the fiddle and the drink — nor even to the shy lovely darkness of bed. They were thinking of the hot nettled broth two hours away.

Chapter 5

'Sean,' Moira said to her brother, 'it's understanding you must be about the coat. Colum is littler, he needs it more than you.'

'I'm cold as him.'

'But you're bigger, you have more blood in you.' She tried to appeal to his vanity. 'You're braver.'

His wise smile came. He said nothing.

'You *love* him. You want him to be warm.'

He looked down, fiddled with the string of his pants.

'I don't say Colum should wear it all the time, like when you need it to go out to the bushes. But when you're both inside, he should wear it.'

Sean made no response. In exasperation, she bent to shake him; then, meeting his eyes, pulled back. Why in the name of God should she be afraid of a boy she could whip with one hand tied? Yet, unaccountably, she was afraid.

He seemed to read her thought. 'I'm not after doing anything,' he said, and threw off the coat and ambled out of the bedroom to join the others by the dead fire.

The turf was hoarded for cooking only, but still they grouped about the fireplace from habit, remembrance, the ghosts of cheer.

Under his blanket Sean wore the long brocaded robe and under her quilt Moira's little velvet capelet hugged her throat and the pink-feathered slippers, too large for her, slapped the floor as she moved to Colum to put the coat on him. Granny and Sally crouched together for warmth, heads in their old, ragged shawls, sharing a blanket. They could hear the wind pounding and the swift, metallic sound of hail.

'I wonder what the time might be,' Sally said.

'About nine,' Moira said.

Fifteen hours until they could eat . . .

'We should sleep,' Granny said. She looked at Cathleen, snug in her box. 'It's lucky she is, sleeping as much as she does.'

No one spoke. The wind rose in tantrum. Moira braided, unbraided her hair. Sally worked a tiny, pearl-buttoned glove on to her hand and the seam split.

'Do you remember,' Sean asked Moira, 'the blood puddens your mother made at Easter?'

'Da — you mustn't talk of food.'

'No,' he said.

They heard the hail, pelting the house like gravel. Colum climbed into Moira's lap and went to sleep. Little Sean stared at the empty hearth.

'Well,' Sean said, and his voice trailed off.

Granny spoke on a sigh. 'I'll be after asking Paddy to come for me funeral dress. You tell him, Sean. Tell him to come after dark.'

'Aye, then.'

'So's I'll get a better price.'

Paddy came the next afternoon wearing a good heavy coat and a tweed cap. He apologised for his fine appearance — these were clothes the gentry had traded, that no one could afford to buy. 'It's like I'm wearing me shop window,' he said.

He spoke of his poverty. 'Look at me, all bones.'

'You're no thinner than ever you were,' Granny said accusingly.

He was defensive. 'I'm losing me hair.'

'You never had none much to start.'

139

'Now, Granny,' Moira said, anxious to keep Paddy in good humour, 'he has nice red hair there on top, two lovely strands as ever I seen. Won't you take a seat, Paddy Nolan?'

He sat on a rock. 'So you're after wanting to sell something?' He looked around the room, bare save for the rocks, the barrels, the legless stool and the baby boxes. 'There ain't nothing here.'

'Me funeral dress,' Granny said softly, caressing the phrase. 'Me lovely frieze with six buttons on.'

'It's warm,' she said to Paddy's silence, 'real heavy.' She went to the bedroom and brought it out. 'Just feel. That frieze'll last forever and make a shift afterwards.'

'Why do you want to sell it now?' he asked suspiciously. 'You was after being buried in it.'

'When I'm dead I have a black silk dress the English give me, it don't matter it's cold. It's not much I'll be feeling anyway.'

Paddy examined the frieze. 'True for you, it's warm. But who's to be buying it?'

'Sure you can sell it to *someone*.'

He shook his head. 'Not now I can't. It's better you're wearing it yourself under that quilt.'

'Alive!' Granny said, shocked.

There was a rap on the door and Tyrone Schwartz came in without a greeting. Abruptly, he said, 'The mill's closed. For good.'

They stared at him in dismay.

'Captain Nevin sent me off the canal to fetch some axes from Mr McLamb. And Mr McLamb says he's closing the mill tomorrow.'

'Why?' Paddy asked. 'There's plenty rain.'

'It's not that. He says now the town's gone and the farmers gone he's going too. Back to Belfast.'

'My God,' Moira said, 'then how's men to work if the canal stops?'

Tyrone shook his shaggy black head. 'It's a terrible thing.'

Paddy was thoughtful. 'What oats is sold me there's no way to grind now, being McLamb's was the only mill this side of Longford.'

Granny's dress was forgotten as they discussed the disaster.

Their only hope now was that the weather would hold, for the hail had stopped in the night and the day was sunny and cold. But if gales came, and snow, the canal work would halt.

Moira took Cathleen into the bedroom and was feeding her when Granny came in. She said, 'Let me take the baby. You go out and dig up me poteen.'

'But you'll not be wasting in on visitors,' Moira said. 'It's in case of the fever.'

'You do what I say, I know what I'm about.'

Moira brought the jug and Granny poured for the men. Tyrone thanked her and returned to work. Presently Paddy rose to go but Granny refilled his jar and he sat down again.

'Tell us,' Granny said guilefully, 'why a fine figure of a man like yourself never married? I bet there was dozens of women wanted you — eh, Sally?'

Sally looked startled. 'Oh? Oh, sure, dozens.'

Paddy's eyes were round with surprise beneath the heavy frown of brows. 'There's no woman ever wanted me that I remember.'

'Oh, sure there was,' Granny said, shaking a playful finger. 'You're not after telling it all.'

He pulled at his red-stubbled chin. 'There *was* Jenny O'Regan.'

There was an uncomfortable silence as Granny and Moira exchanged glances. Jenny had acquired odd fancies and been retired to the Madhouse in Ballydonny.

'Why didn't you marry her, then?' Sally asked innocently.

'She was not right in the head,' Paddy said. 'She thought she was a blackberry and they took her away and shut her in.'

Granny spoke silkily, 'Me daughter was in America then, she couldn't be knowing. Nor how all the women was after you.' She poured him another jar. 'Tell us, is it really leaving you'll be for America?'

He hesitated. 'I don't know. The ship fare is twenty pounds. All I have now is a shop full of junk.'

'Oh, you don't want to be leaving anyway,' Sally said. 'Them ships don't give you nothing much to eat and twelve weeks is like twelve years, that ocean's big as a sea almost.'

141

'We couldn't do without you here,' Granny said. 'It's great merchants like you hold the town together.'

'What town?' he asked bleakly. 'There's nothing on the High Street now but me shop, and Murphy's.'

'I know, but —' Moira paused as Sean and Colum came in, pink-cheeked from the cold.

'Look!' Granny said with satisfaction, 'it's getting dark out.'

Colum shut the door. 'We been looking for praties.'

The old search, now only a game for children . . .

'I don't like the dark,' Sean said, sitting beside his brother.

The dark is terrible, Moira thought, without firelight or candles, with only a little oil to burn if one must use the lantern. To sit in the dark, hearing one another's voices, not seeing, only hearing as blind people.

'Now,' Granny said, 'you'll be wanting to make me a offer for the dress.'

'I can't,' Paddy said. 'I told you.'

'Sure you've got a few stone of oats tucked away.'

'But I have no *use* for that dress.'

'Ah, now, you're that smart you can sell anything. There's gentry left, maybe they're a little hungry but they must keep warm.'

'You know what they'd give for that dress? Teacups,' he said bitterly. 'Table linen. I have no *use* for such.'

'So it's to hunger you'd leave us,' Granny said. 'Very well, Paddy Nolan, it's me death will be on your conscience — and after all me hospitality.'

Paddy wriggled uncomfortably, picked up his jar of poteen and put it down again.

'Ah, well,' Granny sighed, 'me time is only coming sooner than I'd thought.'

'What's she mean?' Sean asked.

Moira hushed him. 'Granny was always good to you, Paddy. She is good to all of us, a saint on earth she is. It would be a terrible thing she should be cut down in the prime —'

'Eighty-three's no prime,' Paddy said, 'but I'll give half a stone for it.'

'It's a joke you're making, of course,' Granny said.

142

He reddened. 'Ten pounds, then.'

'There's no fun in the joke.'

'Oh, God, Mrs Cullen, what do you *want?*'

'Three stone,' said Granny.

'Ten pounds only and that's me last word. But —' Paddy lowered his voice, 'I know where there's turf hid. The O'Dowds had it in that cave near their house and they'll never be coming back, so you take it.'

'Much?' Granny asked.

'It will last through March I'm thinking.'

'Dry?' Sally asked.

'As me bones.'

'Done,' Granny said, 'and twelve pounds of oats.'

Paddy groaned, then nodded. Granny treasured the dress in her hand, then gave it to him.

'And now,' she said, 'would you be liking to buy a grand black straw bonnet with roses on?'

'Jesus God,' Paddy shouted, and fled out the door into the betraying darkness.

The few families left in Ballyfearna became closer, visiting more often, and when it was known that the McFlahertys had fuel they gathered there to break the eerie, lonely black of the nights. Moira did not burn more than enough to see by, the fire gave warmth only to their hearts. One evening, after the guests had left, Sean accused her of being a niggard.

It was an insult as well as unfair and they took the argument up into the loft where they could talk in private.

'Is it a child you are, Da, not to be thinking of the future?'

'Is it me own daughter grudges fire to friends?'

'And you called me wilful and heedless!'

'Not only fire you grudge but food for ourselves. We have Granny's oats —'

'For how long? Suppose the storms come and you out of work?'

'They're not come yet. The boys are thin as sticks, we all are, and the cramps on us.'

'Better cramps than death.'

143

'You can bear them, it's young you are. But me and Sally and Granny are not young —'

'But you're not thinking of the fu—'

'Quiet!' he shouted. 'It's me is head of this house and I say you must feed us enough, aye, twice what we're getting.'

'But Da, it's not safe!'

'You have no faith in God, that's the trouble, you don't have no trust.'

She winced. Perhaps that was true . . .

'Next time folk come here we'll have a good fire and if there aren't too many we'll share the gruel. Hear?'

She heard and she must obey. There was no choice.

Hopelessly she asked, 'Do you never think of the rent, and not a penny saved?'

'I think of the spring and the turnips . . . and the Indian corn should be here any day and it free.'

She tried to take heart but she felt that he was wrong; not wrong as people were in health but wrong in sickness, troubled and twisted by hunger as little Sean was. Of course, she reasoned, her father's hunger was greater than anyone's in the family for he worked all day in the cold with only his oat cake to eat at noon and the pond plant broth when he returned at night. He said he felt no hunger, but were not cramps hunger in mask?

The following night, dreading guests, she lit the lantern and turned it low so as not to attract them by roof-smoke. Yet they came — Father Leary and, to her surprise, Eileen Finnigan, who had never deigned to visit here before. Mary the Midwife came and Liam and his parents. If only, she thought, she and Liam could be alone in the darkness, for they needed no warmth but each other.

Sean said, 'Light the fire, Moira.'

She did so, trying to hide her reluctance, and faces sprang alive. Faces familiar yet strange, as one sees flesh stripped from bones. Mary's hair was still its wavy grey-gold, her eyes were large and dark but the face, once moon-shaped, had wrinkled with hunger and her speech was as slow as her step. Eileen, always slender, always erect, stooped a little and her mouth was

144

thin as a string. And Moira's heart went out to Father Leary, white and delicate, frail as a fern.

He said, 'I've come to tell you about the Indian corn. It's at the workhouse. But — it came unground.'

Sally said, 'Well, we have the mill —' And stopped, remembering.

'Unground? How is it, then?' Liam asked. 'Hard-like?'

'Hard like stones,' the priest said.

'So we boil it a long time, like we should have done the rice?' Moira asked.

He turned to Eileen. 'How long did you boil it, Miss Finnigan?'

'Four hours,' she said. 'It's still like rocks. I put it aside to boil again tomorrow.'

'Why did it come like that?' Liam's mother asked, her voice querulous. 'Do they eat it like that in America?'

'No,' Sally said, 'it's like meal there. I never ate it but I saw it.'

'Then why is it not meal here?'

Father Leary said, 'Likely it costs a lot to grind it in America.'

'But they have money,' Sally reminded him, 'and they were sending it free as a gift.'

'That's why it's free and a gift,' Eileen said. 'They have too much corn they don't want but not the wish to spend a bit to grind it. Gifts!' She laughed. 'Have none of you learned about gifts this year? What did we get? Rice to kill a child, turnip seed for our hunger, clothes for the climate of hell!' She glanced at the priest. 'I'm sorry, Father. But it's true. Gifts are what people don't want.'

'Not always,' he said mildly. (What, Moira wondered, had happened to his old, righteous anger?) 'We'll be inquiring about this corn and what to do with it, not throwing it away unknowing.'

'But surely not eating it until we know?' Mary asked.

'Not unless it's soft. Miss Finnegan is after finding out tomorrow.'

'I'll maybe be cooking it all day,' Eileen said, 'and a shameful waste of sod if I must.'

Liam said, 'If it cannot get soft by boiling there's the grain mill at Longford.'

145

'It costs,' said the priest, 'not just the milling, but carting it there and back.'

Liam's father said, 'What about that nourishing powder the English were after sending us?'

'It never came,' Father Leary said.

'Just talk, then?'

'It would be.'

How weary the priest's voice, Moira thought, that used to be so full of fire; and the good looks gone. There was still the perfect profile but his face had sunken like the death mask of the monk in the churchyard. When he raised his arm and the sleeve of his robe fell back she could see a wrist twig-thin.

Moira broke a broody silence. 'How is it at the convent, Father? How is the Sisters?'

'Two is dead of the fever, one of dysentery.' He mentioned names unknown to her. 'It's caring for the paupers did it.'

'And they so near the workhouse.'

'Aye, it's a stream of sickness goes by each day.'

'It's lived in sickness I have all me life,' Liam's mother said, 'I'm surprised at nothing I hear. First, it was me mother dropped me, and me shoulder torn like thread. Then I got this pain —'

'Hush,' said her husband. But she would not hush, climbing to a climax with the loss of her children. 'It's only Liam I have now . . .'

'Moira,' Liam said softly. 'Let's go out for a while.'

She leaned toward him to whisper that it was too cold. 'And I should not leave with the priest here.'

'I said *hush!*' Lazy Lenihan glared at his wife. 'Pardoning your presence, Father, it's a crack on the jaw she'd get, all the time jawing as she does.'

'That's a kind of disease,' Father Leary said, smiling a little. 'Lots of ladies have it.'

How odd, Moira thought. He would never have said such a thing a year ago. He would have ignored the little altercation. And then she thought, but a year ago tempers were calmer, stirred only by poteen.

Liam said, 'Would Your Reverence be minding if me and Moira took a little walk?'

146

'No, and why should I?'

She wrapped herself in the quilt, hooded her hair with the shawl. Outside, something soft and wet touched her cheek.

'Mother of God!' she said. 'Snow!'

'It won't last.' Liam drew her toward the ruins of Granny's house. 'See, it's like white raindrops.'

He took her into his arms; her mouth trembled under his, she could not lose her fear in his kiss.

'How do you know it won't last?'

'Because it's wet and thin.'

She tried to make a little joke. 'Everything we have is thin — our bodies, our clothes, our gruel, even the snow.'

His kiss drove deep, obliterating thought. Warmth poured back into her, and hope.

'Come to me house,' he said. 'We can be alone there.'

'I couldn't. They'd miss us for so long, they're waiting, the priest and all . . .'

'Let them wait.'

But she would feel rushed, uneasy, embarrassed by her absence. 'I'll come to you soon, but not now.'

'When, then?'

'When I can get away. I'll stop by your shed or your house.'

'Why must you stay home, with Granny to mind the children?'

'Well then — maybe tomorrow or next day if I can.'

'In times past you never said "maybe" and "if." You'd come with me whenever I asked.'

'I am coming, only what excuse could I find in bad weather?' She reached up on tiptoe, drew his head down and kissed the wet waves of his hair. 'I'll come as soon as the snow stops.'

'It will stop tonight,' he said.

But it didn't. By morning it was falling heavily, a marvel to the children, a panic to Sean for fear that work would stop on the canal. But when he did not return Moira took confidence. And after the noon gruel, on the excuse of looking for food (were not animal tracks clear in snow?) she left Granny and Sally and took the path toward Liam's house.

The snow obscured familiar fences and trees. Her feet in the

147

thin slippers were freezing but there was exhilaration in the cold and she could forget the hollow ache in her stomach in the battle to get over snow drifts without falling. But when she reached the house Liam's parents told her he was not there. Likely he was out hunting for food.

Or waiting for her in the barn? She went to it, opened the door and peered into darkness. Then she heard a muffled sound and she stood uncertainly.

'Who is it?' Liam's voice from the shadows.

'Moira,' she said, and started forward but he called 'Wait!' and came out, shaking straw from his jacket. 'My God, I didn't think you'd come on such a day.'

She started to shut the door but he said, 'No, we'll go to the house. It's warmer there.'

'But Liam, it's not so cold. And we can be alone here.'

She started to pass him but he blocked her way. 'Go on to me house, alanna, and I'll finish me work and be there in a minute.'

What work, in this empty darkness? Far in the back of the shed she heard a stir, the merest whisper of straw. Surely he'd not be hiding a pig or chickens . . . ?

'Liam,' she said, 'tell me true, I'd never inform. Is it a animal you have?'

'Now why would you be thinking that?' He pushed her gently toward the door. 'Go, now.'

'I'd be glad for you, as God's me witness.'

Someone sneezed.

'Holy Mother!' she said, and evaded his grasp and ran back into the dimness. Faint light came through and she saw Bridget Reilly lying on a pile of straw and the pale gleam of shoulders before the shawl hid them.

'Well.' Bridget's voice was a squeak. 'Nobody asked you here.'

Moira turned abruptly and walked back to Liam.

'Let me past,' she said, but again he blocked her way. 'Let me go!'

'Now, what on earth could be ailing you?' He smiled in the face of her fury. 'It's Bridget was out hunting for food and turned her ankle in the snow, and me trying to bind it —'

148

'May God damn you for a black liar.' She spoke with deadly quiet as befit the curse. 'Let me by.'

In the snow-light she could see his eyes, direct, honest as ever. 'How could you be so, Moira?'

'How could *you*?'

'It's limping she is,' he said loudly. 'See for yourself.' He called to Bridget. 'If you can stand come here and let Moira see the evil of her thought.'

'Ah, no,' Bridget said. 'I can't stand, I can't.'

'You see?' Liam said, 'I've not bound the ankle tight yet.'

'Anyway,' Moira said, 'you got her bodice off. *That'll* help her ankle.'

'Sure it will, it's the bodice we're using to bind it. We was just after tearing it when you called. Were we not, Bridget?'

'Oh, my!' Bridget said, 'it do hurt awful.'

Moira said, 'Is it you're thinking me a fool?'

He shook his head. 'Not a fool, no, but terrible suspicious and that isn't nice. It does you no credit at all. Well —' he shrugged sadly, '— if you don't believe us, you don't, and it cuts me heart.'

He stood aside. 'Go if you want. But I'm thinking you'd best tell Father Leary of the sin on you.'

'Sin on *me*?'

'The sin of doubt. You have no trust. You believe lies. You curse the poor innocents.' He moved toward the rear of the barn in weary silence. 'All right, Bridget, you can tear it now, but mind in one strip.'

Moira wept her way home. She wept all that night, secretly and in silence. She remembered what her father had said of her: 'You have no faith, that's the trouble, you have no trust . . .'

Oh, God, if only Liam would find it in his heart to forgive her.

Liam came on Sunday when the snow stopped. He was generous. The incident, he said, was forgotten. Would Moira like to search for food in the woods?

'There's nothing,' she said.

'I saw tracks up the hill.'

They set out over the calm, crisp snow and came to hare-marks, following them far up on to the road to nowhere Moira had taken in December, but they saw no animals. The cabin of the lone woman stood in its patch of pines.

Moira had told him about the woman. 'I'm sure she'd be welcoming company,' and she tapped on the door.

There was no sound within. The trees moved in the wind, and snow powdered from their branches.

'Perhaps she's out searching too,' Liam said.

But no footprints led from the house.

'She'll not mind if we take shelter,' Moira said, and opened the door.

The woman lay on her back near the hearthstone. Moira screamed at the sight of the shredded face and hands and ran outside and was violently sick in the snow. Liam lingered a few moments, then came out.

'There, alanna,' he said, 'she was probably dead of the hunger before the rats came. Likely she never knew . . .'

Moira wept, chiding herself for having ignored this lonely, nameless woman whom she might have helped, might even have saved. 'I'd promised to come back . . . I might have helped her down to town, or found her food.'

'Hush, it's no blame on you.' He took her arm. 'Come.'

'We can't be leaving her like that.'

'We must.'

They hunted for two straight sticks and made a little cross outside the door and knelt in the snow and begged God to grant peace to a woman who had died without priest or prayers. Then Liam came out and took off his cap as she murmured the Pater Noster.

To the relief of the men who worked on the canal the snow melted quickly in bright sun and February brought gentle weather, almost May-like. Hazel catkins climbed the hedgerows, coltsfoot and celandines appeared on the river banks. The coltsfoot on their woolly white stems shone like gold along the green of the meadows. In this strange, false spring the people were stirred to hope. The turnips would liven any day now, aye, any moment.

150

And the birds were back.

'It's a omen,' Sally said one noon as they heard the harsh quark of a bluejay. 'There's life where birds are, so the creatures will be coming back.'

She was so thin that Moira could see the very bones of her throat as she talked. But one came to accept how people looked — imitations of themselves or ghosts of themselves, and she herself a stranger to her own mirror with her eyes too big for her face and the shape of her skull plain when she lifted her hair.

'It's me cats kept the birds off,' Granny said. She had finished her gruel and was staring at the empty pot.

'But we should be glad they're back.' Moira wiped Cathleen's mouth and watched her creep over the floor on a voyage of discovery. 'They are good to eat.'

'I'd die first,' Granny said.

'No, you wouldn't. Mary says they're good, baked in the ashes with salt on. Only they're so small it takes one for each person.'

'How do you kill birds?' Little Sean asked.

'With a gun if you have one, or a slingshot like Liam has.'

'I'd die if I was to have to *touch* a bird, much less be eating one.' Granny's finger explored the empty pot, found a bit of oat crust which she ate. 'I was that way all me life.'

'But you ate a whole duck at that wedding.'

'Ducks are *nice* birds, they don't fly, they are more like fish.'

'I'm going to fish today,' Moira said. 'Maybe they have come back too.'

'Can I go?' Sean asked.

'And me?' Colum asked.

'No, it's quiet you want when you fish and it's too serious for boys playing.'

'We'll be quiet,' Colum said, but she was taking no chances, and bade them stay at home.

Sean moved about restlessly. 'What'll we do?'

What you often do, she thought — sleep. It was like the boys were old men, dozing through the hours. But she wanted to encourage them. 'You can gather sticks.'

Sally rose from the floor and gathered up the meal bowls.

Granny yawned and went to lie down. Moira sent Sean and Colum out into the foggy field. Then she took the old, home-made fishing gear and walked to the river.

Nothing pulled at her line, though she was patient. Nothing rippled the calm surface, she could see no minnows, no flies. Why did the flowers blossom on the bank, yet no life in the water?

Hours passed. At sunset Tyrone came along. She greeted him and he sat down on a rock nearby and baited his hook with a worm.

She said softly, 'But nothing seems any use.'

'I know,' he said. 'I've not much hope. But it's company I'm wanting.'

His knees were bare through the tatter of his trousers, his black hair shaggy on his neck. Gone was the sunny, copper-toned skin; he was dun-coloured. She remembered him as she had first seen him, gaudy in his cart, his ear-rings a-sparkle, and she mourned the loss of his gaiety for his eyes were sunken and sombre.

'I'm poor company,' she said, 'but it's glad I am you're here.'

He cast the line, 'It's poor company we all are.'

They spoke in whispers. 'I thought it was to Dublin you were going,' she said.

He shook his head.

'You've still your horse?'

'No.'

She understood. 'Are you still living at the hotel?'

'No,' he said, 'I couldn't be taking off the Murphys and giving nothing.' He hesitated. 'It's at Bridget's I've been these two weeks.'

A year ago she would have been shocked. Now she nodded. The simple need for shelter was beyond moral judgment.

He said, 'I gave her my horse, and the cart for firewood.'

'Does Father Leary —' she tried to form the question tactfully, 'know how it is?'

'Aye, I'd think so, for it's everything he knows about us all. But he's not said one chiding word. And he greeted us at Mass.'

'Why don't you marry?'

152

'I've asked her that.' He turned from the water to face Moira. 'She says she has no reason to say no. Only she says no.'

So it *was* Liam she loved . . .

'She says to wait and maybe someday she will. She says she's grateful. *Grateful!* As if it's that I'm wanting. She says to wait for better times.' His fierce black brows grew together. 'It's times like these folk should marry for the warmth of one another, for it's only love is left us. And if we wait too long, who knows what will happen?'

She spoke of Sally and Patrick. 'People like them wait 'cause they're old. They have old ideas like they should live in a nice house and have what they always had — pigs and praties. I don't think it's love they feel, Tyrone — not like we do.'

'Has Liam not spoken of marriage yet?'

'No.'

'It's wasting yourself you are.'

She smiled wryly. 'Who else is to be asking me? Paddy? Jesus? Or is it old Brian to come a-courting from the workhouse?'

He said, without flirt, 'You are beautiful, I never seen a woman like you. It's like your hair was oak leaves in fall with the sun shining through. Is it blind Liam is?'

'He talks of me hair and all, but he's used to me like one gets after years of seeing. Only I'm not used to his looks. I watch him like' — she pointed — 'like that sky. I seen it all me life but it's always new.'

They were silent. The sky turned to deep gold, the water slowly darkened.

'If you didn't love Bridget,' Moira said finally, 'would you be staying on here?'

He thought for a while. 'Aye, I would. Since I was ten I had no home but the road and when I seen this town I knew somehow I'd stay.'

'Me father says he'd never leave the land.'

'Would you, Moira?'

'No.'

'Suppose somebody give you a ticket to America?'

'I'd not go.'

153

'Because of Liam?'

'It's not just Liam. Like you said, it's home.' She strove to explain, perhaps as much to herself as to him. 'I'm thinking it is no different from other places hereabouts. You see the same hills in Ballydonny, the same stars and gardens. Only here me mother and her mother and her mother before her planted them gardens and looked at them stars and walked them hills and was buried in the churchyard where I'll want to be part of them. Did you know, there's a little flower came up on John the Basket's grave where his father's father lies?' She groped for clarity of thought. 'You know?'

'I know. But Moira, it's like there's a curse on the land. Three famines since '22, and terrible ones too before that. It's not safe to live here any more. It's mad we are to want to stay.'

'Then we're mad together.' She drew in her line and he helped her to her feet. 'It's good to talk to you, Tyrone.'

He kissed her on the cheek. 'It's friends we are?'

'Truly.'

She looked into the dying sunset, the bright too-early flowers, the lifeless river. 'It's strange, there's times a fright comes on me, not just for the hunger or fear of the fever but something else.'

'I think it's part of the hunger,' he said.

'Maybe.'

'If you should ever need me, Moira, you know I'll come to you.'

It was good to know. It was good to think of him as she walked homeward through the twilight. She felt tired, hollow, yet not hungry. As she approached her hut she had a curious sense of calm as though nothing could disturb her.

Until she heard the screaming.

In the kitchen Sean was holding Granny, but her scream pierced the wall of his hand and her eyes were wide and wild. The baby was crying, Sally and the boys stood motionless as though tranced. Moira said, 'My God, what happened?'

'We don't know,' Sally said, 'she's not able to tell us. She was outside and she came in screaming.'

Moira scooped up Cathleen and tried to soothe her.

'It's out of her wits she's gone,' Sean said, and winced as Granny wrenched his hand. 'Come,' he said, releasing her, 'tell us what happened.'

The old mouth chittered but no words came, only an animal shrill. She was shivering and Sally brought a blanket, draped it about her and made her sit on the hearth stone.

'Queer in her head, she is,' Sean repeated, 'she been like this ten minutes.'

Moira put aside the baby and knelt by Granny. 'What is it, darling one? Was it you seen something?'

Granny wailed and shivered.

'Maybe —' Moira took a deep, frightened breath '— The Gorta?'

Granny tucked her head into the quilt.

'A wolf?' Sean asked. 'I never saw a wolf yet, but then the weather's queer.'

Little Sean said, 'What's a wolf look like?'

They ignored him, petting Granny. Moira ran for the buried poteen, forced a few drops through the burbling lips and saw colour return to the face.

Moira clasped a frigid hand and rubbed it. 'It's only hoping to help you we are, and there's nothing to be feared of. Only you must tell us to get the dark off your mind.'

'Maybe it was soldiers,' Colum said. 'Maybe she saw soldiers.'

Moira asked Sean, 'What was the start of it? What was she doing outside?'

'She and little Sean was after meeting you on your way home to see if you had any fish —'

Moira whirled on her brother. 'You were with her, then? What did *you* see?'

'Nothing,' he said. 'I didn't see no Gorta nor anything.'

'Then why did she scream?'

He shrugged.

'What did she *do?*'

'She just screamed and begun to run and I run after her and we came in.'

'Where were you when she begun to scream?' Moira asked. 'Out. Outside.'

'But *where? At Granny's house? The well? Or beyond?'

155

'I don't know. She scared me so I ran too.' He covered his face with his hands. 'She scared me!'

'Ah, poor boyeen!' She put her arms around him. 'Come, don't cry.' She pried his hands from his eyes and found them tearless.

'Maybe it was just a bird,' Sally said. 'She was always terrible afraid of birds. Now, did a bird light on her, Sean?'

'No,' he said. 'There's no birds.'

'There are,' Colum said. 'I saw them.'

'There were no birds,' Sean said, lunging out to cuff his brother.

Moira caught a swift blur of red and bent to grasp the boy's hand. 'What's this? Blood?'

'You're hurting me!' he shouted. 'Let me go!'

His father came quickly to look at the captured palm. 'It is blood.' He licked his finger, touched and repeated, 'it is blood. Fetch a rag, Moira.'

She brought one, wet from the pail, and scrubbed the little hand. 'It's not his,' she said grimly. 'He's not so much as scratched.'

Granny tried to fight them off but they removed her shawl, lowered her ragged bodice, lifted her skirt to look at her legs. There was no mark on her.

Moira waited for her father to question Sean, for it was his place to do so, but Sean had sat down tiredly on his rock. 'Anyway, they're not hurt,' he said, 'God be praised.'

Granny, back in her cuddle of quilt, was sobbing quietly.

Moira took her brother into the bedroom. She begged him to tell the truth — if he had pranked Granny, then he must admit it, apologise. She would not beat him, she promised. No one would.

'I didn't do a thing —'

'But that blood was on your hand. What blood? Something you picked up dead?'

'It was you hurt me.'

'It was not! And if you don't tell me now, Granny will tell us later. She'll have a long sleep and she'll be able to tell us later.'

He said nothing, staring at her with narrowed eyes.

'If you tell me now you'll not be whipped. Was it a bird you

156

found, Sean — maybe dead — and squashed it in your hand and plagued her with it? And made her run in the terror of it?'

'No. I did nothing.'

'All right,' she said. 'You've had your last chance. For when she eases Granny will tell us.'

But Granny never spoke again.

She would eat, as always; go to the bushes at need, cover herself to sleep, but she did nothing else. Mourning the death of her mind, Moira tried to cheer her to speech; Sean and Sally coaxed her confidence but she would sit in silence staring at nothing, and the boys avoided her. Moira suspected that Sean did so in guilt, Colum in uneasiness, in fear of this quiet creature who had once been warm arms, a warm lap to sleep on and was now so changed.

Sean insisted that little Sean could not be punished — for who knew what had happened? Granny was nearly eighty-three and minds failed in the back end of the years. It was not fair to suspect Sean. Boys were always being bloodied, dirtied. He could have tried to climb a tree that day — bark in the palm might bloody but not scratch.

'Oh, Da,' Moira said, 'if only you would —'

Be head of this house, not talk of being. Or allow me to be, if you won't. But this way we drift, and meself in a sea of suspicion of Sean, and Sally nervous as a hurt cat.

Day after day Moira tried to lure Granny to words. She gave her extra gruel when no one else was about; she used the last of the poteen in the hope of sparking speech. Granny ate and drank greedily but she said nothing, and the only sounds she made were animal.

Moira thought, For years someone is close as your own skin and you think you know them; there can surely be no surprise and no mystery. Yet they can change as Granny had, as little Sean had, strange as the paths of mountains you have never climbed. And because you love them you set out on the new path in hopes of finding them again but though they may look back or call your name you know they have taken another bend of the road and you are left behind.

157

If the first spring was false, the second seemed true. It came in late March, riding the back of the wind, on the wings of larks and starlings. It came with good tidings — a soup kitchen had opened at the workhouse. It was rumoured that women were needed to cook and serve the soup, which would be distributed free.

On a Monday Moira and Sally set out for Ballydonny before dawn. They had been uneasy about leaving Granny and the children but little Sean had begged to take responsibility for them. Besides, his father would be home for the noon meal and if he were needed again before dark, Sean knew the way to the canal.

Moira and Sally walked in the half dark until the sun rose. The road was good for three miles, pressed by the wheels of carts, the hooves of horses and donkeys, the recent footsteps of refugees. But the fourth mile was rocky and cruel to the feet.

Sally sank down on the grass. 'It's shamed I am but I can't go on.' Tears rolled down her cheeks. 'I'm too old to walk ten miles and work all day and walk the way home. Not even for Patrick can I do it.'

Softly she added, 'It isn't hungry I am for the soup. I'd love the work-pay but most of all I was after hoping to see Himself or have word of him.'

Moira said, 'Go home, then.'

'Alanna, you're angry at me!'

'No.' Moira was not angry. She could scarcely summon anger from a cramped and hollow stomach. Strange how it was with the hunger — one hour you were ravenous, the next surfeited as though fed, or else close to nausea. 'Give me your pail, then.'

Sally gave it, one they had borrowed from Liam for the soup.

'Promise me you'll bring me news of Patrick,' Sally said.

'I will try. But mind, I can't be hunting for him. If they'll give me work I'll not be out of the place till sunset.'

'God give you strength.'

They clasped hands and went their separate ways.

Six miles, seven . . . The hedgerows were a-bloom and a-chirp with the shy life of the woods. In the gnarl of blackthorn, dog-rose and bramble Moira could hear the stir of voles and shrews.

A weasel ran out, a partridge whirred up from a tussock of heather. The sky, ragged with wind-driven clouds, was lightening.

She set down the lantern near an elder, hiding it under the hedge to pick up on her way home.

Eight miles, nine? She sat by a stream, soaked and cooled her tired feet, then lifted the pail and walked on. God grant it would be heavy with soup for her family when she carried it home.

She had no idea of what to expect when she reached the Workhouse nor any recollection of what it looked like, though Sean said she had seen it as a child on the way to Ballydonny Fair. She knew it was off the main road to town; she must watch for a clump of oak trees to find her way.

Ten miles — oh, God, surely it was ten miles by now? Yet she plodded on and on, the sun in her eyes. Finally she saw the oak trees and a fine level road to the right and a sign which she could puzzle out because she expected it:

WORKHOUSE . . . and a plump, pointing arrow painted in black.

She took the road to a clearing and climbed a slope. The workhouse sprawled, stark and grey, between ancient oaks. It was L-shaped, weathered with years but bare of ivy. Its three storeys were pitted with windows small as goblin eyes, and smoke puffed from its chimney. Beside it was a lean-to, open to the wind which she guessed to be the fever shed. An unpainted wooden house must be the new soup kitchen; its heavy door was barred with iron. The buildings, raw and ugly in the harsh sun, seemed surrounded by a vast lawn of black leaves.

But as she came closer she saw that the lawn moved. She was looking at a sea of dark rags, of slowly stirring people. Hundreds of people, moving like weeds in the wind, rising and sinking back, rising and tottering forward to push at the great barred door of the kitchen, hammering with their weak fists, and their weak voices echoing along the long, sad corridors of the wind.

Why, she thought, the sun is high yet they are just awakening.

But she realised why. Sleep was escape from torment, food for dreams. Where there was no food, God placed sleep.

She moved through the slowly-wakening crowd, stepping over

159

children, fearful of trampling them. People on their feet passed
her silently. No one spoke. She thought, if they did not move
from my way I'd think they walked in sleep.

She did not know where to apply for work but she decided on
the main building, since what appeared to be the kitchen was
barred to dozens of supplicators. So she walked to the door of
the Workhouse and banged the rusty iron knocker.

No one came. She waited.

Then she turned to look at the crowd and was caught in horror. A woman was feeding a child at her breast but the child
was a young boy with swollen legs and belly. A man covered his
wife with his body for she wore only a shift. An old man lay
face up, sobbing, his feet greened by rot. A girl her own age
wound her long black hair over a naked infant to keep it warm.

The door opened suddenly and an aproned woman said, 'No
soup, not till noon,' and started to shut the door.

'Wait!' Moira said, 'I've come to work. To work,' she repeated,
fearful that the door would close. 'See, I'm strong, healthy —'

Sharp black eyes appraised her. The woman was about forty,
once plump, now a mass of oddly hanging fat, with hunched
shoulders shawled in faded blue.

'I'm from Ballyfearna,' Moira said, 'so you *see* I'm strong, ten
miles I've walked to come here.'

The woman said, 'We have enough help.' But her voice
wavered.

'Please,' Moira said, 'I'll do anything, I'll work me hands off.'

'We have ten women.' But the door remained open.

'And some will be sick,' Moira said quickly, 'what with the
fever and all. But there is no fever in me town.'

'Ballyfearna? I hear there is no town there any more.'

'There's still a few of us yet, and all healthy.'

'Well,' said the woman, and opened the door wide. 'Come in.
But I'll have to ask the Master.'

Moira followed the woman into a hallway, gasped at a sudden,
sickening stench. It came from a large room across the corridor.

'Wait here,' the woman said, and left her.

Moira looked across into the room. Crowds of men, women
and children lay naked or half-covered on piles of straw. A

160

woman in a blue apron, evidently a nurse, moved among them offering jars of drinking water. A man, perhaps a doctor, bent to listen to faintly spoken words. The room was unnaturally silent, like a holy picture in church — ashen bodies on yellow straw and the glare of sun streaming through goblin windows.

She felt that she was going to be sick; the stench was nearly unbearable. Then a voice spoke behind her.

'Make way and let me by.'

She moved quickly aside. An old man pushed past carrying a load of calico, dumped it on the floor and left. Soon he returned with a younger man and another load of calico. The old man whistled into the room and the doctor looked up and came to the door.

'There's three adults,' he said, 'and two children.'

'We have more than enough,' said the young man.

Calico, Moira thought, even in mild weather scarcely warm enough for the chill of starvation. At least, she thought, it will cover the poor naked women.

But the men did not take the calico in; they followed the doctor and were lost to her view.

The woman reappeared. 'The Master will see you.' She motioned Moira to the left corridor. 'You'll see a door open. Mind you call him "sir" and make your curtsy.'

'Thank you.' Shyly, she went as directed, stood hesitantly at the designated door. If only she looked decent! But despite its many patches her petticoat was tattered and under her shawl her bodice was rags.

'Come in.' A middle-aged man spoke from a chair by his desk. 'I am James Grant.'

'Sir,' she said, and curtsied and came timidly forward.

He did not look frightening, in fact he was smiling, but he was Master of the Workhouse, he was English, he wore a fine black suit and a white stock that came high to his whiskers. He was very pale, almost waxen. His fingernails were pink and polished.

'What is your name?' he asked.

She told him. He asked her age, her birthplace. How many were in her family?

'Seven,' she said, counting Granny and Sally.

'Does anyone in your family work?'

'Me father, sir.'

He made notes, dipping his pen into a pewter ink well.

'Have you had typhus among you?'

'No, sir.'

'Dysentery?'

She lied. 'No, sir.'

'Relapsing fever?'

She did not know what he meant but she shook her head.

'A charmed life, eh?'

She smiled because he did.

He stroked his curly black beard. 'Well. So you want to work here, eh?'

She nodded. 'Please, sir.'

'And walk — how many miles a day?'

'Twenty, but oh, sir, I'm strong.'

'We'll see about that,' he said. 'We'll test you for a week and if Mrs Goggan says you'll do, then you'll stay. The pay is three shillings a week and all the food you can eat.'

Heaven!

'But you'll not be taking food home. Since your father is employed you must pay for anything removed from these premises. Or else send the others of your family here to get their own tickets for a pint of soup a day.'

But neither Granny nor Sally nor the boys could walk so far.

'It costs a penny a quart,' he said, and frowned at her dismay. 'You'd thought it free? The gossips have been blabbing comfort, eh, before they know the facts? Well, you know the facts now. And don't steal. If you're caught stealing you'll be penalised.'

Penalised — what did it mean? Jailed, whipped? 'I'd *never* steal, sir.'

'Good. Now come to me Saturday for your pay.'

'Thank you, sir,' she said, but he had already bent over papers on his desk and her parting curtsy was not noticed.

Mrs Goggan met her outside the door. 'You're taken? I thought so, he's got an eye for a pretty woman though I will say he's not one to step below himself. He's a Friend.'

'A friend? Of your—'

'Get along with you for a fool! He's a Friend of God, a Quaker, one of them religions they has in England and America and all. Only he's not a priest or a minister, he's just plain holy on his own. I will say he's better than the Workmaster we had (he died of the drink in January) and he's part of the Relief Commission so we get our food. What's your name, girl?'

'Moira McFlaherty.'

They walked toward the main hallway. 'Well, me name's Lily Goggan and you're to call me "Ma'am" and I take no impudence. You can work the rest o' the day and be here tomorrow at seven.' She looked at Moira's shawl. 'Is that a bodice you have on?'

'Aye, but it's coming to pieces, Ma'am.'

'I'll get you a big apron to cover you.'

They were in the hallway where Moira had first entered. And coming out of the crowded room was the young man bearing a corpse on his back.

'Holy Mary!' Moira crossed herself.

The young man heaved the body upright against the wall, then helped the old man to thrust it into a calico sack. They were quick and deft; the old man carried the corpse outside and the young one returned to the room for another.

'Five,' Mrs Goggan said, 'five gone since midnight.'

'Of fever?' Moira asked fearfully.

'That is not the fever shed, that's just one of the common rooms. Those people died of other things like dysentery. And some have come in dying of eating the Indian corn they were too hungry to wait for cooking. That corn's terrible hard on the children. Here we have it ground into meal, but it's too late for some.'

They walked on past other common rooms. At the end of a corridor Mrs Goggan opened a door that led outside, took a key from her belt cord and locked it behind them. Moira followed her, past the lean-to fever shed, a stable and a mud hut. She had not realised there were so many buildings — mainly of stone, with poorly thatched roofs.

'What are they all, Ma'am?' Moira asked.

'A schoolhouse — we have seventy children still alive. The house for nurses and doctors to sleep in when they're too tired to go home . . . and that there —' she pointed to a barred stone house, 'is where the lunatics live.'

'The madhouse!'

'The Master don't like it called that but that's what it is, all right. A lot has died of the fever, though. They give it to each other 'cause we don't dare move 'em into the shed.'

She led Moira to the back door of the soup kitchen which she unlocked.

'You'll be getting your own key,' she said, 'and remember, always bolt the door behind you. Some of the people out there is crazy from hunger.'

But they had seemed so quiet . . .

The kitchen was huge, dominated by steaming 200-gallon wooden boilers which sat on the stoves. Two girls tended the fires from piles of turf on the floor. Other women stood at long deal tables cutting, paring, slicing or kneading dough. Through whirls of steam Moira could see a low shelf glittering with dozens of knives. There were barrels of meal.

At the end of the room closest to the front door ten tables were set with chained iron spoons for the paupers, and piles of wooden bowls.

'Good,' said Mrs Goggan to a woman who was placing the bowls, 'good and early for a change. Now get me a apron for this new girl, she must hide her bodice.'

Moira hung her shawl on a peg and put on the apron.

'You hungry?' Mrs Goggan asked. 'You walked a long way. You can have a bit of bread before you start work.'

'No,' Moira said, 'thank you.' She put her hand to her mouth, willing back illness. The stench here was of meat soup, of onions and turnips and baking bread. 'I'm not hungry, Ma'am.'

'Then come here.'

Mrs Goggan led her to a wooden butcher's table which was piled with ox-heads. 'Now you take them to that pail, Moira, and wash them well. Then you pick out the eyes with a knife . . .'

She indicated the knife shelf. 'Do you see?'

I must not sicken, Moira thought. I must not faint. I must keep me mind, I will not lose it. If I did they'd take me to the Mad-house . . .

164

'. . . now, we don't waste nothing here. We keep them ox eyes for the — the dogs.'

I *must* keep this job. I must not lose it before I've even started. It's safer work than Da's for spring is treacherous with storms and if the canal should stop we've not a penny.

'What's the matter?' Mrs Goggan asked.

Moira swallowed, blinked, spoke in a steady whisper. 'Nothing, Ma'am. Which knife do I use?'

It seemed, during those weeks, that she reached home in the dark only to close her eyes before it was time to set off again in the dark. And spring was as treacherous as she had feared. She stumbled through hail, sleet, the gales of early April or steady, relentless rains. Work halted on the canal. Sean and Liam watched their turnips drown, and the death of other gardens. They sat in the parlour of Murphy's Hotel with Dennis and Tyrone and Jesus and found scant comfort in Jesus' poteen.

Sometimes the men walked with Moira to the workhouse, standing in line with their tickets to pay for the soup, but they soon realised the folly. The long walk nagged their hunger and the penny a day was ill-spent, for the soup was mostly water. The recipe varied from week to week as the Relief Commission sent supplies. Basically it was ox-head and entrails, turnips, onions and salt. With luck, a bit of Indian meal to thicken it. Folk could buy ground corn at the kitchen if they could afford three shillings a barrel. No one could but the few fortunate gentry. They boiled it with water and called the mush 'stirabout.' On Fridays the kitchen served bread and salt herring.

With her stomach full by day, accustomed to the evil-smelling soup, Moira's body strengthened but her spirit sickened at the sights she saw. She could not tell Liam nor Sally nor her father, she denied them to herself as one denies the reality of nightmare. The workhouse, built to accommodate a thousand paupers, now had twenty-two hundred. In the fever shed people suffering typhus, cholera and relapsing fever lay four to a quilt on the damp ground and the children died at the rate of five a day. In the common rooms of the workhouse, and in the stable, unde-tected typhus patients infected others before they were moved to the shed. Debility created gangrene and pain caused suicides. Old Brian O'Donnell watched his toes fall off and stabbed himself in the throat. Kitty the Basket, mad in fever, walked out into the rain to meet her phantom husband and died in the mud.

'Patrick Kane?' Moira asked from her first day there, 'Does anyone know of Patrick Kane?'

Aye, they knew of him. He was the brown-bearded man with the house on Ballydonny Hill, him with the hooky nose and gold tooth. But no one had seen him since his house was tumbled in January. He's gone like smoke and left no trace — likely taken to the road like thousands of others.

'He couldn't have,' Sally said, 'not without telling me. Moira, if he was fit to take the road he'd have taken it to here. And then, his brother Peter gone too — it do seem like they gone together to America.'

Moira could not follow this reasoning and it seemed cruel to encourage her. 'Why do you think that?'

'It's a feeling I got,' Sally said vaguely. 'It's his fortune he's gone to make in Boston, and him coming back for me.'

Oh, darling, Moira thought, don't go queer else I'll think the fever's on you. And don't try to build on bog.

'You say Annie Dumbie has heard nothing from Peter either,' Sally said triumphantly.

'Annie doesn't hear much of anything,' Moira said, 'she's that weak.'

'The fever?'

But Sally knew, she had been told time and again of Annie's illness. Relapsing fever, they called it, with agonising headaches and ringing in the ears. Annie was in a common room at the stable, begging for water, rejecting food, her skin darkly yellowed.

'It ain't typhus, Sally. If ever she can eat maybe she'll get well.'

Sally was curiously blithe. 'Of course she will! Me and her and Patrick and Peter is going to be married when they come back from America. I got me red velvet dress . . .'

Did Granny hear? Moira wondered. If she did she made no sign, staring at them mutely, set and still as a gravestone.

To Moira, Sundays were the one release, looked forward to

every hour of the week. Aware of her exhaustion, Father Leary bade her not come to Mass but sleep the whole morning. Usually she went to the abbey at dusk to make her confession and Liam accompanied her. They were together from her awakening until ten at night.

'We must talk of the future,' he said one day as they sat among the flowers above Miller's Cave.

She felt the pleasant panic of her heartbeat. She had waited so long . . .

He looked up at the limpid blue sky. 'Have you noticed how it storms all the week and clears when the canal is shut on a Sunday? I've earned only two shillings this month and me father only one, him being — sick. We've not been able to save but sixpence for the rent.'

'We've saved nothing,' Moira said. 'Every penny goes for food, even with me eating free we've not enough. But Liam, you was after speaking of the future.'

'Aye. What I mean is, nobody has one. Not here, anyways. Even if this weather holds and the canal goes on, it's too late to save anything for the rent.'

Due the tenth of June. Five weeks away.

'We can't be fooling ourselves, Moira. We'll be evicted. So we have to plan what to do. It's better, I'm thinking, to leave our houses before Mr Pond comes, for then he'll not tumble them. To hide in the woods a week or two and then, when it's safe, to sneak back. He can't be watching every house in seventy miles.'

'Maybe not. But my God, Liam, why must we go? What does he *want* the land for? It does him no good.'

'It's not his, it's Lord Mountjoy's and Father Leary says most of them landlords wants to lease the land to some other lord or else put it back to grazing and send over cattle and sheep from England. Anyway, we must get out by June.'

'To hide in the woods — where?'

'Here.' He looked at the entrance to the cave, secret, beautifully hidden by bracken and heavy creepers. 'Nobody would think to be looking for us here and they don't care about us anyway, only the land. Why, it's big enough for five families, let alone yours and mine.'

'It's ghosted.' She shuddered. 'And it's cold.'

He laughed. 'Ghosts don't walk among ten people, they like it quiet. And it'll be warm enough for summer. Mind you, there's the hearth where the priests used to cook.'

'Well, maybe . . .' She was bitterly disappointed; she had hoped something different from his talk of the future.

'Father Leary will know when it's safe to return to our homes and when to hide again if Lord Mountjoy plans to graze the land. I'm thinking it would take months to buy stock and ship it here. I'd say we're safe till autumn.'

'And you men hiding by night, working on the canal by day? Is that safe?'

'It's none of Mr Pond's puff where we work so long as we leave his land.'

He said to her silence, 'Alanna, I want to see you safe.'

She moved to him and he gathered her close, nuzzling her cheek with his lips. She thought, if only Da would plan as Liam did — plan however vaguely — she would feel safer. But Da's world was changed with Cathleen's passing; it was bounded by four miles of canal, a mush cake at noon and a pint of broth at night.

'Moira,' he said, 'I must see you safe through the summer before I go.'

'Go? Go where?'

'To America.'

'Oh, no!' She grasped his hand so tightly that he drew back. 'You can't, you can't leave me!'

When had she ever known such despair before? Ah, yes. Last year she had dreamed of God's hands tied and Himself helpless. Cities crumbled under falling mountains, seas flooded the land. The world had fallen apart — like this.

'I'd be back,' he said casually. 'And I could send you money.'

'But you have no money to go!'

'True for you. But I'd work me way like Danel did.'

'How do you know he did?'

'Well, he never came back. And I'm younger'n him and stronger. Likely a lot of men fear the autumn storms so I'd try to ship out then.'

She argued vainly. Finally she said, 'Talk to Sally, at least. She'll be telling you America isn't all roses and gold.'

'It's gold, anyway and I'll be sending it home to you.'

She closed her eyes. If only this were a dream from which she could awaken, smiling in relief that the world was sane and orderly, still in God's hands.

'. . . and I'll find it not so strange in America, there's thousands of Irish there to be helping and advising —'

And loving? Liam would find a woman, not a Bridget in rags but a lady in white ruffles and pink sash with seven pink petticoats under. She would carry a sunshade of white lace trimmed with little pink buds and she would be asking him to drive in her carriage.

'You'll soon forget me,' she said, tearless in certainty.

'Forget *you*?' He laughed and pulled her close again. 'Is it I'd be forgetting to breathe, then, or eat or say me prayers? Aren't you knowing you're hot in me heart like blood?'

'But Liam —'

He kissed her, kissed her silent. And she thought, in love born of desperation, before he goes, some night in summer, I shall belong to him and when he leaves for America I shall carry his child in me body and birth in pride. No priest shall make me do penance for mortal sin. For the sin is God's uncaring.

Chapter 6

June came in gentle mist and wild roses opened, fattening the hedgerows where honeysuckle grew. Yellow water lilies floated in the pools and on the river, and yellow iris flaunted from bogs and pathsides. But on her walks to and from the workhouse Moira saw the lovely lushness mocked by the plight of the people. Refugees crept the roads from dawn until dusk, those too weak to rise dragged by their families toward the soup kitchen. Wild dogs scavenged the empty huts and ran in packs at moonglow. Moira carried a big blackthorn stick lest she meet dogs on her way.

Liam insisted that they and their families should move to the cave before June tenth and Moira reluctantly agreed. She had only to convince her father.

'Da,' she said, 'we should move this week.'

'There's time enough.'

'There is not! Liam says —'

'Liam is not head of this house. Let Liam move, then.'

'Please, we must leave to protect our house. Then we can sneak back, and Mr Pond not knowing.'

'He knows everything, daughter.'

She fought against his calm acceptance of doom. 'What's changed you so?'

'What's changed *you?*'

'But I can't —'

I can't reach you, she thought. You're like a man sleep-walking, sleep-eating, and if I passed a hand before your eyes you'd not be blinking. Maybe it was the queerness of the hunger that shrivelled the mind.

She gave up the argument but the next night she appealed to Sally. 'You must help me — we *must* hide ourselves this week.'

'But suppose Patrick comes back from America? How would he be knowing where to find me?'

Moira looked into Sally's eyes, round and innocent and curiously bright. Bright with a gleam she had not noticed before.

'If Patrick went off to America he won't be coming back for a long time. Why, if he left in January he'd only have been there a month or more.'

Sally burst into tears. 'He will be back and it's not leaving here I am.'

'You'll not be the cause of me house being tumbled,' Moira said. 'You'll leave here when we do.'

'If we're not wanted here then it's to our own house we'll go. Eh, Granny?'

The old woman stared at them from the hearthstone. Her lips did not move nor her eyes flicker.

'Sally,' Moira said gently, 'if you go to the ruins of your house Himself will find you there and push you off — or worse. You must hide with us.'

Sally turned and went into the bedroom.

'Where'd we hide?' Little Sean asked softly.

Moira had not known he was in the room, so quiet he was in a corner. Now he crept out from under the blanket where Colum lay asleep. 'In the woods?' he asked.

'In Miller's Cave.' She stretched out her arms and he came into them and she stroked the bright curls of his hair. 'But Da won't let us.'

She spoke to his wise little face as though he were old enough to comfort and understand. 'If we don't move, Mr Pond will

171

come here and tumble the house and then we can never live here again.'

'Will there be soldiers and the burning?'

'Aye.'

He wriggled out of her arms. 'I'd like to live in the cave.' He whistled softly. 'That's the sound the river makes underneath. No, like *this*.'

'We can cook at the old priest's hearth,' she said.

'Rats is there,' he said. 'Me and Colum saw a big one there.'

She shuddered. 'But there's rats everywhere.'

'Aye, I killed one yesterday. In the loft.'

'You didn't!'

'Sure I did.'

'I told you not to kill things for fun!'

'It was dying anyway. I beat it with a stick. You want to see it?'

'No!'

'I'm hungry.'

'Then you know what to do till time to eat.'

Obediently he returned to the blanket and lay down with Colum.

She thought, I should remove the rat before it rots, and she lit the lantern and went up the ladder into the darkness of the loft.

She saw it at once, stiff near the empty oat sacks, lying on its back with a bloodied neck. Big as a cat, but thin. She picked it up by the tail and came down and went toward the door. Then she paused. It was meat, after all. Rats were served the lunatics at the workhouse, shot by the dozens in the grain cellar. Mrs Goggan said they were no worse to eat than ox lungs and ox eyes and they tasted like hare.

'Plenty of people is eating things they don't let on about,' Mary had said, 'but you must keep your mouth shut.'

Moira skinned and cleaned the rat, plunged it into water. She tried to move quietly as she lit the hearth fire but Granny awakened and stared at her, blinking at the sudden glow of turf. The pot began to steam. Granny's mouth opened wetly.

Sean spoke from the rim of the quilt. 'Isn't it a fine big one?'

172

Moira bent and whispered, 'Don't you be telling nobody, not even Colum. Promise?'

'Aye.' He raised up on an elbow. 'I can get lots more. They's all over Granny's place and they go so slow they're easy to kill.'

'Oh, God, Sean.' She knelt beside him. 'I have to trust you, and you so young. Don't ever tell.'

He was excited and eager. 'If I get you some tomorrow what'll you be doing for me?'

'What is it you're wanting, then?'

'One for Colum, all to his self.'

'He can be having mine,' she said. 'But what are you wanting?'

'Oats. More oats.'

'Aye, then. But no one must see me giving you more. And you must hide the rats for me.' She mentioned a spot in Granny's pit. 'I'll be cooking them at night and saying they're hares I've found on the road . . . It's a secret, just for us.'

He looked at Granny and smiled. 'She'll not be telling.'

'No.' Moira could never become accustomed to Granny's silence.

'But she knows,' Sean said. 'She knows.'

Two nights later Jesus visited, bearing a jug. 'Let's be having a shine, eh Sean?'

'No,' Moira said, 'Da's off his belly. He sickened on stew.'

'Hare stew,' little Sean said.

'He should not be drinking,' Moira said.

Sean glared at her. 'Was it me daughter spoke for me? Bring the jars.'

Moira brought two.

'Fill them all,' Jesus said. 'It's we'll all be drinking.'

'Not me.' Little Sean grimaced.

'Or me,' Colum said.

'Nobody asked you,' their father said, and handed jars to the women.

They drank. Granny's poteen dribbled down her chin and she wiped her mouth on her sleeve.

Jesus said, 'As God's me witness a miracle happened to me not an hour ago.'

173

'What?' Sally asked, leaning forward.

'I helped a poor woman . . .'

He said he had been to his cave at moonlight to get the poteen and this woman lay there on the grass, partly concealed by brambles. Poor thing, she was fifty years old, clad only in her shift and you could see every bone of her body. Starving she was, nor words in her either, moaning and shivering like it was winter. He had forced poteen in her and covered her with his jacket and run to Murphy's for a bit of oat cake or whatever they had to eat. He hadn't been gone thirty minutes, aye, he ran all the way and back. But when he returned the woman was gone.

'And your jacket,' Sally said with an edge to her voice.

'Aye, but the miracle —'

'It ain't no miracle when you done something foolish,' Sally said.

'Foolish!' Jesus stared at her as though she were mad. 'Foolish! Wait till you hear. Look what she left me.'

He dug in a pocket of his ragged trousers. 'Look!'

It was a turnip, small and fresh and round.

Moira gasped. Folk said there wasn't a turnip alive in three counties.

'It's a omen,' Sean said reverently.

'It is that.' Sally's voice was humble.

'I heard of such miracles before,' Sean said, 'and they always happen in time of the hunger. Me mother used to tell of the woman all in rags who begged alms and was given maybe a penny or a crust and who left a pail of milk or even a pig. It was said she was Our Lady in guise of a human and when she vanished she left such things; and she blessed your land, too, and the praties came up next season and your garden bloomed ten years . . .'

'Aye,' Jesus said, 'I heared such things from the old men at Murphy's but I never thought none would happen to me.'

Moira said, 'You must save that turnip for it's like a holy thing. You should be after taking it to the abbey.'

'Oh!' Jesus said. 'To put on the altar me father robbed! Only —'

His voice was timorous, '— maybe Father Leary won't be wanting it there.'

'But it's holy,' Sally said.

'I'm thinking so.'

'May I touch it?' Moira asked.

Jesus allowed it to be passed from hand to hand. Even the little boys were respectful and Granny in her silence seemed awed, holding it gently until Jesus rose to take it back.

'I'll go to the abbey before me work starts,' he said, 'at dawn. For I'll not be wanting the holy thing in me poor pocket and maybe sitting on it. Why do you think,' he mused, as though talking to himself, 'such a thing would be happening to me?'

'Maybe to right your father's wrong,' Sean said.

Moira said, 'Or because you always wanted to do something big. That was your wish for St Martin, remember?'

'Aye, but I didn't really do nothing so big — I just gave her me jacket.' He seemed suddenly sobered, his exultation gone. 'How do we know she was Our Lady, what would she be doing in a shift and the burrs in her hair?'

Sean said, 'There was a time she was in a shed with the animals and only straw for her baby and God knows what clothes to her back. You must go to the abbey, you must tell the good father and give him the holy turnip.'

'I will that.' Jesus caressed the turnip with big, stubby fingers. 'But will it be safe on the altar? Nobody'd steal it to eat?'

'Nobody,' Moira said.

Jesus said, in a sudden burst, 'I have kept my bad news till the last — tried to drown it. But I cannot. First a miracle comes to me, but also a most terrible tragedy. I'd be sparing you if I could.'

'Who's dead?' Moira asked. Then, hopefully, 'Eileen?'

'My God, it's far worse,' Jesus said. 'I was into me cave this noon and — I've but one barrel left.'

There was a mournful silence.

'No praties, no poteen,' Sean said sadly. But Jesus' stricken face made him add, 'Still, no one can take your miracle from you. The blessed turnip is a grand omen, I'm thinking.'

175

They saw the turnip safe at Sunday Mass throned on a little puff of lace above the altar cloth. Candlelight circled it, candles so precious that they were lit only at Christmas and Easter. In the past years funerals had raised candles but now they were too frequent and wax too scarce.

Moira was tired and sleepy but she would not have missed Mass for the world since all of Ballyfearna had come, drawn by word of the miracle. Bridget and Tyrone, Dennis and Biddy, Paddy and Mary and Liam and his family and hers. There sat the wretched, nameless roadlings who worked on the canal and even the English engineers, though it was rumoured they were Blackmouths. Jesus and Eileen sat near the altar as befit the family closest to the miracle.

It was a warm day and the congregation wore its English finery — high stocks over ragged shirts, a red hunting coat here, velvet breeches there, a blossoming of bonnets and pale silk dresses. Moira and Sally were saving their dresses for their weddings, Granny for her funeral. Only they, of the women, were patched and tattered. One of the roadlings wore torn trousers and a plum-colored waistcoat with silver buttons. Others wore satin dressing jackets over oat sacks.

Father Leary celebrated Mass. Then he said, 'Jesus Finnigan has told me of what happened to him this Friday last. Will you be telling of it again, Jesus?"

Jesus said, 'I have. I told everybody.'

'But maybe some here have not heard.'

He meant the roadlings, Moira thought — no one thinks to tell them anything. To us they are only strong backs and arms to swing a pick axe and lift stone. Until they weaken and die and their places are taken by others.

Jesus stood. 'Well, I was in the woods . . .'

Delicately, he did not mention why. '. . . and I seen this woman . . .'

The marvel of it was still on him. 'I ran to Murphy's and Biddy give me a bit of stirabout but when I got back the woman was gone.' He pointed to the turnip on the altar. 'She left me that.'

The silence was absolute. You could not hear the catch of a breath or the wisp of a shawl and the few children were quiet.

There was no lift of wind to stir the cherry trees outside.

Biddy said, 'He didn't eat that stirabout. He was after bringing it back.'

'And he was after bringing this turnip to the altar,' Father Leary said, 'and I have blessed it. But it is a living thing with a need to share its life. Now that we have all seen it and know of its meaning, I want Jesus to be taking it home.'

'Home!' Jesus said. 'Why?'

'To eat.'

'I can't be eating a holy turnip!'

'As you wish. But it will nourish you as God intended, as your act has nourished us all. You gave a stranger your jacket; she gave you food. That is the miracle of sharing.'

Eileen's harsh, husky voice teetered on laughter. 'Was it Our Lady he saw, Father, or the drink that made him think so?'

'Does it matter?' The priest's voice was so cold that Moira shivered in the warm church and she saw Eileen pull her shawl close. 'Does it change the truth of the sharing?'

Mary forgot where she was and leaned across the pew to poke Eileen's shoulder. 'Why do you be mocking your brother's turnip? Is it jealous you are of his miracle?'

Sally said, 'Aye, she is, jealous and mean.'

'I am not!' Eileen said furiously.

'You are,' Biddy said, 'and as for the drink, you're a fine one to be talking. Souse!'

'Ladies,' said Father Leary. 'Ladies!'

'What's Eileen ever done so grand she can scoff at her own brother?' Mary asked.

Bridget pounced from another angle. 'Teases the men is all she does, not that it gets her anywhere.'

'You should talk,' Eileen screamed. 'Slut!'

'*Ladies!*' Father Leary's voice rose above the furore. 'You are in church!' Moira could see the old anger back in the burn of his eyes. 'A sin and a shame! You will kneel and ask God's forgiveness.'

They knelt and bent their heads in penance but not so low as to fail to observe Eileen. She had a smugness on her for all of her drooped shoulders and downcast eyes. She wore a blood-coloured

177

dress the English had sent; through the holes of her shawl they could see it buttoned at the throat with little garnet frogs. When the prayer ended she lifted her pale eyes and stared straight at Moira.

I did not say a word yet all her hate is on me. Why?

The congregation was blessed and dismissed. Jesus carried the turnip from the altar and when he reached the churchyard the roadlings gathered about him. Graciously, he allowed them to touch it for luck. Captain Nevin, standing near Moira, spoke softly.

'I've seen queer things in this land but never a deified turnip.'

Liam heard but kept his resentment leashed; after all, this was his boss. 'It's surely a queer thing, sir, with the blight everywhere.'

'It could not be everywhere. Obviously it could not. The woman must have carried turnips from far away, eaten them on the road and had one left.' His smile included Moira. 'Got to be reasonable, you know.'

'Yes, sir,' she said. She had never seen him this close, never spoken with him.

His eyes were admiring. 'You're Sean McFlaherty's girl?'

'Aye, sir.' She turned back to look for Sean who was coming toward them with Sally and Granny and the children. It was terrible embarrassing to have to talk to this lofty Englishman in the stiff black clothes and tall hat.

'She's me girl, too,' Liam said, delighting her.

'Well,' Captain Nevin said, 'why don't the two of you come to the hotel and have a spot before dinner?'

Dinner! 'Hares' and gruel. Only she and little Sean did not eat the 'hares.'

'Come,' Nevin said, 'a bit of whisky, eh, Lenihan? And wine for the lady.'

They could not refuse. Moira spoke briefly to Sean, explaining the invitation; then she and Liam crossed the wooden bridge with Captain Nevin. It trembled under their feet.

'Collapsing,' he said cheerfully. 'Some of you men should strengthen it.'

178

'Oh, it always been shaky,' Liam said. 'We taken a bridge-drink since I was only a lad.'

'Bridge-drink?' Nevin looked puzzled.

'When we left each other's homes we'd always have one for the bridge. For courage, kind of. Only it was like a joke, sir.'

'I don't notice that the village needs an excuse for drinking. It *brews* drinking. I never drank much until I came here —' He had a way of interrupting himself. 'The Hebrides . . . Egypt . . . godforsaken places. But I never really drank till now.'

They were silent until they sat in the gloom of the bar parlour. Biddy brought the men a bottle and a glass of wine for Moira. She tasted it, amber-coloured and heady. Slowly her embarrassment ebbed. Nevin was nice — for an Englishman.

He was about thirty-five, nearly as tall as Liam but fair, with a thin austere face and a sparse moustache. His skin, naturally pink, was reddened by the sun and his eyes were a light, lashless blue with only a trace of brow.

'God,' he said, 'it's good to talk to people.' His smile showed big yellow teeth. 'Even if none of you are real.'

'Not real?' Liam asked.

'Don't real people see you, talk to you? None of you talk to us.' (By 'us' he meant the other engineers, Moira thought.) 'We're like members of an exclusive club and we get tired of each other. There in that bar we hear the same old stories night after night. We'd be glad to talk to you — only none of you are real.'

He paused at their silence. 'Do you know what I mean?'

'Oh, sure,' Liam said, but Moira knew he did not. He was just being polite. 'Sure we do. It's not a bit real we are.'

'It's because of the queer things you think.' Nevin reached for the bottle and refilled his and Liam's jars. 'Like believing in ghosts and miracles and not knowing what goes on beyond your own fences. I'll wager you don't even know who's prime minister.'

'We don't have no ministers here,' Moira said, 'only priests. Not that ministers aren't grand,' she added tactfully.

'Ah,' he said, almost fondly, 'you see? You don't — do you

179

know who's Queen?' he asked, as though hoping they didn't.

'Victoria,' Liam said, 'the last I heard, anyway.'

'Right.' Nevin lifted his jar. 'God Bless her! Do you know what she's done for you? She sent two thousand pounds for Famine Relief.'

'Jesus Mary!' Liam said, 'Here? Is it oats, then, or corn?'

'Money,' Nevin said. 'But not here to Ballyfearna — I meant here to Ireland. Now you see, anybody else on the face of Empire would have known what I —'

He saw Moira's crestfallen look and touched her hand lightly. 'No matter, I don't mean to carp. It's just that I can't —' He started again. 'I was in the East three years, in a desert place. I couldn't understand a word they spoke. But they were real. I never felt left out. And they didn't hate us. They brought us goat cheese and eggplants and oil — I didn't eat any such stuff but they *asked* me to eat. They asked me to their huts. The same in Scotland. Tea and all. Big buttered buns and tea and jam.'

'They weren't starving,' Liam said, 'but the hunger is on us.'

'Perhaps we're different because of the hunger,' Moira said.

Nevin chuckled. 'I think you're different anyway — no harm meant.'

No harm, Moira thought, but a great loneliness on him.

'Where is your home?' she asked.

'Once it was Cornwall, on the sea. I travelled about England and then my wife died —'

'May God rest her,' Moira said. 'Did you have children?'

'No. And I began to wander. Women — well, anyway, I haven't married again. I just get to know a place and then the work is finished. Only here — it will take a long time and I don't know anyone.'

No wonder he's sad-like, Moira thought, drifting the world like fog. She fancied that she saw pity in Liam's eyes, or was it only a softness put on, the look one turned to please a boss?

'Another shine?' he asked Liam, using the word self-consciously.

'It's been a honour, sir,' Liam said rising, 'but me and Moira must be to home now. And we thank you kindly for your hospitality.'

180

'We do that.' Moira rose and curtsied.

'My pleasure,' Nevin said.

They left him there in the bar parlour and Biddy followed them outside.

'Well!' she said. 'He never asked another soul in here but Bridget Reilly and she only having a whisper with him and coming out fast. Is it queer you think he is, then?'

'Aye,' Liam said, and Moira nodded.

'Not queer of the drink,' Biddy said. 'He has no more than six or seven jars a day. He's queer because he's English.'

Liam said, 'But he's not queer in his head. You work with a fella all day, you get to know him a little. Only he don't get to know us. He thinks *we* are queer.'

'Aye,' Biddy said, 'Him thinking we're queer is part of his queerness. I only hope it don't be growing on him.'

Moira made a final plea to her father. 'It's only two days and Himself will be here. We *must* hide. Tonight. Now!'

The door was open, the dark had swallowed the hills. She was nearly too weary to beg, the long walk had been tense with fear of dogs for folk said they were mad with hunger and she had hurried, hurried . . .

'We'll go,' Sean said, and ran out into the night.

She stared after him. 'What's wrong?'

'It's the stew,' Sally said. 'He came home early, he's been sick. So's Granny.'

The change from oats to meat would account for that and she had no time for sympathy. Time enough when they were safe in the cave where Liam and his parents waited.

'Sally,' Moira said, 'I'm taking Cathleen and the boys, then I'll be back. Surely you'll be coming with us?'

'Aye,' Sally said on a sigh. 'What else can we be doing?'

'You bring them stools to the door and all the other things for Da to carry . . .'

Pots, cutlery, jars, meal, turf, wedding and funeral finery, the holy picture, the scrap of mirror, the baby boxes.

She spoke to her brothers. 'Sean, you and Colum bring the quilts, quick, now, and carry them careful.'

She picked up the baby and waited impatiently as the boys dragged in the quilts. 'Lift them!' she said, and saw that the burden would be too heavy. 'There, take one each,' and hurried them out the door before Sean could return to change his mind. For if he were not sick, he would change his mind. He was too weak to protest the move. But gruel would cure him as it had before.

The moon rode calmly over a star-splashed sky.

'Moira,' Colum said as he trotted to keep up with her, 'I'm cold.'

'Then wear that quilt,' she said. 'But it's a soft night.'

'I'm cold too,' Little Sean said.

'Oh, fuss! You'll soon be warm from walking.'

But the woods were damp to their bare feet and a wind came soughing from the loughs. Cathleen began to cry. Moira put down the lantern, cuddled her closer in the shawl and the baby hushed.

'I never seen it so dark,' Sean said.

'You've never been out so late so long.'

They walked on.

'Is there ghosts out?' Colum asked.

'No.'

'Soldiers?'

'No.' But the boys were lagging toward the bridge and she used the soldiers as a spur. 'Not if we hurry.'

'Me stomach hurts,' Colum said.

'Sure, we all got pains for the hurry of it. You'll soon be snug. Maybe with gruel in you,' she said, knowing it false, for Da must bring the sack of it. And Colum would sleep the moment his head hit the quilt.

They crossed the trembly bridge into the deep woods through the smell of dewed mayflowers and trampled grass. Then Colum stopped, dropped his quilt and was sick on the path.

Sean threw off his quilt and stood by his brother. 'He's awful sick.'

'It's only the meat.'

'Like Da.'

'And Granny. Sean, can you be carrying Cathleen?'

'Sure.'

'Take care.' She placed the baby in his arms. 'Take care for the love of God.' She bent and caressed Colum. 'Here, dear one, I'll be helping you now.'

The quilts, the stumbling child and the worry about Sean carrying Cathleen . . . Why in heaven's name had she set out so burdened? There was no such rush, there could have been time for many trips with Liam to help. But she could not risk Da changing his mind.

'It's not far now,' she said, but it was. Half a mile by day was endless by night; a silver birch by day was a specter by night. And the owls — or were they owls? Was it the baying of dogs she heard?

'What's that?' Sean asked.

'Just the hoots. You heared them before.'

'I have not.'

It was cruel, but she had to make them hurry. 'They're a long way off, but if they're dogs we have no time to waste.'

They stumbled faster, faster. Then, mercifully, she saw Liam moving toward them and the heavy wall of creepers that concealed the cave. He was quick; before she could greet him he was carrying the children down the treacherous steps, relieving her of the quilts.

'Come, alanna.' He held out his hand.

'I'll just get me puff for I've got to go back.'

'For what?'

'There's things to bring.'

'I'll bring them.'

'Da and Granny and Sally —'

'Have their own feet. Why should you be going back?'

She did not know. She was too tired to know. 'To say goodbye to me house.'

'It's not goodbye, you'll be back afore you know it.' He put her lantern into her hand. 'Be careful going down, mind it's wet and slippy. Me mother will show you your room.'

She was able to smile. 'Me room?'

'We have three big rooms. We even got a fire. *Go* now.'

He pushed her toward the entrance and she went obediently

183

but, wary of her exhaustion, she descended slowly feeling the moss-slime on her feet and the cave-cold rising under her petticoat. Finally she heard the soft rumble of the underground river, saw a gleam of light and came to the ground. The ground was damp but there was turf smoking in the old hearth. Liam's handsome father moved to meet her, Liam's mother stirred a pot. Rats? Broth? It did not matter. She was not hungry; she wanted only to sleep.

Far back in the cave she joined her brothers and sister on their quilts.

It was strange to awaken in the cave-dark, stranger still to see in the faint glow of the turf's embers a painted ceiling and walls hung with crystals. Gold, silver, ice-blue — and the ceiling had no end, it vanished into its own height up there among its own stars. Somewhere far below the river rushed secretly.

Her sense, clock-taunted, told her it was time to go to work and she smoothed her clothes, passed Sean and the sleeping children and went into the next chamber.

Here Granny and Sally slept, here, too, crystals rose to an unseen dome. Beyond, in the third chamber, Liam was already up tending the fire. His parents lay on a pile of straw in a corner, quilts drawn to their faces.

'Poor girleen,' he said, 'to start your day with a long dark walk.'

The thought of the dogs terrified her. She must never forget to take the blackthorn stick.

'Did Da bring me stick?'

'Aye.' He brought it from the foot of the steps.

'Them dogs we hear about — what am I to do if I meet one?'

'You must walk past that dog as if you're not feared at all. Dogs is cowards, they only try you. If they see you're not scared they'll give over.'

'But if they do?'

'Don't use the stick lest you have to.' He cursed. 'Jesus God, why can't it be me taking that walk?' He looked at her lantern. 'You ain't got much oil.'

184

'I only need it to use till sunrise and then again coming home at dark.'

'But you must have more oil. Can you be buying it at the workhouse?'

'Maybe. But I've no money.'

'Here,' he said, and gave her tuppence. 'It's not just light for your walks, you'll need it down here until your eyes grow kin to the dark.'

'Will they ever?' she asked.

'Sure, me mother can find her way already. Remember Blind John?'

'I do that. He was cooking his praties three days after the accident.'

'And we not near so bad.'

'No . . . but it's fey down here. We should have moved to the house by the Pool of the Waterdogs.'

'It's too small for ten people and it's no hidey place. Now — a bit of broth for a road-drink?'

'No,' she said, but she loved him for wanting to heat it, for wanting to help her. 'I'll be having food when I get there.'

'When you come back tonight, throw down a stone and I'll hear it and come to meet you.'

It was almost as if they were married, alone by their own hearth.

'God,' he said again, 'why can't it be me taking that walk?'

He could not know how often, in dream, he walked with her. Sometimes she even talked to him to ease the miles.

'Come here, alanna.'

She went her way with his kiss warm on her mouth.

'Mrs Goggan,' Moira said, 'would you be kindly selling me a little oil for me lantern?'

It was late afternoon and they were eating soup and bread at a table recently vacated by the paupers.

Mrs Goggan pushed away her soup half-eaten. 'No, Moira. There's no need.'

'But I do need it, Ma'am. And I have tuppence.'

185

'Save it, then. You won't be taking the path after Saturday. The kitchen is closing.'

'Closing!'

'There's no more money.'

'God help us! Will the workhouse close, then?'

'No, but we can only feed the residents and the sick that's in here, not the crowd outside. They must go away. Mr Grant will tell them tomorrow.'

Moira thought of that dark, hungry sea forced to some other shore. And the black-lapping tides that swept them from pain to peace and back again to pain. The kindest prayer, she thought, is that they might not awaken.

'Please,' Moira said, 'let me stay. Sure you'll still be needing help.'

'But we can't pay. Not even in food. You'll have to go. I tell you, there's no money.'

'Why's there no money, Ma'am? I heard the Queen sent two thousand pounds of money.'

'But Ireland's big. You know how big? Mr Grant says more'n eight million people. Mayo's only like a spoon to a barrel.'

'What will be happening to us all?'

'Weep for yourself, girl. Them —' she motioned outside — 'some of them people is tricky as Judas. A girl made believe to be her sisters three times and she got her rations three times over. I mind a man christened his dog Kate so as to get extra food for his "mother" . . . There's some don't tell of deaths in the family for the sake of the extra food tickets — they bury their dead in the ditches at night.'

'It's the hunger makes them tricky, Ma'am.'

'It's the way some are, hungry or not.' Mrs Goggan stirred her soup with a chained spoon, then drank it from the bowl. 'Is your father working still?'

'Praise God he is, Ma'am.'

'You can always come here on penny-a-quart. And I'd not be above putting a bit more in the pail.'

Moira thanked her, then smiled wanly. 'Is it tricky *you'd* be?'

Mrs Goggan threatened her with a raised fist. 'Go on with you and make the prawpeen.'

Moira cooked the watery porridge which would not firm. The women who helped her joked about it. 'A mule couldn't leave the mark of her hoof on it.' 'It will run a mile on a plank.' 'If it won't fill your belly it will scald your throat.' The old, sad jokes.

The bantering stopped. They were all to be dismissed, they would all remember the warm kitchen as luxury and their work as play. Where else could they eat free food or be paid wages?

'Times has got to soften,' they said, and 'God will see to us,' and 'It's not long till the good crops.'

'I heard of a garden blooming in Ballintubber,' one said, and everyone exclaimed at the wonder of it and how soon all the little gardens would be plump with praties.

There is an ache in us to believe these things, Moira thought, an ache that goes deeper than hunger. We have *got* to believe. But no one does.

It was strange to spend the days in cave-darkness with the ghosts all about.

'It's not the priests or the wee men haunt this place,' Liam's father said. 'It's Captain O'Duffy's women.'

'Who's them?' Little Sean asked.

The families were gathered about the tiny turf fire on a night of rain.

'Captain O'Duffy was like us, hiding, only from one of them rebellions against the English. Fifty years ago it was, and me not quite born. When the English left, O'Duffy come out of this cave and went back to his house. But he wasn't safe from the ladies. They thought he was a hero, being a captain and all, and they bothered him so that he was wishing to be back here alone in this cave. Finally one day he lost his temper with one of them ladies and he lured her here and strangled her outside and pushed her body down. He done in twelve that way.'

'God save us,' Sally said. 'A round dozen.'

'But wait. Me grandmother knew Ollie Malone who loved him too, and maybe Ollie pestered him the most, being old and ugly as —' he glanced at his wife '— as can be. Ollie kept on bothering him, bringing him puddens and butter pats and all, till finally he slew her here on a night of moon.

187

'Now nobody could ever guess why Ollie was suspicious. Maybe she'd heard about them twelve vanished ladies or maybe she was just cross with him. Anyway, when O'Duffy started for her throat she threw her whole weight on him and then kicked him hard down these steps where he died of a broken neck. They found him lying on all them bones.'

'And his ghost is here?' Moira asked.

'Sure it is, with the twelve terrible ladies after him, why wouldn't it be? If you'll listen in the night you'll hear him sobbing for mercy.'

'Oh, my,' Sally said, 'I'm hearing him now!'

'It's the river you hear,' Liam said.

'It is not,' little Sean said. 'I hear him.'

'Me too,' Colum said.

'Why must you be telling of it?' Mrs Lenihan asked her husband. 'It's not fit.'

As his parents squabbled Liam rose and took Moira's hand. 'We'll go out for a bit of a walk.'

She shawled her hair and followed him and his lantern up the steps. Outside, light rain met them.

'You'll not mind me father's tale,' Liam said. 'There's no ghosts down there.'

'He shivered me.'

'He told it to shiver me mother. He'll do anything to perk her anger and she'll do the same to him.'

They walked toward the stone bridge. 'Why?'

'They stopped loving.'

'When?'

'Since before I can remember.'

'Why does that happen, then?'

'I don't know. Maybe the knowing of each other too well.'

'We know each other well. And I never stopped —'

But Liam was not listening. He was standing utterly still and staring through the woods. Then he pulled at her hand and she followed him, running through the trees and across the bridge and now she too could smell the smoke. And she knew where it came from before they reached the Crossroads of the Shoes and looked down into the embers of her house.

188

No one was about. There were only the smoking red entrails of roof and walls. She could feel her teeth chattering with shock at the sprawled stones and ashy thatch. One fence still stood; the rain had saved enough to see and weep for.

Liam cursed, the same sickening curse Sean had once used to her. He hurried her down the hill, past the debris through the dark green of the woods to his shed.

'My God,' he said. The shed loomed grey and solid and around the bend of larches the house stood safe.

He marvelled, circling the house, touching it lovingly, holding the lantern up to door and window. Moira tried to share his joy. 'It's a miracle, alanna. Now you can go back.'

'Aye.' He seemed dazed. 'But I can't see how they missed us. Why they didn't ride on here.'

'Them soldiers aren't used to this land. Maybe Mr Pond told them of your place but they lost their way.'

'Likely they'll come later.' But he seemed too happy to believe that. He was patting the walls, the brown thatch. He could not keep his hands from the house and she thought, he is in love with his house, his land.

But so was I, so was I. I did not know it then, but every corner was loved, every inch of the acre. The rambling rose me grandmother planted, the hearth her mother tended, the high, snug loft. It had been a staunch little house. The rain had not dripped through and Peter the Thatcher had come only once in her memory, when the Big Wind of '39 had shaken the roof.

Where were Cathleen and Grace to visit now, spirits without a hearth? And the shy wraiths of animals — the pig, the chickens, Two and Three . . . ?

'Liam . . . '

He came to her swiftly, held her so tightly that her ribs hurt. He said nothing but she felt his need to comfort. And when they turned to go he led her the long way back through the wet meadow flowers knowing she could not bear to see the dying house.

Jesus clambered down the steps with a sort of banshee howl. 'Moira! It's another miracle happened!'

189

She ran to meet him. 'What? What happened?'

'I was after chasing a hare down into St Francis' cave — and what did I see?'

'*Two* hares?'

'Poteen! Barrels of it!'

'May God be praised. But who made it, then?'

'Meself, long ago. Only in a way of speaking I'd hidden it in me drunkenness and forgotten it. And that's the miracle of it.'

Now she could see the jug in his hand. 'Moira, me darling, let's drink. It's a sure omen of better times, I'm thinking. You'll see . . .'

The Lenihans moved back to their house the next morning. In the evening Sean complained of headache and pain in his back. Five days later he was unable to go to work, too weak to move from his pallet. His face was swollen. His skin, ordinarily so fair, seemed darker — or was it the reflected darkness of the cave, with only the sod fire brightening one corner of the enormous front chamber?

The walls were damp and cool yet he complained of heat and Moira bathed his face with cold water but the burning persisted. Late in the afternoon she left Sally to tend him and ran for Mary.

The midwife brought her fardel of medicines. She showed no surprise at the cave (likely the whole village knew of their hiding) but descended cautiously and said a thankful Hail Mary when she felt the ground under her feet.

Moira tried to make a little joke. 'It's you we hail, too, Mary of me heart. It's not many we can count on in time of the trouble.'

'It's me business.'

'But we have nothing to give —'

'Hush. Bring the lantern close and let me be seeing him.'

Sean had moved from his quilt and lay on the damp earth. Mary peered at the sleeping face and drew back the rags of his shirt. 'He has spots on him, Moira. And he smells.'

Moira turned away, aware of the smell now. 'What is it?'

'You'll be knowing as well as me. You've seen it.'

190

But never close and never freezing the heart. 'What are we to be doing?'

'Running,' Mary said grimly. 'I'll tell you true, you must get him to the fever shed — and quick.'

'But how?' Sally asked. 'Tyrone has no cart now.'

'Paddy has his yet. And it'll soon be dark.'

Moira clutched Mary's hand. 'Will you be asking Paddy, then, on your way home?'

Mary hesitated. 'I don't know if I can.'

'Why not?' Sally asked. 'He's a good man when it darkens.'

'He's scared of me. He's after thinking I'm after him for love.'

'Oh, fuss!' Moira said. 'What do you care what he thinks? And you don't love him noways.'

'No,' Mary said, 'but I must be prudent in me old age. Well — I'll be asking him. But if he is not here by the darkening you must find some other way.'

The boys came in from the next room but Moira ordered them back, explaining that Da was sick.

'What has he been eating?' Mary asked as she started up the steps.

'Hares — you know?'

Mary nodded understandingly.

'We had great luck with catching hares,' Sally said.

In innocence? Or did she know?

Mary said, 'Give him nothing to eat. He'll be begging for water but you give him only a little. Don't be touching him more'n you can help. Keep Granny and the boys out. I'll tell Paddy to put a rag on his own face when he comes — *if* he comes.'

'Bless you,' Moira said. 'You'll be in me prayers.'

Mary said, 'I'm thinking He's hearing too many.'

Moira covered Sean with a quilt. To her relief, Sally seemed calm, or was this a queerness on her that didn't perceive the danger to them all? In any case she managed to keep Granny and the boys out of the chamber and her presence was a com-

191

fort during the hours of waiting. Sean slept restlessly, tossing off the quilt.

'If Paddy's not coming,' Moira said, 'I'll have to be asking Liam to carry Da there.'

'How can you? To cart him is one thing, out in the fresh air, but to be carrying him, with his face so close and all — it's Liam could sicken next.'

'But how can I get Da to the fever shed then?'

'I don't know.'

They were silent in the faint light of the lantern near the stairs. They could hear the flow of the river and Sean's rough breathing.

'It's a choice you must make,' Sally said finally. 'Your Da or Liam. For Liam would go if you ask him.'

'I know.'

I cannot make such a choice, Moira thought. There must be some other way.

'If I walked to the workhouse and told them, maybe someone would come and bring him back —'

But the words broke on her certainty that no one would. The drovers were busy with corpses and even if a cart were available who would go twenty miles unpaid to risk Black Fever?

Little Sean spoke from the shadows. 'Me and Colum's hungry.'

'We told you Da's sick,' Moira said. 'You stay with Granny till I bring you food.'

'It's so dark, we have nothing to do in there.'

'Better the dark than you get the fever. Go back.'

She heard her voice echo in the high hollow cave-dark. '*Go back.*'

Another hour passed. Moira made gruel and Sally took it to Granny and the children.

'Paddy's not coming,' Moira said.

'No.'

Sean moved and murmured under the quilt.

'Sally,' Moira said, 'I must ask Liam for help, I *must*.'

'Then you're for fevering him, for putting him toward the grave.'

True and terrible. But she had to save Da. She took her shawl and the lantern, then paused at the foot of the steps. 'Who would you save if you was in me place? Granny or Patrick?'

They could not see one another for the separating dark. 'Granny's old,' Sally said, 'she lived her life, she's no use to anybody now.'

'So you'd not be sending Patrick on this errand.'

'No. And yet Granny's me own mother, like the baby-cord still joined us. And you must think about food. It's your Da makes your living, not Liam.'

'I can't be thinking that way —'

'You got to, for the children. If your Da dies there'll be no money for the food.'

'I'll not risk Liam for your food!' Moira said furiously.

'For the love of Christ, I didn't mean it that way!'

'You did! What else could you mean?'

'Moira, I am only saying what's true. It's Liam's work bears his own family, and your Da yours. What's to happen to you and the children if your Da dies?'

'Or to you and Granny.'

'Me and Granny will go then, and tonight!'

'Good. Get your mother and go!'

'We'll go, and forever.' Sally disappeared into the next chamber.

Moira waited in the darkness. Her father called for water but without light she could not see him nor find her way to the water jug.

Colum's voice. 'Moira —'

'Go back,' she said.

Go back, echoed the strange hollow cave-voice.

'Water,' Sean said.

She groped toward the barrel where the jug was, found it, lifted it, went in the direction of his voice. Then from the cavernous steps she heard her name called, put down the jug and ran toward the sound.

'Paddy!'

'Moira, it's meself, Jesus.'

'Wait!' she called from the foot of the steps. 'Don't come down! The fever is on Da.'

'I know. Mary told me. I come to take him away.'

He blundered down the steps and Moira went to meet him.

'It's a terrible chance you'd take,' she said, 'but you'll be in me prayers all me life.'

He carried the lantern over to Sean, watched Moira lift his head and give him water.

'He'll be no weight, Moira, so thin he is. It'll be like carrying a babe on me back.'

'Oh, God, but ten miles! Couldn't you be getting Paddy's cart?'

'He's scared to lend it.'

She moved close to Jesus, looking up into the big scarred face. 'That wish you made on St Martin's Eve — it come true.'

'Now what was I after wishing, Moira?'

'To do something so big and grand nobody'd ever forget it.'

She went into the chamber where Sally was. A quilt stood packed with the wedding and funeral clothes.

'Jesus came and took Da away,' Moira said.

'I heard.'

'Ah, Sally, it's times like this we must be together, not angry with each other.'

'Angry? There's no anger in me. But I must go.'

'*Where* will you be going, alanna?'

'Why, me and Granny is going to Patrick.'

'But how can you? You said he was in America!'

Sally laughed. 'Now where did you get such a idea? You know as well as me he lives in Ballydonny.'

'Sally! It's not in Ballydonny he is.'

'He's not there *now*. He's waiting for us outside with his cart. He's been calling this half hour.'

Moira felt a shiver of fear.

'You heard him call.'

Slowly, Moira lifted the lantern, thinking, it was as well that they had been prudent of the oil. She also thought that it had been a long time since she had seen Sally's face.

Sally blinked, then smiled. Her gums were like sponge, and bloodied. Her face was swollen.

194

Moira gasped and put down the lantern. 'You ain't well,' she said. 'You have — you must lie down and rest.'

'I must go to Patrick.'

'He'll wait a while, alanna. Please lie down.'

Sally was silent.

'You have a long trip ahead, you should save your strength.'

To her surprise Sally went obediently to the quilt where Granny slept. 'Moira, you go and tell him to wait.'

'I will that.'

'Tell him to mind them steps when he comes down.'

'I will, darling.'

She went into the farthest chamber where the children were. Little Sean's voice met her in the darkness.

'Is Da still sick?'

'Aye,' she said. 'Jesus come and took him to the fever shed. Colum, are you awake?'

'Yes. I was awake a long time.'

'Listen,' she said, 'listen to me careful and do what I say. Stay in here and don't come out for the love of God. Promise?'

'Why?' Sean asked.

'Because I'm thinking Sally got the fever too. She has no spots yet but her mind's queer. And maybe Granny's sick too. You must stay away from them and if they come in here you yell for me and I'll get them back to their room.'

She sensed Sean's excitement. 'Everybody's sick but us.'

'Maybe Granny's not but I'm taking no chances. I'll bring your food and you feed Cathleen for I was too close to Da and Sally . . . do you understand?'

'Sure,' Sean said.

'I like to feed her,' Colum said, 'only she spills a lot.'

'Can't we go up outside?' Sean asked. 'We have nothing to do here in the dark.'

'You can go up tomorrow a while, but don't you get near Sally and Granny.' She did not want to frighten them but she felt that she had to assure their obedience. 'If you get close to them you could turn black and die.'

She addressed Sean through the darkness. 'You're the oldest, next to me. You must take care of Colum and Cathleen when

195

I'm not here. Tomorrow I'll be walking to the fever shed to see how Da is. You must be like him, you must be responsible like a father.'

'Aye,' Sean said.

Moira longed to hug them, to kiss the sweet-sleeping Cathleen, but dared not. She groped her way back to Sally's chamber, picked up the lantern there and went into the front of the cave to wait, For what, for whom? Liam on his nightly visit. Jesus, perhaps, back to tell her that Da was safe in the shed. The lantern oil was low, too precious to waste. She blew out the wick and sat down on the damp earth. She did not know which of the two quilts was hers, which her father had used. It was said a fevered person left fever on all he touched, so she dared not risk a cover.

The underground river lulled her toward sleep. Was it true the fish there were blind? Were there bats folded against the high dome of the cave? Did God hear every prayer or was He too busy as Mary said?

She slept.

She said to Liam that night, 'It's as if Sally's mind is rumpled.'

'I noticed that before. She said something queer last week, I'm forgetting what . . . but why didn't you be coming to me to take your father?'

'I'd not risk your life.'

They were sitting close to the tiny fire and he leaned to kiss her. 'You are me life. I'd do anything you asked.'

'Then how can you be leaving me to go to America?'

'Because there's no other life here. The gardens are dead. I got to go — but I'd be back in a year, maybe two.'

'Aye,' she said bitterly, 'that's what they all say. Granny told me Sally said a year — she was gone twelve years and then only back because her husband died.'

'But Moira, even if I wasn't loving you I'd be back.'

Because of your land. Your buttercupped meadows and your loughs padded with lilies and your woods and your hills. And your house, though no better than others, is the house of your heart.

196

'Why is it you're not asking me to go with you, Liam?'

'How could I, and not a pound for me own passage? I'll be working me way, God willing. And then, you've the children.'

She felt suddenly angered by her inheritance. Her mother dead, her father ill, and their three children left to her. Yet she loved them, sometimes achingly. It was hard not to stroke the boys' crisp curls, not to rock Cathleen; to sever closeness for the sake of safety.

'Liam,' she said, 'it's the bloom of summer now but the weeks go rushing. Soon it will be the back end o' the year and you wanting to go and nothing —nothing —'

Nothing settled between us. Words of love but no vow of marriage.

He patted at her tears. 'Some day we'll have something, it's only the bad luck. Some day —'

'Some day!' She drew back from his arms. 'And what is this "some day" to mean to Da, to Sally and Granny unless it's now? How can I be feeding the children or meself or anyone?'

'Hush, the dark is on you. Father Leary said —'

'He's a holy man, but I'm no holy woman. He has no three children and two women to care for and a father maybe dying.'

'It could be worse. Your Da's safe in the shed.'

'Is he?' She thought of that shed, open to the cool, moist night and the three tired doctors tending the hundreds. She could only hope that Da was noticed, maybe not helped as yet, but at least noticed, so that in the morning someone would think to go to him and do what they could. 'Is he safe just because he's there? Plenty die there, I seen them carried out.'

'You must have faith, alanna.'

The old accusation — no faith. But she would not quarrel with Liam. This was a time for clinging. For a while she lay with her head on his shoulder. Then she felt him move away.

'I wonder what the time can be,' he said.

There was no longer a way to tell time by the sound of the Castlebar Coach or the look of the sky.

'There's a smell of lateness,' he said.

'Don't leave me, Liam. Sleep here.'

'I will, then.'

197

'Will Jesus be coming, do you think?'

'I'd hope he goes home to drop asleep . . . Have you a quilt for us?'

She explained her fear of using one, and they snuggled together on the hard ground. He was asleep almost at once but she lay awake thinking of Da, of Sally, of the emptying oat sack. Suddenly she was hungry, ravenous, but she managed to lie quiet for the fire was dead, the lantern out. She could not cook in the dark. She must not think of food.

What to ease the longing? Daydream. The house at the Pool of the Waterdogs, and herself carried over its threshold in her wedding dress and a pallet soft with goose feathers and a coverlid like velvet and Liam's arms around her like this . . . like this . . .

'When I was a young man in Dublin town'

She sprang up. Liam was gone. (Had she slept, then, and was it dawn?) She could see Jesus' big feet coming down the steps.

'There wasn't a shine I did not down . . .'

'Ah, Jesus, come and rest you. How is Da?'

He wagged a bottle. 'Drink, Moira, me love.'

'No. Tell me what happened.'

'Nothing.' They sat down. 'He's lying easy, they took him in at the gate. He didn't be knowing nothing on the road.'

'But they took him in?'

'Aye. I never seen so many people, like a fair it was, but all quiet. And no horses, no horses only people and no one laughing or passing the jug.'

She realised he was deep in the drink. 'Why should they be laughing and drinking, sick and hungry as they was?'

'I seen a little girl eating the grass.'

'Sure, I've seen that too.'

'Her mouth, it was green.'

'Aye.'

He offered the bottle again but she shook her head. 'You can't be swilling with the work coming on you. Is it nearly day?'

'It's day.'

'Jesus, you must go. Oh, if only it was Sunday and you could sleep till Mass!'

'I'm not sleepy, I feel grand. I could finish this canal meself today.'

'Don't,' she said, trying to smile. 'It's the work on it feeds the town.'

'Captain Nevin tole me we're working too slow. He's got to make a re — report and he says he must lie about how we're going faster.'

'Why would he be lying for us?'

'Maybe he likes us. Some of them English do. I heard about some soldiers who tumbled houses at Castlebar and give the people shillings. Some soldiers even left houses stand hereabouts.'

Perhaps they had left Liam's on purpose, then . . .

'I'll be on me way now,' Jesus said. 'And don't you be fretting.'

She did not mention Sally's queerness lest Jesus, in grandiose mood, would offer to carry her to the shed. He must work, then sleep. 'I'll not fret save for you. Don't be drinking your way off that canal today.'

He dismissed this with a wave of his hand. 'Them English may be crazy but they're not in their heads. They're not letting to let their best man go . . .'

After he left she slept again, a strange deep sleep as though induced by poteen. She thought that someone was climbing the steps but she was not disturbed. After all, she had told the boys that they could go out today.

But when she awakened and went in to see if Cathleen was all right, the boys were there. And passing the packed quilt in Granny's chamber she saw that Sally was gone.

Moira fed Granny and the children but her own hunger had left. Softly, she talked to the boys, then went to Granny and sat down beside her.

'Maybe you can hear me, maybe not, but I must pray you can hear. Sally's gone. I think she's gone to seek Patrick, so that would be to Ballydonny. I must go there and find her and if she's sick I got to take her to the fever shed, where Da is. So I'll be gone all day.'

She lifted the lantern slowly so as not to startle the old woman.

Thank God there was no swelling, no darkening of the skin. But the skin was only bones and the eyes sunken in the grave of the face.

'The children won't be bothering you,' Moira said, 'because I told them not to. They'll be going outside to play. There's nothing you should do, only remember me and Sally's gone for a while.' She paused. 'Darling, could you be showing me you understand?'

The open eyes, the mouth, the hands, were still.

'Then goodbye. I'll be leaving the lantern with you.'

Up in the light of day she blinked, for the sun hurt her dark-accustomed eyes. Then she set off through the woods and took the path to the workhouse.

Twice she passed refugees who begged for food or a penny; once she thought she saw a wild dog hiding behind a hedgerow but as she approached with her stick she saw it was only a stretch of bones. The sun grew hot and she stopped at the brook to drink and cool her feet. Always she strained her eyes into the distance hoping to see Sally walking ahead, dreading to find her collapsed on the path.

Although the soup kitchen had closed there was still the sea of near-naked people lying on the sun-scorched grass. A crowd in front of the fever shed stood, sat, or stretched out in delirious sleep. There were changes — newly turned earth on the slope to the right, obviously graves. At the workhouse an armed guard stopped her.

'You must wait your turn,' he said curtly.

'I want nothing but to see Mrs Goggan. I used to work here.'

'I have me orders.'

'Please,' she said, 'it's like I'm one of the help, I ain't begging nothing but to see her. Please, your honour.'

Perhaps the title softened him. He stepped aside and allowed her to use the door knocker. Presently a slattern admitted her, one of the scrubbers she knew by sight, led her into the familiar stench of the hallway and went to summon Mrs Goggan.

The common room had changed, Moira thought. Once used for the lesser diseases of starvation it was now, obviously, a typhus ward. She could see the darkened, swollen, spotted faces of patients who lay near the door.

Mrs Goggan came along the corridor carrying a tray of sponges. 'Moira,' she said, 'we have no money for help, so be off with you. I told you before —'

'It's not that, Ma'am. Me Da is here with the Black Fever on him and maybe me friend Sally Mullen come in today. I'm after trying to see them.'

'You can't.'

'Then just asking how they are.'

'And who should be telling you?'

'Why — the doctor. Or the Master.'

'Do you think they'd be knowing names? Do you think we can be keeping records here? Aye, once we did, but now there's so many we can't even keep count.'

'But surely, Ma'am, when somebody — dies — you got their names, you know who they are?'

'How should we? And most of them raving when they come here or too sick to be talking?'

'Then what am I to be doing?'

'Go home, girl. If your Da and your friend get well then they'll take the road home.'

'But — How can I wait, not knowing?'

'Go home, Moira.'

'How long must I wait for them, then?'

'God knows. Two weeks, maybe. Three, even four. According to how sick they are and when they come in here.'

'They just come in . . . could I be looking through the wards, Ma'am?'

'No! The Master lets nobody in but the help. And now I must be going.' The hard eyes softened. 'But if you're wanting a bit of soup for yourself —'

'No.' She moved toward the door. 'But could you be telling me where is Ballydonny Hill?'

'A league from here to the east, it starts from the Market Cross. You have friends there?'

'Maybe me friend Sally went there instead of here.'

201

'Pray she has,' Mrs Goggan said, and went off down the hall.

Moira passed through the silent, slow-moving crowd and returned to the road. Walking east she found the hill which rose steeply to a path of larches. After a few minutes she saw a tumbled house — Patrick's or his brother's? At the summit another hut stood firm to the winds. The dead garden was grown to weeds, but neatly fenced. She rapped on the door but no one came. Pushing inside she saw that the two rooms were bare except for rock seats and a rat-chewed pallet. There was nothing to show that this had belonged to Patrick or his brother. If Sally had been here her footsteps had not troubled the soot near the hearth.

Back down the hill she walked past the Market Cross into what remained of the town: a grocer's, boarded up; a blacksmith shop and livery stable without sign of life. A row of mud huts with smokeless rooms. A big building, perhaps a hotel, now deserted. A waterless horse trough. A sign — the coach stop? But no coaches came here now, nor perhaps ever would.

More cabins in browned pratie gardens. And at the end of the long, twisty street, a little stone church overgrown with ivy.

Its door was open and she went in. No one was there. The altar was stripped of cloth and holy statues. There was the ghost of incense.

Outside again, she stood uncertainly, shading her eyes from the sun. Then she saw an old priest hobble around from the flower beds that edged the graveyard and she ran toward him.

'Father!' she called.

He looked up, hand to his ear. Then he saw her and smiled and met her at the broken gate.

'What are you wanting, child? Speak up, the way I can hear.'

She described Sally and asked if he had seen her.

'I might have,' he said wearily, 'but so many roadlings flow past, how would I be knowing?'

'She'd have been asking after Patrick Kane, him who lived on the hill.'

He shook his head. 'There was no one asked for him. He hasn't been here a long time now, nor his brother neither.'

202

'Where have they gone?'

'Who's to be knowing? The town's gone.'

'Is there nobody I can be asking?'

'You could knock on the doors still left but there'll no one answer. They're afraid of the roadlings carrying the fever.'

'Would the nuns at the convent let me in?'

'If you're not asking food or shelter — they have none to give. They got two hundred sick inside, and no beds.'

She thanked him and trudged back through the desolate town, seeing no one. If eyes watched her from the cabins she was not aware of them. Three miles from home she turned off the path and walked up the gravel road that led to Our Lady of the Flowers.

The gray convent buildings lay cushioned on banks of rhododendrons but the once-formal gardens were overgrown with wildflowers. Here, too, she found supplicants in the yard, eighty or a hundred people clinging to hope on holy ground, trusting to be let in. No one barred her way to the main building. There were never protests, she thought, that a person walked over them, past them; likely they were too weak to care. She had a curious feeling of invisibility, that no one really saw her climb the steps and clatter the door knocker.

A nun opened the door a cautious inch. 'Aye?'

'I'm not asking nothing but to see Sister Angelica or Sister Charity.'

'Why?'

'To ask after a friend.'

'They's busy.'

'I'll wait, then.'

The girl shrugged. 'Go 'round to the back and wait by the sundial. Only I doubt anybody'll come.'

Moira waited at the sundial for half an hour, then moved to the shade of the cloisters. Once, she thought, it must have been beautiful here until the gardens had grown shaggy. Their flowers had been the nuns' pride, brought in profusion to the weddings and christenings and funerals of Ballyfearna.

Her long walk and her search had prevented too cruel a worry

203

about her father. Now, resting, she felt engulfed by it. There was, as Mrs Goggan had said, nothing to do but wait for his homecoming. And if he did not come . . .

'Moira!'

A nun hurried toward her, both hands outstretched. At first Moira did not recognize her. This emaciated woman could not be plump, pretty Sister Angelica Kelly. Yet the hazel eyes were the same, and the voice.

'Moira McFlaherty! Is it really yourself?'

So I too have changed. The shock is plain on her face.

'Come,' Sister Angelica said, and led her down the arcaded walk to a bench beneath the willows. 'Sit down. I can do with a little rest meself.'

She inquired of Moira's family and Moira poured out her story. 'I can't bear to think of Da buried somewhere and me not knowing . . .'

'You can't be fretting for a month. Likely he'll be home before that.'

'But if he doesn't come home where will they be putting him?'

'In the common graves, alanna. What else can they do? Nobody has names now and if they did nobody has time to put up stones. Aye, it's a terrible thing, but we must care for the living.'

Moira spoke through the tears in her throat. 'Is Sally Mullen here?'

Sister Angelica frowned. 'Am I knowing her?'

'Sure you do. She was married and went to America —'

'Ah, yes, I remember her now, Granny Cullen's girl. But she's not here. I'd know. I'm the one decides who comes in.'

'And how do you decide? There's no line out there.'

'No. When we have room for one more I go out there and look around and I take in one I think has a chance. Them with the Black Fever I don't — ah, Moira, may God forgive me for saying it, but you asked, you asked me, and me too weary to watch me words.'

'It's me own fault, sister. I should not have asked.'

'Could you be having a cup of water, child? It's all I can offer.'

204

'No. Thank you.' Moira rose. Her legs seemed unsteady. 'I must be getting home to the children.'

Sister Angelica followed her part way around the building. 'I'll be praying for you and your family.'

'We'll be grateful.' Moira leaned and kissed the soft, sunken cheek. 'Give me love to Sister Charity.'

'I will that.' Her chin trembled. 'Times will change. They must. Nothing stays the same.'

Moira thought about that as she plodded home through the slowly falling dusk. The words meant to comfort were a mockery, even a lie. For the brown, blighted gardens were the same, and the hunger on the people. No, not the same — worse.

She thought of God, bitterly. *'Our father . . .'* Even Da had been a better father. Bereaved of Cathleen, tired, hungry, sick, he had supported two families — and the jealous, inhuman Father had struck him down. The habit of prayer was strong, natural as breath, but now she felt that He did not deserve reverences. She would not beg from an indifferent source.

Never.

And yet the next day she went to Father Leary and confessed her sin.

He listened for a while. Then he said, 'It's too bright a day for the shadows. Come out and walk with me and we'll talk.'

Moira was astonished that he would break the ritual of the confession but she waited for him under the wild cherry trees until he came out to join her. They followed the bend of the river and sat down on the bank near the stone bridge.

'Do you believe what the Bible says, Moira — that man was created in God's image?'

'Aye, I suppose I do.'

'Then you had ever thought that God, like man, could be fallible?'

'Fallible?'

'Mistaken, prone to error, deceived.'

'God mistaken!'

'Couldn't you forgive and understand a mistake?'

'Of course, but I thought Himself so powerful he couldn't make one, nor be deceived either.'

'Maybe He can be. Maybe there's times He longs for *our* forgiveness and when we do forgive why then His power is back again and He starts to correct the mistakes.' He smiled at her wide eyes. 'I think He's needing us like we need Him.'

'But if man was made in His image —'

'Man is often cruel and capricious and sometimes it seems God is too. We got to understand that the best way we can. Now, I'm not saying I believe this meself, Moira. But when I find someone like you about to desert Him, why then I raise the point, for it's better to accept Him as He is than to leave Him.'

'Has your own father ever been cruel?' he asked.

'Not often. Sometimes, maybe.'

'And you forgave him. You have two fathers, Moira. You mustn't give up either one.'

She felt a flood of tears that she could not stem.

'Weep,' he said gently, 'you'll feel the better for it. And don't be in guilt. We've got to question sometimes and in me mind it's no mortal sin to do so.'

'Then you're after absolving me?'

'I am,' he said, 'if you can begin to trust again. You'd do as much for your human father. Why not for Him?'

'I will, then.' She smiled and dabbed at her eyes. 'You've made me almost happy. It's *three* Fathers I have!'

He blessed her and helped her to her feet. 'Miss Finnigan will be making soup. Shall you be joining us?'

She longed to but one did not accept hospitality these days. 'No thank you. I must get back to Granny and the children.'

'What do you eat?'

'A little oats. Hares —'

But she could not lie to him. 'Rats, Father, when we can get them.'

'I was fearing so. You must stop that. Dr Thrush thinks the rats are maybe sick and that they sicken us in turn. It's not safe to take the chance.'

'But what will I —'

She broke off, for Eileen had approached silently on bare feet.

206

Her hair was its usual snarl but she was oddly elegant in the blood-red English dress.

'I was just wanting to know should I be waiting to make me confession or the broth?' she asked.

'Both, Miss Finnigan,' the priest said. 'I'll be along soon.'

Eileen's voice was warm but her eyes on Moira's were ice-cold. 'I didn't mean to be bothering you.'

'No matter,' Moira said, 'I'm going now.'

She thanked Father Leary and turned homeward, aware that she was shivering, the strange inner shivering she always felt when Eileen lanced her with those sharp, pale eyes. *Why should she hate me so? Whatever have I done to hurt her?*

Maybe it's because she loves Liam. But so does Bridget, and when we chance to meet, Bridget is only a sulk and a head-toss or an uppity nose. Bridget would like me gone, aye, or better, never born. But Eileen's hate is toward murder. She wants me dead.

Chapter 7

Days passed without word of Sean or Sally. Moira's lantern burned out and time was measured by little morning hunts in the woods, the nightly visit of Liam. She slept apart from the children in the front chamber and Granny kept to her own quarters, climbing the steps occasionally to sit in the sun outside the cave.

When Liam left and Moira lay down to sleep, the haunting began. Not Captain Duffy nor the long-dead priests, but her father. Once she heard him moaning on the quilt near the hearth; often she awakened to hear him call her name. Always she welcomed him, for who could fear a loved one?

She told Liam of this and he said, 'He's not dead. It's you thinking of him keeps him alive.'

She thought, I was too close to Da to know him, too near to see him. Like when you stand close up to a tree you can't see it clear, only the bark and the top, not the middle, not the root-spread. I suppose I never knew him whole, only the little boughs.

Alone in the darkness she tried to build the tree from the little boughs she had seen as a child.

He had been happy, she remembered, always a-tease and a-whistle. Aye, and a great one for pranks. Like the time he had gathered the hens' eggs and boiled them and put them in a box and sold them to Biddy. Biddy had tried to cook them for hotel guests, tried to break one and couldn't, and tried others and couldn't and Dennis went on a drink a whole two days when Sean told him the hens were in heat and had boiled the eggs in the nest. . . . And the time Sean pranked John the Basket whom he saw hiding a jar of poteen in the river-reeds. Sean waited until John was out of sight and drank up the jar and filled it with water and John returned and swallowed a pint of minnows. But a gypsy once pranked Sean by giving him a horse at Ballydonny Fair in exchange for a little pig. Sean raced that horse on the High Street against Paddy's mare, and the horse was away ahead till it saw Murphy's water trough where it stopped so sudden it pitched Sean in the ditch. It drank that trough dry and then sat down on a pratie bed and had the hiccups and went to sleep. That horse never did Sean any good. It cost him a lot of shillings one way or another but it was grand having a racehorse even if it never did anything but eat and drink.

'Me racehorse,' Sean used to say with all the pride of gentry. 'You never seen such a horse before.' And truly no one had. It died, finally, of eating Annie Dumbie's bonnet right off her curls. Annie was charitable and asked only sixpence but Sean gave her eightpence as befit the dignity of a man who had owned a bit of a stable.

That was Da at twenty-six, twenty-eight — irresponsible. Maybe he fought that weakness of living for the moment; maybe that was why he feared it in herself. God knows he had sobered, perhaps too much. The light had gone out of him like a blown candle. Why? Not Cathleen's death; it had happened before that. He, who had cheered Jesus on to magnificent fights, indeed had started them, and joined in them, began to pacify. He urged quiet settlements, he refused the broils at Murphy's. And he stopped drinking, only three or four jars a day.

She asked Liam if he had noticed the change in Da, and if so, when. Being older than she, Liam might remember.

And he did. 'It was about six years ago. We was at Murphy's one night and he told us he'd not be having another jar. He said he couldn't afford it because a baby was on the way. Well, of course Dennis give him drinks on the house to celebrate the event but a blue ruin was on your father and nothing could cheer him up. It was me walked home with him and he said, "Me and Cathleen and Moira has been happy, we need no-one else." It was almost like he was jealous of the baby coming, and he saw the good times gone and him with another mouth to feed.'

'But times was good when Sean was born.'

'Sure, but not for your Da. Quieter he was, and sad, and when he did drink his heart wasn't in it. Bitter he was, and broody. He told me once it was hard to be loving a woman and not touching her.'

'He told you that!'

'Aye, and later, too. He wished there was some way he could bed Cathleen without fear of a baby coming . . . Years after, when she died, he blamed himself in a terrible way.'

'I thought he did but he never told me.'

'It's them things you don't be telling a daughter; you tell another man.'

'Do you think,' she asked, feeling the pain of the question, 'that in the last year he been a little queer?'

'Why do you ask?'

'He wasn't making up his mind, he put things off, like moving here. He didn't take charge of the boys like a father should. All he did was go to work, like his whole life was the walk from here to the canal. I'd be talking to him, asking him something, and he was looking just beyond me shoulder.'

'I'm thinking your mother's death tore him up more'n you know. He was a grand man, Moira —'

He stopped abruptly, hearing her sob in the darkness. 'I mean, he *is*. We must go on hoping.' He groped toward her hand, clasped it. 'Now let me tell you something makes me love him more'n me own father. You're remembering that September after little Grace was born when your Da told me I couldn't be seeing you but two nights a week? I thought he was suspecting me of trying to harm you and I was red-mad. I said if he didn't trust me he could go to hell, that I'd see you anyway. And he put his hand on me shoulder and said, "It's Moira's life I'd trust you with but it's her mother's health I'm fighting for . . ." and he told me why you got to stay at home till she was stronger. I was thinking of that trust he had when I slept here that night with you in me arms. He'd not have been minding, he'd have known you couldn't be alone in the dark, not that night.'

Moira moved closer. 'I wonder why I have to begin to know Da now? Why I didn't never try before or care so much? Because I know in me heart he'll never come back?'

'No, darling, you're only missing him.'

They were silent, close in a new way, she thought, deep beyond the need to kiss. 'You told me your mother and father had stopped loving. From knowing each other too well.'

'Aye, they did.'

'Can love die of age, then?'

'I don't know. All I'm knowing is, they like to be hurting each other, it's hate they feed on.'

Mindful of hate she told him about Eileen. 'One look of her eyes and I'm scared. Does she be loving you?'

He laughed. 'If she does she never said so. Sometimes we meet on the road and she asks me in for a shine but never a loving word or touch. And me only staying a minute or two.'

'Then why does she hate me?'

'Maybe you done something —'

'Never.'

'— you don't be remembering. Something long ago. Why don't you ask her?'

'I'd as soon be asking a dog that's run wild. I've thought and thought why it could be . . .'

'Let it be then. There's no sense to being broody.'

He was right.

She wished she could see him for the darkness seemed no comfort now, she was sick of it, mired in it, but the fuel was low and it was dangerous to fell a tree lest Mr Pond find it out. Hiding on his land she dared not steal more than twigs. 'Liam, you said the house at the Pool of the Waterdogs is no hidey-hole but so far as I know Mr Pond never went there. If Da doesn't come back in — time — I'm thinking of moving there.'

211

'The sun,' she said to his silence. 'The dry ground. There's wood all around just for the taking. Frogs, otters maybe.'

'There's nothing there but the wood and likely he'd be seeing the smoke rising. There's no life in that pool, you know that as well as me.'

But there was no life here in the dark, living like moles; no one to talk to all day but the hunger-drugged children who needed the sun and the change of light to prevent them from sleeping too much . . . or was it more merciful to keep them here?

When Liam left, Moira lay awake wondering what to do. She mistrusted his youth and her own. If only Granny could advise her . . . If only she could draw on some wisdom beyond her own. Surely her parents had said something she could use as guidance . . .

She searched the pockets of the past but found them empty.

By chance she met Mary hunting on the road to nowhere. It was not long since Moira had seen her but her hair, once grey-gold, had lost its glow and the moon face sagged with wrinkles. Only the big brown eyes seemed the same as though a younger woman looked out of them.

'I found nothing,' Mary said, extending a slingshot. 'I aim at a bird but I never get one.'

'Me neither, nor fish on me line.'

'Rats —'

'Father Leary told me they're sick and we shouldn't be eating them.'

'He told me too. But the grass and the plants don't hold the hunger and some is sick from them too.'

Moira said, 'Maybe it's them sicken Cathleen. She been so good up till now but lately she's been crying. I took her out in the light to look at her close and she's got swollen — not her face, thank God, so it's not the fever. But her little stomach's filling out in a way's not natural.'

'And the boys?'

'Them, too. What's wrong, Mary? Their stomachs is empty but all swollen up.'

212

'It's the bursting sickness,' Mary said. 'I seen children burst from nothing but the water in them. You must find them something solid to eat.'

'How? Where?'

'Me mother told me once after the time of the last hunger that she eased us children just by the boil o' the water on the hearth. Stones she put into the pot and us soothed to sleep by the very sound of cooking. And somehow it was a comfort to our stomachs. Maybe it would be helping Granny, too.'

'Just the sound o' the stones?'

'Aye, a-bubble in the pot.'

'I'll be trying it, then. Now, is it safe for them to be sleeping in the chamber where me father sickened?'

'Why not? It's twelve days now.'

'Da used two quilts but I've been careful, I use neither one but sleep without.'

'Use them, alanna, for sure the fever is gone from them now.' Mary stared along the quiet path. 'There's some life, I seen it. Like the birds sometimes, and the rabbits. I was hoping to find something for Paddy's supper, something besides the oats he'll bring.'

'Well! So it's courting he is! I mind you said he's afraid of you.'

'He is, only I'm thinking he's afraid to be alone, too. Maybe it's lonely he is now that the town's gone. People aren't buying or selling or borrowing, so he has nothing to do. Mopey, he is. So I'm after hoping, in his poor condition, now's the time to get him if I can.'

'Ah, Mary, he'd be lucky. But you're not loving him.'

'I *told* you, I must be prudent. Fifty-three years of age I am, giving or taking a little, and I can't keep me looks forever. And these bad times have done nothing to help me baby business, them folk that's left here haven't the energy for — nothing. So I'm down to me last shillings. But Paddy still has his house and cart. He doesn't let on, but he's even got seed praties.'

'Oh, go on with you!'

'He has. I seen them meself under his pillow.' Her broad face flamed. 'Me kindly patting up that pillow when he had a cold in his head. I think he has seed praties hid all over the house, only don't you be telling a living soul.'

213

Moira promised. But she was dazed, almost unbelieving. 'Where does he be getting them?'

'God and Mary know. He's dark about his doings, and of course I'm never asking.'

'Is he after planting them?' Moira asked, marveling.

'Now is that pimple on your shoulder never coming to a head, girl? Put your brains into a fish, it would go crazy. Of *course* he isn't after planting them for folk to see and beg of. It's me is proud of him for his good sense.'

'But where is he getting these seeds? From England?'

'Who's to be knowing? He doesn't even know *I* know.'

'Well,' Moira said, 'there's one thing I'm knowing — we must get you married to him, and fast lest he feels better. It's not only prudent, its *wise*. Is there something I can be doing to help?'

Mary considered. 'You might be asking us over some night — like as if we was a couple.'

'Sure and I will. It's a frolic we need, all of us, and even if we have nothing to eat, Jesus has the drink always. Queer it is — Jesus is after helping everybody these days, so I'll be having a word with him.'

'Now what will you be telling him?'

'That if he can help get Paddy to marry you, he'll be doing something real saintly.'

'May the Lord bless you, Moira McFlaherty! Could we be coming soon, then?'

'Tomorrow night,' Moira said.

Secrets were kept in Ballyfearna — grim ones, guilty ones — but news of a frolic spread no matter how careful one was. So it was only natural that when Moira had a private word with Jesus, he should tell Tyrone who worked beside him on the canal, and that Tyrone should tell Bridget who chanced to see Biddy on the bridge; and what on earth is a wife to do but share the news with her husband? If Eileen heard (and likely Jesus told her) she did not come, for Father Leary had the cough on him and she remained to tend him, making hot poultices for his throat.

All the women but Granny and Moira wore their English finery, for it was a warm, starry night. Jesus was generous of the poteen and Biddy and Dennis brought a pound of oats which thickened Moira's pond broth. Paddy brought an oil-filled lantern so they could actually see each other in the cave when the stick fire died. 'Is it a occasion?' Liam's father asked Moira. 'Is it good news you're surprising us with about your Da and Sally?'

She wished he had not asked. 'No, only a bit of something to cheer us up.'

'Well, it's meself can do with some cheering,' Mrs Lenihan said, 'what with me stomach and all — and I haven't healed yet in that place where O'Ryan's goose got me.'

'It was your own fault to meddle with that goose to begin with,' her husband said. 'Now you hush your mouth or go home.'

It wasn't the happiest start for a frolic but Jesus' poteen soon eased the Lenihans and Moira was pleased that Mary seemed radiant, almost like the bride she hoped to be. She wore a blue bombazine dress with lace at the neck and if the lace was a little yellow (them English ladies didn't seem to be liking it white) still it made a lovely lot of frills at the throat. She even had part of a bonnet on, with a feather to cover what was missing, and pink lace gloves.

'Mary,' Jesus said, 'I never seen you look so beautiful. I could marry you meself.'

Moira thought, He's off too fast, like he was a horse at a race. He ought to ease in slow so Paddy won't be suspecting anything. But Paddy looked scared.

'A fine wife you'd make any man,' Jesus said.

'Sure,' Liam said helpfully, 'she made Donald happy.'

'Now what was it Donald was after dying from?' Bridget asked. 'It's so long ago I'm not remembering.'

Mary said, 'He got fallen from Hallihan's hayloft — a pitchfork was up on its arse and caught him terrible, poor man.' She bent her head into the lacy collar. 'It's terrible sad to be a widow, and alone. But at least I have no children to support so if I'd consider to marry again the keeping of me would be cheap.'

'And would you be considering to marry again?' Jesus asked.

'Only to the right man.'

215

'It's wise to be aiming high,' Moira said, 'to be choosing the finest man hereabouts. One with a trade, maybe?'

'Och, it's not money I'm after,' Mary said. 'I'd not mind if he had only half a acre.'

'Or not even a shop,' Jesus said.

'Shop?' Mary asked, shocked. 'Who cares for a shop, Jesus Finnigan? It's love I'm after. I'd be loving every hair of his — well, I'd love him any way. And when times get better, why then I could help him with me trade, for babies must be born when folk gets stronger.'

Bridget said, 'True for you,' and Tyrone took her hand as though it were some little light thing like dandelion fluff that might break in his fingers. Then Bridget pulled her hand away and Moira saw the despair rise and flood his face. His face is so thin, she thought, that it seems all dark eyes and it hurt her to look at him.

Jesus filled the jars and Moira resumed the vital subject. 'Mary, where would you be finding such a man as you'd consider to marry?'

'Oh, I don't know about that,' Mary said subtly. 'I wouldn't be after chasing anyone.' She moved from her rock near the hearth and went to sit beside Paddy. 'Now what's making you so quiet, Paddy Nolan?'

'Oh, nothing,' Paddy said, 'except me lungs and me liver and me heart and all. I'm a dying man.'

'*You are?*' asked Mrs Lenihan with vast respect.

'Then it's some woman you're needing to nurse you, Paddy,' Jesus said, 'some skillful woman. Like Mary here.'

There was sudden silence around the little fire. Then Paddy said, 'But Mrs O'Hara's spoken for.'

'Spoken for!' Mary stared at him. 'What in the name of hell are you talking about?'

'Why, you and Jesus. All night he's been saying how he's in love with you and you pretending not to hear.' Paddy rose, kissed Mary's cheek and slapped Jesus on the back. 'Why didn't you come out with it, boy? It's me ghost will dance at your wedding.'

It was amazing, Moira thought, how fast Paddy sprinted up those steps, them being slippy and him being close to death.

216

Jesus gulped another jar and Moira knew the fright was on him too. But Mary made it all right. 'Jesus,' she said with dignity, 'I thank you for your proposal of marriage but I think the years between us would make it wrong. I'm old enough to be your mother.'

Then Jesus said something really saintly. 'Sure and you grieve me to me heart. You're sure?'

'I'm sure,' Mary said.

How long had it been since Da had fevered, since Sally had left? It was hard to measure time in a lightless place. But on her daily quest for food Moira felt summer ripen toward its end and fogs swirled in from the sea, prescient of autumn.

Again she journeyed to the workhouse asking of Sean, and again she was turned away. But she could not relinquish hope that he was alive and she told the boys to pray for him and for Sally.

The scant food had queered both boys. Once devoted, they quarrelled constantly. Cathleen wailed her own distress but if Granny heard she made no move to comfort. Often she climbed the treacherous steps to sit outside in the sun, wrapped in her shawl against the moody weather, wrapped in her dead-eyed silence.

'Sean,' Moira said to her brother, 'it's you must watch Granny when I'm not here and see that no harm comes to her. She could fall on them steps and break, for her bones are frail as reeds.'

'Aye, but if she fell what would I do?'

'You'd run to Liam at the canal and tell him to bring help.'

His voice sulked. 'I have Cathleen and Colum to watch.'

'Sure,' she said, 'and Granny too, for till Da comes back it's you are the man of the house.'

What was that word she had been — irresponsible? Aye, but Sean must not be. Only the hunger was on him and his youth and so she could not blame his bickering with the other children. But it wasn't good, the high wrangling voices, the tears, the slaps, the eternal tattling. Colum had hit Cathleen — not so! Sean had hit her, and lied. Not so, Colum had lied . . . and so it went until mercifully sleep took the children and the cave was quiet at last.

217

On Moira's birthday (how could he count the days?) Liam brought her a present of oil for her lantern. She wept, holding him close in the light-shifted shadows and he kissed her wet eyes and her hair and said to save the light; and took her up into the pale starglow.

'How did you know it was me birthday?' she asked. 'I didn't.'

'Nor meself, darling. But the sunsets are red and the leaves are golding and the crickets beginning and so it's your birth month.'

'September,' she said, 'the back end o' the month.'

'On your birthday,' Liam said, 'you make three wishes, and always true they come on the first star of your sight.'

She knew and chose the star. 'I wish —'

'But don't you be telling or the wish will wither.'

I wish Da will come back in health; that the hunger be off us; and that Liam will ask to marry me this very night.

They walked up the hill and paused there, hearing the chitter of night things in the trees. Ballyfearna lay below them, silent, dark, its lamps bereft of oil, its candles gone. Wind rose and she thought of storms, of the coming winter. 'God and Mary keep us if the canal should close for weathering.'

'Aye.'

'How many men are working on it now?'

'A hundred, maybe. Some drop out for tiredness and new ones come in from the roads. It's few of us started are still on it.'

She knew where her questions led but was helpless to stem them. 'But you will be on it, Liam?'

'Until I go.'

She took a deep breath. 'Go — when?'

'The ship from Galway Port leaves the end of next month.'

'Oh, God! You meant it then.'

'It's me only hope for money. Just think, once I'm in America it's two pounds a month I'll be sending, maybe more. And I've told me father to take care of you.'

'Would you —' She paused, for it would shame her to beg for marriage.

'What, alanna?'

'Have someone write from America so I'd be knowing you're safe? And Father Leary reading me the letters?'

'Now what did you be thinking I'd do?'

They saw a lantern move through the darkness, heard a call and Paddy hurried toward them. 'Quick, Moira, you've got to leave this place. Dennis told me Mr Pond has heard of folk living in caves hereabouts and says he'll smoke you all out or seal them caves, they being his property. So you'd best get out this very night.'

Liam cursed. 'Where would she be going?'

'Off this land.'

'But it's all his land,' Moira said, 'clear to the edge of Galway.'

'You could hide in me house,' Liam said.

'With the children noisy and Granny bumbling outside? No, I'd not dare it.' She thought for a moment. 'I'm believing no one knows of the hut at the Pool of the Waterdogs, for secret it is.'

'Aye,' Paddy said, 'I'd even forgotten it was there.'

'It wears bushes and trees, it's hidey,' Liam said, 'only you must be careful of the smoke from the chimney for fear he'd see it.'

Moira said, 'God knows it's only a hour a day I cook.'

'But soon you'll be needing fires to warm you,' Liam said. 'It's warm now but the woods go contrary any time soon. It's hot one day so you think it's summer, then the frost and the terrible cold. You'll have to be having the fires.'

'Then I'll chance them,' she said, 'and plenty of twigs there to burn, and there's a old tree fell you can be making me logs of. Before you go.'

Before you go — like saying 'Before I die . . .'

Yet because of her long love of that house it seemed an adventure to leave for it this very night and the dream of someday living there with Liam made it more closely hers. 'Come,' she said, 'let's go and waken the children and Granny and go.'

They met Jesus on the path and he helped hide the few household belongings in the bushes to return for later. No sense, Paddy said, to be burdened by more than the bits of food and the cooking pots and quilts. And then he was gone with a 'God speed, may your shadow never grow less.'

Then they were on their way. The boys, petulant and sleepy, lagged through the woods and Liam carried Cathleen. Granny, for all her stiff joints and her silence seemed her old self, following obediently the lantern Paddy had left with its bit of precious oil. Sean carried Granny's funeral dress and Colum Moira's bridal gown. Over stiles, past hedgerows and the bridge, through guardian blackberry bushes and finally into the little clearing.

The pool was dark and lifeless but then who knew what night creatures might not have dived for cover or scuttered into the thick brush? So happy a house it was in her memory, despite the sad end of the schoolhouse. And never forget, Moira said to herself, a priest once taught here and blessed it. Sure and it must still have a holiness on it.

Jesus beamed the lantern into the hut. 'You can't be sleeping here this night,' he said. 'It's stuffed full o' the woods.'

Moira knew. 'It will take a time to empty, so we'll be sleeping on the ground tonight, for it's warm.'

'But tomorrow night,' Liam said, 'then what if it rains?'

'It won't,' she said confidently. No evil could come here in the love of her long dream and of the priest's goodness. Until the hut was cleaned there would be no rain, no fog, no heavy dew, only this bearable calmness.

'It's queer I feel here,' Jesus said. He set down the lantern and looked up at the hut with its tracery of dried wild roses.

'Is it scared you are?' Sean asked, sitting beside Colum.

'Not scared, no, but queer, as if part of me life was left behind. I've not seen this place since I was a boy.'

'Were you a boy once?' Colum asked.

'Sure I was no girl.'

'What were you doing here when you were a boy?' Sean asked. 'Fishing?'

'Well, to tell you honest, I was larking. It was me time off from the workhouse — two days a month I had — so I come to see me friends in Ballyfearna and I stays here, it being empty. Now I was thirteen and maybe a little wild-like. I sneaked in the hotel and stole Dennis' gun to go shooting with, and a jug o' poteen.'

'And drunk you got and shot nothing,' Moira said.

'No, in me way I shot meself. You see on this night — it was hot June — I had me drinks and took off me shirt and hung it on a long stick and goes to sleep on the floor. Then I wakes up in the dark and sees something tall and white. My God, I thought, a ghost! So I takes up the gun and I shoots that shirt. It's a miracle I wasn't in it at the time.'

'You were lucky,' Sean said.

'Next day,' Jesus said virtuously, 'I gave that gun back to Dennis and tole him the truth, but the poteen was all gone so he gave me a drink on the house to celebrate me honesty.'

Liam smiled and yawned. 'It's home I must go.'

It saddened Moira how early he left these nights. Sure, a man tired from the long day's work and not much food in him. But the image of Bridget entered her mind and would not leave it and the thought that they met in secret nagged like an ugly wasp.

He kissed her and left. Jesus helped her bed Granny and the children on to quilts and she prepared her own pallet in the shelter of the bushes. She was far from sleep and did not want him to go and he sensed the dark trouble on her for he said, 'You're in a fret. It is scared you'll be here after all?'

'No.' They walked a little way into the woods. 'Not scared like you mean, not of Mr Pond finding us even. But —'

'What?'

She shed her pride. 'I'm scared Liam doesn't love me.'

'But why?'

'He comes after supper and leaves only a hour later, and that wasn't his way in the old days. I'm thinking he meets Bridget.'

'Bridget's got Tyrone.'

'But Tyrone hasn't got Bridget, not in her heart. If I thought Liam was with her now I'd—'

'But he's not. And if he was, what would you be doing then?'

She smiled wanly. 'Nothing. Scraps of him is better than none.'

'I'm believing he loves you truly,' Jesus said firmly, and emphasised the statement with a fist to his hand. 'So why can't you believe?'

'Maybe because love's so hard to believe in.'

'Is it, then? I never had any from a girl, so I'm not knowing.'

She looked up into the poor raggedy face with its huge nose and said, in love and pity, 'But you will! When the good times come back there's sure to be a girl . . .'

'Yesterday I took a jug to the hotel — and Dennis gave me soup

221

in exchange — anyway I passed by a looking glass and Great God! I jumped at me own self! I looked like that fella I seen once carted off to the Blackmouth Cemetery, all bones. He deserved it though, I mean, looking like he did. Even Danel Powderley couldn't argue me down about them Protestants. Why, I'd *die* before I'd be buried in a Blackmouth Cemetery.'

'You're no bonier than the rest of us,' she said, 'and it's sure I am that a girl will make you happy someday.' Standing on tiptoe she kissed the bristly cheek. 'A good night to you, Jesus.'

'And to yourself. And don't you be broody on Liam — he's a fine grand man.'

She groped toward sleep on that assurance. When she awakened the mist was not heavy, but tender, and the sky turned gold. It will be an early autumn indeed, she thought, for yellow leaves drifted in the pool, and as the sun rose high it caught the red of the oaks that reflected in the water like blood.

She loved each leaf, each grassblade, each crumpled toadstool — though these be poison as food. Stretched on the quilt, her hand caressed the lace of a fern, a swell of emerald moss. Then she looked at the little house — old, aye, but alive with the flaunt of the dropping leaves and firm to the winds these countless years. A house to live in, a house to live for in hope. And hers.

'Mr Pond,' she said, 'afore you get one toe in that door I'll pull the roof about you.'

It took four days to empty the forest-filled rooms and to wash them out and she thought, If we were in health it would have taken one. So tired they were, almost crawling, and the pains in their bellies until — praise be — Liam brought three pounds of oats.

'Where on earth did you be getting them?' she asked.

'Oh,' he said vaguely, 'I had some hid away these many months.'

She did not believe him and she worried through her delight of them. Maybe he stole but from whom — Paddy? Dennis? Ah, well, if that were so he'd repay them some day and he had no sin to confess until Father Leary recovered from the cough and Mass was resumed.

The oats were a boon for there seemed no life on the ground. Birds fluttered, but high, as if they knew folk waited with slingshots. The creatures sensed the hunger of the humans for the squirrels kept to the tall branches and shrewed from there, when once they had frisked at the doorway. And whatever lay in the pool hid deep.

And deep lay Liam's thoughts — if he had any about her. Gone was the swagger and the fun and what was worse — the strength. Sure, his arms were strong when he felled the tree and brought her the wood on a Sunday but so many trips to carry it and he tired soon as an old man would. And then, when he had rested, his kiss was a wisp as though it were given in duty.

She thought, I cannot go on this way, not knowing his mind. I must do something, for the days are short until he leaves for America.

And so, one afternoon when the work was done she stripped and bathed in the dark blue pool which still held the warmth of the sun. At twilight, when the household was abed, she took off her rags and put on the white shift and blue-ribboned petticoat, then the blue silk dress with its festoons of violets on the wide skirt. It was that queer pause between summer and autumn when the woods were still holding August but she drew the furred velvet capelet about her shoulders and tucked her hair under the bonnet with its little white plumes. God grant no one awakened to see her for she could not explain . . . except to herself. And so used was she to bare feet that she nearly forgot to slip on the pink velvet slippers tipped with feathers.

If only she had a looking glass! And yet, mindful of Jesus' shock at seeing himself, she was thankful. Perhaps Liam would mirror her in the past when she was maybe pretty . . .

She tiptoed from the house and, lifting the heavy silk skirt, took the wooded path where Liam would come as he usually did at this hour.

It was near the stone bridge that she heard footsteps and paused, waiting to surprise him, waiting as a bride waits in her brightest beauty. But no — it was a woman coming toward her and she stood dismayed.

'Eileen! Whatever are you doing here?'

223

The thin mouth curled. 'I could be asking the same of you.' But Moira saw envy of the blue dress and capelet and bonnet and thought, So I'm looking me best . . .

Moira would not admit she waited for Liam. 'How is Father Leary and his cough?'

'So you're fussied up to visit him, eh? Well, you'll not go.'

The last words were spoken quietly but as a dog growls quietly and Moira felt the rise of fear. If only Liam would come, for she dared not pass Eileen on the path.

'So you're turning back, Moira McFlaherty. Now.'

'I was only waiting for Liam,' Moira said, her voice a squeak.

'That's a black lie. He's on the canal and you know it.'

'Not after dark.'

'No? It's him is back at work soon as supper's over, so don't be giving me that.'

There was truth in her face and Moira thought, So that's why he's been leaving me so early. But why didn't he tell me?

'That cape hides nothing. You're wearing that dress to show Father Leary your tits — like a twopenny whore.'

Red rage rose in her and she lost her cowardice in the need to kill, and ran forward. But Eileen ducked aside as Moira tripped on a root and fell on her back. A bare foot stamped her hard in the ribs and for a moment she lost her breath and gasped for air. Then she wavered to her feet and felt Eileen's fist on her mouth. Through a fog of tears she could not see Eileen but lunged at her wildly, was thrown off balance and fell again, her face in the leaves. Now she wanted only the peace of lying there, to tunnel like a worm into the safety of the ground. Blood filled her mouth; she gasped and vomited.

Eileen bent over and ripped the cape from her, clawed off the bonnet, tore the dress and petticoat from neck to hem. Moira heard the slashing of silk, then words that beat and sickened. 'And if you be telling one word of this to anyone I'll not rest till I cut out your . . . and your . . . and your womb.'

Then she was gone, turning back on the darkening path.

Moira lay for a long time, dazed, sick on the shreds of her gown. Finally, ribs aching, she managed to rise and holding to the little trees, stepping over the ruined clothes, weaved her way home like a woman in drink.

Painfully she bent to the pool to put her face in the dark water. Or was this heavy, puffed thing a face at all? She felt inside her mouth — thank God her teeth were safe. But each breath cut her ribs. She wanted desperately to slip into the house, on to her pallet, but she could not trust her clumsy body to carry her in silence. Granny and the children must not awaken in terror and she could not explain what had happened.

Better to stay here near the pool, half-naked as she was, for the night was soft as the moss beneath her. She spat more blood and stretched out, knifed with the pain. And though sleep seemed as far off as heaven, she slept with her face in the ferns.

It was Sean who found her at dawn when she awakened to his scream.

'Hush,' she said through thickened lips. 'Let them be sleeping. Come here, darling.'

He stared at her. Was it horror on his face, then? And why did he creep forward so slowly unless her own face was . . . broken.

'Was it a mad dog?' he asked.

She was thankful for the thought. 'Aye, it came on me in the woods last night and tore off me clothes and I ran and fell on me face. Is me face — terrible?'

'It's like the colour of berries.' He shrank back. 'It's all fat.'

'Puffed like?'

He nodded. 'What was the dog like, Moira?'

She said, 'Me mouth hurts to talk. Now go in and heat the water in the pot and tell them what's happened so they won't be scared to see me.'

But first he had to know more about the dog and she fed him lies and repeated those lies in the house as they ate their porridge. Colum sat near her pallet and patted her hair and dragged over a blanket she didn't need. Granny must have understood, for she brought hot rags for her mouth.

'It's that dog I will find and kill,' Sean said.

It hurt to speak but she spoke sharply. 'You'll not go far in the woods alone, not further than the broken fence.'

'Then Liam and Jesus must kill it.'

'Sean,' she said, 'they must not see me — nor anyone — until I've healed. Promise me you'll be keeping them away, tell them I'm sorry of my looks, and vain.'

'They'll not be minding me.'

'Tell them I said you're the man of the house. For you are.'

She regarded him anxiously, realising he was young for such responsibility but thinking he must take it. 'It's soon Liam will be going to America,' she said, 'and it's you must grow fast to the needs of us here. This is why you start to be helping.

'Like a real man,' she said, for the big eyes held wonder and the small fists were clenched too tight for ease.

'Sean, it's me eyes you must be, too, and watch over Colum and Cathleen and Granny if they's outside. And it's me looking glass you must be too, to tell me when me face is well.'

If ever it is. Would only a berry-colour bruise make both jaws so sore and pain up to her forehead?

'It's the man of the house I am,' Sean said gravely, and kissed her — so rare a thing that she felt the tears wet her lashes. Odd he was, and sometimes sly and hurtful but maybe that wasn't his fault. What with remembering his mother's death and the dogs and his father's leaving — and the hunger and all. And maybe guilty because surely something happened that day with Granny . . .

'Then I'll be sleeping in peace,' Moira said, returning his kiss. 'Take Cathleen out to the sun, and then you and Colum see what's stirring by the pool. Maybe you'll be getting a frog.'

The familiar story tale, she thought, as Sean left with the children. Wherever frogs were, they weren't here, yet she could remember the song of them courting and loving among the plants of the pool. Her mother had said it was the bullfrogs made the noise, the lady frogs just stayed quiet and took the tribute and maybe if they was in the mood, they went off with the frog of their choice.

She closed her eyes, hearing the creak of old bones as Granny lay down to sleep again. But Eileen was between Moira and sleep.

She is mad, Moira thought, mad as the dog I made up. And I

think I'm understanding why — it's love for the priest she has, jealous, passionate love, and no way to feed it. Maybe she hates me just because he's always been kind to me though he never favoured me above anyone else.

The Bible said 'To understand is to forgive,' or something like that, but she could never forgive Eileen and some day she would take vengeance. Her hatred was the stronger for having been punished for no fault. True, Eileen was the stronger, bigger of body but, Moira thought, I've all me wits and she has not. I've me cool mind to plan with while hers is hot in the broil of madness.

Later, at twilight, she heard Sean run to the door and Liam's voice, loud and arguing and the doors swept open as she hid her face.

'I can't show meself,' she said. 'Now you heard me brother, he's man of the house and he *tole* you not to be by till I'm well.'

'It's not to look at you I've come,' he said, 'it's to hear your voice and to know what happened from your own words.'

Again, the lies.

'But where were you going wearing them good clothes? It's meself picked up the scraps of them and brought them to you.'

'Oh,' she said, 'I just had a fancy to wear them and thought I'd walk out to meet you. Now, Liam, don't you be telling anyone about that dog for it could put the heart crosswise in the women and nothing to be gained. Sure it's far off now in the hills.'

'I'll tell no one but Mary and it's meself will bring her there tomorrow, being Sunday and me off the work.'

She said impulsively, 'It's working two ways you are now — light and dark.'

'Who told you?'

'No matter, I know.'

'Jesus? He promised he'd not tell.'

'No, I just knew of myself somehow.' Another lie. 'It's me mother's second sight I have.'

He believed her. 'Them engineers is trying to get the work done fast before the winter sets in and it's the wages I need. Darling, I've a bag of oats for you there in the corner and I bought a bit of bacon from Paddy.'

It was too great a gift and she began to weep, but quietly, lest he come too close and hold her in his arms and see her face.

'Thank you,' she said when her voice was tear-cleared, 'Now you'd best go, it's your suppertime and you need food for your strength. Are you well, Liam?' she asked anxiously, 'well enough to work the two ways?'

'I'm grand but I knew you'd fret your head over me, that's why I didn't tell you.'

'And you're sure you've enough oats for yourself?'

'Sure. Now, Mary and me will be here early, there being no Mass. It's worried I am about Father Leary, he been sick now two weeks.'

'We'll pray for him, Liam.'

'Aye.'

Then he was gone. As she rose to cook supper she thought of a vengeance on Eileen. When the priest recovered she would confess her hatred of Eileen (for hatred was a sin) and explain why, thereby exposing Eileen in all her terribleness. He might even send Eileen away. But no, the vengeance was too soft. She must think of something far worse . . .

Mary visited twice that week and at the end of it stated that Moira's face was healed. There was no news save that a group had gathered last night at the church to pray for Father Leary. As to her plot to get Paddy, she saw no hope even though she had explained that she would not marry Jesus. Clearly he was a man of no sense whatever.

She asked to see the scraps of the English clothes and agreed they were beyond repair but a pile of ripped silk was better than none.

And the memory of those clothes, and why she had worn them came to Moira over and again. If Liam loved her then it did not matter that she wore rags on the night which must be soon. For now the crickets were clacking and the wild geese flying south. And Liam saying, 'Next week I'll be leaving.'

She was bringing out the quilt when she found Da's dressing-gown tucked inside — now how could she have forgotten that? Except of course he'd never worn it. Beautiful it was in its flowered silk and the velvet collar and not so very long on her when she tied the belt.

That Sunday night when Liam came he told her she was grand in that robe but was it an occasion?

'Aye,' she said, 'it is. I want us to walk to the cave tonight and say goodbye, for we'll not have much time before Wednesday.'

'But why the cave, alanna?'

She blushed. 'To be alone, like.'

They took wood for a fire and a blanket to sit on and it was warm when the fire flared up but cold inside her for she knew she was putting a sin on them both when she returned his kiss in a new way.

He drew back in astonishment and she said, 'Liam Lenihan, I want a child by you this night.'

'My God!' he said, and held her so close that her healing ribs ached again. 'You can't be meaning that.'

'But I do. I want a child for the comfort of me while you're gone.'

'But you can't be meaning that.' He released her and looked into her face. 'You've never been like this.'

She smiled. 'You're thinking the fever is on me and me head gone queer, but you're wrong. It's not the child I want only, but the part of you that's never been mine, the sacred part women have of their men that makes them whole women, not just half.'

'I'd not hurt you, alanna.'

'I'm wanting the hurt of you.'

His eyes marvelled. 'You're sure?'

'Sure as I'm alive.'

'Then we should be married.'

She had no words, only a feeling of wanting to thank God for his. He pulled her down on the firelit blanket, pulled apart the silken robe, and though his hands were warm on her body she shivered under his kiss. His mouth on her breast was soft as the lips of their child would be.

Pressed under him she heard the rise of the wind outside and its long sigh down the steps of the cavern. His mouth on hers was hard, his arms nearly cruel — and yet . . .

'Darling,' she said, lifting from the depth of the kiss, 'is it that I'm not right for you? Am I somehow wrong?'

He spoke on a curse. 'It's not you, it's meself . . . I can't bring meself to you.'

'But we'll marry. There's no sin on us if we marry.'

He turned and lay beside her in silence.

'Liam, I'm sure in me soul it's no sin.'

He sat up suddenly. 'Sin! I'm not caring a God damn of the sin — it's *me* that's wrong.'

She put her arms around him, fearful for him because he was cursing the saints, and she felt the flood of his tears on her throat and held him closer.

'Now what could be the matter?' she asked, crooning as though to the child. 'Tell me, darling.'

She could scarcely hear the wisp of his words. 'I can't tell you.'

'Is it maybe,' she asked hopefully, 'that you don't know how to do this, never doing it before?'

'*No!* It's not me ignorance of it.'

She drew away. Of course he had had other girls and he did not want her. She was not beautiful enough for him. It was Bridget he loved. She felt numb, a dead thing beyond tears. He could weep, aye, for love of Bridget and remorse that he had nearly been unfaithful.

He reached for her hand. 'I love you. How I love you I can't begin to tell and so you'll never be knowing.'

'Aye,' she said bitterly, 'like a sister.'

He turned on her in a rage and called her a bloody liar, but his fury was soon spent. She looked at him, bare as herself in the dying firelight and she saw his terrible thinness and his dark-circled eyes and his mouth, once so full-lipped, queer and pinched. And suddenly she knew what was wrong and why it was so.

'Liam Lenihan,' she said, 'it's tired you are, tired past loving any woman, tired near to death — and all because of meself.'

He made a little gesture with his hand, like saying 'No,' but he couldn't deny the honest truth of it for his eyes said yes.

'It's your nights working on the canal have ruined this night

230

for us,' she said, 'and you too proud to say so. But love, me love, there will be other nights when you come back and the potatoes flower and the hunger an old dream. Don't you be seeing that?' She leaned toward him, so anxious to give comfort, so afraid that he would not accept it. When a man could not mate he must feel lower than dung and somehow she had to raise him.

'It's oats you put in our bellies,' she said; 'you've kept me and Granny and the children alive, so how can you be alive in love when you've spent your body for a love that's deeper?'

'It's not deeper,' he said, and now his voice was calm, and his eyes too. 'It's the same love, I'm thinking, like the same tree has different leaves.'

'Aye.'

'Moira.' He moved her close in his arms. 'Not to be a man is a terrible thing in love.'

'But you're more a man for what you've done for us. And some day . . .'

They kissed, the old soft kiss of the old soft years yet somehow new and wise with the wisdom of what had happened. A kiss, she thought, that me mouth will remember always.

'I'm no saint,' he said, 'I've me wildness like any man, for when I'm meself the seed is hot to sow. But you'll be knowing this when the seas are between us — it's you I'll come back to.'

She knew, knew for sure; and again she cradled him in her arms, but not as a child. As a man, hers, who had known her body even though he'd not locked it for a child.

'Maybe it's best like this,' she said, 'that there'll not be another mouth to feed. But later it's many children we'll have, won't we?'

He stroked her hair. 'Aye, as many as you like. And tomorrow we'll be married.'

'But Father Leary's sick —'

'Not too sick, I'm thinking, to take the sin off us if we confess.'

She laughed, then sobered as she put on her father's robe. 'I could be happy if only Da was back and knowing Sally was safe somewhere.'

'I haven't the second sight,' he said, 'but I never did think they was lost. And even if they are, you know what Danel Powderley

231

said one night at the bar? In the drink he was, but I keep thinking on it. He said nothing and nobody is ever lost, only forgotten.'

'And we're never forgetting.'

In the morning Moira told Granny and the children. 'It's me and Liam is going to be married!'

The boys laughed and capered and it did her heart good to see how a few meals of oats had strengthened them. And Granny must have understood because she pointed to her funeral dress.

'It's beautiful,' Moira said, kissing her, 'but would a bride be wearing black? It's me will be making over Da's robe like a dress and I'll get the sewing thread from Paddy and the scissors and all. And I still have me velvet slippers with the feathers on.'

She sang through the day and at twilight Liam came and took her to Father Leary's house to arrange for the wedding. Eileen met them at the gate.

'He'll see nobody,' she said.

'But it's to talk of our marriage we want,' Liam said.

She stared at Moira. 'Marriage? To *her*?'

'And why not?' Moira asked, not scared now because Liam was with her. 'We want to be married tomorrow, before Liam leaves for America.'

'Aye,' Liam said, 'we've only two days before I go to Galway Port.' He put his hand on the gate, 'So you'll kindly be letting us in.'

'I'll not. The cough is on him hard.'

'Too hard to be saying a few blessings on us?' Liam asked. 'I'm not thinking he'd grudge them even if he whispers.'

'He can't whisper,' Eileen said, pale and queer-like. 'There's nothing he can do for you now.'

'We'll just be seeing for ourselves,' Liam said, and he opened the gate and pushed past her, taking Moira's arm. But in the house, even before they reached the common room they heard the gaspy cough and stood silent and sad.

Eileen was behind them. 'It's Doctor Thrush was here last night and said he's in a bad way, close to dying.'

It's hard to believe a madwoman, Moira thought, but I believe her sure for the tears in her cold, pale eyes and the truth on her face.

'He's in the high fever,' Eileen said, 'there's nothing he can do for you now.'

'God and Mary with us,' Moira said, crossing herself. 'Is there nothing to do?'

'Aye,' Eileen said, 'you can be going.'

'We can't be leaving you alone with the sadness,' Liam said.

'*Go!*' Eileen said. 'Go to America. You'll find your sluts there too. And they say all of them red flannel petticoats is made of satin.'

'Hush,' Liam said, 'the dark is on you for worry of him and you don't know what you say. Don't be tearing us in your trouble, for we love Father Leary.'

Eileen turned to Moira. 'And he loves you.' The words hissed and scalded. 'Aye, he told me so years ago when I come here. He says, "Moira McFlaherty is a example to all the young girls of this town — good, pious, beautiful." He said *beautiful*, he did —'

'Meaning me spirit, surely, not that I am,' Moira said, frightened.

'I know what he was meaning.' Suddenly the hot voice turned to embers. 'And to meself that works for him so hard and got no life but his, he says, "Thank you kindly for the porridge, or for the fish, or for the scrubbing, Miss Finnigan." But for you and your mother when you comes to tea that spring he says, "Get out the pink china, Miss Finnigan" . . . and he asks me to cut the roses like you was the queen coming and he — and he says, "That's a small little bunch of flowers, Miss Finnigan, get more." '

She turned to Liam. 'And this is the truth.' The voice was still embered, even ashed. 'She was after wheedling him, Moira was — and she do be doing it after you go, if it's still living he'll be.'

Liam said, 'You're daft with worry. Is there food for him?'

'The bishop's seen to that.'

There was revulsion in Moira, but pity too. 'And food for yourself?'

'Is it begging alms I am of you?'

233

Liam sent her a long, cool look. 'You can live on your brother's poteen. And now you'll be apologising to Moira for the evil you've said of her.'

The old fire was back. 'That I will not.'

Oh, God, Moira thought, her pity shrivelled and her fear back. Now that Liam's wanting to marry me she'll hate me the more, and he gone and no one to be helping me against her. She had a wild thought — but no, it would never do to tell Sean. What could a small boy do if it came to grave trouble? And she could never tell Jesus for in the drink he might tattle and, in his anger at Eileen, make things worse.

'May God forgive you,' Liam said. 'Never will I. Come, Moira, let's be getting the clean air.'

On the walk home she said, 'I always knew she hated me but not why.' Lest she say too much she stopped in the path and kissed him. 'What will we do now that we can't be marrying?'

'Nothing, I'm thinking. But I'm wondering if he's really that sick? Sure, we heard the coughing but I was of a mind to walk in his room and see for meself that she wasn't spiting us.'

'Ah, no, it's best you didn't for if Dr Thrush was really here, then it's bad he is, poor darling.' They walked on in silence through the darkening trees. 'Liam — there's a way we could marry like folk in America do when there's no holy man to help. It was Sally told me.'

'How?' he asked. 'What? I'm thinking there's dozens of priests in New York.'

'Not there,' she said, 'out in the country where there's them Red Indians and all. When people love each other they makes a promise and has a Bible to touch and they're married as good as if a priest done it. And when a priest do go through that land, then he ties it up proper.'

He shook his head. 'That must be a Blackmouth way.'

'But it's a way.'

'We have no Bible to touch.'

'True for you,' she said, 'but we have each other to promise.'

'Aye.' He kissed her. 'I promise you.'

'That's not the way Sally told of. You go to the church if there is one, and you promise there.'

'Then it's to the church we'll go,' he said, 'and this very night.'

Bright leaves were gusting the darkness as they walked back toward the abbey, and their feet crisped the leaves of its garden. Old and desolate it looked in the far shine of candles from the parsonage, and bats flew up and the river wind was cold.

Liam pushed at the massive door. 'It's locked,' he said. 'My God, it's never been locked before.'

'It'll be because the cold's coming and roadlings trying to sleep here.'

'It's not Father Leary's way to do that.'

'It's like Eileen to be getting his key and him not knowing.'

They paused at the door. 'Maybe if we just touch the church,' she asked, 'while we promise?'

'Aye.' He took her free hand. 'I promise to be your husband, Moira McFlaherty.'

'Wait,' she said, 'it's rings we're needing.'

She bent and plucked grass blades, twining them on his finger, then on hers. 'Keep this in your pocket, always, Liam, for it grew on holy ground. Now, touch the church with me.'

She tried to remember the words of long-ago weddings. 'In health and in sickness, for good and for worse . . . I promise you, Liam Lenihan, to be your wife till I die.'

They took their hands from the door and kissed, hearing the mourn of the wind from the river and the sigh of the shedding oaks. And in silence they walked the red carpet of the leaves.

Part Two

I am like the solitary tree which stands at the end of the road
Giving shadow to the wolves.

Gypsy lament

Chapter 8

With Liam gone the light left Moira's days but it was a glad thing when Father Leary recovered, and some said a miracle. In late November he was back celebrating Mass and hearing confessions. And in the darkness of the abbey Moira told him of her sin with Liam and how, because of his illness, they had married themselves.

This angered him for he said such a marriage was mockery, and she could not remember so terrible a scolding.

'And is there anything else you'd be telling me, Moira?'

The sternness of his voice frightened her into blurting her hatred and fear of Eileen and all that had happened between them. 'I think it's love for yourself makes her jealous of anybody you been good to and wild as that mad dog I lied about.'

Coldly, he said, 'We'll not be discussing the feelings of Miss Finnigan, but yours. You must snatch the hate from your heart and forgive her. You must make her your friend.'

'I can't be taming a mad woman.'

'You must try. For that is to be your penance for the marriage mock. And you will start today — now — for it's her time off and she in her cabin.'

'But I dare not!'

'You must.'

'And must I be telling her I confessed to you about her attacking me?'

'No, cleanse it from your mind and make her your friend.'

'But what on earth shall I be saying to her?'

'Pray as you go and the words will come to you.'

She had to obey him but she was trembling long before she crossed the woods from the wooden bridge and though she tried hard to pray her thoughts were a jumble. Nearing Bridget's cabin she thought, I might just stop off for a word with her now I know Liam don't love her. Besides, it was as well that Bridget and Tyrone knew where she was in case of trouble. Eileen's cottage was not far and perhaps a scream could be heard.

It was a gaunt grey day, the woods hushed and queer-like and she was cheered to see smoke puffing from Bridget's roof. As she went to the door it opened and Bridget came out with a broom, chasing the leaves outside.

'Oh!' she said, startled. 'I didn't hear your steps. Come in and be warmed.'

Moira followed her in and sat on a rock near the fire.

'Himself is out hunting,' Bridget said, and she must have sensed Moira's disappointment for she said, 'Were you wanting to see him?'

'Well — no. I just come by to visit on me way to Eileen's.'

Bridget's glossy brows rose. 'I didn't think you'd be after visiting *her*.'

'It's a penance,' Moira said. 'I told Father Leary I hate her and now I must go and be friends with her.'

'Och, but she's a bad one, always after insulting people.'

'Aye, it's scared I am of her.' Impulsively she told Bridget about the attack in the woods.

'My God!' Bridget said. 'Well, I'm not meaning to say Father Leary is wrong but I think the hell he is. The penance is terrible dangerous. He never troubled Tyrone and myself so hard, and we living in sin. Maybe he keeps on hoping we'll marry and make it right.'

'But you won't?'

'Not meself. I'm clinging to Tyrone for the hunger of food, not for love. And if ever times change I know I'll be leaving him and it's not right to marry knowing that.'

'But if there be a child?'

'Praise the saints I've been lucky and these days Tyrone isn't so much for loving as for sleeping nights.'

It was queer to be talking so nice and intimate with her old rival. 'Would you have married Liam?'

Bridget smiled. 'I would that, but I give up hope a long time past. It's you he loved, not meself. I was only for his — flirting.'

It was another word she meant, Moira thought, but the pain of it was small for no matter what the priest said, she felt herself Liam's wife.

'Bridget,' she said, 'you and me can be friends now, can't we?'

'We can that, and truly.'

'It's me was jealous of you,' Moira said. My God, she thought, I've done nothing but confess this whole morning. 'You were — are — so pretty.'

'Once, maybe. But I lost me figure to the hunger.'

'You still have them black curls and eyes.'

'It's your red hair I'd be wanting.'

They laughed and then Moira said, 'I must tell somebody so I'll tell you . . .' And she confided her marriage to Liam.

Bridget understood and the warmth of that was a grand thing to feel. But now Moira must go and she rose reluctantly.

'Shall I be going to Eileen's with you or maybe waiting just outside?'

The offer was tempting but she shook her head. 'Eileen mustn't be guessing we're friends or she'd hurt you too.'

'But how will I be knowing you're safe?'

'I'll come back this way on me way home. If I'm not here in an hour then I'm not safe.'

They kissed. 'God keep you,' Bridget said. 'And maybe Jesus will be to home.'

But he was not. It was Eileen who came to the door, a jar in her hand and her eyes cloudy from the drink.

'So it's you,' she said.

'Aye.' Please God, might the right words come. 'I'm here to be

241

asking your pardon if ever I hurt you. Can I come in?'

'It's me curiosity says you can, not me longing for your company.' She motioned Moira in and shut the door against the whirl of leaves.

Moira stood near the door in case of need. 'I'm come,' she said, 'to tell I never loved any man but Liam — I mean, hot love — and you were wrong to believe Father Leary ever give me a thought but for the good of me soul.'

She paused, uneasy of Eileen's queer, set smile and her silence.

'Now that pink china and the roses set out for tea, they were for me mother, not meself, he thought her a real good woman.' My God, she thought, the words are coming fast but mostly lies. 'When me mother died he told me she was close to a saint. And if he ever told you I was beautiful, well, he was meaning me mother's spirit.'

Still the smile and the silence of Eileen as she stood near the loft ladder.

'Well, so that night when you saw me dressed up to meet Liam you took it all wrong and I'd no time to be explaining before we was fighting and me hurt bad.'

Eileen drank from the jar.

'Before God, Eileen Finnigan, I never meant any harm to you. The truth's between us on that.'

Still silence.

'And now, Eileen, I have no more to say but that I'd be friends if you would.'

Eileen spoke like the slash of the blue silk in the woods. 'Aye? Friends with a mad dog?'

Now how had she heard that? Surely not from Liam. Blast and damn the rattling tongue of someone!

Moira moved a step toward the door. 'I never called you no dog.'

'Not to me face. But you told your brother Sean who told Jesus — so I know.'

'Faith, I had to make up some lie since you said never to tell on you so I thought up this wild dog —'

Eileen set the jar on the ladder. 'Moira McFlaherty, you'll not come crawling here again with your lies and your pious look.

242

Mad, am I? But not so out of me wits not to know what you know.'

Moira was at the door. 'And what is that?'

'That some day I'll be killing you.'

She was panicked as she fled to Bridget's house where she was soothed and petted. And then when Tyrone came in with a squirrel in his bag Bridget said the most beautiful thing that Moira ever heard: 'Tyrone, here's Missus Liam Lenihan who's for staying to eat.'

Moira's family ate the oats Liam had left but they went so fast, even stretched with the pond greens. Liam had said his parents would help her but though she went to see them each week no help was offered and she saw that they had little for themselves.

As the raw cold came, so came the old sickness and the stomach cramps and the tiredness, the dismal sameness of crawling through the days. And then one morning Moira awakened to the sound of rain and Granny had gone.

Moira searched the woods and, suspecting Sean of some prank, begged and threatened him to confess but he said he'd last seen Granny asleep on her pallet. She believed him because she had to and because the funeral dress was gone. To die in? Where but on holy ground? Yet she was not at the abbey nor could Jesus or Tyrone find her anywhere. In time the pool or the river might rise her but in the long time from December to February the water was still and secret.

And secretly and sadly her going kept them alive, Moira thought, by extending the scant food a little further. But soon a day would come when there was nothing at all but the broth, unless Liam sent money.

Each week she asked Father Leary if there was a letter from America and finally he said, 'Don't you know I'd bring it the minute it comes?'

'But suppose the runner-man comes and you not to home and Eileen gets it and burns it, seeing the mark of the post of America?'

He snapped at her that Eileen was too much on her mind and

that her fear of her was 'unreasonable'. Yet he knew of what had happened that day at Eileen's cottage and of her threat to kill. It seemed he had some queer faith in Eileen like masters have of their beasts. She remembered the farmer who once lived back of Miller's Cave, and he so loyal to his bull he wouldn't chain it, wouldn't believe it would kill a man until it did.

Something had changed Father Leary for sure — the hunger, maybe, and the hard work of trying to help people — for he had sold all his things now to Paddy and his house was as bare as others. He had lost his gentleness too and his eyes held a hard gleam.

Well, she'd never mention Eileen to him again and, as for thinking him her friend, she could no longer. And a sly thought entered her mind that maybe he loved Eileen as a priest should not — why else did he defend her?

Spring, hazy and flower-soft, came early on the winds of March. The lands of Mayo and Galway bloomed pale yellow with cowslips and primroses and the blue cobwebs of harebells. Beyond Ballyfearna The Moor of the Blood — once used for the blood-letting of farmers' stock — had returned to its naked plain, shed and fences crumpled. And scattered through the woods and in the lanes and hedgerows and in the huts the people lay dead or dying or stirred sluggishly. And the roadlings who came to work on the canal fell from weakness, were replaced . . . and re-placed . . . replaced.

Moira awakened at dawn to a strange sort of silence and listened and knew what it was. Cathleen was not crying for food.

She dragged herself from the dregs of sleep and went to the child and saw that she had vomited the broth of last night. The lips were blue. Fearfully she touched the little heart and felt its faint beat.

The boys heard Moira as she moved to dress as quickly as she could.

'I'm hungry,' Sean said from his pallet. 'I've got me pain so bad I can't —'

He began to cry and so did Colum. Her own pain sharp, Moira

said, 'There's nothing to eat and you know it. It's food I'm going out to beg, for Cathleen's dying.'

'Dying.' Sean repeated the word as though it were new.

'Aye, keep her covered and rub her hands. Keep the life in her till I get back.'

Outside she met the dazzle of the flowers and trees. Her head felt queer, like once when she'd had too much poteen, and the springtime spun about her in waves of green. The young leaves spoke softly and somewhere far off there was music.

It was cool in the woods but her forehead dripped sweat and a great thirst was on her. But soon she would reach a well or the house of Annie Dumbie who'd had a whole pig for the wake. Sure some had been saved from last night since Father Leary had broken the frolic early because Liam and Jesus had fought and the corpse been tumbled, and them all in disgrace for the drink.

Aye, Annie would have some pig left, enough for Cathleen and the boys, maybe enough for her parents and Granny and Sally. But she couldn't find her way to Annie's, the path was fey going on the way to Liam's. At Miller's Cave there was a little stream and she knelt and drank and cooled her hot face. Then she rose, shaking the hair from her eyes and there was a great gnarled tree before her and low in its crotch was a nest of eggs in their grassy cup of mud. She would go to Annie's later and take the eggs home now.

On tiptoe she reached them easily and cradled them in her cupped hands. Robins' eggs, bluer than the sky and all about her was the flower of the gardens. The pratie plants were white as bridal blossoms and she walking past them, Liam's bride in blue silk trimmed with violets.

She found her way home singing for the joy in her and as she came to the house by the pool she heard the dogs, Two and Three, growling and arguing as always they did and she smiled at their silly old ways for they were only playing.

Carefully she put all five eggs into one hand and opened the door to the house and saw Sean and Colum at Cathleen and heard their growling and dropped the eggs and stared.

'*No!*' she said, and moved to stop them. 'For the love of God —'

245

But then her senses came back and she willed herself to walk to the door and close it. Outside she sat on the grass and licked the broken eggs from her hand.

It was Bridget who found her hours later, staring into the pool, spent of tears, and she told her what had happened.

'I'll not go in to that house ever again,' she said.

'But you must. They'll be needing you more than ever they did. And it's all beyond sin, I'm thinking, for they couldn't help it and you did right.'

Bridget said to her silence, 'She'd maybe have died anyway. You did what you had to for the good of the living. Now I'm going to the canal and meet Tyrone and bring him back and he'll find out a way to help you. And if anybody comes by before we're here, why, you just keep them out of the house, that's all. Tell them Cathleen's in fever.'

She touched Moira's forehead. 'And it's yourself too, I'm thinking. I'll bring you a quilt.'

'No!' Moira called as Bridget turned to go into the house. 'You can't be going in there!'

But she was already in, and then out with the quilt, face ashen, voice a whisper. 'They're asleep. Now, wrap in this and keep warm.' She put the ragged wool over Moira. 'Stay quiet, alanna. Stay quiet till we're back.'

Moira heard her footsteps go and lay rigid. Pray, she told herself, for them and for yourself. But prayer was not in her, only a nothingness. She thought, I passed prayer a long time ago. It's only words, after all, and Him not hearing anyway. And a mockery worse than me marriage.

Oddly, she felt the need of water on her body and slipped out of her bodice and skirt and went into the pool. Shivering, she came out of it and wrapped herself in the old quilt and lay there until Bridget and Tyrone came to her.

'Me cart is gone,' Tyrone said, 'and me pots and pans and all I had. But I have something left and that's the things I learned when I travelled this land and I heard stories — history they called it — if the stories are old. Moira, this isn't the first time it

246

happened for it happened before in time of the hunger and it's happening now, only nobody talks of it. They keep it all secret. It wasn't little Jack O'Ryan drowned. He was —'

'Hush,' Bridget said, 'don't you be telling her that.'

'It's only to be comforting her, the way she won't feel so alone. Now I'm going to bury Cathleen in the woods and let it be known she died of the fever, and tomorrow folks can come and pray with Father Leary at the grave. I'll send the boys out here.'

Bridget saw her wince. 'You must face them, alanna, and they you.'

'Not now.' She turned to Tyrone. 'Tell them I'll be walking in the woods with Bridget a while. And don't let them be expected at the funeral, just tell folk they're too grieved and sick, too.'

He nodded and went inside and she and Bridget took a path toward the wooden bridge.

Later she forced herself to return to the house alone. She could not speak to the boys, nor they to her, and they avoided one another's glance. As night fell she made a stick fire and in silence they went to their pallets and lay down.

Her bed was closest to the fire and she lay there watching the light bloom and the shadows dance on the ceiling. The little house she had loved so much was ruined for her now. If only she could go to Liam, alone, without her brothers . . . And where was Liam now and how was he living? Poor, maybe, but surely not too poor for the cost of a letter. He'd send it even if he thought Father Leary had died of the cough, he would know it would come to her somehow for the bishop always sent runner-men to the parish.

'Moira.' Sean's hand was on her hair, and he so quiet she had not heard him rise from his pallet. 'Moira, oh, talk to me! Please be saying something, anything. I know what we done was terrible and it was me begun it. It was me.'

She lay silent.

His kiss brushed her hand. 'Only I never meant to. She was there dead . . . I knew she was and Colum, he knew too. We — had to.'

247

She caught his hand and held it.

'It was me who . . . but I never hurt Granny. That bird, it lit on me arm, it was queer some way, for I never knew a bird to do that before. She screamed and I crushed it and showed her it was nothing, only like a little bug but then she runs in the house as queer as that bird was.'

Her hand tightened on his.

'I never meant to scare her. And when you wasn't around I'd try to tell her so, the way she'd talk again but she never did. And Moira, I had nothing to do with her leaving here.'

His tears burst on to her hand. 'I love you.'

She sat up then and took him into her arms and held him tight, tighter. If his thin body was hurt he seemed to want that and snuggled close, closer in the mix of their tears.

'Darling,' she said finally, 'as you're man of the house I'm asking you what to do. We can't be staying here now.'

'No. There's nights I hear moaning, like Granny.'

'That's only a owl, like sad-sighing women. But we must leave here anyway.'

He drew back, manlike and full of thought. 'But where?'

'To Liam, in America. To a ship from Galway Port. If I ask Paddy at dark o' the moon when the good is in him likely he'll cart us there. We can't be walking twenty-five miles.'

'Colum can't.'

'No.'

'I could.'

'None of us can. But somehow we must go.'

Colum awakened suddenly with a soft scream as though roused from nightmare. 'Hush, now,' she said, 'and come here to us.'

He ran to them, nearly upsetting them in his need to be close, and she held them both, patting at Colum's tears, soothing him, and thinking, My God, the three of us can't get close enough, locked so deep in love it aches like the hunger.

'Now promise me something,' she said. 'I'll be telling you about Cathleen's funeral tomorrow, and what Father Leary will say over the grave. But after that we'll never be speaking of her again. Promise.'

They promised.

Then Sean said, 'Colum, as man of the house I say we're going to leave here and go to Galway Port and take a ship to America where Liam is.'

Colum smiled and the new dream was bright in his eyes.

It was a sad day, with the funeral in the woods, but Bridget brought comfort. Maybe it wasn't nice to be thinking sin of Bridget but how on earth did she wheedle a bag of oats out of Paddy — and why bring them at night while Tyrone slept?

Moira went to Father Leary and told him that Paddy had agreed to cart her and the boys to Galway Port. (She did not add that Jesus' poteen had encouraged the enterprise.) If a letter came from Liam, please to hold it until she had someone write to him. Only of course she'd be seeing Liam in New York, maybe before any letter came.

'You're daft to leave here,' he said. 'The ships are full to bursting. You have two boys and not a penny for fare.'

'Ah, but I'll cook me way over and the boys are sharp, they'll do whatever a ship's needing.'

He begged her not to go, warned her that New York was so big she'd never find Liam, it would be like searching a pebble in a haystack. But she was going no matter what he said, and finally he blessed her and — my God! — gave her half a sovereign.

There were the sad goodbyes to Jesus and Mary, Bridget and Tyrone and Liam's parents. But, on the day they left, the sun smiled down and the white clouds puffed like featherbeds. Somehow the little house by the pool seemed innocent as long ago, twined in the sweetness of its roses. She looked back at it from Paddy's cart and thought, I'll return here after all. Some day, with Liam.

A sadness to leave but hope, too, and pride in the way the boys had turned men, watching to see that the pans and quilts, roped together with Da's robe and the feathered slippers, were secure to the gait of the horse. Over the wooden bridge they rattled, past the priest's garden. There stood Eileen hanging out clothes on the line. She turned at the sound of the horse's hoofs and called out something Moira could not hear. As well, she thought, for it's surely no blessing but a curse.

Then they were on the High Street and here was a surprise with those friends not on the canal gathered to see them off. Mary and Bridget and Mrs Lenihan and Biddy outside the hotel, and Dennis lifting up jars for the road, big ones for herself and Paddy, wee ones for the boys.

'We'll be back,' Moira said, knowing it so. 'You'll be finding us back in me house some day.'

She saw Bridget's startlement. 'Aye,' she said to the warm black eyes that held tears, 'I'm thinking it's a fine house after all. Liam, he'll be fixing the roof.'

'It is a fine house,' Bridget said, standing very straight, 'and it's me will be keeping the woods out of it.'

'You'll be sending word from America?' Mrs Lenihan said, 'word of me son?'

'I will that.'

Mary said, 'I hear people gets sick in them ships since them ships run in storms and gets theirselves messed up in tides and all. So here —' she handed up a bottle. 'It's medicine made of me own herbs and willow.'

'Moira!' Bridget brought up a larger bottle. 'Jesus give me this for you if it's cold on the boat. And me — I have nothing so grand to give but the kiss o' me heart.'

'That's grander, even.'

'We must be getting on,' Paddy said, sour by daylight as always, and handed down the empty jars to Dennis.

'To Galway Port,' Sean said, as man of the house. 'You know the way?'

'I only been there fifteen times,' said Paddy, sarcastic. 'But maybe you'll be showing me?'

He started up the thin old horse and blessings followed them, old and lovely as the tired country they travelled. *May the wind always be at your back and the road rise with you, and may you always lie in the hollow of God's hand.*

A new smell, the smell of the sea, the tar and the salt of Galway Port. They entered it by the water road and Moira said, 'Paddy! Look! Ships!'

250

'Ships?' He spat. 'Them's only little cockleshell boats for the fishing. Ships are big as hills and them ships don't be coming every day here.'

He could not blunt her excitement, her hope. 'Tomorrow, then.'

'Do you know what they call them ships?'

'Boats?' she asked.

'Coffins. Coffin ships. They're not safe. Half the folk they take out die on the way. They bury as many as land.'

But he could not tarnish the gold of her happiness. 'They're old, we're young and thanks to Bridget and yourself, we have oats in us.'

He flushed. 'Those two should marry, Bridget and Tyrone. It's not right the way they live.'

'Nor you and Mary neither.' Happiness — this great adventure and this great sun and sea emboldened her. 'It's Mary loves you, Paddy. She'd never say so, proud as she is but she does, for even if you're not so good by day there's something grand comes over you by night.'

'It's me nemesis,' Paddy said.

'You're not sick, Paddy Nolan, or Mary'd be knowing of it. But if you *were* sick, she'd be nursing you right to your grave and well you know it.' She turned again to look at the sea. 'It's the biggest river ever I saw!' And she roused the sleeping boys to watch the fishermen spread their nets on the quays and to see the sweep of the gulls.

Then they came to the heart of town, bigger than Ballyfearna and Ballydonny put together. Paddy slowed the horse because there was so much on the road — horse cars carrying their passengers back to back, with the sea breeze whirling their scarves and shawls, and donkey carts and men riding mules and all along the yellow dust rising. It was a town of yellow, Moira thought, even the houses that colour with the roofs going out at queer angles and stairs climbing the outside walls. Gardens were full of daffodils and yellow mud under the cool of the trees.

'I never saw so much yellow,' Moira said.

Paddy spat from the side of the cart. 'A long times ago, so they say, some Spanish people got spilled out of a ship and settled here. And they made this town like the towns in Spain, which is yellow, with funny kinds of houses as you see.'

Yellow were the markets, too, painted that way, and the vendors with fish that they brought and flapped in your face. Sixpence they wanted for the big ones and Paddy said, 'No!' and Sean echoed 'No!' and ducked the tail of one. There was something strange about this street, Moira thought; no, it was the people on it, not creeping about as they did at home but walking upright and brisk. Aye, most were thin but it was the thinness of poverty, not hunger.

Paddy drove on to a road that went uphill where it was quieter and asked a woman on the path where could a family be staying until a ship came in?

Her eyes, half-hidden by her shawl, were kindly. 'You mean, for paying?'

'I have half a sovereign,' Moira said, 'till a ship comes in.'

'Don't you be telling you have a penny,' the woman said, 'or robbed you'll be.' She motioned uphill. 'There's a hotel up there where the sign has a pig on it dancing a jig. Maybe they'd let you sleep on the floor if you work.'

'I'll work!' Moira said.

'But I'm not knowing if they'd feed you. They're queer women, Mrs Calicoe and Mrs Milks. Sisters they are, widow women who hate each other. Maybe one would be taking to you and the other not. But there's likely plenty of work with all the people in there waiting for the ship.'

'And when is it coming?' Sean asked.

The woman shrugged. 'Nobody's knowing.'

They gave her thanks and a good day and moved on up the hill. 'Now don't be talking of your money,' Paddy said, 'just be asking to work.'

The hotel was big and its sagging porch was thick with the ivy of years. Windows stared out like goblin eyes above a sprawl of unkempt gardens. A lovely smell came from the chimney — fish.

'Mind,' Paddy said, as Moira and the boys climbed down from the cart, 'don't be talking hungry. Roadlings aren't welcome anywhere, so you must seem proud. And if they don't have work then you must stay here tonight and pay what you must, and tomorrow —'

'What?' Moira asked.

'Sleep on the beach and wait for the ship there. You have your quilts and you'll find driftwood for making a fire and maybe you can buy tackle cheap . . . Now get along with you.'

Moira thanked Paddy for his kindness and reached up to clasp his hand. 'God and Mary willing we'll be back to home some day.'

Something like pain flickered over his face and he started to speak, then nodded. She and the children stood in the brown tangle of bushes, waving as he turned his horse and was gone.

'I'm hungry,' Colum said, sniffing the fish.

'Hush,' Sean said, 'you heard Paddy. We can't be seeming like them roadlings.'

But we look like them, Moira thought, ragged and barely patched together, dirty, with wind-tossed hair. As they carried their bundles up the steps to the porch she said, 'Now look proud, and smile.'

A tall woman of about thirty answered their knock and opened the door a few inches. She was grey-eyed, grey-faced, shawled in black over a dingy black petticoat.

'Well?' she said warily.

'We're from Ballyfearna,' Moira said, 'and we come to wait for the ship, me brothers and me. Is it work you'd be having for me? I'm strong, and we have oats, so we're not after begging.'

The smell of the frying fish teased the saliva to Moira's mouth. 'We just want a place to sleep and to cook our oats. Are you Mrs Calicoe, Ma'am?'

'I am not.' The grey eyes stormed. 'I'd not have that sin on me soul. It's Mrs Milks I am and there's no room here. We have more than a hundred people lying in there with beds for twenty.'

'But sure you need help looking after them?'

'Them that's strong enough helps.' She measured Moira's slenderness, shook her head at the little boys. 'You do be looking like pond reeds. And don't be lying to me about your oats, I've heard that story before.'

Sean bent quickly to the quilts, untied them, and held up the precious bag. 'Look, oats they are, and plenty.'

'To last three days,' Mrs Milks said on a sigh. 'It's sorry I am but you can't stay here for God knows when the ship comes and we haven't a spare inch on the floor.'

The door flew wide and another woman stood there, pretty in a dark way but haggard and fierce-eyed. 'What's this, and the wind coming in?' She slammed the door and stood outside with them. 'What's it you're wanting, girl?'

'Now that's a mad question,' Mrs Milks said, 'what else but work and shelter and I told 'em we have none, and to go.'

'*You* told 'em? It's half me hotel, is it not? My, who's the high and mighty one turning away people into the wind.'

'They're roadlings, and you know it.'

'*Are* they, now?' She looked at the bag Sean held. 'No roadlings have oats, and the girl looks strong as a ox.'

Moira blessed her for the lie. 'I am strong, Ma'am.' She decided to trust this savage gypsy-looking woman. 'And we have a shilling, too.'

'Ah,' said Mrs Milks, 'then why didn't you be saying so before?'

'Because she has sense,' the dark woman said. She turned to Moira. 'I'm Mrs Calicoe. Come in and be welcome to me hotel.'

Mrs Milks bristled. 'It's *me* hotel.'

'I'm sure there's two sides to any hotel,' Moira said tactfully.

'True for you,' said Mrs Calicoe, 'with a eternal rope between, and you'll work on me side of it.'

She swept them through the door into what seemed darkness. Then as her eyes adjusted, Moira saw a few oil lamps set dimly into the far corners of a large room carpeted by people.

'Mind how you step over them,' Mrs Calicoe said. 'We wouldn't want to be waking them.'

Families lay clasped on the floor, seemingly asleep, but there were open eyes, too, and a little stir of sitting up and staring. Mrs Calicoe led the McFlahertys up a left side staircase and at the top were more people, and still more visible through the shadows beyond. It was then that Moira saw the rope which divided the house swinging from a roof beam.

'You always stay to this side,' Mrs Calicoe said, 'for it's me own. Now up there's a loft.' She moved carefully over a huddle of bodies and picked up a candle-dip. 'I'll hold it here at the ladder the way you can see your way up. And when you've got your fardel there, girl, you leave your boys to sleep and come down to the kitchen, you'll find your way by the smell.'

The loft room was tiny, likely once a hidey-hole for persecuted priests. In its blind darkness Moira fumbled to lay down the quilts and the boys, trying to help, only hindered. Finally she had them bedded, soothed with promise of oats to come, and she took some with her to cook, cradled in her petticoat and it held high. No one would notice her bare legs in the darkness below.

Her journey was slow, down the creaky ladder, over the people, hearing a sigh or a curse as she stepped on someone. Far in a corner folk were singing softly:

> *Come back to Erin, Mavourneen, Mavourneen,*
> *Come back, aroon, to the land of your birth . . .*

Of course she would. But the song was sad, like someone pleading from far away. The ghosts of Grace and the two Cathleens, perhaps of Da and Granny and Sally and those other lost ones who had once been her world.

She reached the steam of the kitchen where a rope swung from a beam between fireplaces that blazed from both ends of the room. Mrs Calicoe turned from a bubbling pot as Moira came up to her.

'I'm ready for work, Ma'am.'

'Good. What's your name?'

Moira told her.

'Shake your oats into that pan, cook them and feed your boys. Then come down and I'll give you a bit of fish for yourself. for it's a long night you'll be working.'

The night seemed endless, feeding those awake, avoiding those asleep, caring not to pass beyond the rope of Mrs Calicoe. At midnight, after the other four servants had retired, Mrs Calicoe offered a little jar of poteen which she and Moira shared by the fire.

'You can sleep till five, Moira. Then you work again till star-time . . . When a ship comes, how do you plan to be going on it?'

Moira's eyes were heavy with sleep. 'To cook, Ma'am. Or to serve.'

Mrs Calicoe sighed. 'You can try at the shipmaster's when the time comes but . . . never mind, you've my blessing. And if the ship won't take you, you can stay here till one does.'

'You are good,' Moira said, half asleep.

'Most of me good is just to spite me sister Ollie. Only there's nobody going to win, not as long as we have to share this place. Me father left it to us and he fixed it so's we can't sell it — he thought it would bring us to Christian love. Love!' Her laugh rasped. 'We've been here in hate ever since our husbands died and I can tell you this — it's hate wastes and sickens you like the fever, only the fever ends or kills.'

Moira thought of Eileen. 'At least it's not mad hate. I mean, you must have some reasons.'

'Plenty since childhood. Then she took me man and married him and left me the dregs of Michael O'Hoolity — but that's a long story not fit for a girl's ears.' She paused and looked at Moira's weary face and drooping eyelids. 'Go, sleep. Can you be finding your way in the dark?'

'Aye,' Moira said, 'I'll be finding me way.'

Rumor had it that the ship was in and at dawn hundreds of people left hotels and rooming houses to crowd the shed of the shipping agent, waiting to beg or pay passage to America. But he was not there and Galway Bay was bleak of all but fishing boats and floating gulls. Along the shore rose the soft mourn of shivering people. Wearily they returned to their lodgings but most were rejected, for a new wave of roadlings had come. Gradually the beach covered with men and women and crying children who had no quilts but locked bodies for warmth in a vast embrace against the night cold of the sea.

'Why were we told the ship was in?' Moira asked, thankful to return to the safety of the hotel.

Mrs Calicoe said, 'It's those criminals banded together own the lodgings and the other hotels. They want out the ones who can't pay, and so they trick them with hope of the ship. It happens once a week, but each time I'm believing of it or I'd not have let you go.'

'Then may a curse be on those landlords.'

'It's queer you should say that, for cursed they are. In '46 the Cullin's Hotel was cursed by a old woman who lived there. They roused her at six of the day and hurried her out, saying a ship was there and she, sick with the fever, ran her old bones two miles to find it was all a lie. When she got back to Cullin's they thrust her out, knowing she'd worn out her pennies.

'She stood at that locked door and cursed them, them and all their descendants and everyone heard . . . Nobody knows what happened to that old woman, for she wandered off. But the Cullins, these scant years, have fared in queer ways. Joseph Cullin was rich on cheating but he died in a fire at Kinvarra with all his money on him. His wife, in her sixth month, bore a monster and killed it and herself with a knife. The son, Padraic, of the age of sixteen, hanged himself, and he was the last of them, praise be. Cursed as it was, nobody wanted that hotel. So the roadlings stay there for free as if it was just a barn in the bogs.'

'Then they don't know of the curse on it?'

'Roadlings are grateful for any roof. There's no fires now or lamps or candles but it's shelter for the poor and full to bursting and nobody there tricks anybody about the ships. The old woman would have liked that.'

'Aye,' Moira said. 'It was a grand curse.'

'Makes you sure of God,' said Mrs Calicoe.

Rainy days later as Moira was stoking the fires for breakfast Mrs Calicoe hurried into the kitchen with a fardel of fish.

'The ship's in. I saw it myself.'

'Holy Mary! Does it go today?'

'No, it will unload and bide a bit. Now, get tidy and run to the shed fast as you can and tell Mr Fogarty — he's the ship-agent, and me friend — that I said you were a good cook, and strong. If he signs you on, don't be mentioning the boys but pay your shilling to somebody at the gate for them when people be going aboard. Then they'll be part o' the crowd and the man tipped won't be saying anything.'

Moira thanked her, jerked off her apron, combed her hair and snatched up the fragment of quilt that served as her shawl. At least she wasn't bare like some women she saw in the streets with only a strip to hide their breasts. Hawkers were trying to sell them bits of blanket as cover, but few could buy. Like herself they were running, a brown-black tide — here a red petticoat, there a bonnet, but mostly just scarecrows running with their children past the tip-tilted yellow houses, through the yellow rain-swollen mud. Their men carried boxes, bundles, carpet bags, and she marvelled to see a few goats and pigs, and my God, a chair, a black stove, a table. Even the rich were off to America . . .

A guard kept order at the shed, or tried to, but as the crowd swelled he was joined by two more who used canes to rap the people into line. From her place Moira could see the great wooden ship lying at anchor and dock hands removing its cargo. Cotton and grain, people said, but who could tell from the long distance, and the sailormen black dots through the rain?

The line inched through the mud of morning into the mud of noon. And then she was in the shed sniffing the oil lamp that burned above a big table where a man sat perched on a high stool with a pen in his hand and a heap of papers before him.

'Mister Fogarty?' she asked, as her turn came.

'Aye.' He scarcely glanced at her. 'Seventy-five shillings it is, paid now, not including food or water. Forty days at sea. You've a family?'

'No, sir,' she said, 'but I can't —'

He thrust a paper at her. 'Make your cross here.'

Bewildered, she asked, 'What's a cross?'

'You can't write, can you?'

'No, sir. But I was wanting to say —'

'The cross marks your name. Now, do you want to sail or don't you?'

258

He looked at her with such impatience that she shrivelled, nearly lost her voice, finally found it. 'I can't be paying those shillings, sir. I want to work me way over as cook. Mrs Calicoe at the hotel told me to tell Your Honour I cook just grand.'

'Steerage passengers cook their own food.'

'Then I'll do anything, anything, sir.'

He was silent for a time, staring at her. 'Anything, you said?'

'Aye, sir, that I would.'

He shrugged, lit a pipe, pointed a thumb at the door. 'Go in there and wait.'

She went to the door, entered a small room to find a pretty girl of her own age sitting on a bench. They waited, not smiling, not speaking, and Moira sensed that they were rivals for the work. Pray God this blonde was fragile as she looked, and stupid . . .

A small bull-chested man opened a door and called, 'Next.'

The blonde went in. The door closed.

Another girl came in and seated herself near Moira. Pretty, too, with bright brown hair spilling over the rags of her bodice.

Ten minutes passed. The door opened. 'Next.'

Moira went into a wood-panelled room lit by candles. The bull-chested man in a tight blue coat with brass buttons was sitting in the one chair. He was about forty, she thought, bearded darkly, with harsh, scarred skin. Ugly . . .

'So what's it you're willing to do on this voyage, miss?' he asked.

'I hear you don't be needing cooks, sir, but I'd scrub or serve or anything.'

The corners of his full lips lifted, the blue eyes married. 'That's what they all say — anything.'

'But I'm meaning it, Your Honour.'

'The voyage may be rough.'

'That don't matter, sir.'

'Just give you an apron, eh?'

'Oh, yes, sir!'

'But I'm not liking aprons on women.' He pointed to a wooden screen. 'Go behind there and put on the clothes you see.'

Well, she would wear anything he wished, and a maid's clothes would surely be grand. She remembered the old days at Dennis' hotel and how the girls wore red petticoats and starched white collars.

Behind the screen on a stool were dark blue garments — breeches and a woollen jacket. She looked around; there were no others.

'Your Honour,' she called, peeping out, 'these are for a man.'

'Put them on, or go.'

She removed her rags and put on the clothes, feeling foolish and bewildered. But if this was what maidservants wore on ships, why then . . .The jacket was too big, the breeches too tight, as if made for a slender boy.

Blushing, she stepped out.

'That's better,' he said. 'Come here. Let's see how they fit.'

His hands swept over her hips and thighs. One finger poked up her rectum. She lurched away but he spun her around, laughing as she spat at him.

'So,' he said, releasing her so suddenly that she fell. 'You don't want to be my cabin boy, eh?'

She stumbled to her feet and ran sobbing behind the screen, changed clothes and hurried past him to the door.

'Not that way,' he said good-humouredly, 'the other door.'

As she fled to it she heard him cross the room and call, 'Next.'

Outside she was in the rubble of the docks, of tar and rope and overturned barrels, boards splintering her bare feet. And there was the great brown ship that would sail without her, bobbing in the rainy water.

'Looking for someone, miss?'

She turned, startled, but it was only a boy, grinning and friendly.

'You can get lost in this mess,' he said.

She dabbed at her tear-stained eyes. 'Do you be knowing of any way a girl can get aboard to work over?'

He shook his head. 'I'm not crew. I only work the quay.'

'Do you know where the captain would be, then?'

He pointed back to the room she had left. 'He's in there.'

'Oh, no! Was it him I — dark and little with a beard on him?'

'That's him.'

Hopelessly she turned and left him, trudging back through the mud, back through the people that crowded the shed, back toward the hotel. As she started up the hill she saw a tall man coming down and screamed, for sure as hell it was the ghost of Danel Powderley, the Protestant poet, who had wandered from Ballyfearna so long ago.

'Moira!' The voice was real and the clasp of the long, thin hands on hers. 'Moira McFlaherty, whatever are you doing here?'

She stammered his name, incoherent with surprise, joy, relief.

'Come,' he said, 'come to me little house, it's not a throw from here.'

This was a further marvel — he had a house, and it by the sea. An egg shell of a house made of bits of boards and crates. Only one room but a shelter from storm, and his very own.

'Now,' he said, when they were cosy inside sitting on barrels, 'I'll brew you some tea and we'll be talking."

Tea! One should not question heaven, and more heaven of a bit of bread and butter. But naturally suspicious of Protestants she asked, 'Did you steal it, Danel?'

He laughed. 'In me way, I did — from the feelings of people. Here did I come seeking a ship to America but they needed no man over fifty so I starved near a year, begging of beggars. And then I thought of the sad poetry of leaving Ireland and what would appeal to folk who would never see these shores again. Something to make and to sell.'

'What?' she asked.

'Sod. Sod in boxes with a shamrock on top.' He rose and went to a pile of things in the corner. 'Here's one.'

She handled it — a thin little thing but full of real sod and the shamrock marked on in paint. 'It's beautiful.'

'And here's the poem goes with it.'

'I can't read, Danel.'

'No matter, it's not a good poem but it makes them cry. Lucky it is that God rhymes with sod. Anyway, the box and poem sell for threepence, which is tuppence profit . . . Now tell me of yourself.'

She told him all that had happened since she left Ballyfearna. 'And today that terrible captain . . .'

He comforted. There would be other captains of other ships.

261

Meanwhile she and the boys must leave the hotel and live with him here and make the little boxes and learn to paint on the shamrocks.

'Oh, dear,' she said, 'I never lived alone with a man. Liam wouldn't be liking it.'

'He'd be understanding. I'm not asking your love, Moira, only the warmth of a family.'

Like a good dog who'd put his great vasty paws on your lap, giving love but not asking it. And protecting . . .

'Well, then, Danel . . . but we'd not wish to be a burden.'

'It would burden me if you went back to that hard work.'

'Then we'll live here.'

She rose and kissed him gently and his curly brown beard brushed her cheek. 'We'll make you a good home, Danel, that I promise. Until another ship comes,' she added, anxious to set it squarely.

'Until a ship comes.'

The ship she could not take sailed with two hundred and sixty aboard, berths for thirty-eight. Steerage passengers, packed togegther on bare boards, clung for warmth and spread disease. Typhus . . . typhoid . . . cholera. Live bodies piled like shrouds against the cold swell of the Atlantic, those dead pushed over the rails.

When storms struck they were battened under hatches, closed from air and light. Rigging rotted, hulls leaked. When their food ran out, people starved. Those few who had animals killed them, ate them raw, fought off the hungry humans and the hungry rats. The voyage took fifty days.

At New York Harbour immigration officers went aboard with camphor handkerchiefs over their noses.

'We're a refuse dump for Ireland,' one said.

'Yes. We've landed thirty per cent dead since 1847.'

'Good at figures, aren't you? Look.' He bent to examine a little girl whose eyes were open. 'How'd she get a brown leaf in her mouth?'

'That's no leaf. It's her tongue.'

262

Ships came and went that winter but there was no passage for Moira. She leaned on the hope that Liam would send money so that she could pay their way but though Danel had written Father Leary the reply came: 'I have not heard from Liam. Be patient and pray and thank God for your haven with Danel . . .'

Moira was thankful, for Danel was patient with her clumsy attempts at making the little boxes and the evening Sean painted a perfect shamrock the family celebrated on Jesus' poteen, and even the boys had a sip.

Cosy it was that night with a driftwood fire in the slanty fireplace and the long sigh of the sea outside.

'A story?' Sean asked, stretching out on the floor at Danel's feet. 'You always tell such good stories.'

'What kind?' Danel asked.

Colum said, 'Something scary.'

'We live scary enough, lad.'

'Then a animal story?'

Danel puffed on his pipe, used only on special occasions. 'Well, it happened in a November of my young manhood. I was felling trees for a laird in that part of Scotland that's called the High Lands because mountains there are.

'November it was, as I said, and me coming back to my hut after a revel in the village. The moon was full so I saw through the dark woods without a lantern. Suddenly I hear this noise in the brush and I stop and I stare.

'There were two deer — bucks they were, with white tails. At first I thought they were fighting, for bucks go mad to mate in rutting time and seek to kill their rivals. They'll even kill a man when the moon-lust is on them. But they weren't fighting now, not even trying to, because their antlers were locked and they were only pushing feebly to get away from each other.

'Seeing them helpless, I came close and knew they'd been at it for days, maybe weeks for the ground was trampled bare. The two were mostly bones, starving to death together, and their eyes were green with agony and their tongues out with the long breathless tiredness of them.

'Now I heard of a man gored when he unlocked the horns of

263

deer and I'm no fool. But in the morning I went there with my gun to put them to peace. One was dead, dragging the other. And the other was fighting ravens from its eyes, and it I killed.'

'Oh, God,' Moira said, 'that's no tale for children.'

'But it's a moral tale — how enemies fighting can finally come to help each other for the simple hope of living. It's said that when a horn-locked buck can reach for leaves of a tree, and eats, then he tries to move the other toward those leaves to keep him alive too.'

'But not from love,' Moira said, 'from fear the ravens will come.'

Danel smiled. 'Who knows for sure? I like to think that in the long struggle a buck's heart goes out to its enemy and understands its pain.'

'Did you kill that raven?' Sean asked.

'It flew off at sight of me.'

'If I was God I'd not make them ravens,' Colum said.

'God knew ravens keep the woods from rot, lad, and the fields too.'

'How is your God different from ours?' Moira asked shyly.

'He doesn't need saints,' Danel said, 'or images. Only faith . . .'

Queer Protestant talk, she thought. And as the weeks passed she learned more of Danel's queerness. He loved them as a family, she was sure, but rarely was he home. At the day's end when he had sold his boxes he ate quickly and was out to walk on the seashore no matter what the weather and was out again at dawn. Sometimes he brought in things swept to the beach — bits of wood which he made into a bench; a jar of green glass, a broom handle, a keg of sour wine, a rusted knife. It wasn't queer to seek treasure but it was to cherish some crazy old shell and peer into it and listen to it as if it had some message for him no one else could know or hear.

Gradually she came to know his moods; never to intrude when he was silent in thought, never to ask where he was going when, after one late walk, he set out on another. Restless he was, that was all, and a poet to whom the sea was like the hearing of Mass.

Gradually, painfully, she realised that his moods were because of her, that he loved her as a lover. He gave her the beloved shell

264

and made her a bracelet of others, spending hours in the fashioning. He bought her a petticoat — second hand, he said — but she knew it was unworn. He lied too about the bodice which he claimed he'd found in the sea. It was wet, but it had no salt marks. Shyly he gave his gifts, gently she accepted them. And to prevent his building on dreams, she spoke of her love for Liam.

Liam who did not send word. Was he dead then in some pauper's field of America? Five months it was, and no letter and her heart was stiff with fear, her mind afraid to think. She kept busy, gathering sod and making the boxes, cleaning, cooking, searching the beach for firewood. On Sundays she and the boys went to the Catholic Church on the hill and afterwards she called on Mrs Calicoe for a bit of gossip, always interrupted by the needs of the hotel guests.

In the spring Danel taught the boys to fish, but secretly, for they had no money for a licence and the port fishermen would beat anyone caught poaching in their waters. And so there was food that spring.

In May came a letter from Liam written by a parish priest from a place called Killala.

'But that's in Ireland!' Danel said when he saw the mark.

'Praise God! And read it to me.'

'Dear Miss McFlaherty,' he read, 'I am to inform you that your friend Liam Lenihan has only this half sovereign to send you, having also to help his parents but he will send more as he can. He says to tell you he is well and waiting for a ship to America as he could not get one from Galway Port, He is working on the docks and expects to ship out any time now. He sends you his love. Sincerely yours, Michael Maurice McClafferty (Rev.)'

He sends you his love. 'Read it again, Danel.'

He did so. 'Written April second. It's been a long time traveling.'

'Aye,' she sighed, 'if I'd only known he was here in Ireland I'd have gone there. But now he's likely on a ship.'

'Don't be sad, alanna.' He rose to give her the coin but it fell from her hands.

'Here,' he said, 'you must put this away. In time he'll send you more so you can go to America too.'

265

Sean and Colum sensed her despair and sat quietly, watching Danel place the money in her hands.

'Save this?' she asked 'Why should I, then? I'll spend it this day.'

'Ah, no —'

But a dark wild mood was on her. 'It's poteen I'll buy and bacon and candles and a ribbon for me hair.'

'A green ribbon,' Sean said.

'Red for her hair,' Colum said.

Danel frowned and told the boys to go out and gather wood. Alone with Moira he sat by her feet and took her hand.

'You're not yourself, alanna. You should be glad for Liam's caring. Likely he's little money for himself.'

'Money!' she spat the word. 'What do I care for it? It's what he didn't say, about us being married and someday together in America. The important things . . . but that letter's cold as snow.'

'It's the priest wrote it, formal as clergymen do. It's not Liam's fault.'

'No?' She looked down at him, her hand limp in his. 'If he'd said to that priest what he should, that priest would have written it down like the Bible, aye, that he would have. But —' Her voice crumpled, 'Liam had no more to say.'

'He's young. Maybe he misunderstands women, that's all.'

But you understand, she thought, and her hand came alive in his. He loved her, that she knew. In the nights on her pallet near the boys she could feel his love beating like the sea, and like the waves of the sea, moving away but always coming back.

'How do you be understanding women, then?' she asked. 'Were you ever married?'

'Aye, thirty years ago. She died. But it's not marriage makes a man understand. It's women you read like poems and feel what they are and then you know what they need.'

'What am I needing, then?'

He was silent for a while. Her hand tightened but his eased.

'You need the love of Liam. You've got to believe in him.'

'How? As I believe in God?' she asked bitterly.

'It's the same kind of faith, I'm thinking.'

She stared at the money. 'You can say what you like, I'm spending it. I've a rage to go somewhere, anywhere that's bright, where fiddles are and drink, and spend every penny. Like Slattery's.'

His eyes, darkly blue, kindled to her own anger. 'Hush, Slattery's is no place for you.'

'And why not? I've seen women go in there.'

'Not your kind.'

'Women are women and me no different from others.' She opened the back door that led to the beach and whistled for her brothers. 'I'll feed them and send them to bed and we'll go.'

'Not to Slattery's.' He was tall beside her, and though he had not touched her she felt gripped.

'It's me money and if you'll not go, then I'm going alone!'

His voice rocked her. 'I'm master of this house.'

'But not of me.'

'Of you while you're here.'

'Then I'm leaving here.'

He swooped to take her in his arms and though she struggled he held her fast. 'Weep,' he said, 'that's what you're needing. And when your tears are dry, why then you will tie up your hair and adorn my arm to the Jolly Tuppence on Dingel Street.'

She pressed her face against the rough wool of his jacket.

Another ship was in, *The Bristol Queen* and Moira prepared once more to take the familiar way to the shed. As she fluffed her petticoat Danel said, 'It's no use you're trying until you know where Liam is in New York. Suppose you do get passage, how would you ever find him in a city so big? It's got nearly six thousand people.'

'Father Leary told me that too, but I know I'll find him somehow.'

'Listen, alanna. Even if you had money and a carriage and a driver to help you search, you'd never find Liam. But you'll be landing with nothing but what's on your back and not a friend to help you. Can't you see the sense I'm talking? And would Father Leary be advising you wrong?'

'No,' she said. She looked down at the petticoat. 'Go out a while the way I can change to my old one.'

'That's a good girl.' He moved to the door.

'But oh, Danel, it's hard to be just waiting for something that never happens.'

'I know,' he said. 'I know.'

Summer flowered and faded. Liam sent word from Sligo that it had been impossible to work over from Killala, so he was cutting turf until a ship came. He enclosed a sovereign and sent his love. He hoped Moira was well.

She burst into tears. 'I could have spent that to go to him in Killala! Now Danel, write him to this priest in Sligo and say I'm coming to him and to wait for me.'

'Moira, let's see — it's up in the north, miles and miles from here, and you don't have —'

'I have me mind made up and money for the donkey car and if that isn't enough me and the boys will walk.' She turned to Sean. 'Won't we?'

'Aye.'

'Me too,' Colum said, but he went to Danel and hugged his knees and Danel swung him up into his arms. Over the red-blonde curls he looked at Moira and said, 'I'll not stop you if you're set on it.'

'I am.'

'Then I'll write this moment. But you must wait for his answer.'

'Wait, wait, wait! That I'll not, I'll go this very day if I can. Sean, you and Colum run down to town and ask the donkey car man how he charges for the trip to Sligo. Make sure you both remember the price right and find out when the car's to leave. Hurry!'

When they had gone Danel said, 'Promise you'll send word from Sligo so I'll know you're all right. And if it's not all right you must come back here.'

'I won't have money to come.'

'Somehow I'll raise it.'

'No, Danel.' She tried to smile into the sadness of his face. 'We'll be seeing each other in Ballyfearna some day when times are better. Liam and I aren't going to be staying in America once we know it's safe to come back, no more'n you'll be staying here.' She said to his silence, 'You want to go back, don't you?'

'Aye. It was a place my poems bloomed. Remember, I even sold one.'

'I remember.'

He walked out on to the cold of the beach and was still there when the boys returned.

'It's a sovereign and a half,' Sean said. 'The mail coach.'

'Oh, God! Then we'll get off at eighteen shillings' worth and walk the rest. When does it leave?'

'At eight tomorrow,' Colum said, 'and the driver he says to be on time. It's him I'm not liking.'

'He laughed at us,' Sean said.

'No matter, we're going. Now listen, if Danel thinks we have to get off and walk it will trouble him and maybe he'll not let us go, so if he asks, you must tell a lie and say it'll cost us sixteen shillings clear to Sligo.'

But oddly, Danel didn't ask. At dawn he packed them a fardel of oat cakes and boiled fish, helped them down the hill to the waiting coach and said, 'God bless you,' in that quick Protestant way.

'Promise you'll have someone write me?' he asked.

'I promise.'

He waved them off with a smile under the deadness of his eyes.

Chapter 9

With three other passengers they rode past the sea, the bogs, the woods of Galway and into Connemara. No wonder the boys had not liked the driver. He was sullen, rough with his whip on the two animals, impatient when anyone wanted to stop for natural reasons. His name, printed on the car, was Timothy Loone.

There was a ragged woman with her daughter and a blond young man who tried to flirt with Moira — the queer speech on him might be English and this was enough to keep her cool and distant. His tweed jacket and black trousers hadn't a hole and this was suspicious too. The son of a landlord, she decided, on the way to collect rents somewhere. Soon he stopped trying to talk to her — and just as well.

At rise of the moon they stopped at an inn where Loone unharnessed the animals in the stableyard.

'Those that can pay sleep in the inn,' he said. 'Those who can't, sleep here in the coach.'

The young man got out and went into the inn. The others remained in the coach, quilts raised against the nip of late September. Leaves blew down through the starlight, red and yellow and weary green. Cuddled with her brothers on either side, Moira slept. At dawn she was awakened by the young man who brought mugs of tea for the three of them, and slices of bread.

'Thank you,' she said gratefully.

'Not at all,' he said in a voice like scissors clipping soft thread. English he might be, but he didn't speak like Mr Pond or the engineer at Ballyfearna. And, to her relief, he didn't seem to be flirting now, or watching her at all. It didn't do to get mixed up with gentry. You couldn't trust them two steps in the furze.

The miles of autumn ribboned by, gold and red, bronze and brown. They bounced over peat hags, strained up hills, clattered through villages. Moira put off the question she dreaded but finally at a stop at Westport she climbed up beside Timothy Loone and said, 'I must talk to you.'

'I was thinking you would.' He turned his mean little eyes on her. 'Well?'

'I have only eighteen shillings.'

'Me heart runs blood.'

'So do be telling us when we must get off.'

'I will that.'

'Soon, is it?'

'Maybe.'

She returned to her seat as he whipped up the animals. A mile, two, three — stony and desolate, with a storm coming on. She gasped as he stopped the coach. But he went off into the bushes, and returned to drive on.

They were hours under the heavy thrash of rain, then its tapping, finally nothing but the far caw of crows. Moira peeped out. The sky was wan and watery, the woods dripping. Night was not far off. She eased her body, cramped from the weight of the boys who were still asleep.

Another mile, dusk softening the hills beyond. The coach jolted to a stop.

'You there,' Loone said, turning to point at Moira, 'this is as far as you go.'

'Oh, sir,' she said, aghast, for it was wild and sad, this country, bare and brown except for the hills ahead. 'Can't we go on a bit further?'

'Your money's run out.'

271

'How far then to Sligo?' she asked.

'Too far,' said the young man. He leaned forward and gave the driver a coin. 'This will take them to Sligo. And you might be quicker about it.'

She stared, astonished and awed by the force of him, by the miracle — for indeed it was that. Loone changed from sullen to fawning but the young man cut in and said, 'Get on with us and spare your blather.'

Loone obeyed and Moira bent across Sean to thank the young man. 'Come,' she said, because it was only polite, 'sit beside me here.'

He and Sean changed places.

'I do thank you,' she repeated, 'from me heart. Me name is Moira McFlaherty.'

'I am Terence O'Toole.'

O'Toole! Now it was the Countess O'Toole was the loveliest girl in Galway, so men said — Liam had seen her once at the Horse Fair, blonde she was like this man, only handsome as he was not. He had a big rough crop of straight yellow hair that looked coarse as straw, a round face and a thick neck that sloped into his shoulders. Soon he would run to fat, for the gentry had seed praties and pigs and never worked off an inch at honest labour. Sure he must be the brother of that countess, what with his clothes and money and all.

'Sir O'Toole,' she said, very formal, 'this is me brother Sean, who's man of the house; and Colum, who's younger.'

He nodded to the boys with grave dignity. Then he asked her what took her to Sligo.

She told him about Liam and how she would seek him through the priest near Union Place. 'Then we'll be working our way on a ship to America.'

'That is —' fear caught her, 'if he's not already left.'

'And if he has, what then?'

'Why then, I'll find work somehow and get a ship meself.'

He was silent and she noticed his eyes, big and soft like grey flowers, with the black pupil like the little eye of the bloom. Beautiful they were, a grey pool you could see into and lose yourself in. She wondered if the countess had eyes like that. Of

272

course she dared not ask him about his family but she could maybe wheedle a bit of information.

'There's O'Tooles in Galway,' she said.

'Yes,' he said, and smiled. And my God, his whole face changed and he wasn't fat at all but young and fair, his hair like sun in the twilight.

Cleverly she said, 'I suppose your family misses you.'

'They're in Sligo now, where I'm going.'

'Is it a grand place, Sligo?'

'For some, like any place.'

The grey flowers had closed a little as though he were tired of talk and she sensed a chill on him. Presently they stopped at an inn for the night and she did not see him again until the journey resumed at dawn. But she thought about him. Queer, how he had flirted at first, then turned cool and polite. Well, she would not be forward; she had thanked him for his kindness and that need be all.

He resumed his old seat for the rest of the journey. Then they were in Sligo at last of the sun, grey and bustling as people went home from their work in the path of the lamplighters. Tall roofs, queer dark alleys, small streets that snaked, wide ones where beautiful houses curtsied to gardens. The coach stopped near a place where other coaches were lined up.

O'Toole helped Moira down, lifted the boys. 'There's Union Place to the left,' he said, 'and the church round its bend another street down.'

'Aye,' Colum said.

She thanked him and he gave her his card. 'If you can't find your friend, come to me for I think I might find you work.'

She thanked him again, tucked the card in her pocket and hurried the boys down the street. Lamplight on the cobbles splashed yellow, not the brash yellow of Galway Port but wan as dying candles. The church, old and crumbly, was taper lit and they entered to a dim shabby emptiness that smelled of incense and urine and set their fardel near a pillar.

Moira genuflected and made the boys do so; then she went toward the altar hoping to see a priest but there was no one about.

'Someone must be here,' Sean said.

'Make noise,' she told them, 'and he'll come. Make noise quietly, like singing.'

Sean began When I Was a Young Man in Dublin Town but she hushed him for that song might rouse a priest but it wouldn't please him.

She thought it better to call out into the darkness. 'Father?'

And then he was there, formless in his dark robes, and smiling.

'I'm Moira McFlaherty,' she said, 'and these is me brothers. Are you Father Carney who wrote to me of Liam Lenihan?'

'Aye,' he said. The smile faded. 'But he's gone from here, Miss McFlaherty.'

'Oh, God! Where? To America?'

'I'm not knowing. He said he'd be trying at another port and someone would lift him there on a cart — three days ago, it was — but he wasn't sure of where he'd be going. He said he'd not be knowing till he was on the road.'

'Oh, God,' she said again. 'What will I be doing, then?'

'That man said he knew of work,' Sean said.

Dazed, she pulled the card from her pocket and handed it to the priest, who peered at it.

'Well,' he said, 'this is an inn and I think it's respectable enough for I've seen ladies go in with their children.'

He gave her directions and told her to look for a sign picturing a harp wreathed in shamrocks. She promised to keep in touch and left with his blessing.

The dusk was deepening as they walked the half mile past slanty old houses, through twisty alleys. Several times they lost their way but at last they saw the inn — brown wood it was, gabled and peaked, tall like an old cocked hat, set back from the road in a scraggy garden. There was a stable nearby and a coach drawn up at the door.

'It's nice,' Colum said.

'Say a little prayer that Mr O'Toole will let me work there,' she told them. 'And when we go in, remember — look proud and smile and don't say nothing about food.'

'He'll know we're hungry,' Sean said.

'But we don't be reminding him.'

They went to the door and knocked and then she remembered

it was a public house, like a hotel, and pushed open the door. The boys shoved in the fardel and stood blinking, for the lamp was turned low in the hallway. There was more light from a room at the left and the sound of people talking. They went in hesitantly to see a long brown bar and men sitting on stools under hanging lamps. A big fat woman serving drinks paused and stared at them and they stared back, so queer it was to be seeing someone fat . . .

'Well?' the woman asked.

'It's Mr O'Toole we're looking for, Ma'am,' Moira said.

'For what?'

'He give me this —' Moira fumbled for the card — 'and told me to come here —'

'Speak up, girl.'

Moira approached her timorously. 'Here's the card, Ma'am. He said we should come here if I couldn't — I mean, we were on the same coach today and he said to come here.'

One of the men laughed and beckoned. 'Why don't you come *here*, sweetheart?'

'Shut your lip,' said the fat woman. 'What's your name, girl?'

'McFlaherty. Moira McFlaherty.'

The woman pointed to a door. 'You go in there to the parlour and I'll be seeing if Mr O'Toole is about.'

The parlour was all black oak and horsehair and a little fire burned in the grate. There were empty tables and chairs and the boys wanted to sit down but Moira forbade them. Better to stand and wait respectful like.

A thin young woman came through with a tray of tea, glanced at them briefly and walked through another door. They could hear her climbing a staircase and people talking above.

'It's a busy place,' Moira said hopefully. 'There was lots of men at the bar and that coach outside, and all. Surely they'll be needing help.'

Sean looked at the vacant tables. 'It ain't busy here.'

'It's only tea-time, alanna.'

'What's that?' Colum asked.

'You had tea,' Sean said, 'Danel gave it to us.'

'But not fancy like,' Moira said. She remembered the day she and her mother had taken tea with Father Leary. 'It's a thing for

275

priests and the gentry, with tea in a pretty pot and little cakes to go with it.'

'I'm hungry,' Colum said.

How often, she wondered, had these two words been spoken during these dark years? Oftener, for sure, than any others.

'Hush,' she said. Maybe she should never have left Danel; at least there had been food. But the dream of joining Liam had been too bright.

Terence O'Toole came in then. He had changed from his travel clothes to a loose jacket and brown trousers. God, she thought, he looks different from only two hours ago — sad and tired and somewhat older as though his back were weighted.

'So you didn't find your friend?' he asked.

'No, sir. I fear he's off to America.'

'Sit down. I'll be back.'

They sat at one of the deal tables, scarred from the markings people had made — their names, maybe, and hearts twined. Presently he was back followed by the young woman who brought a tray of beer and bread and butter. Maybe she's a roadling like us, Moira thought, thin as she is. But her black dress and white apron were neat and clean.

'Thank you, Mary,' he said, and she nodded and left them.

'Drink up,' said O'Toole, and laughed as the boys spluttered when the froth teased their noses. Like herself, they tried hard not to grab and gobble the food.

O'Toole said, 'I don't own this place, it belongs to my mother-in-law whom you saw at the bar. Mary, my wife, is her daughter. It's just the three of us here because we can't keep any help.' He paused. 'Because we can't afford help.'

'But sir, I'd hoped —'

'Mary needs help,' he said.

And sure by the look of her, she did. She's even thinner than meself, Moira thought, and though her cheeks were rosy her brown hair was dead-like and circles shadowed her eyes. A queer looking girl to be married to Mr O'Toole, and sure as heaven no countess.

'She's frail,' he said. 'The scrubbing is too much for her and she shouldn't do heavy work. If you could work for as little as

276

we can pay then we'd try you for a week — or maybe Mrs Bunt won't agree.'

'Surely she'll want help for her daughter.'

He smiled a little. 'We'll see.'

She asked on impulse, 'Are you English, sir?'

'Yes, of Irish descent.' The grey eyes lighted and twinkled. 'My accent is commercially valuable. All I have to do is speak and fights start at the bar. Lovely fights, the customers call them, and come back for more.'

'Do you win them fights?' Sean asked, mouth full.

'Naturally. I don't drink and I'm an agile dodger.' He rose. 'I'll take over the bar and send Mrs Bunt to you.'

'Now pray *hard*,' Moira whispered as he left them, 'and smile at her.'

They waited for nearly half an hour. Then she came lumbering in and eased her fat into a chair. Under the black bodice her breasts were big as balloons and yet, Moira thought, she's more like a man than a woman, for her features are coarse, her chin haired and her voice deep.

'So you want a place here,' she said, and her glance sneered over Moira. 'You don't look like you could pull a daisy, much less a broom.'

'But Ma'am, I can! I worked at the hotel in Galway Port and Mrs Calicoe said I was strong as a ox.'

'I have one sickly girl on me hands, is it likely I'm having two?'

'But I'm not sick, only thin. Try me and you'll see how good I am.'

'In bed? Is it O'Toole you're after?'

Moira flushed but kept her temper. 'I'm after no man, Mrs Bunt. I'm spoken for and waiting for me intended.'

The thick lips pursed. 'Maybe you are and maybe you aren't. Where is he?'

'Off to America, I believe.'

'Jilted you?'

'Oh, no, Ma'am. To make his fortune, the way we can marry some day.'

She looked at the boys. 'Are they yours?'

'Aye, me brothers, Sean and Colum.'

277

Mrs Bunt snickered. 'Your sons, you mean.'

'Now how could that be, and me only nineteen years of age?'

'Some sluts start young.'

Oh God, Moira thought, I can't work for this terrible woman. She wanted to pull the boys to their feet and run but there was no place to run to. If only she had stayed safe with Danel . . .

'Mrs Bunt,' she said, tears close, 'I'm no slut and these are me brothers — sure you're just teasing by what you say. If you'll kindly try me for a week I'll work that week free for only food and roof.'

'And what will these boys be doing then?'

'There's your garden,' Moira said. 'They can pull weeds and plant and all. Can't you, Sean?'

Proud she was of his lie. 'Didn't we make that garden at the hotel just grand?'

There was a long silence. Finally Mrs Bunt said, 'I'll try you for a week. You can sleep in the stable. I'm not after messing up me upstairs rooms and wasting beds.'

'We have our quilts,' Moira said, 'we can sleep anywhere.'

'Well, then.' She heaved her bulk and got to her feet. 'After this week if you work well you'll have eight shillings a month and a half day off on Wednesdays. Wait here. Me daughter will show you the stable. Be in me kitchen at six of the morning — six to nine at night you'll work.'

'Thank you,' Moira said. 'You'll not be sorry.'

Alone with the boys she sighed. Sean caught her hand and pressed it. Colum reached over and took the other one. They seemed to know that she was relieved and scared and sad all at once. And yet they were so young. It could only be her imagining that they understood.

Then Sean released her hand. 'Moira, I hate her.'

'Aye.' Colum was a little echo.

Sean took a sip of his beer and wiped his mouth on his sleeve. 'But as man of the house, I say, we must stay.'

There was no work that was not put upon her — scrubbing, washing the latticed windows, making the beds, cleaning the heavy, greasy pots, carrying trays to guests who wanted food in

278

their rooms, serving at the tables. Mrs Bunt and O'Toole shared the hosting and bar duties and kept accounts. Mary did the marketing and cooked, with Moira's help.

Moira was grateful for food, grateful too that she was kept on and paid. Sometimes Mary gave her extra bread and meat to take to the stable. 'Don't be letting me mother know, she's always one to starve the help.'

Moira thanked her. 'It's you who should be eating more yourself, Ma'am. But you only nibble.'

A wan, sweet smile. 'Food sticks in me throat. It's me sickness does it.'

And sick indeed she looked despite the pink cheeks and eyes like shiny brown glass.

'It's the coughing sickness,' she said. 'It ain't much in the days but it's bad at night.'

Poor lass, Moira thought, soft as her mother was harsh, gentle as her mother was rough. No wonder O'Toole was so careful of her, shawling her heavily when she went to market, fussing that the weather was too raw for her and that she carried as much as the carter did. But she pleaded that she liked to go out, and carried little.

'It was a big bag of turnips Friday,' he scolded.

'Why couldn't Sean come along, then?' Mary asked. 'He could help.'

Both boys helped and it was grand how Mary took to them, especially Sean. She was always after patting his pretty curls and telling him how strong he was and how clever. Lucky that Colum wasn't jealous for in the kitchen after supper the songs Mary sang were always for Sean and the stories she told made him the hero. 'Once there was a handsome little prince named Sean McFlaherty . . .'

Sean was delighted and Colum happy too for if he wasn't a prince he was a great soldier or a brave knight who saved the prince from dragons and wicked mothers. But the stories always ended when Mrs Bunt came in from the bar and Mary and Moira would be talking only of the next day's work, and the boys polishing the guests' boots.

On her first day off she went to Father Carney and had him

write to Danel for news of Liam, but weeks passed and there was none, though Danel wrote often. On other free days she and the boys explored the town. Once they went shopping and bought a few necessities, for Mrs Bunt was embarrassed by their shabbiness.

The snow was not good for business at the inn, for the coaching roads were impassable and customers fewer at the bar. This was when Mrs Bunt was worst, blaming everybody for what couldn't be helped, saying she was tired of supporting them all and for a farthing would sell out and leave them to make their own way. It was wonderful, Moira thought, how Mr O'Toole could master his rage for it burned in his eyes. Likely he did it for Mary's sake, for it was plain he loved her. Any man might flirt on a journey and Moira guessed why he had on the coach from Galway: to try to stop thinking of what faced him here at home.

One afternoon when Moira was cleaning the empty parlour he came in and sat down with a glass in his hand. Poteen it was by the look of it and she stared in surprise.

'I hate it,' he said. 'But sometimes I need it.'

She understood. He was only after a bit of comfort, he wasn't no drunkard. He wasn't much older than she but at times like this she felt like his mother and wanted to smooth the sadness from his face and make the grey-flower eyes merry.

'Sometimes I think we hate what we need, sir.'

Like Mrs Bunt . . .

Snow lazied down and he looked at the window. 'I'm taking over the marketing for Mary now. She needs warmth. Sometimes I think . . .' He broke off. 'Maybe she could get well in a sunny place. I'd like to take her to Hampshire, where I was born. The winters are dryer there.'

'Isn't there some way you could go?' she asked, but knowing that if he did her stay here would end.

'No. I've only the wage she pays me and not enough saved to buy the smallest cottage.' He took a gulp of the drink. 'Do you know I had a good education?'

'Sure I guessed it, sir.'

'But no trade. When my father died he left me fifty pounds

280

and I thought I'd see the world a bit and shipped out of Southampton as a deck hand. I saw the world, all right — more than I'd like to see again. All along I was thinking I'd invest that fifty pounds in a business. When my ship was in for repairs at Sligo Bay I came into town and stopped in this inn for a meal — and met Mary. We were married that same week.'

'And the fifty pounds, sir?'

He shrugged. 'It went for improvements. Drains, the roof, things for Mary. Oh, I've tried for another place. When I met you I'd been in Galway to see about work at an inn but there wasn't anything.'

'I'm so sorry, sir.'

'I'm stuck. But so are most people.'

'True for you.'

'No word of your young man?'

'Not yet, sir.'

'Well,' he said tiredly, 'that's the way of it.'

The stable was not uncomfortable with their quilts on the straw and sometimes, if a coach were in, the warmth of horses. Cosy, too, with the one lamp that burned at the harness room. Here, before sleeping, they ate the extra food that Mary provided and sometimes she joined them, not eating but telling her stories, sitting with them in the straw.

'Where did you learn them lovely stories?' Moira asked.

'I made them up for me own boy. Terence and me had a boy once.' She glanced at Sean. 'He went away like.'

'Where?' Sean asked.

'To heaven.'

There was a long silence, broken by the wind thrusting the door.

'He died?' Sean asked.

'Aye, and only four he was.'

'It's so sorry I am.' Moira leaned to press her hand.

'It was a year ago I lost him in the cold of winter. He was larking in the snow and later he had the sneeze and all and then the fever, and then, well . . .'

'May his soul rest in peace.'

'His name was John. He looked like —' She glanced again at Sean. 'Beautiful he was.'

'Sure you'll be having another,' Moira said, but wished she hadn't spoken for Mary looked off into space and didn't reply. Likely she knew she was too frail. 'It's getting cold in here, Ma'am, and if he finds you cold Mr O'Toole will be giving us the devil.'

Mary rose, shook the straw from her petticoat and covered her hair with her shawl. 'A good night to you all.' She lingered near Sean, as though about to speak to him; her hand hovered over his hair. Then she turned and opened the door, pushing it against the wind and they could hear her steps crunch the snow.

Mrs Bunt was quarrelsome, finding fault where there was none but Mr O'Toole became nicer as the winter passed. Not flirty, just friendly, sometimes seeking Moira out to talk of his troubles and to ask of hers.

'Me big trouble is not having Liam,' she said. 'Now I got me shillings saved I could go part way to him — at least to some port.'

'You'd better stay here until you've more.'

He was prudent like Danel and she spoke to him of Danel one afternoon when she cleaned the parlour and he sipped his hated drink.

'I think Danel loves me. He writes to the priest and the priest reads me the letters which is all about how glad he is we're safe. But it's Liam doesn't send a word — and *he's* the one should be caring most.'

Now in March anger was on her for Liam's neglect. Was he thinking it was only money she needed and not news of himself?

'Maybe he's at sea, Moira, and you know it takes a long time for a ship to cross in the winter and then weeks for a letter to come back.'

'Aye.' He was a comfort to her, her friend now, and God knew the friendship innocent. Only Mrs Bunt looked ugly and suspicious when she found them talking. Mary didn't mind.

And it was Mary who worried Moira, seeming to see her dead son in Sean and sometimes calling him by the name of John.

She said, 'I think about Mary a lot. If only she was well and you could have another child.'

O'Toole plunked down his drink and stared at her. 'What do you mean, another?'

'Another boy like John.'

'John?'

'Aye, him that died last year.'

'She told you that?'

'She did, and I'm sorry for your trouble. What's wrong, Terence?'

'Wrong! You ask what's wrong?' He stood up, but shakily like an old man. 'Tell me just what she said.'

She repeated. '. . . died of the fever. He was a fair curly lad like Sean. Wasn't he then?'

'No. He wasn't at all. He never was, Moira.'

'But I'm not understanding.'

'She made up a dream.'

Once long ago Moira had a dream she could never forget. She was standing on a high ledge over whirly tide-torn water, narrow and slippery with the wet leaves of autumn. And she had to walk that ledge, fearful of every step lest she fall on the cruelty of rocks.

Mrs Bunt was the rock Moira feared now. Nothing could please her, she was forever scrubbing over Moira's clean floor or repolishing some chair or table Moira had already worked on. And when she saw Moira talking with Terence it was like being caught in guilt when you'd done nothing wrong.

On a Thursday while Mary and Terence were at market and Moira scrubbing the upstairs hall Mrs Bunt came in.

'You rotten little thief!'

Moira rose to her feet, the wet rag in her hand soaking the side of her apron. '*What?*'

'It's not enough you steal a husband from me girl — now you steal me silver rosary.'

Moira stood stunned. She had never seen any rosary here, much less a silver one.

'Give it back to me.'

'But I never even —'

'Worth two pounds six, it was, me wedding present.'

'Before God, Ma'am, I don't know anything about it.'

'The law will be reminding you, then. It was in me room, and you pretending to tidy that room this morning.'

'But I never . . . and sure you'd not call the police?'

'Even you'd feel the shame of that, eh? They'd lock you up for maybe a year.'

'How can they when I haven't got it?'

'They got the word of a respectable woman against a dilsy's. Och, it's plenty I could tell them if I wanted — how you and Terence is driving me poor girl sick in the head who's sick in the body already.'

'We never —'

'Aye, it's plenty I can say. So you can be giving me back me rosary and leaving here.'

Trapped I am, Moira thought, panicked. Likely there's no rosary at all or maybe she hid it herself, and all a plan to be rid of me. She could not offer any plea to soften that brutal face, with its eyes like little black knives.

Mrs Bunt was sly. 'Maybe you've sold it, then. So you can pay me what it's worth.'

'I've sold nothing! And I have only one pound halfpenny, and that's all me savings.'

'It's not enough. But maybe that would make me change me mind about the law, for I'd not like to see them beat up any woman and have her blood on me rugs. Now you go this minute and take your brats with you and bring me the money as you leave and don't be taking them quilts you have — I can use them. I'll be watching you, so don't be trying no tricks.'

Mute, frightened, Moira ran past her, down the stairs and across the garden where the boys were playing. She called to them to come into the stable quickly, and it was wonderful how fast they obeyed, maybe sensing how scared she was.

'I have no time to explain now,' she told them, 'but we're leaving here. Put on your shoes and your old clothes and make up a fardel of the rest, all but them quilts.'

She hushed their bewildered questions and took her purse from under the straw. 'Hurry,' she said, for she was not trusting Mrs Bunt.

Then she and the boys were at the inn's front door and Mrs Bunt standing there with her hands on her hips, and smiling.

'The purse,' she said.

Moira gave it to her and started to turn away.

'Wait till I count the money.'

She took her time counting. Then she nodded and turned and left them, slamming the door.

'Come,' Moira said to her brothers, 'hurry, now,' and took the fardel from them.

'But where are we going?' Colum asked.

'Just away from here.' She sped down a side street across an alley into the skirts of the town. Maybe she should seek Terence and Mary at the market but she decided against it. He had no money to spare, he had his own hell and she could not beg of him. And surely she must spare Mary the pain of bidding Sean goodbye.

'We'll go to Father Carney,' she said.

As they trudged to the church through the mud of March she thought, we're better off than some other times. We grew strong on food and the breakfast in us should last till dark . . .

Father Carney and the children listened to her story together, sitting in the little study of the parish house.

'So what should I be doing, father?' Moira asked. 'I've not a penny now and Danel so far away.'

'I'll write him today, Miss McFlaherty. Maybe he'll be sending you money. It's a good man he is, I'm thinking, and wanting you back safe.'

'But till then?'

'There's an old room under the church, a basement where we store things. But it's dusty and cold and you've got no quilts for sleeping there.'

'It won't be long till spring.'

'Maybe me housekeeper can find you some covering but it's

285

little food we have — I'm begging alms for a dozen families and every cabbage spoken for. You could be using the kitchen if you had anything to cook.'

'Somehow we'll find it,' she said, so grateful for shelter that she did not think of food.

'You've me blessing. And the prayer that Danel Powderley will send for you soon.'

'Or Liam.'

'It's Danel I'd be trusting,' he said, and twisted her heart.

It was a terrible thing but they had to be doing it and so she told the boys that evening, lying in the dark of the basement, snuggled together under the housekeeper's rags.

'You know that market Mary goes to on Thursdays? We'll go there too, but not on the day she does because we can't be having Mrs Bunt know we're in town and Mary might tell—not meaning to. But listen to me plan . . .'

'Oh, my,' Sean said. 'But that's stealing.' He didn't sound shocked, only excited.

'Aye, but Mrs Bunt stole from us so she makes us steal in turn. It's not right at all, but we must do it. Don't we, Colum?'

'Aye,' he said. 'We must eat.'

'God knows we'll never do it again when we're safe.'

'We must be very careful,' Sean said. 'We'll not be after taking anything too big.'

'And playing like we're just looking,' Moira said. 'And we don't go there together, but one by one, for sure if just one boy was caught they'd only think it mischief and not a family plan.'

But if it's me that's caught, she thought, it's likely the jail house.

There wasn't much they dared steal—a cabbage if it was small, a pickle from its vat, a little loaf of oat bread, a bit of cheese. It was Moira who got a blood pudding and a sausage pie, hiding them under her shawl and once a cart dumped some meal bags by chance and she made off with enough to last them a week.

Each day she waited for a letter from Danel but none came and after a month Father Carney's letter to him came back marked with something that meant no one lived there any more.

286

There was a week of rain and both boys had colds so Moira went to the market alone. She had snatched a turnip and put it under her shawl when the old whiskered owner sidled up beside her, quiet as a cat.

'It's often you're here,' he said, 'but I'm thinking me things ain't good enough for you.'

'Why, sir?' she asked, trying to smile.

'You never buy.'

'True for you,' she said, hoping to God her voice was steady. 'But it's the hunger makes you look.'

He said, 'Wait here and don't you be moving a step for me son is watching from the counter.'

She waited in terror, staring into the dark drizzle of the street. They could take her away and the boys would never know where, waiting scared as she was now.

She dared not turn to look at the man at the counter but kept her glance on the street. Carriages passed, a donkey car; people looked at the herring vats and dried beef.

Now why had she admitted to hunger? Why hadn't she said that her mistress was prissy and particular? He might have believed that. If those shrewd blues eyes would believe anything . . .

No, she thought hopelessly, he's used to roadlings like us, he's likely jailed dozens or even hundreds, who knows what this town has been like these past years?

Why hadn't she gone to the other markets, the ones on the other side of Sligo where they wouldn't have been noticed so much? But Mary had said they weren't as good as this one so Moira had thought, if we're going to steal, then we steal from the best. Oh, but she had been a fool.

The old man came back carrying a brown paper box. 'Now,' he said, 'it's me who remembers me hunger in the old days when I was young like yourself. And so here's me memory of what I wanted and needed and never got. Take it. It's yours.'

Still trembling, she bent to look. Bread and eggs, bacon and ham, oats and cheese and sugar, dried fruit and tea.

'Oh, sir,' she said, 'it's so much I can't thank you!'

'Don't be thanking me dream.' The old eyes were merry. 'And don't be coming back here until you got the money to buy. And

287

now, if you please, you'll be giving me back me turnip.'

She gave it, full of tears and laughter and wonderment that she was free and soon to be eating. Then she blew a kiss to the old man and carried the heavy box through the rain, pausing to rest on the pooled cobbles, uncaring that her shawl fell from her hair, and it a long wet rope. Men stared at her curiously, smiled or spoke, offering to help with the box. But she paid no heed, entranced by the thought that she was wrapped in love.

The market man. Her brothers. Danel. Liam . . . for surely Liam's love was strong and steady as God's and to be taken on faith. But this was a queer way of thinking for she did not trust in God at all — much.

The housekeeper summoned Moira from the basement into Father Carney's study and she hurried up the stairs, sure of news from Liam or Danel.

But he held no letter. There was a small, shabby man with him whom he introduced as Michael O'Beirne.

'Tell Miss McFlaherty what you saw on the road, Mike,' said the priest.

'I was last week in Galway, miss, and the praties was blooming.'

'Thank God!' For Galway was near to Mayo and if the praties bloomed there, likely they bloomed at home.

'You're sure?' the priest asked.

'Sure, father. Me eyes is good as ever and I seen them in the gardens.'

'You were not in the drink, Mike?'

'Oh, no, I hadn't the cost of it. I was begging me way for bread.'

'So,' Moira said, 'I can be going home!'

Mike nodded. 'I'd say so, miss, if you live Galway way.'

'I'm from Mayo.'

'Then it's only next door.'

'Did other folk see the blooming and talk of it?' Father Carney asked.

'Aye, there was singing in the streets of Oranmore. Then I turned east to Meath and I seen the plants there too, not many, but some.'

288

'And you sober?'

'I told you so, father, on me word.'

'Miss McFlaherty has got nothing to trust but your word.'

'She can trust it.'

To go home and wait for Liam there! No more wandering or stealing, no more hunger. But no money to get there unless they walked.

'Thank you, Mike,' the priest said, and the man shuffled out smiling, likely with a coin in his ragged pocket from the charity of the church.

'We'll be walking there,' Moira said.

'Walking that long way? Now I'd like to trust Mike but he loves the poteen more than the truth. It was him said he saw a vision of Our Lady at the altar and swore on the Bible of it but it was only Biddy McKallop with a sweet white shawl on her head. Another time he said he saw St Paul move in his niche — it was just the wavy of the candles in the breeze.'

'But now I think he's speaking for true.'

'Maybe so, but your wish to believe is stronger than his word.'

'Couldn't we be finding out for sure, then?'

'It would be sure if the newspaper said so but it hasn't.'

Moira said, 'I'm going, for my heart says to. Me and the boys go tomorrow.'

'Wait, for I'll write your priest — he'll be knowing the truth.'

But her mind was made up. 'I can't stand no more waiting, I'd rather be walking. And we've still got food, enough for a week.'

'Well, then, may heaven forgive Michael O'Beirne if he's lying again. And I hope your faith in God is as strong as your faith in a drunkard.'

She laughed. 'Oh, it is! I'll have Father Leary write you soon as we're there and you'll kindly be sending Liam's letters to him?'

'Aye,' he said, but shortly, as though he never expected any, as though Liam were nowhere at all but in her mind. Maybe, she thought as he blessed her, he didn't quite know what love was.

The boys faced the first few miles laughing and teasing, for it was a great adventure to be going home, and when they tired it was a happy thing to eat and sleep in the sweetness of the hedgerows. But after three days it took all of her own tired body to prod theirs and they dawdled along, taking refuge from the rain where ever they could find it. An old deserted barn . . . a burned out hut still stinking of char . . . a house whitewashed to show that fevered folk had lived there, but safe now surely and empty of all but meadow grass.

There were no pratie flowers but surely they lay ahead . . . No one in the villages they passed had heard of the blooming but when she told them they wanted to believe as much as she. Aye, few coaches went through, what with the recent floods, so how was the news to travel?

Another day, another night. Thank God there was still food — the boiled eggs and boiled ham and cheese. After a damp sleep in the hedges they forced their stiff bodies on and came to an inn where the landlady let them brew their tea in her kitchen while she finished her morning work.

When they went outside to resume their journey a carriage was ready to leave — shiny brown it was, with fancy gold trim — and as the driver waited in the sun Moira ran to him and asked if he had seen the praties in Galway or Mayo.

He had not been that way, he said, but he was going that way. 'I'm taking me lady to County Clare.'

'How far is Mayo from here?' she asked, hoping their shoes would hold.

'I'm not knowing these parts at all but I'll ask me lady. No, you can be asking her yourself.'

He pointed as a black-cloaked figure came down the steps with the landlord bowing like she was a queen. And indeed, Moira thought, she looked like a queen if queens wore black. She was all velvet from throat to slippers and her pale silver hair was webbed in black lace.

'I'd not dare ask her,' Moira said, awed, for now she could see the dazzle of jewels on the long white fingers as the lady waved to the landlord and moved toward the carriage.

'Go on,' said the driver, 'she'll tell you the way. She was born in the west.'

Timidly Moira approached her and curtsied and asked please, where was County Mayo?

The lady was pale and tired looking but she smiled. 'Why, my dear? Are you going there?'

'Aye. Me and me brothers' — she motioned to the boys who waited nearby — 'is walking there.'

'Walking!'

'We've walked clear from Sligo.'

The beautiful violet eyes opened wide. She glanced at the boys, then back at Moira. 'I am going through Mayo. Would you ride with me?'

My God, a miracle. And when that happens, can folk speak for the lovely shock of it?

'Well, girl?'

'I'll bless you the days of me life for it, Ma'am.'

The lady beckoned to Sean and Colum. 'Then come.'

As the driver opened the coach door and the lady entered, Moira paused, seeing the velvet of the cushions. 'Ma'am, we're dirty from the road, we'd spoil —'

'Nonsense.' She spoke to the driver. 'Tim, take up their fardel and lower the curtains.'

Heavy black curtains at the windows shut out the sun and the view and as they settled in the lady sensed Moira's thought for she said, 'Perhaps it's like a hearse but I want it that way. I've long thinking to do and it's best in the dark.'

She was silent then as the coach rolled and rattled, sank and lifted along the miles. The boys slept but Moira was wide awake in the darkness that smelled of roses. What were the lady's thoughts? Sad ones, surely, for once or twice was a sigh, or maybe a sob.

Finally the lady said, 'We stop at Castlebar for the night.'

'Is that far from Ballyfearna, Ma'am?'

'I don't know. What town is near Ballyfearna?'

'Ballydonny.'

'Then we've not far to go, for Ballydonny's on my way.'

Silence again and the darkness. The boys awakened and Moira whispered to them to be quiet. At last they came to Castlebar and as they walked toward the lantern-lit inn Moira said, 'We'll meet you here in the morning if we may, Ma'am.'

'But where will you go?'

'We'll find a place to sleep. The stable, maybe, or —'

'You will be my guests here. I shall see you at eight.'

Oh, heaven to eat hot food, to lie in a featherbed all her own, and the boys in the next room. At breakfast there was gammon and eggs by the tap room fire.

'Tell me, sir,' Moira said to the landlord, 'is the praties back in Ballyfearna?'

'Where's that?' He sounded impatient, doubtless disgusted by their rags. 'Now I've no time to be chatting,' and he was off to another room.

They waited outside with the coachman. All around were stone houses huddled together like the ones on the streets of Sligo. Presently the lady came out accompanied by two nuns who kissed her and watched as the coachman lowered the curtains.

'I am sorry to keep you in the darkness,' the lady said as they drove off.

'We like it,' Moira lied, for she knew it was hard on the boys not to see out but she had explained to them the night before that the lady was likely in mourning.

They said nothing more, until the driver stopped and called out 'Ballydonny.'

'We're only ten miles from home!' Moira burst out, 'straight as the crow flies. We could walk it, Ma'am.'

'No, we'll go on,' and she told the coachman to drive straight ahead to the next village.

The boys were restive, but behaving as Moira had told them to, though she knew they longed for the sunlight. First, she thought, we'll go to the hotel and hear all the news from Biddy and Dennis, and maybe if the praties are out we'll frolic to-night . . .

But what if the gardens were still dead and everyone moved away? Fool, she thought, you should have minded Father Carney as you should have minded Danel. And if it's hell you find you can't even be blaming God or a drunk but only your own self.

The coach stopped and they heard the thump of the driver's boots as he jumped down and his tap on the door, which the lady opened.

'Would this place be what you're after, Ma'am?' he asked.

'Is it?' she asked Moira.

'Aye,' Moira said, glimpsing the road, 'it is, and you'll be in our prayers forever. And,' she added, bold in departure, 'I'm sorry for your trouble but sure it will pass.'

'I think it will — in the peace of the Church.'

So she's entering a convent, maybe, after some deep grief, and meditating here in the dark . . .

'Then a nook in heaven to you, Ma'am.'

Then they were out on the road, the fardel beside them, and the coach moved on through the sunlight.

'*Look.*' Sean said and she saw him pointing beyond the old sheds to the slope of the fields.

They left the fardel and ran past Paddy the Pawn's and the Market Cross and the well. At the Corner of the Shoes they climbed the hill and stared down, shading their eyes from the sun.

Between the black rubble of roofless huts the gardens were blooming white and everywhere were the frills and flounces of spring — the daffodil ruffles, the lilac plumes and far off at the abbey, the pink froth of cherry trees.

They clung together and kept on looking as though their eyes were starved.

'Colum,' Moira said, with the wet of tears on her cheeks, 'Look down there next to them rocks. Maybe you was too young to remember but that was our garden and now it's alive again, that was dead.'

'It hasn't the look of a ghost,' Sean said.

'It's no ghost. It's bad times haunted them gardens, but now it's all over. You can't be seeing the green of the plants from here but I know they're green and strong as oxen from the very look of the bloom. Da told me . . .'

Could it be that Da was back too, and Sally and Granny? 'Come,' she said, 'we'll go to the hotel and ask all the news.'

They hurried down the hill and met Dennis coming up.

'We seen you getting out of that coach,' he said, hugging them. 'Now me and Biddy wants you for tea and a grand long talk. You're home for good?'

'Forever,' she said.

'How long is that?' Colum asked.

293

'It's 'way beyond tomorrow,' Dennis said.

Moira told the boys to run ahead and take the fardel into the hotel. 'Dennis,' she said, 'is there news of Da?'

'No, alanna.'

'Granny? Sally?'

He shook his head. 'It's too long now to be hoping. And we done our grieving years ago.'

She sighed. 'Has the Lenihans or Father Leary heard of Liam?'

'Not since the Lenihans had word from Sligo . . .' He patted her shoulder. 'He'll be back, don't you worry, with all them American shillings and him in a tophat tall as a tree. Now, we'll be saving our talk for Biddy, she saw you from her winder and was hopping fit to piss!'

A grand talk they had in the shabby rose-papered parlour, with tea and oatbread and a bit of poteen when their throats grew hoarse from the gossip.

Danel Powderley was back and had sold a poem for six shillings, living in his old house these past four months. And Annie Dumbie had returned with her husband Peter the Weaver. Mary the Midwife and Paddy was still peculiar friends — some said they were engaged but Biddy said no, they didn't seem any different.

'And Bridget and Tyrone?' Moira asked.

'They're married,' Biddy said. 'She never wanted to, but Tyrone, he was after doing anything to keep her so he made her begin a baby and Father Leary noticed and raised such hell they had to marry. Three weeks ago, it was.'

'I wish I'd been here,' Moira said.

'Aye, it was a pretty wedding,' Biddy said. 'We pulled and tugged but she couldn't get into her English dress so we tore up one of me old white tablecloths and made one. It turned out there was a stain o' sloe in the front but she held her flowers there so it didn't show, and all the flowers o' the fields was piled at the altar. Jesus gave her away.'

'And Eileen?' A shadow fell on Moira's heart. 'Is she still here?'

'Aye, but let's not be talking of her,' Biddy said swiftly. 'There's new folk have come to town — the O'Shaugnesseys from Longford. He's a widder man used to farm and he got two

294

daughters, Cathy and Deirdre, and pretty as sunflowers they are
. . . but oh, you never heard the *grand* news. Mr Pond died.'

'He did? How?'

'He took a fit in his cart.'

'Not two miles from here.' Dennis poured more poteen. 'It's
said something scared him so bad his heart split.'

'Was it wild dogs?' Sean asked.

'Who's to be knowing? Some says the ghosts of all the folk he
threw off the land but I'm thinking just one ghost could do it. Or
maybe The Gorta.'

'Hush,' Biddy said, crossing herself. 'Don't even be rousing the
thought of him.'

The outside door banged and as Dennis rose Jesus came in and
at sight of the McFlahertys gave a great astonished bellow and
kissed the three of them. Then he joined them at the table and
asked for tea.

'Tea?' Dennis asked accusingly. 'Is it drunk you are, then?'

'No, last night I took a pledge of Cathy O'Shaugnessey. She
says I may brew me poteen but not be drinking it for love of her.'

'Is it engaged you are then?' Moira asked.

'Aye, if I don't be drinking. Oh, I know she's too good for me
— a fine big girl she is with yellow hair and two big — dimples.
But tell us of you, Moira.'

She told me all that had happened since she left. And then she
asked, 'How did them praties come back?'

'Well, now,' Jesus said, 'I can't rightly say. Maybe it's just
nature did it by itself, like the birds and animals is back. But I
think Paddy had seedlings hid and I *think*,' he lowered his voice,
'someone did be stealing them and planted them at dark o' the
moon.'

'Mary, maybe?' Moira asked.

Jesus accepted a tea mug from Biddy. 'I'll say nothing. But
Cathy thinks maybe them English engineers set seed praties on
account of they wanted to make up for that canal.'

'What do you mean?'

'Well, it's a grand looking canal — higher than a house and four
miles long. It got finished last month and there was flags and a

295

speech and all. But you see there's a little thing wrong with that canal.'

'What?' Sean asked.

'It won't hold water.'

'And should it?' Colum asked.

'Sure it should, but it don't. Danel says it's built on pore-rock.'

'Porous rock,' Dennis said.

'Aye. Now that canal was meant to bring in ships and help us be a port but how can a ship come in on dry ground? It's a embarrassment to the town, that it is. So maybe Cathy's right, them English felt kind of guilty for wasting all our time and raising our hopes, so in secret they sent to England for seed praties and planted the praties. Don't you think so, Moira?'

She smiled. 'I'm liking your Cathy already. Now tell me, is me house in the woods all right?'

'Aye, Bridget's there every so often to sweep the woods out of it,' Biddy said.

'And you should see me new house,' Jesus said. 'I'm putting the roof back on John the Basket's to make it snug for Cathy. We don't be knowing who the new land agent is — Mr Pond, he died —'

'They were telling me.'

'— but whoever he is he can't move us out now our praties are growing.'

'Did I ever eat a pratie?' Colum asked.

' 'Course you did,' Moira said, and leaned to kiss his cheek.

'Now,' Biddy said, rising to clear the table, 'you and the boys will stay here tonight and tomorrow you can go back to your home.' She glanced at the little fardel. 'Is that all you have?'

'It's bits of food and clothes. I told you Mrs Bunt took our quilts.'

'Then I'll be giving you some and rags to make up your beds and there's old pots you can clean up for cooking. We'll lend you oats so you haven't got a worry now.'

Eileen.

Biddy wouldn't talk of her, but surely Jesus would. 'And how is your sister?' she asked.

He shook his head. 'Not good, alanna. Queer-like.'

'How, then?'

'Well, she's —'

'Hush,' said Biddy, 'it's to be a happy night. Now, Jesus, you
go and tell everyone they're back and the frolic's on us. Don't be
sitting there like a gawk — go!'

'I'll just see you to the door,' Moira said, and when they were
in the common room she said, 'Why is Eileen queer-like?'

'She do be like the old woman at the workhouse who said the
same things over and over and forgot what she had to do. Only
that woman was eighty years of age, and Eileen not twenty-five.'

'It's the poteen makes her forget.'

'No, for she promised the priest not to drink after she broke
the holy images.'

'In the *church?*'

'No, the ones in his house, over his bed. She hasn't drunk since,
and she couldn't anyway 'cause I hide the jugs. Times there are
she doesn't even know her own name but thinks she's — someone
else.'

And the shadow on her heart grew darker, for Jesus said,
'There's no way to be saying it soft, Moira. She's mad.'

Danel was first to arrive that night and Moira drew him aside
into the hall. 'I'm scared of Eileen,' she said, and told him why.
'I can't be out there alone in the woods with nobody but me
brothers.'

'Suppose I was to live there with you?'

Oh, the joy and the safety of that! But she told him that when
Liam came back he might be angry and Father Leary had never
understood her fear.

'I think he will now. He's sure to come tonight so I'll talk to
him myself.'

'But will others understand?'

'You've only to explain. You don't keep a pledge of silence to
a woman who's pledged your murder.'

So it was settled, at least between them, and it was lovely to
be talking to Danel as though there hadn't been months between
but only hours the way you could pounce on a problem without
so much as a 'How have you fared?' He had fared well, by the

look of him, for his beard was trimmed and he had a new jacket.

There was not such a frolic since the old days, but nobody fighting or even quarreling, not even the Lenihans, and not once did Mrs Lenihan complain of feeling bad except they hadn't heard from Liam since the shillings from Sligo; and oh, the O'Shaugnesseys were a ornament to the town. Jesus' Cathy and her sister Deirdre were as Biddy said, pretty as sunflowers and sweet, too, and their father could play the fiddle as if it had all its strings and even more. Annie Dumbie's husband Peter was nice and lively as a hop-toad, and polite too, coughing into his sleeve when the fit took him, and he danced every jig.

Mary and Paddy came together, almost like lovers they were, for a kind of comfort was on them as if everything was understood and he no longer running. Best of all was Bridget's warm kiss, Tyrone's hug, and she looking so happy you wouldn't know she was married at all.

Father Leary came late, at nine of the clock, and this was odd because he was usually early to bed. He took Moira's hand and said, 'I'm thankful you're home safely,' and he seemed his old self but for a great sadness in his eyes as though he had seen too much of hurt and horror.

The music was playing when Danel took him off to the empty bar and closed the door.

I love Danel, Moira thought, but it's not enough for him and maybe I'm wrong to live with him again. It's not right to ask a man to protect you when you can't feel a deeper thing. But it's never hope I gave, only the love I could.

And what was love, then? And how many kinds were there, all of the same name but different as praties were different, not one sized the same? And why do folk call it love when it is really need?

She danced with Jesus, with Paddy and Dennis, but all the time she watched for the bar door to open. Finally Danel poked his head out and beckoned and she left Peter the Weaver and went into the long, dim room.

'Moira,' Father Leary said, 'you can't be living with Danel here. In Galway there was no other place to go but his, but now you're home with a home of your own.'

'But Eileen —'

'Can't you be trusting me about her?'

'No,' she said, amazed by the blaze of the truth, 'I can't. I trusted you once and took me life to her hands and it's not your doing I wasn't killed that day.'

'Aye,' Danel said. 'Moira knew she was mad then as she is worse now. But you wouldn't see it.'

'I see it now. I see it from dawn to dusk.' He pushed a tired hand through his hair. 'I see that I failed you, Moira. But I won't again.'

They were silent and he said, 'You're thinking how will I keep me promise? It's not me, though it is me saying it. It's —'

'God?' asked Danel, hard and sharp. 'Where's God been these past years? Down below the pratie beds? And now on a whim does He make them bloom to His glory and then maybe cut them down again? It's not as a Protestant I'm asking. It's just as a man protesting that a woman needs safety and you denying it on the sham of morality.'

The priest's voice was soft. 'Danel —'

'I shall live with Moira and be damned to you, for it's only Liam I must answer to, and he alone has the right to anger.'

'Danel. Listen to me. Eileen Finnigan is mad, but not in violence. She feels her mind slipping from her like a shawl and the terrible thing is, she has the wit to know it . . . She is even afraid to say "Yes" or "No" for fear it will be the wrong way round — like when I asked her if supper was ready and she said "Yes" and it not started, and "No" when she meant aye, the altar cloth was washed. So she is in silence, scared to speak lest she betray herself for if she's not better there's nothing I can do, nothing but send her off.'

'To Marytown?' Moira asked, but sad now, not scared, not thinking of the past, only the future of Eileen.

'Aye, Moira. I wish to God she had no wits at all. For she talks of the madhouse. She knows, she knows.'

On a soft day of mist the folk of Ballyfearna dug their potatoes. Some knelt in the sweet brown earth and thanked God for the harvest, others rejoiced in church. Oh, they'd be prudent to store them well, to cherish the seedlings as if they were gold. Never again would they waste or idle or spurn other plantings. Cabbages weren't just for pigs nor turnips for cows. There was even some talk of raising carrots, but that was tipsy.

Tyrone carted Moira's crop from the old garden to the house in the woods where they dug a pit to keep them safe from the rain. Bridget, big with child, helped make the house cosy, sewing oat sacks to cover the pallets and calico cases for the barrel seats. And never had Bridget been so beautiful, her black hair shiny as satin and her black eyes soft with content.

'It's me loving the baby inside makes me love Tyrone too,' she told Moira. 'Now isn't that queer after these years of not caring?'

Many things were queer that summer but queer like a happy dream. Mr Grant, the new land agent, was polite and patient as could be and would not bother them for rents until the second crop was in. Paddy turned generous by daylight and bought Mary a pig for her birthday. At his marriage frolic Jesus drank not a drop, thirsty as he was from the heat of the jigs. And one August night a shooting star burned across the skies of Mayo, sure sign of God's blessing.

The grain mill opened and roadlings came to settle, but as Deirdre O'Shaughnessey said, even the young men looked old from the years of the hunger. She had her choice of them, pretty as she was, but being only sixteen could bide her time to marry; a girl should be prudent. Ah, that lovely word 'prudent', drummed into them by Father Leary's sermons. They'd not waste so much as a blackberry. And since they all had hopes of heaven, it wasn't prudent to lie or cheat or fight or drink too much. But of course it was prudent to gather the sloes for wine before the blackbirds got them.

Moira could not quite lose her fear of Eileen and rarely ventured far from the pool without both boys, for Father Leary and Jesus couldn't be watching her all the time and the mad were said to be cunning as foxes. And always when she visited neighbors Danel was with her.

They were gossiping at Murphy's after a long day's work when they heard screaming in the street and ran out. There was

300

Paddy's cart and Father Leary and Jesus in it holding something on the seat that squirmed and twisted. Then its dark covering came off and Moira looked into the face of hell.

The eyes were only sockets, like a skeleton's, and the lips, once thin, had sunk into nothing. But from them came the screaming stifled now by Jesus' hand. The cart moved past the gathering crowd and was lost in the darkness.

'May she rest in peace,' Moira said on a sob for she felt how Eileen felt, sick of soul and scared past anyone's knowing. Strange it was to share the mind of someone — as Da had with Cathleen on the night of her child-pains.

'Come,' Danel said, and took her arm. 'I'll tell you my new poem.'

Mutely, obediently, she walked along with him.

'The poem is to you, Moira of the Scarlet Hair.'

But in this moment she was not Moira. She was Eileen Finnigan screaming her way to Marytown.

The young men, chilled by Deirdre, came to court Moira but she told them of Liam and that she was pledged to him and they did not press her. But it was as if they respected a widow, not a waiting woman; as if, like Father Carney, they didn't believe in Liam at all.

Often in the fall of leaves she went alone to the church to touch the door they had touched, to whisper the words they had spoken. 'I, Moira, do take thee, Liam . . .' but she could not feel their substance nor the ghost of his arms or his kiss, or anything at all.

She prayed, looking up at the torn sky through the old torn windows of the abbey. Once at the red rags of sunset she thought she felt Liam's hand, but it was only the wind from the river troubling her hair.

Over the land dropped the mists of October, sneaking like thieves through the fields. Mist softened old black stumps and silvered the larches and willows. The gardens loved the mist and in the earth grew the seeds, safe as babes in the womb. The squirrels sensed this safety and stored their prudence of nuts. Badgers

301

and weasels tunneled in trustfully. Young deer roamed the high hills. And the frogs, old in wisdom, crept back to the pools of the past.

Moira heard the stir of the trusting animals as she sat at dusk by the pool and she called to her brothers to come outside.

'Listen!'

There was the deep boom of courting frogs, the splash of an otter.

'Isn't it grand?' she whispered. 'It means the land is safe now.'

They were silent for a while, bemused by the whir of wings in the oaks and the sleepy trill of the birds. Then, from a distance, footsteps crackled the leaves.

Sean peered through the deepening twilight. 'It's Danel, maybe.'

'No,' Moira sprang up from the bank.

'It's Jesus, then,' said Colum.

'No,' she said, close in the wisdom of the animals, 'it's Liam.'

Epilogue

The hills purpled with twilight and swans slept on the river. Between mud huts and rock fences potato plants flowered white and through the grey of dusk the candles of Ballyfearna welcomed men home from the fields.

In the abbey cloister Father Leary strolled under the cherry trees and prayed for the soul of Eileen Finnigan. On the road Paddy the Pawn closed shop and stopped for a dram at Murphy's. Across the bogs Jesus Finnigan drank half a jug of poteen and chewed a bunch of grass lest his wife smell the shame of it. At the Crossroads of the Shoes Mary the Midwife put on her boots to make a fine appearance in town. In the woods Liam Lenihan kissed Deirdre O'Shaughnessey and laughed at her slap.

Three miles away Sister Angelica and Sister Charity gathered flowers from the convent garden and hitched the donkey to its cart. In her hut Bridget Schwartz fed her daughter and tucked her into a travelling shawl. At her well, Cathy Finnigan drew up water and washed her hair. By the river Danel Powderley pondered a poem in his mind and ripped it out.

At seven o'clock all of them met at the wake of Peter the Weaver, and the women loud of the keen, this being Annie's fifth loss. The corpse, circled by candles, lay in a hay-lined coffin made by the hands of Mick McLamb and Terry Regan, new to the town but anxious to help in its sorrow.

Father Leary blessed the house and the nuns told their beads. Everyone talked of Peter's goodness and all was quiet and reverent until the third round of poteen when Deirdre O'Shaughnessey told how Peter had kindly cut turf for her and Annie asked why?

'You're jealous,' Cathy Finnigan said, defending her sister, and Annie slapped her and Bridget got into it and then such a squealing and hair-pulling as made the priest hurry the nuns outside for now the men were roused. Mick pinched the behind of Cathy and Jesus thought Liam had done it and hit him and then the two fighting like they never had before, fighting out the back door and clear to the hen run where Paddy and Tyrone ducked them in the well.

They came out splashed and sober to face the fury of the priest, who gave them penances clear to Whitsuntide. 'It's a bloody blooming disgrace you are.' He turned to the others. 'Now all of you go home.'

'And don't any of you be coming to the funeral, either,' Annie shouted, 'ruining me nice house as you did, though thank God, Himself wasn't tumbled *this* time. Not through any fault of yours, it was as the mercy of God.'

She and her broom and the priest dispersed them and they picked up their lanterns and went their separate ways. Cathy gave Jesus hell all the way to the hill and up it, but Liam took the blame for forcing poteen on him and Deirdre made peace.

'Now me and Liam will smoke a pipe together,' Jesus said, and gave the girls his lanterns. 'Go on home and we'll watch you safe over the bogs.'

They watched until the lights were lost to sight. Far off they could hear the rumble of the Castlebar coach as it crossed the bridge.

'Well,' Jesus said, 'here's me hand, old friend,' and Liam shook it. 'It's sorry I am I blacked your eye.'

'It must be a grand one,' Liam said generously.

'Not so bad as I could have.'

They puffed at their pipes and looked down on the town. Candles went out, hut by hut, but those of Murphy's still blazed against the darkness.

'I'm a happy man,' Jesus said. 'Cathy isn't one to hold grudges. Forgiving as a saint, wasn't she, when I told her I'd never drink again?'

'Aye, you could be searching the world and never finding a better wife.'

'Do you be regretting you never got to America?'

'No,' Liam said. 'I've seen all the ports of Ireland and most of the land. It's a travelled man I am, so now I can say this is the grandest place of all.'

'No greener over the hill, then?'

'No greener.'

'Maybe,' Jesus said, 'we should be going down to Murphy's and having a dram on that thought.'

For waiting there were philosophers all, able and willing to examine the beauty of Liam's thought, for spiritual it was to hear a man praise what he had.

'No,' Liam said, 'it's home to Moira I am.'

'It's only after ten of the clock.'

'Aye, but it's her ninth month.'

'So come to Murphy's and we'll drink to her and I'll pay.'

'Thank you kindly, but it's home I want to be.'

Oh, God, Liam thought, I must still be drunk for I never spurned a drink yet, and it from a friend and free. He left Jesus and ran down the hill through the deep woods. Somehow he couldn't wait to get home, where the pool lay like a mirror in the lap of leaves, and his woman and her brothers snug inside.

Acknowledgements

Many people have helped with this book. Charles Beatty of Beaulieu, Hampshire, suggested the haunting lines of Michael Innes and put me in touch with special material at the National Library in Dublin. Professor McDowell of Trinity College in Dublin contributed his valuable time, and is one of the writers who made *The Great Famine* the definitive book about those tragic years. It was published by the New York University Press in 1958, edited by T. D. Williams and R. D. Edwards and I recommend it to anyone who wants the complete story, for it covers the politics and economic problems of the period as well as its emotional ethos.

My warmest thanks to Peter Foy of County Mayo, who walked me through a dry canal and talked me through many miles of the country I describe; who showed me its secret caves where only recently human skeletons have been found — victims of the famine. Mr. Foy is a very old gentleman but spry as a hill goat and impervious to leprechauny legend. When, once in a while, I thought he might be faulty in memory of his parents' stories I checked the text books and found him accurate. So accurate, in fact, that the value of a book was proven when it agreed with the recollection of Mr Foy.

I am grateful to Beverly Balin for Irish peasant folk lore and to the wonderful folk of Ballinrobe and Castlebar, Knock and Galway. Their gardens, once 'haunted' by the blight of fungus, bloom to the sea.

Oldcraighall, Scotland.   ELIZABETH BYRD
1972.